MW01139539

CHARLIE

ELIN PEER

CULTIVATED #1

Books in this series

For the best reading experience and to avoid spoilers, below is the recommended order of the Cultivated books.

#1 Charlie
#2 Atlas
#3 Lumi
#4 Nathan
#5 River
#6 Maximum

For a full overview of my books and to be alerted for new book releases, discounts, and give-aways, please sign up to my list at
www.elinpeer.com

PLEASE NOTE

This book is intended for mature readers only, as it contains a few graphic scenes and some inappropriate language.

It deals with the subject of suicide so if you know that's a trigger, this book is not for you.

All characters are fictional and any likeness to a living person or organization is coincidental.

DEDICATION

To my good friend Bolette

Thank you for flying to Ireland and helping me with my research.

Seeing Dublin, Trinity College, Howth, the cliffs of Moher, and the medieval city of Galway was amazing, and so was staying in an old Irish castle for a few days.

Not least because of your amazing company.

Elin

Prologue
Coffee Confusion

Charles

The comforting aroma of coffee hit me as soon as I opened the door and stepped into one of the coffee shops on campus. For a Wednesday morning the line wasn't too long, but most of the tables were taken by study groups who preferred the informal setting over the study hall at the library.

Without making eye contact with the guy behind the register, I gave my order. "I'll just have a large Americano."

"Any snacks or pastry with that today?"

"No thanks."

"All right. What's the name for the order?"

"Charlie."

"Okay, we'll have your coffee coming right up."

Moving over to let other customers give their orders, I scanned the room but saw no one that I knew. It wasn't surprising, since I was no social butterfly and the people that I considered friends were few. With thousands of students on campus it was rare that I ran into anyone I knew by chance.

The loud sound of a chair scraping over the floor drew my attention when a young woman got up from her group and walked to the counter to study the coffee shop's display of cakes and sandwiches.

The knitted sweater she had on was dark blue and looked worn, which made me think this was one of her favorites. It fell over her left shoulder revealing her smooth skin and a thin white lace bra-strap that made it

1

impossible for me not to envision what the rest of that bra looked like on her. She wasn't wearing any make-up and her long curly brown hair was damp as if she'd showered and hurried out the door, but with her feminine curves and symmetrical features, she stood out to me as an example of natural beauty.

"Can I have one of your cinnamon rolls and a hot chocolate?" The natural beauty pushed her right hand into her back pocket to fish out some crumpled-up dollars. It was impossible not to notice how round and perfect her behind was. Calculating the amount of sugar that she would be indulging in, I wondered how she managed to look like she lived off broccoli and seaweed.

She talked with the barista as if they were old friends and they laughed about his claim that he could eat a whole cinnamon bun in one bite. He was flirting with her and I watched in fascination how easy he made it seem.

I would've shaved off a whole grade point from my last exam to act that natural and relaxed around women. For me it was the opposite as beautiful women like her made me nervous, which was stupid since they never even looked in my direction.

A female barista interrupted them when she addressed the guy at the register, "You need to take your break now before the lunch rush comes in. I'll handle the store."

"Yes, boss." He gave another smile to his cute customer and handed a cup to his colleague. "She wants a hot chocolate."

"Okay, I'll take care of it."

He nodded like it was no big deal, while I sighed because I hated waiting on my coffee and now there would be one less employee working.

The young man left and the noisy coffee machine drowned out conversations around the café. When Miss

Natural Beauty looked over at me, flames shot up my neck and my tics kicked in so I turned my attention upon a community board, focusing on reading notes about tutoring, cooking classes, roommate opportunities, and sales of school books.

"Hey."

Turning my head, I saw that she had moved over to stand next to me.

"Hey." I avoided eye contact and pretended to be very interested in the information on the board.

"Are you looking at that support group? My friend Brian is involved in it. Have you been?"

My heart was pumping and I felt my shyness pull up the protective shield of indifference that I'd perfected in my twenty-four years of living.

"Been where?"

She nodded to the note that she must have thought I was studying.

Break your porn addiction!
Join our support group
Mondays and Wednesdays from 8 to 9 p.m.
Everyone is welcome.

"No, I... ehh..." I frowned and crossed my arms. "I don't have a problem with porn."

With a playful smile, she tilted her head. "As in you don't watch it or you don't think there's anything wrong with watching it?"

Jeez! My heart was beating fast. I'd never discussed my view on porn with anyone.

When I didn't answer or smile back, she withdrew a little. "I'm sorry. I was just trying to be funny. My friends say I lack a filter and I guess I just proved them right."

3

"Charlie." The barista placed my order on the counter in front of us, but before I could react, Miss No Filter reached for my warm drink, gave the barista a "thanks," and lifted my cup of coffee to her lips.

My brow rose in surprise at the same time her face scrunched up.

"Excuse me but I asked for hot chocolate, this is coffee."

The barista looked over. "I'm sorry, did I get it wrong?"

"No, it's my order."

She turned to me. "Yours? No, it's mine – see, it says Charlie on the side."

"*I'm* Charlie."

Her eyes widened and then she burst out, "Shut up. You're called Charlie? Me too. It's short for Charlotte but I never liked that name. My friends call me either Charlie, Liv, and sometimes Chris."

"That's a lot of names for one person."

"I know, right." She smiled. "Liv is my middle name and Chris is short for Christensen which is my last name. What about you? I bet you're a Charles. You look like a Charles, being so stoic and serious."

My arms, which had been folded, dropped to my sides and I shifted my balance. I only appeared stoic and serious to people I didn't know, and the bubbly personality of this woman was like a feather tickling and teasing me to let out my humor. If only she didn't make me so nervous.

"Yeah, I'm Charles. Charles McCann." So much for coming up with a funny or clever response; and to make it worse, my tics kicked in again. *Come on, say something clever and interesting. Ask her a question.*

There were a few seconds of silence and then she played with her hair. "I'm a freshman. An *old* freshman, but that's because I took a few years after high school to work and travel. You?"

"Not a freshman." My tics were driving me insane. *Just look normal for once.*

I looked to the door, mentally marking my escape route from this fail of an encounter with a woman who was everything I dreamed of when I was alone.

"I bet you're a numbers guy or a law student."

Nodding my head, I confirmed it. "International law. Finished my undergrad last year."

"Oh, so you already did the first four years. Then you only have what... three years left?"

"Something like that." I looked down at my cup of coffee that she was still holding. It made her jolt.

"Shit, I'm so sorry. Here. I don't know what's wrong with me today." A faint redness spread in her cheeks, just as the barista announced:

"Here's your hot chocolate with whipped cream."

"Thank you, ehm, I also paid for a cinnamon roll." Charlie took the cup and brought it to her nose, sniffing in the scent. "Yup, this is much better than coffee." Her smile revealed that her teeth were white, straight, and as perfect as the rest of her.

"Did you have braces?" I could have face-palmed myself, but Charlie didn't seem to mind my random question.

"I did." She flashed another big smile that unleashed another annoying round of tics for me.

"Did you just wink at me?" She was still smiling, but the way she tilted her head so as to figure me out made me so bloody nervous that my tics went crazy. My right shoulder lifted, my nose wrinkled up, and my eyes winked again. All in quick succession and with me leaving her hanging and saying nothing.

"Here's your cinnamon roll," the barista told her.

Charlie reached for the plate and was just about to walk off when she stopped and looked down at the cup in my hands. "Are you okay drinking that? I don't have any diseases or anything, but I can buy you another cup if you want me to."

I should have been charming and flirtatious and told her that putting my lips where hers had just been would be a pleasure, but I'd never been a smooth talker, so I just shook my head.

"So, we're fine then?"

"Yeah, we're fine. I can just take off the top."

There was a micro expression of embarrassment on her face. "Right."

I had my coffee and should get out of here, but as if Charlie were the sun of this campus, I was pulled in by her strong gravity, eager to stay in orbit a bit longer, just so I could feel her warmth.

Tell her it came out wrong and that any man would be honored to share a cup with her.

"Okay then. It was nice meeting you, Charles. I'm going to go back to my studies so I can one day become an influential anthropologist."

"Yes, very nice meeting you too, Charlie."

Come on. Ask for her phone number. Say something.

This woman was stunning and charming and my instincts told me that I'd regret it if I left without a way to get ahold of her.

With the same scraping of the floor as before, she pulled out her chair and joined her group again.

Come on, just man up, and ask her out. I closed my eyes, regretting that I hadn't done it earlier. Now she was surrounded by people and walking over there would be ten times more challenging for me.

Stretching and fisting my hands, I pumped myself up, but just as I took my second step in her direction, the guy next to her pulled her in.

"Babe, come on, give me some of your delicious bun. I know you want to."

She laughed and tried to protect her pastry, but he opened his mouth trying to take a bite. The playful energy between them made it clear to me that they were intimate.

Of course she's not single. That would have been a fucking miracle.

I abandoned my mission of asking her out and headed to the exit.

CHAPTER 1
Mr. Robertson

Liv
5 Years Later

The black interior of the limousine with the wet bar, the large sunroof, and the partition glass was all luxurious and a far cry from my own small Volkswagen beetle.

It had been almost forty-five minutes since the driver had picked me up at my building in the center of Chicago. We were now in the suburb of Winnetka.

With a major in anthropology, I was fascinated with the different demographics in neighborhoods. Winnetka shouted money: the beautiful view of Lake Michigan, the stately houses, and the lush golf course where well-dressed players drove golf carts and enjoyed time with their friends.

The glass partition lowered between the driver and me. "We're almost there, Miss Christensen."

"Thank you."

Opening my bag, I pulled out my phone and looked at the mysterious email I'd received three days ago.

Dear Ms. Christensen,

We trust you are well.
Mr. Robertson, chairman of Solver Industries, would like to meet and discuss a private matter with you this Thursday, October 22nd, at 5 p.m.
Are you available?

Regards,
Damon Green,
PA for Mr. Robertson, Solver Industries.

The email didn't give me any more details than it had the first time that I'd read it. Not even my response to Damon Green asking for an agenda had resulted in answers.

All he had been able to say was that he didn't know the agenda, as the meeting was of a private nature.

I wasn't one to jump when rich people asked me to, but Robertson was among the hundred most influential men in the world and a benefactor to Harvard, which I'd graduated from. He was known for his sharp intellect and his impressive rags-to- riches story.

The limousine took a sharp turn and continued up a gorgeous driveway where tall trees formed an arched canopy above us.

My parents had money but this was a different level of wealth than what I'd grown up with. It was certainly in stark contrast to the modest life I lived now. With my student debt and a job as an International Nonprofit Administrator, I was lucky to have my two-bedroom apartment in a decent building in downtown Chicago.

The car came to a stop in front of a wide staircase in white stone. Before I had a chance to open my door, a man in a dark suit opened it for me.

"Welcome Miss Christensen. I'm Damon Green. We corresponded."

"Hello." Stepping out of the limousine with all the grace my mother had instilled in me from early childhood, I offered my hand to Damon, who was in his fifties and reminded me a little of an old-fashioned butler with the way he stood straight.

"How was the drive?"

9

"Fine, it's a pretty area."

"Yes." Waving his hand to the staircase, he gave me a polite smile. "Mr. Robertson is ready to see you."

We walked up the stairs and into the grand entry, where two curved staircases provided symmetry in a room created to impress.

"May I take your jacket?"

"Yes, please."

Damon waited for me to shrug out of my soft green leather jacket, which had been high fashion three years ago.

"Thank you. It's right this way." With my jacket across his arm, Damon walked over and opened two French doors into another opulent room with a lit fireplace and four large floor-to-ceiling windows that provided a breathtaking view of the pristine garden and the lake in the distance.

"Ms. Christensen is here, sir."

An old man rose from a reading chair close to the window.

I recognized him as Mr. Robertson from the research I had done, but he looked tired and older than in the pictures I'd found of him online.

"Thank you for coming. Would you like something to drink?"

"Yes, thank you. Water would be fine."

Robertson was dressed in an expensive-looking suit but it was loose on him, making me think he'd lost weight recently. Walking over to an oval-shaped free-standing bar made of mahogany, he poured me a glass of water from a jug that still had ice cubes in it. "Here you go."

I stepped closer and took the crystal glass. "Thank you."

After pouring himself a glass, he motioned for us to sit down.

"You have a very beautiful house, sir."

"Mmm." Robertson gave a minuscule nod of his head.

I sipped my water, impatient to hear what he wanted to talk to me about.

"I need your help." He tapped his index finger on his glass. "And I think you need mine."

Shifting in my chair, I licked my lips, feeling nervous.

"You come from money, but now you're in need of it."

I frowned, not liking that he knew this about me.

"You grew up with easy access to funds. Your parents were described to me as rich and generous by nature. But then they cut you off a year and half before you graduated. That put you in a rough situation."

"I manage."

"Yes." Robertson lowered his glass and looked thoughtful. "You're a resourceful woman."

I wondered how many details he knew about the time my parents gave me the ultimatum to either break up with my boyfriend or be cut off financially. It had broken my heart, but I hadn't hesitated in choosing my independence and my self-respect.

"Can you confirm that you're no longer in a romantic relationship?"

My throat felt dry so I took a bigger gulp of water from my glass. "I'm not."

The relationship with Miguel had only lasted four months after the split from my parents, but I didn't regret standing my ground. Never had I imagined my parents would hold their money over me as leverage. It had infuriated me. Especially, since their argument that he wasn't good enough for me was based on the things that mattered to them and not to me. So what, if Miguel was a broke musician? He was kind and funny and we were great at laughing together. On our first date he took me salsa dancing and made me feel pretty and adored. When

11

I twisted my ankle four weeks into our relationship, he carried me seven blocks on his back.

I didn't pick him so he could make my parents look good among their friends, I picked him because he was transparent, funny, and kind.

And yet, over time, my parent's criticism had weighed down on our relationship. Things that hadn't bothered me before began to annoy me. Like the fact that Miguel couldn't pay his share of the rent. Or that he would box our food and give it to homeless people, which was a sweet thought, except I was the one paying for the groceries.

I couldn't afford to feed the neighborhood. Hell, I couldn't even afford to pay for Miguel and me.

My scholarships didn't cover my full tuition, and being financially cut off by my parents, I had been forced to obtain student loans and work on the side to not lose my apartment.

If it hadn't been for my friend Sydney, who introduced me to her lucrative side business, I wouldn't have graduated.

"I could use your services and you could use my money." Robertson had built the Solver empire and he was a man used to getting what he wanted.

My chest heaved in a deep intake of air. Of course he wanted to talk to me because of the services I could offer him. I should have known. "I'm very particular over whom I offer my services to. To be honest, I've only had four clients and they were regulars. Our age difference is something I'd have to think about before I agree to this, but what I can tell you is that I charge two thousand per event you bring me to. I have dresses for most occasions but if you require me to wear something specific, I'll have to approve it and the cost will be yours to cover on top of the two thousand. There are no sexual services included of any kind. No touching and no kissing but dancing is fine, as long as it's clean."

Robertson had straightened up in his seat and there was curiosity in his eyes now. "You're a very attractive woman, Ms. Christensen, but I'm seventy-six and you could be my granddaughter. I'm not asking you to escort me to a function."

"But you said that you needed my help."

"I do."

Crossing my legs, I admitted, "I'm confused."

"Mmm… yes, but before I reveal the nature of my request, I must ask that you sign a non-disclosure agreement. This is a private matter and I don't wish for the press to get a tip." Turning in his chair, he reached for a brown envelope and took out three pieces of paper for me to sign.

When it was done, he took his time to put them away before he folded his hands in front of him. "I've called you here because of my grandson, Charles. He went to Ireland to participate in a conference, and enjoy a few weeks of traveling around the country. The plan was for him to stay in Ireland for three weeks and then come back home and continue his work for Solver Industries. He's been gone for five months now and it's become clear to me that he's fallen prey to a cult."

He trailed off but I kept waiting for him to tell me more.

"I suppose Charles being involved with them is proof that having a high level of intelligence doesn't always come with a developed critical sense."

"Are you sure it's a real cult?"

"I've done my homework on the man who runs the cult, and I can spot a Machiavellian character when I see one. He's a charlatan who has Charles enthralled."

"It's not one of those religious doomsday cults, is it?"

13

"No, but there are a few factors that define it as a cult. Conor O'Brien preaches his own philosophy on spirituality, and on most evenings, the members sit for hours listening to his speeches that no one is allowed to question. Former members talk about worshipping O'Brien and his having control of their careers and money. The members are asked to cut off contact with family and friends, and should a member no longer be able to produce riches for O'Brien, he gets rid of them."

I'd leaned forward, engulfed in Mr. Robertson's pain. "That's awful. Have you warned your grandson?"

"Of course, but now he has stopped answering my calls." The old man looked out the window with sadness showing in every wrinkle on his face. "The first time he talked about the mastermind group that he'd joined, I was on my way into a meeting, so I didn't ask many questions. After that I didn't hear from him for several weeks until he finally returned my call."

When Robertson took another sip, his hands were shaking. "I was shocked at the things he said."

"What did he say?"

Robertson's eyes glazed over. "He talked about finding the family that he never had and he blamed me for not caring about him." A flash of pain crossed his face as he lowered the glass to his thigh. "Charles is my only grandchild. My late wife and I took him in when our son and daughter-in-law died. Charles was four."

"I'm so sorry for your loss."

"Thank you." His chin shivered a bit as if suppressed emotions were trying to find a way out. "I'm a busy man and looking back, I didn't take as much time for Charles as I should have. It was hard for Emmy and me; she was already sick and Charles had all those issues."

"What issues?"

With a sigh, Mr. Robertson threw a hand up. "There were the night terrors that would have him screaming from nightmares. Then there was his extreme shyness, which I suspect had a lot to do with his Tourette's. Of course, we gave him all the help money could buy, but for every year he went through therapy and treatments, it seemed the doctors just added more diagnoses to his chart. That boy had so many letters attached to him. ADHD, OCD, Asperger's, Tourette's, I don't know." He shook his head. "Sometimes I wonder if they blew it out of proportion, but for what it's worth, he got better over time."

The name Charles and Tourette's brought back a memory of a man I'd met at Harvard, but his last name had been McCann and not Robertson.

"As I said, Charles was only four when his parents died. It was a motorcycle accident. A drunk driver missed his red light and caused a frontal collision. My daughter-in-law, Rose, was killed on impact but my son hung on for a few more days until the doctors advised us to turn off the respirator. It just about killed Emmy. She mourned every day and then sixteen years ago when Charles was thirteen, we had to bury her too."

"And Charles' maternal grandparents; where are they?"

Robertson cleared his throat. "His mother, Rose, was Irish and that's why Charles wanted to travel around Ireland for a few weeks. He has an aunt and a grandmother on his mother's side, but they haven't heard from him in months either."

"Are you worried that he's hurt?"

"I know he's alive. My team looked into it and made me a report." He turned again and handed me a green file case. "Charles has moved into a commune. It's like the damn hippies with everyone calling each other family and sharing. Have you ever heard of a mastermind group that lives together? The moment I read that Charles now lives there, I knew that the Red Manor Mastermind Group is a cult."

"You really think your grandson joined a cult?"

"I know he did. My sources confirm it. It's run by a man called Conor O'Brien who sells himself as an enlightened genius." Robertson scoffed. "He's clever all right, targeting people from Ivy League colleges around the world who all think they're too smart to fall for something as cliché as a cult. Of course, it's not a coincidence that most of them come from rich and influential families either." Shaking his head with sadness, he looked away. "Young people are so naïve."

There was another moment of silence as if Robertson needed to collect himself.

"I'm more than happy to help any way I can, but I have no connections in Ireland. I'm not sure what it is that you want me to do."

He turned his face and pinned me with those intelligent eyes of his that shone with determination. "I want you to get Charles out of the cult, of course."

I jerked back and squeezed the arm rest of the chair I was in. "How? I don't even know your grandson. What makes you think that he'll listen to me?"

"You've met him. You attended the same university."

"I assure you, sir, that I didn't even know we had a member of the Robertson family on campus."

"That's because he enrolled under his mother's maiden name, McCann." From his inner pocket, Robertson pulled out a picture and handed it to me.

It was the man from the coffee shop in a serious pose from his graduation day. His dark hair was a bit unruly but he looked confident, handsome, and as well built as I remembered. I nodded. "Yes, I've met him."

The memory of our first encounter still made my toes curl. I had been a freshman blown back by the stranger that had walked into the café, exuding intelligence and elegance. But no matter how much I'd tried to make eye contact with him, he wouldn't look my way. With the confidence of a young woman used to being hit on, I had gone over to order, just so I could have a chance to talk to him. It hadn't worked out, since Charles had shown zero interest in me. In my eagerness to start a conversation with him, I'd made a big fool of myself and when I proceeded to take a sip of his coffee, the humiliation had been complete.

"I looked into your background and found a few details that makes me optimistic that you're perfect for the job." Turning in his chair, Mr. Robertson pulled out another set of printed papers and handed them to me. "You should recognize this paper. You authored it."

I let my fingers run over the title: *Mind control: Myths and Facts.* It was a paper I'd written in psychology.

"You have seventeen pages describing the ways cult leaders brainwash their victims."

"Do I?"

"Yes, and quite a few describing unhealthy company dynamics that take place in modern-day business. Some of which I'd like to discuss with you another time."

I moved in my seat. "As I said, I'd like to help, but just because I know a bit about how cults work doesn't change that I've only met your grandson a few times, and that was years ago. What makes you think that he'd be interested in anything I have to say?"

"Hmm… come with me. There's something that I want you to see." Mr. Robertson got up and swung a hand, gesturing for me to go first.

He took me back through the grand entrance and into a small elevator. "I used to run up and down those stairs, but now, my hips don't like them much."

On the second floor, we got out and walked to a bedroom with large, robust furniture in dark wood. Unlike the rest of the house, it was a little untidy in here with random-looking objects spread around.

"This used to be Charles' room." Robertson walked over and touched a globe on the desk that stood against one of the three windows in the room. "After our last conversation when he cut me off, I came in here hoping to find clues… and maybe to feel a bit of a connection because I missed him." He sighed. "But either way, I found something that led me to you."

My heart did a flip as I kept listening.

"I never cleared out this room after Charles bought his penthouse apartment in downtown Chicago. Turns out that he left some boxes here and in one of them there were some of his diaries and a few objects." Robertson moved to the bed and picked up a blue journal.

"I didn't take Charles for a guy who would keep a diary." Maybe it was the mystery of it all that had me on edge and making such an insensitive comment. "I'm sorry, it sounded like criticism, but I just meant that it's unusual, that's all."

Robertson held the journal in his hands. "Emmy taught him to use it as a tool when he was younger. She kept a diary from before I met her and over the forty-two years of our marriage, she often tried to get me to keep one of my own. According to her, journals offer a safe place to vent out the thoughts and emotions that we find it so hard to share with the people around us. With Charles being painfully shy and introverted, I suppose writing down his feelings became a stress reliever of sorts." Robertson lowered the book and frowned. "I don't believe

18

in snooping around in other people's diaries, but in this case, I'm trying to find a way to help my grandson out of the claws of a cult, and I'll do whatever it takes."

"I understand."

"Good. I don't need to remind you that you've signed an NDA. I'm going to leave you here to read what he wrote about you."

Charles wrote about me? Butterflies tumbled around my stomach as if a sudden gush of wind had knocked them off course.

Feeling like I was in a surreal trance, I watched Robertson place the journal on Charles' bed before walking past me and stopping by the door.

"I'll see you downstairs. If you decide to take the assignment and help me get Charles out of the cult, his journals will give you important insights into his personality and background that can serve you in winning his trust."

"Thank you."

The old man stood for a second with his hand on the door handle. "If you get Charles to leave the cult for good, I'm prepared to give you a million dollars."

My jaw hung low. "That's… a lot of money, but it's not necessary. I assure you: I'm happy to help if only you pay my expenses."

"I'm getting old and my health is declining fast. Believe me when I say that a million dollars is nothing compared to what I'd give to make peace with Charles before I die. The sad reality is that I've worked my entire life to create an empire for my heir, and now he doesn't want it." His shoulders sagged and he looked thoughtful.

"Did Charles say that?"

His eyes glazed over again. "He said he needed to do some soul searching. It's ironic, isn't it? I never did much of that, but these past months I've had a lot of time to

19

think. I worked so hard to give him a privileged life but at the same time, I made him a target for charlatans and criminals like O'Brien. That's why I've changed my will. If I die before Charles is outside the influence of the cult, he won't get his inheritance."

"Nothing?"

"Nothing. I'm hoping O'Brien will release his claws on Charles once he learns there's no inheritance. If he does, I'll have given Charles something worth more than money."

"So, you're saying that if I don't get Charles out of the cult, he'll lose his entire inheritance. How long do I have?"

"If we're lucky, a few months."

I stared at the old man. "Are you... dying?"

"We all are. My time is just coming sooner. Or at least, so my doctors tell me, but I'm not convinced." He didn't stay to elaborate but walked out. When the closing of the door clicked behind me, I moved forward and picked up the book on the bed. A bookmark stuck out on top, marking where Robertson wanted me to read from. My hands were shaking when I opened it.

December 16th.
I ran into her again tonight. Charlie from the coffee shop.
She was standing with some of her friends outside Lucy's Bar. One of them was smoking and they were tipsy.
It surprised me that she called out to me because it's been over a month since that awkward meeting at the coffee bar. It's stupid how much I've thought about her and all the witty things I wished I'd said to her that day. Twice, I've seen her on campus and both times she smiled at me, but I was so stressed about the pep-talk in my head to go and talk to her, that she was gone before I mustered as much as a smile. I've been so certain that by now she would have categorized me as either stuck-up and arrogant or a complete basket case.

That's why I was surprised when she called out to me.
She's gorgeous! I mean, even wearing a red nose and a hairband with reindeer horns sticking straight up, she looked stunning. As always, I'll try to write everything down as detailed as I remember it.

I was alone, sober, and on my way home, but I stopped and took in her outfit, which matched what her friends were wearing.
"Ugly Christmas sweater theme," she told me and pulled at the red and green knitted sweater she was wearing with the text "Jolly AF" on her front. And then she introduced me to her three friends. "Everyone, this is Charlie, my name twin."
One of the three nodded and grinned. "Ah, the one whose coffee you poisoned with your toxic lips."
It made me want to turn on my heel and leave because, yeah, I'm the idiot who said I'd throw away the lid of my cup after she took a sip, but Charlie just laughed it off and introduced me, "These are my friends, Sydney, Alicia, and Maggi."
The woman she had introduced as Maggi swayed a little and grinned. "You look way too serious and sober on a Saturday night. It's December. You should be celebrating."
Alicia lit up and tapped Maggie on the arm with eagerness. "You know that thing we talked about earlier. The ugly Christmas sweater competition. He should be our ref and decide which sweater is the ugliest."
I stiffened. I have a hard time talking to one pretty girl and right there I had four wanting me to engage with them.
Sydney, a young woman with an impressive afro, pointed to her sweater. "What do you think?" It was dark green with white patterns on the front and it said "Merry Elfin Christmas."
"Mine is better, wouldn't you say?" Alicia, who was another dark beauty, came over to place her hand on my shoulder.

21

Her sweater had two snowmen with carrot noses made of orange fabric sticking out prominently from her breasts.

Feeling uncomfortable with her touch, I moved a little and looked at Maggie's shirt. She was the shortest of Charlie's friends but compensated with high heels and a large bun on her head. Her sweater was blue with a train that said "Bipolar Express."

Charlie spread out her arms and grinned. "It's a tough call, isn't it?"

"Yes. Am I judging the craftwork of the sweater, the absurdity of it, the fit, the colors, or the creativity? I mean what criteria should I base this important ruling on?"

"Just pick mine. It's the only one in 3D," Alicia begged and pointed to the carrots sticking out.

I picked Charlie's, simply because her smile warmed me to the bone. That made Maggie swing a hand through the air and boo at me. "Sober people can't make important decisions like that. You need to be at least a little drunk to appreciate the humor behind these masterpieces."

"Yeah... honestly," Sydney complained.

"Don't listen to them, they're sore losers." Charlie gave me a beaming smile that could have melted all the snow in the entire street. But then her friends wanted to go back inside to dance.

"Let's move, ladies." Maggie with the high bun flicked her cigarette butt into a snowbank and moved to the entrance, where loud music was booming.

"You wanna come bust some moves with us?" Charlie asked me as her friends were dancing up against a bouncer who waved them back inside.

The idea of dancing with her and potentially touching her was exhilarating, but I was stone sober and too fucking aware that I wasn't going to impress her with my dance moves, unless swaying from side to side counts, so I excused myself saying, "Ehh... I can't tonight."

Maybe it was the flash of disappointment on her face that made me burst out, "About that day in the coffee shop."
"Yeah?"
"Remember how you asked if I winked at you? I didn't wink on purpose. It's my... It's my Tourette's."
Her eyes widened. "You have Tourette's?"
"Yes." Right then a set of tics underlined it.
"But I thought Tourette's was people swearing and cursing at random times."
"It can be, but that's rare."
"Liv, are you coming?" One of her friends popped her head out the door and called for her. "Oh, and bring tall and handsome with you. We'll grind up against his sober ass and bring out the Christmas spirit."
That comment made me smile a little.
"I'll be right there, Sydney." Charlie turned her attention back to me. "You were saying?"
I told her about my involuntary tics. "That's why I was blinking that day in the coffee shop."
"Huh. And here I hoped that you were flirting with me." She winked and gave a tipsy grin and even now that I'm writing this, just thinking back to how gorgeous she looked at that moment, red nose and all, I get hard.
I wish I could write that I went inside and danced all night with Charlie, but the shameful truth is that I blew it once again when my shyness spoke for me. "No, I didn't. I don't. I mean I didn't flirt with you."
She made a mock face of disappointment and opened her mouth to speak, and just then we were interrupted by a group of five drunken guys who came singing down the street.
"Hey, Charlie," one of them yelled and came over to plant sloppy kisses all over her face. I was trying to remember if he was the same one who had wanted a bite of her cinnamon bun the first time that I met her.

23

I stepped back and watched her try and push him away, laughing. To my relief he stopped and moved back to his group, who were trying to bribe the doorman to let them in to the bar.

"One of your girlfriends called you Liv. Which do you prefer more? Charlie or Liv?"

She was rubbing her pretty cheeks from all the sloppy kissing before. "I go by my middle name Liv or Charlie. As long as you don't call me Charlotte it's fine. I never liked that name."

"Your last name was Christensen, wasn't it?"

"Wow, you remember? Do you have an exceptional memory or something?"

"Yeah." I didn't tell her that I'm bad with names in general. Her name had just been branded in my mind since I first met her.

The sloppy kisser came back and pulled her with him, insisting that she owed him a dance. It was my cue to walk on, so I raised my hand and told her that I'd see her around.

The first thing I did when I got back home was look her up on social media. Charlotte is twenty-one and from Chicago like me. What are the odds?

I was pumping myself up to write her a message but as I looked over her pictures, the same guy kept popping up and her relationship status said, "it's complicated."

Maybe if I wait another few weeks it'll have changed to single. I hope it does.

Lowering his diary, I felt weird for having read Charles' private thoughts about me.

That night, I'd been convinced that he was out of my league, but felt honored that he took time to talk to me. How in the world had I misinterpreted his shyness for disinterest when I considered myself a people person? I moaned a little thinking about my conversation this

morning with Sydney, who had wor
here alone. I had told her that I was
reading people.

Apparently not!

I looked down at the box, where
bottom. A pair of white lace pa
handwritten notes, a tie, and a black lid to a coffee cup.

I stared.

A lid to a coffee cup.

Is that…?

Picking up the small lid, I felt goosebumps rise on my arms.

He saved it.

As if the sun had broken through the clouds on a hot summer day, warmth spread in my body.

Reading the last part of his entry again from five years ago, I regretted that I'd never heard from Charles.

My relationship status of "it's complicated" had changed to "in a relationship" within two weeks of that night, but it had been a constant struggle between Chad and me, and things had never developed into a strong and committed relationship like the one I had later on with Miguel.

Holding the lid in my hands and having read Charles' words about me, I felt a strong urge to see him again. If Charles was in trouble, I would help him any way I could.

Putting the lid back in the small box, my fingers touched the handwritten notes and curiosity made me pick them up. The writing was feminine and beautiful and my eyes swallowed the words.

Charles,
Please don't push me away.
You know my situation.

25

...ever ask anything of you, but you have needs and
...
...et me today in the laundry room at 3:30.
—T

Concluding that Charles had a sexual relationship with someone who had access to his house, I picked up the second note and arched a brow.

Is it wrong that I'm getting addicted to your body? Thank you for making my workday so pleasurable by sneaking in quickies. I don't want the summer to end and for you to go back to school.
—T

Okay, so it was someone working here. I wondered if Mr. Robertson knew about it and how many years ago this affair had taken place. By school, did the woman refer to college? Or maybe high school? I frowned and put the notes back. It wasn't any of my business. The only thing that mattered right now was finding a way to get Charles out of the cult.

CHAPTER 2
Ireland

Liv

Six days after my meeting with Mr. Robertson, I found myself standing outside a small bed and breakfast in Ireland. The clouds hung low and the air was humid from this morning's rain as I waited for the contact that Mr. Robertson had set me up with.

It had been such a hectic week with my mood swinging like a pendulum between excitement and self-doubt. There were moments when Mr. Robertson's faith in me made me feel like Wonder Woman flying in to fight injustice. But then I'd get these moments of fear that took my breath away. Rescuing someone from a cult was so far out of my expertise... why would Mr. Robertson trust me with something this important when I had zero experience?

The small village where I'd been staying for the night was waking up with a car starting in the distance, a man biking past me with a nod, and a cat strolling toward me from the corner of the house.

It was pretty here. Last night I'd walked around and taken in the lush fields surrounding the village, with its cute houses that spoke of owners who took pride in where they lived. The cat stopped in front of me and meowed as if saying, "Hey there, stranger, I haven't seen you before."

I squatted down to pet him and right away the large cat began to press his body against my leg.

"You like this, don't you?"

His loud purr was answer enough.

"Found any rats lately? I'm hunting for a big nasty one myself."

"Talking to the cat, are ye?"

I looked up to see a woman in her thirties walking toward us. Her cheeks were red and matched her hair.

"Never trust a cat. They tell all yer secrets."

Standing to my full height I shook the hand she was holding out to me. "Hello."

"Hi. I'm Kit. I assume ye're Charlotte?"

"Yes, but you can call me Liv."

"All right." She smiled but then her face fell. "What's wrong?"

"Eh, I'm sorry, but are you K.C. O'Rourke?"

"I am. My full name is Kathy Christiana O'Rourke, but I've been Kit since I was a wee lass." Her Irish accent was charming, but she was nothing like I would have imagined from the report she had prepared. It had been so sharp and precise that in my mind I had imagined a former military man was behind it.

"It's just that after reading the report, I had this image in my head of you being a gruff former policeman or a retired military sergeant with battle scars."

She grinned and began dragging her leg. "I can fake a limp for ye, if that helps, and I could make up a brutal story of being shot by a target that I was surveilling."

I grinned back and instantly liked her humor. "You're fine, don't worry about it."

"Good, but we actually have one of those men in the family. My dad started O'Rourke Investigations. He's been in the industry for over forty years and the shite he's seen has made him battle-scarred in here." She touched her chest.

"You work with your father then?"

"I do, but my brother Tommy and I are in the process of taking over. My younger brother is in the gardaí. He just joined the ERU." There was such pride in her voice that I had to ask:

"I'm sorry, I didn't catch that. Did you say that your brother joined the guard? Do you mean the coast guard?"

She smiled. "No. Our police force is called the garda síochána na hÉireann. It means guardians of the peace of Ireland but we just call them guards or garda."

"Oh, all right and you said he joined the RU, what is that?"

"I said, the ERU. It stands for Emergency Response Unit. It's like yer SWAT team. They're legit badasses with their helmets and big guns, blowing doors off their hinges and taking down armed criminals. It's been Damian's dream ever since he was a wee fella. He only just turned twenty-seven last month and that makes him one of the youngest to ever make the unit." She squared her shoulders. "Ninety-five percent don't even make it through the first two hell weeks. Ninety-five! Can ye imagine how tough ye'd have to be?"

"Wow, that's impressive. A whole family of crime fighters. How come you didn't join the police?"

She flashed her teeth. "Because the pay is rubbish. I can make more as a private detective. Now tell me, how was yer journey?"

"It was fine, thank you."

"Good. I hope ye're not too jetlagged 'cause we have a lot of work to do."

The cat was still trying to get my attention and it followed us when we began walking the way Kit had come.

"Do you think it's hungry?"

"Nah, it looks overweight, so someone is feeding it. About that, did ye eat breakfast?"

I nodded.

"Good. I parked my car around the corner. I'm takin' ye to meet one of the survivors who lives outside of Derry.

29

That's why we're meeting here, up North. I thought about booking ye a hotel in Derry but my da suggested we should expose ye to a bit of the Irish country side. Isn't it lovely?"

"Yes. It's very peaceful."

"I'm glad ye like it. Later today, I'll take ye down to Dublin. It's a four-hour drive so that should give ye time to read my report, in case ye didn't already?"

"I did, and I have questions." Droplets of rain began falling again but this was October and I'd brought my rain jacket. "You said that there's been some mysterious deaths."

Kit walked over to a Toyota and we both got in before she answered, "Aye, there are five children living in the house and I've been trackin' down the mother of one of them. Turns out she's dead." Kit started the car and didn't wait for me to bugle up before we sped off.

"But her child is there?" I said and hurried to secure the seatbelt.

"Aye. It's a boy, and I only know about it because one of the survivors told me about him."

"What's his name?"

"Nathan. He's fourteen."

"How did his mom die?"

"Suicide. I'm trying to get more information. Honest to God, I didn't know we had a cult in Dublin. It's scary." It was fascinating how such a severe subject seemed less threatening because of her up-and-down lilt with each word. "I mean, the more I dig around, the more I worry that I've fallen over a demon or somethin'." She made the cross in front of her face. "That man, Bricks, he's such a menace, ye know, like a weed that keeps poppin' up in yer garden even though ye try to scrap it. When the English police had him on their radar, he just moved on."

I remembered that Conor O'Brien's real name was Conor Brick from the report, but I was getting nervous from the way Kit was driving through the narrow streets of the village, on the wrong side of the road.

My fingers folded around the panic handle on the door. "Where are we going?"

"I thought ye'd like to speak to one of the survivors yerself. There's a woman whom I tracked down a few days ago, and awk... does she have stories to tell."

"Can we trust her?"

"I would na bring ye to her if I didn't think so. I'm cross-checking her stories and it's good. Her name is Eileen and she got out of the cult about seven months ago."

It took twenty minutes for us to reach Eileen, who lived with her grandmother in another village. The woman had a large overbite that made me think of Freddie Mercury. She was a bit plump and looked like a timid mouse.

"Won't you come in and sit down?" She took us through the house to the kitchen, where tea stood ready on the small round dining table.

"Thank ye for seeing us." Kit had already introduced us and was now sitting down, placing the case file in front of her. "Liv is goin' to try and get a man named Charles out, so she can use all the help ye can give her."

Eileen poured tea for us and spoke with a distinct British accent. "I wish someone had gotten me out a lot sooner."

I gave her a sympathetic nod. "How long were you a member of the mastermind group?"

"About four years."

"Can you tell me about the group?"

Setting the teapot down, Eileen sighed. "In the beginning, I loved it there. Everyone was so smart and articulate. They had ambitions of making the world a

31

better place and I was flattered that I got to be part of this exclusive group. My friend had been talking about it for months as a secret society that guaranteed future success. I mean, the names of the alumni alone would make anyone desperate to join. According to my friend, O'Brien had worked with several public figures and people you see on TV. Of course, now I know most of those people were never members to begin with, but at the time I thought that his mastermind group was like a modern-day Illuminati for the gifted. My friend kept telling me that O'Brien would only invest his time in you if he thought you were special."

Blowing down on her tea, Eileen muttered, "I wanted to feel special and so when one day the miracle happened and my friend was invited, I begged her to bring me along."

Kit moved in her chair, "What was it like?"

"I think the best word to describe it would be a love-fest. It was the most welcoming atmosphere, with an interest in me as a person. All night, people would hang on my every word, laugh at my jokes, and make me feel more welcomed than ever in my life. And then there was Conor himself. The enigma of a man whom people were talking about like he was the new Messiah. The excitement I felt when he asked to speak with me and I was led to him..." Eileen sighed again. "That man has a way of looking into your soul and telling you exactly what you want to hear. It all resonated with me. I thought myself lucky to be invited into his mastermind group. He was going to make me into someone others wanted to be like. Not only would I help the world be a better place, but I would become one of the celebrities on TV. Someone with influence and followers." She stopped talking for moment, a small frown on her face, as she looked down at the tea in her hands.

"How would he do that?" I asked.

"The way he described it was that the mastermind group was a network of carefully selected people, like a freemasonry group where everyone were brothers and sisters, sworn to secrecy. We were the enlightened ones with access to resources like no other. And he was right. Some of the people in the room were from affluent and influential families, and I wanted desperately to be part of their so-called family."

"Did you come from money?" I asked.

"My family is wealthy, but nothing like some of the others. I think his interest in me was because of my connections. You see, I bragged to him that I'm related to the royal family on my mother's side, which is true, but in my eagerness for him to like me, I exaggerated my family's influence quite a bit."

"What happened after you became one of his followers?"

Eileen blinked her eyes. "First of all, you have to understand that I never saw it like that. I never suspected that it was a cult and neither does your friend."

I nodded for her to go on.

"In the beginning it was a dream come true. Our conversations in the group were deep and philosophical at times, but for the most part we shared knowledge with each other. Conor taught us how to be influential and read body language. He taught us NLP and the art of conversation and discussion."

"What's NLP?" Kit asked.

"Neurolinguistic Programming."

"Oh, okay."

"I loved it. Like a sponge, I soaked up all the amazing things he taught us. The place was full of gifted people who would share their knowledge of history, art, literature, or whatever they were studying. The house was buzzing with smart people on a mission and there was nowhere I'd rather be..." Eileen's voice dropped, "My social life outside of the group fell apart. I couldn't share what was happening in the group because of my sworn secrecy and when my friends and family asked questions, I couldn't answer them. It created conflicts and within a year, I'd lost the people I considered friends before I joined the Red Manor Group."

I gave a another nod of sympathy. "What about the friend who brought you in the first place?"

Eileen zoomed in on me. "She didn't join."

"Why not?"

"The whole thing gave her the creeps." She shrugged. "I guess she had a much better developed sixth sense than me, but back then I bought into O'Brien's story that he'd asked her not to come back. According to him, she wasn't the right fit for the group and he didn't see enough potential in her. I remember thinking that her warning of the place's being weird was coming from a place of jealousy."

Eager to hear the story, I leaned forward. "When did you realize that something wasn't right?"

"I'm ashamed to say that it took me years. I think I lost my sense of self in there. Whoever I was before I entered was slowly chipped away until I'd bought into the ideology and lived it with my whole being. My greatest goal was to make Conor proud of me, to be of service to the group, and to prove myself worthy." Her voice slowed down and tears formed. "It's like that saying about boiling a frog. The pressure starts out slow but then it increases. Conor would question my loyalty to the group and him. His reminders that the group was only for a select few and there was no room for doubters made me sob in my room, where I would come up with desperate ways to prove how much I trusted and loved him. I'd meditate more, study harder, volunteer for cleaning and kitchen duty, I'd offer my body to him, and donate all my money. I gave him everything I had, and he took it, sucked me dry, and still wasn't happy."

The pain in Eileen's voice made me swallow hard and fold my hands to fists.

"When O'Brien kicked me out, I was friendless, money-less, and had cut all ties with my family. He even convinced me that I was unworthy and that it was better if I left my friends inside the mastermind group alone. I was a mess. I guess I still am, but at least I began reaching out to other members who had moved out without saying goodbye, and I learned that they too had been kicked out."

"You didn't know?"

"No. When someone left unexpectedly, it was assumed that they had left on their own accord. Two times, I remember a public fight. One was River's mum, who embarrassed herself by clinging to O'Brien's feet and refusing to let go. She begged him to let her and River stay but he accused her of stealing from the group. Little River tried to comfort her mother while crying herself. We all loved the girl so Ciara, who has two boys with O'Brien, asked him to at least consider letting River stay.

"It was horrible to watch when Julie left with her head bowed in shame. She was outside the door with tears down her eyes, telling River that she loved her, when Conor slammed the door shut before she could finish the sentence."

"That's pure bollocks!" Kit rocked back and forth with anger on her face. "That man is a weasel of the worst kind. To separate a mother and child like that, and ye did nothin'?"

"There wasn't anything I could do except comfort River and help her move on. It wasn't until I was kicked out myself that I reached out to Julie to find out what really happened."

35

I arched an eyebrow. "Let me guess – she didn't steal any money."

"No – well, yes, in a way. You see, like me, she ended up without a penny in her eagerness to satisfy O'Brien. Millions of her inheritance had been transferred to his funds, except for a portion of three hundred thousand that was earmarked for River. It was when she refused to give him that money that he accused her of stealing."

"That's not stealing."

"No, except at one of her weakest moments she had told him he would get it, and when she failed to follow through, he cut her off."

"So, hang on. Is River one of the five children that lives in the house?"

"Yes. Her mother, Julie, is in a psychiatric hospital after she tried to kill herself three times."

I knew this from the report and nodded. "Did you meet Charles while you were there?"

"No, it's been seven months since I was inside the house. Your friend wasn't a member then."

I crossed my arms. "I need to find a way to get Charles out of O'Brien's claws. Do you have any suggestions?"

Eileen watched me closely. "I've been thinking about it ever since I heard you were coming. The sad truth is that I don't think you can. Conor O'Brien isn't an ordinary man. Some days I doubt he's even mortal. He will make you think he's the kindest person in the world while he's stabbing your heart. It's almost like witchcraft the way he holds power over people. If Charles has already been there for months, he'll be in too deep."

My shoulders sank. "You think it's hopeless?"

"I'm afraid so."

"I don't!" Kit sat up straighter. "Ye've just got to give Charles the hottest sex of his life and make him desperate for more. Men do stupid things for sex all the time."

Eileen turned to Kit. "I don't think you understand the kind of spell O'Brien's followers are under."

"Maybe not, but I know people go crazy for love. My cousin Richard left his wife and three babes because he fell in love, and my friend Andy moved to Finland to be with a girl he met in Ibiza. I mean if that's not some powerful love voodoo, I don't know what it is."

"What if Charles is in a relationship with someone inside the cult?" I asked.

Eileen snorted. "He's not."

"Why not?"

"Because O'Brien doesn't like to share attention and I've never seen him allow couples in the group."

"But you said that you offered your body to him and that one of the other women has two sons with him, so clearly O'Brien allows sex in the house."

Eileen looked away. "I offered but he rejected me. I'm not as attractive as some of the others." Again, her tone was heavy with sadness.

My heart went out to her and I placed my hand on top of hers and looked deep into her eyes. "In the US we have a saying. Sometimes a rejection is God's protection."

"I like that." Kit nodded. "And in this case, it's the truth. I wouldn't ride that man if he came with pedals. Ye should be relieved that you didn't give him yer body. He might have been inside yer head, but at least he never got inside yer fanny."

I liked Kit. She had to be at least five years older than me, but she was feisty and opinionated and her accent alone was amazing. "The more I hear about the mastermind group, the more I want Charlie out of there."

Eileen tapped the armrest of her chair. "I've seen friends and family show up and demand that members leave with them, but that never works. One mother once had her daughter kidnapped, but that backfired when the

37

daughter pressed charges. Not only was the mum convicted of kidnapping but her daughter never wanted to see her again. How well do you know Charles?"

"I don't. Well, we met five years ago and there was chemistry but it never evolved to anything."

They both stared at me and then Kit exclaimed, "But I thought ye were his girlfriend."

"No, I'm not. I'm just a girl he had a crush on once."

"Oh, for God's sake." Kit stared at me. "What made ye think ye had a chance then? I mean, friends and family of the members haven't been able to get them out. Ye hardly know the bloke."

"Charles' grandfather asked for my help and I'm here to try."

They both sighed but it was Kit who spoke, "Aye, ye might as well give it a go, but when ye do, it has to be all or nothin'. Ye'll have one chance to seduce the hell out of Charles and make him fall in love with ye. To get him out, ye've got to bind him to ye in a stronger bond than anything Conor could ever offer him."

Eileen looked thoughtful. "Do you know anything about what he likes or doesn't like? What his dreams are?"

"No, not really. I mean, I've read some of his diaries but I'm still not sure what he wants out of life."

Eileen looked at me with a grave expression. "I guarantee that O'Brien knows and it gives him power over Charles. Never forget that."

The two women were looking at me, and the silence in the small kitchen made the sound of the clock on the wall sound louder. "Tick, tock, tick, tock."

Kit's bright red hair stood in contrast to the green flowery wallpaper she was sitting against. Her raincoat was in her lap and the sleeves of her thin knitted sweater were pushed up on her forearms.

"I can't make Charles fall in love with me on purpose. It's been five years and he might not like what he sees anymore."

Kit studied me. "I'd do ye."

It was so forward and unexpected that I didn't know how to respond. There was no flirtatious smile and I hadn't taken Kit for a lesbian.

"Yes, I would too," Eileen muttered. "There are no men to fancy here anyway."

I put both my hands to my chest. "Aww, aren't you two being nice to me."

"Just trying to pump yer self-esteem a little 'cause when ye meet Charles, ye'd better knock his pants off with a wink."

"I'm not here to have sex with him."

"Why not?" Kit wrinkled her nose up. "Don't ye fancy him?"

"Yes. I had a massive crush on him, but I can't just throw myself at him."

Kit crossed her arms. "Then tell us yer plan."

"I'm going to befriend him and hopefully be invited inside. Once I'm there, I'll start to ask him questions to make him see how strange it all is."

"You can't do that." Eileen rested her elbows on the scratched-up kitchen table. "If you're not a full-on believer, O'Brien won't allow you to hang about. And if you push Charles too hard, he'll be caught between you and them. He might find you dramatic and not worth the trouble."

The kitchen fell silent again as my shoulders fell.

"I think..." Eileen paused and looked thoughtful. "I think your best chance of getting Charles out is to get *everyone* out."

"Ooohh, ambitious. Keep talking!" Kit sat up straighter.

39

"Conor is a criminal who thinks he's above rules and laws. If you could get inside and observe for a while, you might be able to help Kit and the gardai build a case against him. I mean, if Conor goes to prison, the Red Manor Group falls apart and that would free not only Charles but everyone there."

Kit turned to me. "What do ye think?"

"Well, I like the idea of saving everyone of course, but I'm not sure how to do it. Eileen, how do I get invited to stay there?"

She scratched her cheek. "I'm afraid there's no set formula. There has to be a room available. Conor is like a collector of people. If he sees someone he wants, he'll look at the people already occupying his rooms and get rid of the ones he likes the least to make room for his newest addition. It's unlikely that he'll invite you to stay, but if you get a chance, take it. And another thing..." Eileen leaned forward and took my hand. "See if you can get close to the children. They observe a lot more than the adults realize, but they don't always understand what significance it holds. You might get them to tell you things that no adult would."

"All right." I nodded. "I'm going to seduce Charles, try and become a member of the group, and lure information out of the children."

"Aye. Now, don't ye look so terrified." Kit rubbed my back with her hand. "Let's just take one step at a time. Charles works at Trinity, and tomorrow, I'll help ye bump into him and make it look like a coincidence. Maybe things will work out."

I gave a skeptical glance and rubbed my neck.

"Or maybe..." Kit looked to the kitchen counter, where a butcher block stood with large knives in it. "Maybe we should cut off a beloved part of O'Brien."

"You want to castrate him?" Eileen's tone lifted at the end of her sentence, expressing horror, but her eyes lit up with excitement.

"Naw, I was thinking about cutting out his lying tongue so he can't bewitch and trick more people. If we work together, I think we could do it."

I was trying to read Kit and looking for any sign that she was joking, but there was no smile or wink.

"Ehm, okay, let's keep within the law for now, and avoid any blood if possible. I'd love to know more about the people living there and any tips you can give me about do's and don'ts."

Eileen nodded and pulled out a notebook. "I've written down what I think might be useful to you."

Over the next hour and a half, she talked me through the different members, including the five children. She kept pulling her pink cardigan closer around her like a safety blanket to protect herself from the pain of reliving all that happened to her.

"Thank you so much for taking the time to brief me."

Eileen gave a small smile. "I don't like to talk about it, but Kit said that she's working on collecting evidence to take down Conor, and I support that. The man ruined my life."

Kit narrowed her eyes. "That bastard is so bad he'd even steal the blessin' from the holy water. Someone has to stop him and why not us three?"

Eileen nodded and put her hand in the middle of the table. "I'm in. I'll reach out to anyone I can remember leaving the group while I was there, and I'll search my memory for things that might help the case against him."

Kit covered Eileen's hand with her own. "Good! I'll help Liv meet Charles and then I'll keep searchin' high and low for any mistake Conor might have made, so we can bring him to justice once and for all."

41

I placed my hand on top of theirs. "I'm ready to open Charles' eyes and bring him home to make peace with his dying grandfather."

In that moment, Eileen's grandmother walked in with two dogs trailing after her. She came to a full stop and looked at us three women sitting around the kitchen table with our hands stacked. "What's this?"

"We're making a pact to bring down Conor O'Brien," Eileen answered, and I quickly added,

"And save my friend Charles."

The old woman was plump like Eileen and she looked well into her eighties. "Ah, I see..." she crossed her arms. "An Irishwoman, a Brit, and an American sittin' in a kitchen cooking up plans together. There has to be a joke there somewhere."

We smiled and Eileen said, "No, I assure you that we're serious."

"Awk, aye, I'm sure ye are. But it's a sad affair when women have to banter together to kill the dragon and save the prince. I do not like these modern times."

I laughed low. "I assure you that this is no fairytale and Charles is no prince. He's reserved and a little intimidating, to be honest, and he has Tourette's."

The old woman moved one of the dogs with her knee and came closer. "And yet when ye speak of him, yer face lights up."

"That's just because I haven't seen him for five years, and tomorrow, I finally get to see him again."

"Five years." Her wrinkled face scrunched up. "That's a long time."

My heart pumped faster, and I swallowed a lump in my throat. "I know, and it might sound strange to you all that I came when Charles and I only met a few times. I'm not sure I understand it myself, except that over the years, Charles has popped into my mind so many times. And now, after reading his diaries, I feel like I know him and we've been friends for years. There's this urgent pull in me to find him, and that *has* to mean something."

"Aye, sounds to me as if he's yer Owen."

"My Owen?" I frowned in confusion, but Kit gave a sad sigh.

"The one who got away. Owen was mine. Tall and rugged, with a large scar on his chin, and a devilish, gleam in his eye that made me cream my panties. Every time I can't sleep and need a good quick release, I fantasize about Owen. Is Charles yer go-to man?"

I felt my face heat up but nodded. "Definitely."

Eileen's grandmother had taken off her jacket and was eyeing me. "Aye, I can see how besotted ye are with him, but are ye certain he even remembers ye?

I filled my lungs with air and gave her a brave smile. "I guess we'll find out soon enough."

CHAPTER 3
Trinity College

Charles

A group of tourists passed me as I walked from the old historical buildings of Trinity College where I'd just taught a lecture on International Law.

The male student leading the guided tour talked about Trinity College being Ireland's oldest university and how it was once a monastery. The young guide was wearing the brown robe that used to be mandatory until the early seventies. He was charming and seemed very confident in his presentation.

"The Victorian buildings that you see now are not the original from when the daughter of Henry VIII founded Trinity College back in 1592. The oldest building that we have left is from 1699." He turned and pointed. "This statue is of one of our previous headmasters, George Salmon, also known as Grumpy George. It is said that he was so adamant about never allowing women into his fine school that he said, 'Women will enter Trinity College over my dead body.' This turned out to be an accurate prediction since despite his veto, the board eventually forced him to sign the papers opening up enrollment for women, but true to his word, George died a few days before the first woman, Isabel Johnston, arrived to study here.

"Now, it's become a tradition for the women who graduate here to climb up on his statue and have a photo taken with Grumpy George."

44

The group moved as the tour guide waved a hand. "Follow me, and I'll tell you about the time some students got fed up with a professor and shot him. It's this way."

I turned my head to the tour guide. *What? No one has told me about a professor getting shot! Was it recently?*

A quick look at my watch told me I had time, so I followed the large group to hear the rest of the story.

Some tourists were commenting to each other right in front of me. "Don't you just love the old-world charm with the cobblestones and the Victorian atmosphere? It's so adorable. We sure don't have anything like this back in Texas."

The guide stopped and waited for his audience to gather around him.

"The Rubrics building behind me is legendary because of several things. One, it's the oldest, more than three hundred years old. Two, it's the cheapest place to live on campus."

"Why? It looks so cute," a tourist asked.

"Oh, don't let the red bricks, the charming windows, and the central location fool you. This place has twelve apartments with four students in each. Yet there are only two bathrooms and they're outside. If you get here in the morning, you'll see tenants coming out of this door and walking all the way to that door. If they're lucky a bathroom is free. Otherwise they'll have to line up, and if that weren't bad enough, these buildings are freezing cold and drafty. But what makes these buildings truly legendary is the ghost that haunts them."

I smiled a little, enjoying the showmanship of the student guide.

"In 1734 a Fellow named Edward Ford lived in this building. He was hated by the students and one night there was a confrontation between him and a group of the young men. When they threw rocks through his window,

45

he shot at them, so some of them went back and got their own guns. Edward was shot when he came to the window to admonish them and it's said that he haunts this place."

"What about the men who shot him?" a man asked.

"Good question. An interesting twist to the story is that there were no witnesses. Despite fifty students living here, no one saw a thing. Do you think that's possible?"

A man with a German accent spoke up. "No way. The other students were just covering up for their friends who shot him."

"I think so too. The four men that the police named as the culprits were acquitted by the court, but the board still expelled them. Our next stop is the old library, which has been in a lot of movies."

I'd been standing on the outskirts of the group and was just about to walk away when a woman turned her head and met my eyes.

Charlie.

It had been years since I'd seen her, but I would have recognized her anywhere. She did a double take before her lips spread in a bright smile.

As the group moved on, we stayed behind, with me coming to stand in front of her. "Small world. What are you doing here?"

She grinned. "I know, right? I should be done with universities, but a friend told me that you can't visit Dublin and not see Trinity Library. Turns out you can get a tour and access to the library for almost the same price, so here I am – soaking up the ghost stories." She laughed and reached out to touch my elbow for a second. "And you, what are you doing here?"

"I teach here." My tics acted up, but the joy on her face to see me made me continue. "It's a long story, but my mom was Irish so I came to learn more about that side of my family and I just loved it here, so yeah, I decided to stay."

Her eyes widened. "As in permanently?"

"Maybe, I don't know."

"Wow. I thought I was being adventurous by taking a trip to Europe, but you just had to outdo me and move here."

We laughed together and then I looked after the group, who were turning a corner in the distance. "You're losing the group."

She looked back over her shoulder and then to me again. "It's okay, the tour was almost over and since you're a local now, how about you show me?"

"I'm afraid I'm not much of a historian." I scanned her hands for a wedding band and couldn't decide if the ring on her finger was only decorative. "Ehm, are you traveling alone or with someone?" I was half expecting some guy to come jogging and pull her away again.

"Alone." She bit her lip. "I needed some time to clear my head, you know. Things have been hectic these last years and…" She stopped herself. "I'm sorry, you're probably busy and I don't want to take up your time telling you about my sad love life."

Her words empowered me to ask what I should have asked the first time I saw her. "No, it's fine. I was going to grab some lunch and get some work done. Are you busy or do you want to have lunch with me?"

She lit up. "I'd love to."

"Great. Should I call you Charlie or Liv?"

"You remembered." She looked genuinely impressed and surprised. "I prefer Liv, if you don't mind."

Lifting my hand, I swung it to the main entrance. "All right, Liv. I know a nice Italian restaurant. Will that work?"

"Pizza always works for me."

"Yeah? Which pizza is your favorite?"

47

We made small talk as we walked the ten minutes to the Italian restaurant that I liked so much.

"This is so cute." Liv was doing a full spin, her head leaning back as she looked up at the old brick buildings surrounding the covered patio with the string lights, heaters, and brightly colored chairs and tables. "It's like a hidden gem."

"And they make amazing food on top of that."

Liv sat down at the table that the host had led us to. "I can't believe you recognized me after all these years."

"You haven't changed that much." I sat down too.

"No?" She shrugged. "That's because you only see the outside of me. Inside I've grown old and cynical." She followed her statement with a small wink that made my heart beat faster.

What was it about this woman? I'd only ever had brief encounters with her and every time I'd been spellbound by her.

"I hope you don't mind me saying this, Charles, but you've changed a lot. You look so grown up with your professor outfit."

I looked down at my black turtleneck and expensive gray blazer that was formal enough to follow dress code but allowed me not to wear a necktie.

"Your hair is all stylish. I like it."

"Does that mean you didn't like my hair before?"

"No, actually, I remember that I had this thought..." She trailed off and shook her head with a laugh. "Please don't judge, but the first time I saw you in that coffee bar, I remember thinking that I wanted to slide my hands through your hair. It looked so thick and soft."

That had me smiling more. "Why didn't you ask me?"

"Would you have let me touch you? I was a complete stranger." She wrinkled her nose up. "I'm outgoing and forward, but I'm not without social filters. Even I know that walking up to a hot guy and asking to touch him would be making a bad first impression, which of course I still did when I took a sip from your cup." She held both hands to her hair to underline how embarrassing that had been to her.

I smiled and couldn't get past the fact that she'd called me hot. "Don't worry about it. I was entertained by you."

"You were?"

A waiter brought us a basket of bread and asked for our order. I went with a salad while she ordered a pizza.

She looked around. "I'm so happy I ran into you, because I don't like going to restaurants by myself."

"No? It's not so bad. You just have to get used to it."

"Maybe, but I'm telling you that I've had the strangest guys approach me. It's like a woman sitting alone at a table is seen as an invitation for them to join me. One of them wouldn't stop talking about his collection of dried flowers, and another was a feces donor, which I didn't even know was a thing. I mean it's fascinating and admirable that he gets to help people with bowel problems, but I was eating when he brought up the subject."

"A feces donor. Really?"

"Yup."

"You sure he wasn't making it up?"

"That's what I thought, but I looked it up and it's true. Doctors use fecal transplants where they clear out the patients' digestive tract and then they infuse a dose of healthy stool containing the bacteria needed to digest food."

Picking up a piece of the warm bread, I broke it in two parts. "Interesting."

"Oh no, I'm doing it again. You're eating and I'm entertaining you with stories of stool. I'm so sorry, Charles. I don't know why I always behave so awkwardly around you. Maybe it's because you make me nervous."

49

I stopped my hand halfway to my mouth, and lowered the bread again. "I make you nervous?"

She was wearing a sweater again, this time gray and cozy-looking. "Yeah, you have such a refinement about you that's a bit intimidating."

I tasted the word. "Refinement."

"Mmm, you just look like you've read a thousand books and that you're eternally bored with us mediocre human beings."

That made me laugh. "That's your impression of me?"

"Am I wrong?" She flashed those perfect teeth of hers and swung her long brown hair back. I had seen her without make-up in the coffee bar, and with make-up outside of Lucy's bar. Today, she was somewhere in between, with a discreet amount that emphasized her natural beauty without being overpowering.

"I certainly have read thousands of books or at least it feels that way, but I wouldn't say that I'm bored. Didn't I just tell you that I found you entertaining at the coffee bar?"

She picked up her napkin and placed in it her lap before giving me a playful smile. "Sure, but we both know that you and I have chemistry, so I'm different than all the other sad humans you have to endure."

A tingle ran up my spine, and tics made me blink a few times. I should respond and keep the flirtatious energy going between us, but her comment about us having chemistry threw me off.

"Or maybe not?" She licked her lips, looked down, and shifted in her chair.

An awkward silence spread between us.

"Ehhm, you studied anthropology, didn't you?" I asked to change the subject.

"Yes, I graduated with a major in anthropology and a minor in psychology. Now I work for an NGO but I'm not loving it as much as I thought I would." She smiled at the waiter who brought us our drinks and then she took a sip of her Pellegrino.

"So, what are you going to do?" I lifted the cold lager that the waiter had placed in front of me.

"I don't know. This is a weird time in my life. I feel like I'm standing in this huge roundabout with roads going in a hundred directions around me. I've worked so hard to get here. Gotten my degrees, cleaned out toxic relationships, and become independent. I finally have freedom to live my life, but I'm terrified of choosing the wrong path.

"Careerwise?"

She planted an elbow on the table and rested her chin in her palm. "Career, relationship, family, what city to live in. I'm unsure about where to go from here."

"Having choices can be stressful." I thought about it. "I was a bit lost myself, but I've found an amazing group of people here in Dublin and things are beginning to make sense."

"When you say people, does that include a partner?" Her tone was soft. "I don't see a ring on your hand."

So, I'm not the only one who looked for that.

"No, I'm not married." I was flattered that she even cared. "You?"

"Nope. That's where the cynical part of me comes from. I haven't had much luck in love."

"Why?" The question flew out of me. People like Liv who were outgoing, intelligent, and beautiful had been blessed from birth. If they couldn't make love work, then how were people like me with a whole boatload of issues supposed to stand a chance?

"I'd love to tell you that it was all because of my awful taste in men, but my therapist wants me to take responsibility, so the honest truth is that I'm a bit much to handle for any man."

"What do you mean?"

"Why would I tell you that when I'm trying to make a good impression? Or is that too late?" There it was again, her easygoing flirtatious energy that reached me like a seductive force of female power.

"What do you have to lose? As I see it, it's better to wear your uniqueness as a beacon. Just lay it all out. The people who can't handle you will move on, and the people who are part of your tribe will have an easier time finding you."

"Oh, I love that." She paused and leaned back to make room for the food that was brought to our table. "I knew you were a smart guy."

Digging my fork into my salad, I shrugged. "I can't take credit for those words. My mentor taught me that."

"You have a mentor?"

"Uh-huh. So back to your theory that you're too much for men to handle. Tell me more." My shoulder lifted and my eyes winked in a series of tics.

A shy smile spread on Liv's lips. "You want to know the skeletons in my closet? All right, I'll show you mine if you show me yours."

I chewed and swallowed the salad in my mouth before responding. "I already told you I have Tourette's."

"Yeah, but that's just part of your charm. We're talking skeletons here. Scary, rattling skeletons that make your lovers run away screaming."

She thought my Tourette's was charming? I didn't have time to process that because she was pointing at me with a slice of pizza in her hand. "I want juicy, dirty details."

"I'm socially awkward."

"Don't tell me that you take sips from other people's coffee cups or you tell them about poop when you want them to like you?"

"No." I smiled at her self-deprecating irony. "But I'm shy and introverted."

"Yeah, no…" She shook her head. "You're going to have to find something better than that."

"I've never had a serious relationship."

She stiffened and raised an eyebrow. "Define serious."

"I've never had someone call me their boyfriend and vice versa."

"Wait…" She moved forward in her chair and lowered her voice. "You're gay?"

"No!" I didn't have a problem with gay people, but I didn't want Liv to doubt that I was interested in women.

"Then why did you say vice versa? That would mean you called each other boyfriend."

"Wrong choice of words. I meant that I haven't been in a committed relationship."

"Oh, okay." Her fingers were picking up some strings of melted cheese and placing them on top of her pizza slice. "Maybe you just haven't found the right woman yet."

"Maybe." I moved in my seat. "I actually met one that I thought could be the right one not so long ago."

"Here?"

"Yes. Her name is Sara and I met her my first week in Dublin. She's a lawyer like me and I met her at the conference that I attended when I first arrived here. She was outgoing, charming, intelligent, kind, and I just had an instant connection with her." I put down my fork and raised my lager again. "She was the one who introduced me to my mentor and the group of people I've come to like so much."

"Nice. So, what happened? I'm sensing it didn't work out the way you wanted it to."

53

"No, Sara isn't in a place in her life where she can commit to a relationship. She says it's constricting for our souls and that love should be an energy shared without labels."

Liv swallowed her food and lowered her brow. "What does that even mean? Is that a fancy way to tell you she wants you to have an open relationship?"

"Could be. But that's not my thing. And besides, she shares her love with O'Brien, so…"

"Who's O'Brien?"

"Conor O'Brien is my mentor. He runs a mastermind group out in Howth, where I live." I leaned back. "Now show me one of your skeletons."

Sucking in a deep breath, Liv seemed to think about it before she met my eyes. "Okay, but anything we tell each other has to stay between us."

Chills ran up and down my spine from the intimacy between us. "You have my word."

"My last boyfriend told me that…" She rubbed her forehead. "This is so embarrassing."

I waited.

"When we broke up, he told me that I… snore." The last word came out in a mumble and I didn't understand.

"You do what?"

She whisper-shouted it. "I snore."

"Oh."

"Not all the time but enough that he threw it in my face when we broke up."

"And you don't think a man can handle you because of that?"

"It's not very sexy, is it?" She looked around. "And I have this thing that drove him crazy…"

"Don't tell me you crack your fingers. That would drive me crazy too."

"No, but I get excited and I interrupt."

54

"You haven't interrupted me."

"Yet. It's something I'm working on, but give me long enough and I will."

I crossed my arms. "I feel like I showed you a big six-foot-seven skeleton and you're showing me these kid ones."

"Hey, snoring and interrupting aren't attractive traits in a person."

"Sure, but you've got to have something worse than that. I've got twenty years of extensive therapy for all sorts of shitty disorders like OCD and ADHD, and my Asperger's alone counts for a whole regiment of skeletons."

"Why? Isn't Asperger's that thing that make people clever, like Rain Man? I'll bet you were a straight A student."

"I was, but being autistic is no joke, Liv."

"No, I'm sorry, I didn't mean it like that." She looked down.

"It's hard for me to show my emotions and I can't always read people. Sometimes I come across as insensitive and arrogant without wanting to."

"Can I ask you something?"

I nodded.

"You say it's hard for you to show emotions, but do you still have as wide a range as other people?"

Looking around at the other guests in the restaurant, I thought about it. "That's hard for me to know, isn't it? Can you say if you have a wider range of emotions than the people at that table, or that one? How do you measure something like that? We Aspies are all different and I'm on the lighter end of the spectrum. I feel anger, sadness, empathy, and frustration just like other people, but it's my ability to express those emotions that can be hard at times. There've been situations where people have called me cold and uncaring, but it wasn't that I didn't feel. I just couldn't be there for them."

Liv took it all in. "Wow." She breathed. "That's a big skeleton to have in a relationship."

I picked a cherry tomato from my plate and popped it in my mouth. "Compared to your puny ones, it is."

We returned to eating a bit more. "I do have one big thing that is very private."

Lifting my gaze to watch her, I waited for her to go on. "It's kind of a fetish really."

"A sexual fetish?" My back straightened with interest.

"Yes. But it's only something I would ever discuss with a lover I trust."

"But it's a skeleton?"

She tilted her head from side to side. "It's something that can be either a turn-on or turn-off."

"What is it?"

Liv smiled. "If you ever become my lover and we grow to have complete trust, I'll tell you."

My napkin lifted in my lap from the mere thought of being her lover.

"If your fetish turns me off, you don't want me as your lover to begin with."

"I suppose you're right about that. My sister says there's someone for all of us, but apparently, my man is playing some lame game of hide and seek because I can't find him anywhere."

My fingers tapped against my glass. "And are you looking to settle down?"

"Yeah, I am. I'll be twenty-seven next, and I want the dream. The partnership and the family." She shrugged. "You?"

"I..." I thought about it. "I've been so focused on my career that it's only recently that I'm starting to reflect on my dreams. Conor helped me with that, and if I'm honest,

I'd love to be in a committed relationship if it was with the right woman."

"And you thought Sara was that person?"

"Mmm, there was a spark of hope for sure... but let's get back to your fetish. You can trust me, you know. I'm good at keeping secrets."

She took a large gulp of her water and thought about it before she shook her head. "For a moment there, I was tempted to tell you. It's weird. I can't figure out what it is about you, Charles, but you do funny things to my sanity."

I felt flattered by her words and wanted to push her and get more details, but knowing that I had a tendency to overstep people's boundaries, I let it go... for now.

"How long are you staying in Dublin?"

Liv lowered the slice of pizza that she'd been about to bite into. "I'm not sure. This trip was spontaneous and I just bought a one-way ticket to Europe. Dublin happened to be the cheapest flight, so I'm starting here before I move on." She bent down, rummaged through her bag, and picked out a handwritten note. "I made this list on my way across the Atlantic."

I took the list she handed to me and read aloud.

"Edinburgh, Liverpool, London, Copenhagen, Amsterdam, Rome, Paris, Oslo, Vienna, Athens. Wow, how long do you have? You realize that these cities are in a lot of different countries, right?"

"Yes, I know. I was studying a map when I wrote them down."

"I thought you said that you worked for an NGO. Are they fine with you staying away for weeks?"

"We made an arrangement before I left. I can work remotely."

"Good for you."

She pushed her plate toward me. "You want some pizza?" Three of the six slices were left and I took one.

57

"How long have you been here?" she asked.

"About five months."

"And have you done all the touristy things?"

"I've been to Temple Bar, the factory where they brew Guinness beer, and a few whiskey distilleries. I rented a car and drove around to meet the few family members I have on my mother's side, but that's about it. The rest of the time, I've been working and getting to know people here."

She pulled a few brochures out of her handbag. "There's this day trip to the cliffs of Moher that I'd love to go on. There's a stop in a medieval town and at an old abbey that's now a ruin. Wanna come?"

"I would have thought you'd go for a full day tour of Irish castles."

She looked up from the brochure. "Oh, that sounds fun. We could do that too if you want."

The thought of spending hours in Liv's company was tempting. "You really want me to come?"

"A hundred percent."

I studied the brochure when she handed it to me. "I've been to Galway, the medieval town you mentioned. It's a cool place."

"We could go tomorrow if you want."

"Tomorrow is Saturday. I have a meeting." My head was spinning to find a way to go with her.

Her face fell. "You have a meeting on the weekends?"

"In the mastermind group. It's very informal and social, so I guess I could be a bit late. How long is the tour?"

"Fourteen hours."

I turned the brochure around. "Departure is at 6:45 in the morning. That's early!"

"But I'll bet it'll be fun, and if you're sleepy I'll let you drool on my shoulder." Liv gave me her brightest smile. "Please, Charles, you're my only friend in Ireland."

58

That did it. There was no way I could resist her. "All right. I'll go with you to the cliffs of Moher, on one condition."

Her eyes were wide and her smile still bright as I had her full attention.

"You'll tell me your fetish right now or I won't get a minute of sleep, just thinking about it."

"No. I want you to come tomorrow."

I narrowed my eyes. "Is your fetish so disgusting that I wouldn't want to sit next to you on a bus?"

"Depends how you feel about it. You may never be able to look at me the same again."

"It's urine sex, isn't it?" I grinned.

"No."

"Is it worse? Don't tell me you like to play with excrement, is that it?"

"Nope."

Tilting my head, I tried to sort through the long list of fetishes running through my mind. "You like to lick feet?"

"Nooo."

"Anuses?"

She couldn't keep a straight face. "I'm not telling you until you show up and the bus is at least an hour away from Dublin."

"It's anuses or you would have denied it when I asked."

"Maybe." She grinned. "Would that disgust you?"

I scratched my neck. "Depends how much soap and water was involved."

Liv pulled a wallet from her handbag when the waiter brought the bill to our table. "How much do I owe for the pizza?"

I snatched the bill. "Nothing, I've got it."

"I'm happy to split it."

Ignoring her, I left money and stood up. "I need your number so we can coordinate."

Liv was getting up too and reached out her palm. "If you give me your cell phone, I'll put in my number."

"Here."

When she returned it, I had a number on my phone with a contact name saying, "The cute coffee thief."

"Text me so I have your number."

Shooting her a quick text, I wrote. "To the girl who likes to lick rectums. Can't wait for our trip tomorrow. Good thing I'll be sitting down so I won't tempt you."

Liv read it and with a smile on her lips, and a raised eyebrow, she texted back to me. "Whatever, Rain Man."

I grinned. "You don't play nice, do you?"

"Sometimes. Why? Am I being too hard on you?"

"No, I'm a big boy. I can handle it."

Humor played in her eyes. "We'll see about that."

My confidence had grown a lot over these five years since I'd first met her, but the strong sensual energy that pulsed between us still made me unsure.

Am I misreading her?

Is she just being friendly?

It felt like she was flirting with me, but I had misinterpreted social situations before and decided to go slow. "See you tomorrow morning then."

"Yes, I'll book the tickets tonight and text you." She opened her arms for a hug and I reciprocated albeit a little stiffly.

"See you later, Liv."

"Yup. Bright and early for a full day of adventure. I can't wait."

CHAPTER 4
Late Night Texts

Charles

I was reading a book that Conor had recommended to me when my phone buzzed. It was a little past ten and I yawned.

Liv: Got the tickets. Departure point is outside Dublin City Gallery at 6:45. Be there at 6:30. The tickets are fifty dollars.

Charles: I'm afraid I don't have any dollars. Will Euros work?

Liv: Yes. Bring a warm jacket. The weather can be changeable out on the cliffs. Prepare for rain and wind.

Charles: Yes, mom.

Liv: You're welcome, son. Now be a good boy and go to bed. You have a day full of adventures tomorrow.

I chuckled at her tone. Liv was three years younger than me and I wasn't used to anyone speaking to me the way she did.

Charles: I might be a rebel and stay up late.

Liv: As long as you're not a grumpy ass tomorrow morning.

Charles: Was that another hint? Your fixation with asses is alarming.

Liv: Alarming or intriguing? I'm starting to think back-door sex is a turn-on for you. Are you hoping I'll lean in tomorrow and whisper that my fetish is to lick butt?

I was grinning from ear to ear and texting as fast as I could.

Charles: I could take it off my bucket list if you did. It would be a first to meet a butt fetishist for sure.

Liv: Prepare for a lot of firsts tomorrow.

Her text made my heart rate pick up. Liv was definitely flirting with me and there had been amazing chemistry between us today at lunch. From the first time I'd met Liv, she had stood out to me. My mentor Conor had told me that with his teachings, I'd be able to attract anything I'd ever wanted in life. Maybe he was right.

Back when I'd met Liv five years ago, I'd been too introverted to make a real connection, but I'd grown more assertive over time and these past months, with the help of my mastermind group, my confidence had skyrocketed.

Liv would only be in Dublin for a few days, which meant that I wouldn't have time to go slow. This was my chance to see if there was a reason for the breathtaking energy that I'd felt between us from day one.

I wrote a few answers and deleted them all. My fingers were tingling to take this correspondence up a notch. It couldn't be a coincidence that the one woman whom I'd never gotten out of my head was here. It had to be a reward from the universe for all the hard work I'd done.

Pushing my luck, I wrote:

Charles: My eyes are wide open now. What kind of firsts are we talking about? Sex on a bus, a cliff, in Galway, what?

I kept staring at my phone waiting for her answer.

Liv: Whoa, whoa, I'm talking about our first time visiting the Cliffs of Moher and Kilmacduagh Abbey.

My face fell.

Charles: Oh.

Tics made me wink and my nose wrinkled up as I added: **Awkward.**

Her answer came fast and I had to read it twice to let it sink in.

Liv: Nahh, I'm flattered. I used to think you were the hottest guy at Harvard. Did you know that?

Was she serious? I had been told I was handsome before, but mostly by older women who were all married.

Liv was naturally beautiful and so outgoing that she could have any man she wanted. What was I supposed to write back? I tried a bit of humor.

Charles: Is that why you licked at my coffee cup?

Liv: Duh... what else do you do when you find someone attractive?

I laughed. Geez, she was cute and I couldn't stop smiling.

Charles: If I'd asked you out that day, would you have said yes?"

My heart was beating fast in my chest. There was a real chance of her rejecting me. I'd taken a risk by bringing it up.

Liv: Sure, and then I would have squealed a little.

Charles: Good thing I didn't then. I hate squealing girls.

Liv: See, I told you I'm too much to handle. The mere mention of a squeal and you're running.

Charles: Not running, just writing ear plugs on my grocery list.

Liv: Promise you'll be there tomorrow.

I felt feather light inside. I had dreamed about Liv and now she was flirting with me. Problem was, I had no experience flirting and every answer I tried to write, I deleted again because I sounded lame or too desperate. Finally, after beating myself up for at least ten minutes for not being able to produce a simple answer, I fell back on what Conor had taught me about never limiting myself and so I reached for the stars.

Charles: It's a date!

I kept looking at the phone for her answer, but it remained silent.

Charles: Liv?

Dammit! Had I misread her signals?

Charles: It doesn't have to be a date.

Charles: Did you fall asleep or are you the one running now?

Charles: Okay, either your phone died, you fell asleep, or I'm going to show up to a bus full of tourists and be the only American because you got cold feet.

CHAPTER 5
Bus Trip

Liv

I was already there when the large tour bus arrived at 6:15 a.m. The driver parked and the guide opened the door to smile at me. "Ah, an early bird, are ye?"

"No. Just still on American time, and to be honest, I get motion sick, so I figured I'd secure seats up front."

"Good thing you came early then. The bus fills up fast."

Getting out of the bus, the female guide brought out her list of names. "Let's get you crossed off, shall we?"

"Liv and Charles."

"All right." She smiled and nodded to the bus. "You get first pick."

I chose the first row, which would allow us the best view, and then I found my phone and went over messages.

It was sweet how Charles had written me after I fell asleep; I was just about to answer him when an incoming call from Mr. Robertson made me sit up straighter before answering. "Hello?"

"Liv, I got your email. Can you talk?"

"Yes. I'm on the bus, waiting for Charles."

A family of four Dutch-speaking tourists came in and took the two first rows on the other side of the aisle. I turned in my seat toward the window, listening to Mr. Robertson.

"So, you're convinced that Charles thought it was a chance meeting?"

"Yes, your contact gave me his whereabouts and I saw him mix in with a guided tour group. It was easy to do the same and make it seem random. It all worked out.

"How is he?"

"He seems fine. A few times he mentioned his mentor, but nothing concrete. I'm hoping to get more out of him today."

Mr. Robertson cleared his throat and coughed. "Forgive me, this damn cough won't go away. I'm impressed with your idea of a day trip. If you can, give me an update when you get back to the hotel tonight."

"Thank you, sir. It's good to see Charles again."

"That's nice." Mr. Robertson coughed again and I held the phone out a bit, nodding back greetings to some of the people entering the bus.

"Are you okay, sir?"

"Yes, yes. We'll talk later, and don't forget to keep me posted." As he hung up, I returned to my messages to answer Charles' text from last night, but just as I was about to press send, a deep male voice with a distinct American accent made me turn my head to look out the window.

Charles stood outside talking with the guide while holding two cups in his hands. I knocked on the window and waved at him.

"How can you look so good this early?" he said as he came up the stairs.

"Oh, you like the jet-lagged look on me?"

"Here." He handed me a cup. "Hot chocolate with whipped cream."

"Aww, thank you. That's so sweet of you."

Charles sat down in the seat next to me and brought with him a scent of shampoo, coffee, and delicious cologne.

"Umm, you smell good."

67

"Yeah?" He gave a shy smile, and it made me think of his diary where he'd described feeling blocked and limited because of self-doubt.

"Uh-huh. Are you ready to go on an adventure and see the rugged cliffs of Moher?"

He leaned back in his seat, placed his coffee in the cup-holder, and nodded. "I am. The question is, are you ready to go on an adventure with *me*?"

"Oh, so it's not a date now?" I wriggled my eyebrows and grinned a little while holding up my phone for him to see me press send.

On the screen were his last messages from last night calling our day trip a date. My answer stood out in blue below.

Liv: I'd love to go on a date with you.

His eyes lit up as they shifted from my phone to me. "It's been years since I've been on a date."

"Me too, but my older sister taught me some tips when I first began dating. Would you like me to share them with you?"

"Sure." He took off his jacket and placed it over his lap.

I held up a finger. "One, go out for drinks or coffee only. A meal takes too long if you have nothing to talk about."

"You're saying that now that I'm about to embark on a fourteen-hour day trip with you." He grinned.

"Right, but you already know I'm great company. Two, have a friend call you twenty minutes in. If you need an excuse you can say that your friend needs you and it's an emergency.

He looked down at my phone. "Is your friend going to call you in a few minutes then?"

I gave a playful smile. "You'll just have to wait and see." I held up a third finger. "Three, don't shave your legs. That

68

way you know you won't be tempted to have sex on the first date.

"At least I have complied with that rule." Charles raised his pants leg a little. "I didn't shave my legs this morning."

"No?" I leaned my head to one side and sighed. "I get it. You don't want to come off as easy. Good call."

Charles was just about to take a sip from his coffee and laughed into the cup. "Yup, that was my great concern. A man has to watch out for his reputation, you know?"

"Absolutely. A woman too, so let it be noted that my legs might be smooth, but that's because I had permanent hair removal done a few years back, not because I shaved them for you."

"I would never assume that you did." He looked relaxed and amused and I found him incredibly handsome with his light stubble, amber-colored eyes, and dark eyebrows that were a few shades darker than his hair. We sat and smiled at each other while people were coming onto the bus.

"Did your sister have any other great rules that I should know about?"

"Yes, rule number four: always bring money for a taxi. You don't want to be stuck somewhere and have to rely on others."

Charles shook his head. "We're going across Ireland. Do you have any idea how much a taxi would cost from the west coast to where I live? Nah, I would find a different solution." He turned in his seat and looked around in the bus. "There's a single woman a bit further down. I'm sure she would let me sit with her if I asked nicely."

"Alright, but at least follow the fifth rule. It's to take a picture of your date with your phone. That way if you end up strangled to death, at least the police will have an easier time finding the killer." I took a photo with my phone and smiled. "Now, if you turn out to be a psychopath, at least the police will know what you look like."

When Charles took a picture of me, I made a grimace, baring my teeth, and looking insane.

He chuckled. "Gorgeous as always." Charles blinked his eyes and his shoulder lifted in a tic. "I'm surprised how much you can remember from your sister's advice, since you seem to blatantly disregard it all."

Around us, white noise quieted down as the guide came on board and took the microphone, telling us that her name was Sinead and sharing practical details about the trip. "You can expect to be home around eight o'clock tonight, but depending on traffic it might be nine or later. Yesterday we got stuck behind a farmer with his herd of sheep and it delayed us by quite a bit, but that's Ireland for you."

People laughed and buckled up as the bus began rolling down the street.

The first half hour was easy since Sinead pointed out sights in Dublin, from Temple Bar, an area full of bars and restaurants, to the Guinness brewery. She talked about the city, and sights not to miss, and all the time Charles and I sat and listened.

Then we hit the highway and Sinead said, "I'm going to be quiet for a while now. Our first stop will be in an hour and a half. If you're tired and want to nap, this is a good time to do it."

"Ah, a nap sounds nice." Charles drank the last of his coffee and fished a packet of chewing gum from his pocket. "Do you want some?"

"No, thank you. I prefer the sweet taste of cocoa on my tongue, but it's very considerate of you to use gum. I'm not a fan of coffee breath."

Charles pursed his lips. "Sometimes I think you have less of a filter than me."

"I'm just being honest."

"And direct."

"Is that bad?" My pulse sped up a little. From the moment I'd seen Charles yesterday, I'd been as eager to make a good impression as the first time I'd met him.

"No, it's… refreshing." He rested his hands on his lap and spread his legs a little, making his left thigh touch mine. It released a swarm of butterflies in my stomach. I might be here by Mr. Robertson's request, but the feelings Charles awoke in me were very real.

"Did you… did you want to sleep a little?" I asked. "You can rest your head on my shoulder if you want."

"No, it's fine. Why? Are you tired?"

"A little; it's night in the US and I haven't adapted to European time yet."

"Then rest your head." He patted his shoulder and the temptation of being close to him made me accept his offer.

The bus drove through Ireland and part of me wanted to keep my eyes open and take in the landscape, but the rocking movements and the warmth and closeness of Charles made my eyelids heavy.

He pressed a light kiss on the top of my hair. Acting on instinct, I took his hand and weaved our fingers together. It made his tics act out, and the shoulder I'd been resting my head on bobbed up.

"I'm sorry."

"Don't be." I smiled at him and looked deep into his light brown eyes. We hadn't even been on the bus for more than an hour and we were sober, but I felt like we were on a dance floor, swaying from side to side in our own little bubble about to kiss each other.

CHAPTER 6
French Pastry

Charles

She wet her pink lips as if inviting me to kiss her. By default, I wet mine too and lowered my eyes to her lips and back to her eyes.

Does she want me to kiss her?

I was scared I'd misinterpret her signals or go too fast, so instead I let my thumb stroke over the back of her hand and squeezed our intertwined fingers. "Your eyes are so pretty."

"Thank you." With a soft smile, she returned her head to my shoulder. I focused on the traffic in an attempt to slow down my racing heart and I positioned both my arms over my jacket in my lap to hide the effect her closeness had on me. Dammit, there had been an invitation to a kiss, and I'd blown it.

After ninety minutes of driving we stopped at a gas station with a restaurant and a mini-market.

Liv found a selection of French pastries and took forever to decide among the five different types of croissants. Biting her lip, she stood with the bag in her hand. "I'm torn between the almond and the strawberry croissant – look at how delicious that filling looks – but then I've never had a lemon custard croissant either."

Picking up a bigger bag, I took one of each of the five croissants, and moved to the large fridge to get us two cold waters.

She beat me to the cashier and pointed to the items in my hands. "Five croissants and two waters, please."

"I'm paying." I looked at the man behind the counter.

"Nope, I've got it." Liv waved her credit card with her right hand and held out her left to keep me from getting closer.

Shaking my head, I waited until the payment was done and she turned to me with a satisfied smile. "You'd better help me eat all those croissants."

"I don't like French pastries." I kept a straight face and walked out of the mini-mart holding the door open for her.

"That makes no sense. Everyone likes croissants."

"Nope, they're too dry and sweet for my taste."

With a hand to my elbow she stopped me. "Try one right now and tell me that it isn't delicious. You can't know if you haven't tried it. Come on, I dare you."

My lips lifted in a sly smile. "You dare me? All right, but then I dare you to taste something too."

"Sure, bring it on." Her face lit up with a mischievous smile that made tingles run up and down my spine.

Moving closer to her, I lowered my voice. "I'll sample a croissant if you sample..." My nerves were making my tics act up and I blinked my eyes.

Come on, she called it a date and held my hand in the bus. Be brave!

She waited for me to push out the word.

"Me."

Her answer came without hesitation and it made me widen my eyes in surprise when she said, "Deal!"

"Yeah?"

Taking the bag from me, she opened it. "Which flavor do you want? Plain, chocolate, almond, strawberry, or lemon?"

"Plain."

"Okay." She pulled it out and handed it to me. "It has to be a healthy bite. Don't just nibble on it."

I followed her instructions and ate half of the croissant. "You're right; it's delicious."

Her satisfied grin spread from ear to ear. "I told you so." And then she rose to her toes, her feminine scent engulfing me as she looked deep into my eyes. "So, tell me, how do you want me to sample you?"

Damn... With butterflies in my stomach, I lifted a finger and pointed to my mouth.

Liv's lips turned upward and then she kissed me. It was slow and deliberate and lasted a lot longer than a simple peck. With the two bottles of water in my hands, I wrapped my arms around her and kissed her back.

Her lips were as soft and amazing as I'd imagined they would be. We kept up the kiss for a long moment until she pulled back.

I couldn't read her expression. "So? What do you think?"

"You taste..." She licked her lips. "Hmm... I don't know. Can I have another taste to be sure?"

I was smiling when she kissed me again, and this time she sucked on my upper lip like she was really doing a tasting. After releasing it, she declared, "You taste of *more.* Yes, that's how you taste."

We laughed together and I tightened my hold around her. "That's funny. I was just going to say the same about you."

A loud honk sounded from the bus and made us look over; the guide stood in the door and waved for us to hurry.

Liv and I ran together, and we'd only just plunked ourselves down on our seats when the bus began rolling again.

"I do have a soft heart for people in love, but please make sure you mind the time at our next stop." The guide gave us a smile before taking the microphone again. "And now with everyone on board, we'll head for the old ruins of Kilmacduagh Abbey, which is also called the seven churches although not every building there was a church.

"On our way, try and notice the fairy forts on the fields that we pass. You'll recognize them as circles of stones, earth banks, or trees that the farmers don't touch. It's said that they date back to the Iron Age and that we have more than forty-five thousand of them here in Ireland. You might wonder how so many have been protected and the short answer is that's it's not because of the law, it's due to superstition. The fairies were believed to inhabit Ireland before they retreated to a different realm. All these sacred places are their portals and if you disturb one, the fairies will take their revenge. Cutting down a fairy tree might mean that a member of your family will die before the year is out. We Irish don't mess with the fay. Personally, I'd never cut down a fairy tree or disturb a fairy fort. It's just not worth the risk."

Some people were laughing in the bus and it made our tour guide raise her brow. "It might be strange to you, but Irish people have a long tradition of embracing the paranormal. For instance, more people believe in spirits than not. Once we get closer to the abbey, I'll tell you why the only door in the tower is seven meters above ground, but for now, I'll leave you with some nice Irish music."

Soft Celtic music began playing and Liv offered me another croissant. "Do you believe in ghosts?"

"Do you?"

She thought about it. "I'll have to say yes to that. Not that I've seen any myself, but my mom did and she's a very credible, no-nonsense person, so I believe her."

"Hmm... I'm skeptical."

"Because you never had a paranormal experience?"

75

"I lost my parents when I was a boy and I used to pray for them to come and visit me. I'd cry myself to sleep begging them to come and talk to me."

Liv gave me a look of deep sympathy.

"If spirits were real, I would like to think that my parents would have answered my prayers."

She nodded. "I'm sure they would have if they could. I'm so sorry that you lost them."

"Thanks, but it's been so many years that I only have scattered memories of them. I grew up with my grandparents in Chicago."

"I'm from Chicago too."

My lip lifted on one side. "I know."

"You do? How? I didn't tell you that, did I?"

"No, you didn't." I scratched my neck, hoping she wouldn't take this the wrong way. "But after I met you that night outside the bar, I looked you up on social media and I saw that you're from Chicago."

"Why didn't you connect with me?"

"You were in a relationship."

She sat back and leaned against the window to face me. "I wish you had, though."

She was so pretty with her long brown hair cascading down her shoulders and those eyes that had caught my attention the first time I saw her. Even now that I got to study them up close, I still couldn't decide if they were blue, gray, or green. "Can I ask you a question?

"Sure."

"What color are your eyes?"

She smiled. "My dad calls them marble balls because they are a bit of everything. It's freaky."

"No, not freaky. I told you. You have beautiful eyes."

She smiled and reached for my hand again. "Can I make a confession?"

"Ahh… you're finally ready to tell me what your fetish is. Let's hear it then."

"No, there was something else I was going to confess."

"Geez, how many confessions can one woman have?" I teased and intertwined our fingers.

"My friends and I all thought you were super handsome and unattainable back at Harvard. That night at the bar they wouldn't stop asking me about you."

"It was the alcohol. You were all drunk and cross-eyed."

Liv shook her head. "No. I think it's because we were used to guys hitting on us, while you would hardly make eye contact. Sydney figured you were gay, but either way, you didn't seem interested in any of us. The problem was I couldn't get you out of my head, and I spent hours at the coffee shop, hoping you'd come by again."

I frowned in confusion. "You did?"

"Yes. I tried searching for you on social media but the only men named Charles McCann that I could find were older or living abroad."

"Damn. I wish I'd known."

"Well, now you do."

"Yeah. Now I do." My heart rate was going at too high a pace for someone sitting still. The ball was in my court now, but it hadn't even been twenty-four hours since we first met at the university and we were moving incredibly fast. "Liv, I'm not sure what to say, except there's definitely a mutual attraction here, but the thing is…"

The tension on her face when I said the word *but* was cute. "You promised me that if I came on this tour, you'd tell me about your fetish."

Liv studied me with humor playing in her eyes. "It's not easy to talk about that sort of thing. Maybe it would be better if I showed you."

"Showed me?" I cleared my throat, which suddenly felt swollen, and then I whispered, "Are you suggesting sex?" My tics were acting up and my heart was racing when Liv leaned in and gently bit my earlobe.

"When we get to the abbey, I'll show you."

CHAPTER 7
Kilmacduagh Abbey

Liv

"In a minute, you'll see the old abbey to your left. Don't be afraid to wander around or crisscross the graveyards; that's perfectly acceptable here in Ireland. Notice something peculiar about the large tower that you should all see now? The entrance is seven meters up from the ground. That's because of the Vikings who used to raid our lands. The monks would use a ladder and when the Vikings came, the monks would barricade themselves in the tower, which by the way is over thirty meters high. That impressive height makes it the tallest pre-modern building here in Ireland."

"When was the abbey built?" Charles asked.

"The abbey is from the seventh century although the stone ruins you see now are from around the tenth century."

We left the bus and walked around taking pictures.

Charles laughed when I began mooing at some cows that were grazing nearby, but I kept at it until they answered me and came to see what I was about.

"So, you're an anthropologist *and* a cow whisperer?"

I rubbed the heads of the three cows who were sticking their heads over the stone wall to greet me while seven others were coming closer at a relaxed pace. "Animals sense energy. I'm telling you that if an animal doesn't want to be close to a person, that tells you something."

79

Charles took pictures of me and the cows. "I thought you said that you're from Chicago? You sure you didn't grow up on a farm?"

"Yup, I'm sure. I just love animals and they love me." Other tourists hurried over to have pictures taken with the cows, so after giving the closest cow a last scratch, we walked on. "Look how picturesque it is." I pointed to the landscape surrounding the abbey.

"Would you like me to take a picture of you?" Charles offered an Asian couple who were trying to get a good angle on their selfie.

When he was done, the man offered to return the favor and Charles and I smiled at the camera with the abbey in the background.

"We only have fifteen minutes and I can't stop thinking about the thing you wanted to show me," Charles whispered in my ear.

"All right." I was nervous when I led him away from the other tourists and around the corner of one of the buildings. "Promise you won't judge."

He nodded.

Looking over my shoulders to be sure we were alone, I walked in to stand with my back to the old brick wall. "You have to come closer."

Charles was quick to comply, and moved all the way up to stand in front of me, his eyes shining with intense interest.

"Give me your hand." I licked my front teeth and felt like I was taking a big chance by revealing something this private about myself. "Okay, so the thing that really turns me on is the way my lover touches me. Some men don't like to do it, others think it's hot." Lifting his hand, I placed it in the middle of my chest and then I guided him to raise it higher and close his large hand around my throat.

Charles frowned and it made me scared that this had been a bad idea. He wouldn't be the first to find it weird. Miguel had once told me I was a freak, but we'd been fighting then and he'd later apologized.

Shit. I should have never told him this soon.

I waited for Charles to say something. His shoulder bobbed up and his face scrunched in a succession of tics. I'd always found it charming when he did that, as it made him more approachable and imperfect like me. But right now, I wanted to know what he was thinking and his silence made me nervous.

"Would you rather it had been the butt thing?" My comment was an attempt to give him a way out, but he didn't take it. Instead he moved closer and lifted his other hand to my throat as well. Lowering his head, he spoke with his lips almost touching mine. "I wouldn't have guessed you to be submissive."

"I'm not. It's just the throat thing. I can't explain what it is."

He wasn't squeezing but kept his hands on my skin. His warm breath on my lips, and his large hands around my neck made Ireland in October feel as hot as the Caribbean.

"Are your panties getting moist from this?"

His voice was low and husky, and although his question surprised me, I met his eyes and answered in truth. "Yes."

"Good." Leaning his torso against me, Charles pressed me against the wall and whispered in my ear. "Do you feel what dominating you like this does to me?"

With the way he was pressing up against me, I could feel something hard pressing at my stomach.

His accepting this part of me made me want him even more. Letting my hands slide down his torso, stomach, all the way to the front of his pants, I touched the outline of

81

his impressive erection. His eyes closed and he moaned against my cheek. "Holy Christ."

"Mmmm." I moaned too.

"If you knew the things that I want to do with you right now," he whispered and moved his face into position to kiss me, yet he didn't.

Our breaths mixed, our eyes weren't blinking as we looked deep into each other's eyes, and then he leaned his full weight on me, pressing me back against the wall and tightening his grip around my throat just a little more. "I wish there was no bus and it was just you and me out here."

I wanted him to kiss me and made a small sound of agreement.

When his lips touched mine, it made my whole body vibrate as if I was a musical instrument that only he knew how to play.

His kiss was dominant and because of his hands around my neck, I couldn't move much. It excited me to be under his control and my brain was trying to figure out how he'd become such an assertive kisser.

Voices from people approaching gave us time to move apart just before they rounded the corner. They sounded Russian and posed on the graves for pictures.

My body was shaking from the powerful experience of what had just happened between us. There had been nothing shy about Charles just now. In fact, dominating me had seemed within his comfort zone.

Does that mean he has done it before with someone else?

Neither of us spoke as we walked side by side back toward the road.

I wished I'd truly run into him by accident because if he ever found out that I'd read a few of his diaries and been helped by a private investigator, it might make

Charles question everything else that was happening between us.

No, he has to know that what just happened was real.

But if he finds out his grandfather offered to pay me to be here, he'll be hurt and think I'm doing it for the money.

"You okay?"

I turned my head to see Charles observing me.

"You look pretty serious. Did I do something wrong?"

I kept walking and let my hand run over the wall of stones that separated two of the grass fields. "No, you didn't do anything wrong. It's more like the opposite."

"You think that you did something wrong?"

"No... I don't know... did I? I was thinking the opposite, as in you do everything right, and it has me trying to process what is happening between us."

Charles stopped for a second with his eyebrows drawn close together. "What do you think is happening between us?"

"That's the thing. It's unlike anything I've ever tried. For me relationships have always been growing from friendships to something more. With you, things are happening so fast."

He crossed his arms and I got scared that he misunderstood, and thought I regretted making out with him. I made my tone a bit lighter, trying to ease his tension.

"Honestly, I blame our chemistry. I'm a sane person on my own and you're probably sane on your own, but when we're mixed together there's an explosion of sexual attraction that takes my breath away." I pantomimed an explosion with my hands. "I mean, have you ever been on a date like this?" I chuckled a little and it made him visibly relax and walk on. "Well, have you?"

Charles placed an arm around my shoulder and guided me to the bus, which was filling up. "Sure, I've been on tons of fourteen-hour dates where I made out against

83

ruins and kissed within the first two hours. Happened all the time back in the states."

I narrowed my eyes and wrinkled my nose. "Liar."

"What? Did you think you were special?"

I shoved him with my shoulder. "Be honest."

He pushed me in front of him in the line to get back on the bus and with his hands wrapped around my waist, he whispered in my ear. "Do we have to compare it to something? Can't this just be our thing?"

I turned my head to look at him. "At least admit that it's special."

Sliding his hand up to my neck, he pulled me in for a quick kiss. "You're special, Liv, and I'm having an amazing time with you. I'll admit to that."

We didn't speak until the bus was on the road again. The guide explained that it would be hours until we reached the Cliffs of Moher on the west coast and it left us time to get to the questions that my tongue had been burning to ask since I met him yesterday.

CHAPTER 8
Worth It?

Charles

I was playing with Liv's fingers, letting the tip of my index finger run along her nails and rings. "Who gave you those?" I asked and pointed to two rings on her ring finger. "Are they old engagement rings?"

She shook her head. "Nope. I got close, but luckily, I woke up in time. These rings I bought myself."

"Do you like jewelry?"

"I do. But I'm more about the sentimental value of it than some large bling diamond."

"Okay, so what's the story behind these rings?"

"Just after Miguel and I ended our relationship, I went on a girls' trip with some of my friends. We all bought one of these in different colors. To me it symbolizes that love doesn't have to be sexual. It's such bullshit the way we've been taught that love only comes in a package of tall, dark, and handsome. Sometimes, love comes in a group of silly, flawed friends who laugh too loud, drink too much, but who will drop anything when you're hurting and need them to be there. We were all having love problems and just decided to get rings and celebrate life together. The idea, of course, was that men would think we were married and stay away because at the time we decided that modern men weren't worth getting involved with."

"Ahh... I see. And how long ago was this?"

"A few years."

"Have there been any other serious relationships?"

85

"Not really. I've dated a bit, but…" She shook her head. "My sister says I'm way too critical and picky."

"If you are, then I'm in trouble."

"Why do you say that?"

"Because of my tics and my issues."

Liv tilted her head. "Don't say that. Your tics are just cute. I think it's what gave me the courage to try and talk to you the first time I met you. I mean you looked older and so sophisticated in your expensive clothes, and you oozed intelligence. I was just a freshman regretting that I was in my old washed-out sweater without makeup on. It was stupid, but I couldn't take my eyes off you… and then you had tics. I don't know, it just made you a bit more approachable. If you hadn't had those tics, I wouldn't have been brave enough to try and talk to you."

"You're just saying that."

"No, I'm not. My friend, Sydney, was there and she watched you from a distance.

I scratched my nose. "It's weird when you say things like that, because I never see anyone checking me out."

"That's because you don't make eye contact with people."

"Hmm… well, it comes with my issues. I'm not a people person, or at least I didn't think I was until I met Conor."

"Your mentor." Liv pulled a leg up under her. "Tell me about him."

"I'm not even sure where to start. Conor is just amazing. He attracts the brightest people from around the world, and he empowers and inspires us to be the best version of ourselves and take leadership in our lives. When I came to my first mastermind meeting it was overwhelming how nice everyone was to me. That thing you said about sharing love with your friends resonates with me because that's how I feel about the group. All of them are accepting and kind. It's like finding one's tribe or family, you know?"

"That sounds amazing."

"It is! On my third meeting they surprised me with a birthday cake and singing. I was so touched because it happened after I'd spoken about missing out on having a big family to celebrate my birthday as a child. And they had listened and gone out of their way to give me what I never had."

"Was it your birthday?"

"No, but they said it was to make up for what I'd missed out on." I smiled widely. "At least thirty people sang for me and then they all made a circle around me and gave me a massive group hug."

"Wow."

"I know. It was a bit overwhelming but one of the most wonderful experiences at the same time."

"How many people are in the group?"

"It varies. Sometimes people move on, and other times, someone oversteps Conor's rules and then they're asked to leave, but thirty-four of us currently live at the Red Manor."

"Is it like one of those hippie communes?"

I shook my head. "No, all the people in the mastermind group are driven and successful people who want to change the world in some way. There are no sex orgies or experimental drugs either."

Liv let her fist swing from her hip and up to her chest. "Ah, darn it, I would have loved that."

"What, drugs and sex orgies?" I grinned at her mock disappointment.

She nodded. "Yeah, so be honest: how boring is your group? Are you all sitting around eating poppy seed muffins and discussing how to outsmart the rest of us?"

"Pretty much." God, it was so easy to be with her. She made me look like a social superstar the way we conversed with no awkward breaks.

"Are there any attractive women in the group?"

I moved my nose from side to side thinking about it. "There are a few, but they all gravitate toward Conor so I haven't been with any of them."

"Did you want to?"

I shrugged. "You can't blame a single guy for being interested in some intelligent and beautiful women."

"Okay, but in comparison, who would you rather be with? One of them or me?"

It melted my heart how Liv sat up straighter and lifted her chin, as if she had to take on the competition in a battle. "Why? Are you jealous?"

"No, should I be?"

I tucked a strand of her hair behind her ear. "That depends…"

"On what?"

"On what this thing between you and me will lead to. If you were my girlfriend and living with a bunch of attractive males, I might feel a bit jealous, but since I'm not, I don't have that right, do I?"

"I'm not talking about whether or not I have the right to be jealous, I'm asking if you're pursuing any of them."

"Well, in that case, the answer is no."

She studied me for a moment.

"What is it? I can see your head spinning a mile a minute."

"I'm just trying to figure out if you're worth it."

"Worth what?"

"Potentially getting burned." She looked down before meeting my eyes again. "Let's face it. You and I have only experienced romantic love that ended in pain. Otherwise we wouldn't still be single, would we?"

"True, but maybe none of the other relationships worked out because it was always supposed to be you and me." My words made her smile a little.

"I like that thought."

"Me too." I smiled back

"But opening up my heart to you means taking a risk of getting burned again. So, let me ask you, Charles: are you worth the risk?"

"Definitely!" My answer was confident but inside I knew exactly what she was talking about. I'd lost too many people to risk getting attached to someone who might leave me. "Are you?"

"Yes. At least I'd like to think so myself."

Taking a sip of my water, I leaned my head back. "I like that my flaws don't seem to scare you. You're the first woman to call my tics cute. And the fact that you speak almost without a filter makes it easier for me to relate to you. I have a hard time reading people." I looked down. "For years, I did therapy to learn how to express myself and read emotions and social cues. I'm a lot better than I was, but it drains me. I feel like with you, I can relax. It's the same with Conor. He reads me like an open book and often finishes my sentences before I do. He's so in tune with people that it's crazy."

"Do you think I can meet him and the others one day?"

"Of course. You'll love them."

"But will they love me or will they think I'm an intrusive Yankee coming to take away their beloved Charles?"

"No, don't worry about that. If you want, you could come and meet them before you leave."

"I'd love to."

I lit up at Liv's excitement. With my having a tiny family, my new group of friends meant the world to me. And since our lunch yesterday my thoughts had been running crazy with hopes that maybe... just maybe... Liv would turn out to be that special someone my grandmother had always told me was out there for me.

The Cliffs of Moher were rugged Irish nature at its finest. We walked hand in hand like a real couple, and that was a new experience for me. I'd been in sexual relationships in the past, but none of them with the prospect of turning into something serious.

Walking hand in hand with the most gorgeous girl in Ireland made me walk prouder than usual. It was a clear but windy day, and we took pictures of the incredible coastline that went on in both directions for as long as the eye could see.

"How far down is the water?" I leaned forward to look down.

"At least three hundred feet."

"Do you think people have ended their lives here?"

Liv pulled me back a little. "Yes, I do, and many probably unintentionally because they walked too close to the edge."

"With this much height, you'd have time to think before you died. How long do you reckon it would take someone to fall three hundred feet?"

"I don't know, maybe four, five seconds."

I leaned forward again. "Huh. Imagine how many times you'd say shit, shit, shit, on your way down."

"Yeah, so let's not do that." As Liv pulled me along with her, I spotted a woman selling Celtic jewelry on the path further ahead.

"Come on, let's see if she has something that can become of sentimental value to you."

Again, it took Liv forever to decide between the necklaces, but she finally picked a green amulet with a Celtic symbol on it. "This one."

90

I paid for it and watched as the local woman adjusted the leather string to fit Liv, while her mixed-breed dog sat next to her and kept an eye on the birds flying above us.

"Thank you, Charles." Liv rose up on her toes and kissed me. "I'll treasure it."

"Good, I figure you can show it to our kids and tell them how I got it for you on our first date."

We laughed together like it was a joke, but on my part, it was more like a wish for the future.

"There's something I want to ask you, but I'm not sure how." Liv bit her lip.

"What do you mean, how? Just use your words. I understand English."

She was battling with the wind to keep her long hair out of her face. "No, I mean, I don't want to sound too clingy and you're already spending all day with me, but it's just that..."

I lowered my brow wishing I could read her mind or that she would spit it out faster, because I was curious to know what she wanted from me.

"When we get back to Dublin... I mean, we'll probably be tired tonight, but..."

"But I could come back to your hotel with you." My wish spilled out when she didn't finish fast enough, but the way a triangle formed between her eyebrows made me add, "You know, to watch a movie and maybe cuddle. Is that what you wanted to ask me?" God, I hoped she didn't think I expected her to have sex with me tonight.

"Well, actually, I was going to ask if you wanted to hang out again tomorrow."

I cleared my throat wishing I'd kept my mouth shut. "Sure, what did you have in mind?"

"Why don't you show me your favorite parts of Dublin?"

"All right."

A large grin spread on her face.

"What's so funny?"

"You are! I can't believe you'd be willing to prolong this date and spend your evening with me. As if fourteen hours of me forcing you to eat croissants and sitting in a bus wasn't enough."

With a grip on her rain jacket, I pulled her closer. "If that's surprising to you then what if I tell you that I'd be willing to spend the night with you? Falling asleep with you in my arms sounds very appealing." I was grinning too, because the truth was that I wasn't just willing to do it, I was eager to crawl into a bed with Liv and cuddle up with her.

She met my eyes, and there was a flash of worry behind the excitement. "I don't want you to think that I'd normally sleep with a guy on the first date, but..." She trailed off.

"But you'll make an exception with me?" Hope made my voice crack a little.

"I didn't say that. But we could count yesterday's lunch as a date, and today is like four dates in one."

"Good point, so if we count me coming back to your hotel as a date as well, it would be our what... sixth date?"

"The thing is; I feel so relaxed with you. If we're talking about a movie night with us cuddling and nothing more, then I'm okay with it."

On the inside I raised my fist in triumph as I hugged her tight. "It'll be the perfect way to end an amazing day."

CHAPTER 9
Movie Night

Liv

It was close to ten at night when we finally walked into my hotel room.

"Fancy." Charles looked around. "I thought you said you were traveling on a budget."

"I am, but I got lucky. They upgraded me to a suite."

"Why?"

"Because the hotel I was supposed to stay at was overbooked. This hotel is further outside the city center and in compensation they gave me an upgrade and free breakfast."

"Nice."

"Are you hungry?" I pointed to the room service menu.

"No, but I could drink something."

Taking off my jacket, I walked over and bent down to open the mini-fridge. "Okay, let's see. There's white wine, beer, soda, and juice. What are you in the mood for?"

"A Sprite would be nice."

I pulled out a Sprite and a Fanta. "What about some chocolate? They have Milka."

"Sure."

Getting up from my squatting position, I turned to give him the soda. "I was thinking about taking a quick shower. Maybe you can find a movie for us?"

Charles picked up the remote control and sat down on the bed. "Scary or funny?"

"You decide, but nothing too bloody. It gives me nightmares."

93

I was back ten minutes later wearing my shorts and tank top that I normally slept in. It wasn't sexy lingerie by a long shot, but Charles still checked out my legs with a quick side glance. When I saw a small smile on his lips, I relaxed. "Do you usually shower at night or in the morning?"

Charles moved over on the bed to make room for me. "That depends. If I've been at the gym, I'll shower at night, but otherwise I do it in the morning." He rolled off the bed. "But since you're all sparkly clean, I'll take a quick shower too."

Charles was even faster than me and came back in wearing his t-shirt and briefs. "You'd better not have eaten all the chocolate."

"No, I left you a small corner."

"I should have known from your sugar addiction that you can't be trusted with sweets."

"My sugar addiction? What's that supposed to mean?"

He raised his brow. "Ehm, the first time we met, you ordered a cinnamon roll and a hot chocolate with whipped cream. Do you have any idea how much sugar that is?" He was teasing me. "And today you more or less ate five croissants by yourself." Holding up his hand, he spread his fingers. "Five."

"Oh, that's not fair. I wanted one croissant. You were the one who got me one of each."

He laughed and got into the bed next to me. "To taste. No one forced you to eat all of them. It's a wonder to me how you can look so fit."

"How could I stop when they tasted so delicious?"

Charles opened his arms to me. "With that little self-control, you have me wondering what would have happened if the guide hadn't called us to the bus when you sampled me. You said I tasted of more, remember? If you can't stop yourself, does that mean you would have eaten me too?"

"Nah, you're not sweet enough." I placed myself with my head on his shoulder, my stomach against his hip, and my hand across his belly.

"Really? So, if I was a spice, I wouldn't be sugar?"

"No way, sugar is a mainstream spice. You'd be something intimidating like chili."

"Really? Why?"

"Because it's a spice that people have respect for. It can overpower most other spices and it makes your blood heat up."

"Hmm…"

"What about me? What spice would I be?"

Charles looked up at the ceiling thinking about it. "Something rare and expensive, like saffron." He intertwined our fingers and turned to look into my eyes.

"What do you use saffron for?" I asked.

"You use it in food and bread baking, but it's labor-intensive to collect and process, and that's why it's probably the most expensive spice there is. As I recall it, saffron also has healing abilities."

"You're just making that up." My eyes were sparkling with humor.

"No, I'm not. Here, let me prove it to you." Reaching for his phone, he looked it up on the Internet and read aloud. "Saffron is a powerful spice high in antioxidants. It has been linked to health benefits, such as improved mood, libido, and sexual function, as well as reduced PMS symptoms and enhanced weight loss. Best of all it's generally safe for all people and easy to add to your diet."

"Hang on, if I'm like saffron, that means adding me to your life will improve your mood and your libido."

He nodded. "Yeah, I'd say it's working. I've been pretty happy today."

"Yeah? Me too. It was hard to stop kissing you at the abbey."

Charles ran a hand through his hair and closed his eyes for a second.

"Shouldn't I have said that?" I asked him.

His chest rose and fell and then he opened his eyes. "You have no idea how much I'm restraining myself right now. I've never tried cuddling without sex, and being so close to you and hearing you speak like that..." He shook his head. "I don't want you to feel like I only came back to your room to screw your brains out. It's not like that at all, but damn, you're putting my gentleman manners under pressure here."

I smiled and raised my leg over his. "Would you think less of me if we made out?"

"No, of course not."

Taking his left hand, I placed it on the back of my thigh. Charles was quick to take the invitation and slid his hand higher to my behind. Boring his fingers into my flesh, he let out a soft groan. "Mmmm."

Our lips met and we were back to kissing just like we had earlier, only this time, Charles intensified it and let his tongue twirl around mine in a way that ignited every nerve ending on my body.

"Who taught you to kiss like this?" My question was swallowed by our kissing, and he didn't answer.

Instead, he raised his hand to my throat and squeezed a little while looking into my eyes. "Before this goes too far, I need to know: do you have a condom?"

"No."

"Are you on the pill?"

"No."

He groaned again and pulled me on top of him. We still had clothes on but his hard cock felt amazing as I pressed against it. With his hands on my hips, he steered me to ride him while pulling me down for more kissing.

It had been years since I'd made out like this with my clothes on. Being twenty-six, I was eager to get to the real thing. I'd complained to my friends about boyfriends not taking their time with foreplay, but with Charles there was an urge inside me to feel him inside me. "Why don't you have a condom?"

He pulled back. "Because I didn't expect this."

Leaning my forehead against his, I kept rocking my hips back and forth against him. "Your briefs are going to be wet from my juices."

"Mmmm... just the thought of your moist pussy makes me want to fucking rip your clothes off." His voice was breathy as he was kissing me down my neck. "We could go out and buy a large box of condoms and stay in bed all night and tomorrow too."

A dazed part of my brain was flaring up with warning signs. "We can't." My voice sounded strange, like I didn't want to say the words.

Charles growled against my neck. "Why not?"

"I'm not that kind of woman. I don't do sex outside of a relationship and we haven't defined our relationship."

Rolling us around, Charles got on top of me and grabbed onto my hair with both his hands. "Then define it!"

"Okay. For me a relationship means exclusivity and trust."

"Good. I want that with you." His eyes were shining with intensity.

"So, we agree that we're taking this to the next level then?"

"We already did when you took my hand on the bus. I'm not fucking around. I want you, Liv, and I want to see where this thing goes."

"Same."

"Say that you're my girlfriend then." Charles had a challenging look in his eyes, like he didn't think I'd do it, but I didn't hesitate.

"I'm your girlfriend."

"Yeah?" It was such a turn-on to hear how full of disbelief his voice was, but then he'd never been in a committed relationship.

"Yes."

"You're my girlfriend?"

"Yes." I bit his lower lip when we kissed. "And you can tell that to all those attractive women at the mastermind group. Don't even think about giving out any more samples of yourself, because you're mine now and I want the whole package for myself."

"Greedy." His eyes were shining with delight. "That's fine because I'm not sharing you either." He pulled my t-shirt off and buried his head between my breasts.

My hands lifted his shirt, signaling for him to take it off. He complied and I was blown away by how sexy he looked bare-chested. Charles was fit, but not in that sculpted way that comes with eating on a diet and living in a gym. He was just right, with meat on his bones and muscled arms and chest that revealed he took care of himself.

"I knew you'd be perfect under that shirt." I smiled at him as he tugged down my shorts. Throwing them down on the floor he placed kisses on my stomach and let his right thumb slide down along my panties.

"You were right. The fabric is soaked." His lips kissed my pelvis bone while his thumb stroked across my clit on top of my panties.

"That's because of the things you do to me."

"I'll take the blame for making you wet all day long. It's boosting my confidence." Lifting my panties to one side, he pushed my legs apart and slid a finger over my folds. "I like that you left some hair. Some women shave it all off and I'm not into that little girl look."

"Good, because I like my triangle... ohhh..." I ended my sentence in a moan when Charles lowered his head and licked me.

"Relax. I just want to taste you."

The TV was showing some movie that neither of us paid attention to. My eyes were closed and I was on sensory overload with his tongue licking me like I was his favorite treat. Looking down it was surreal to me that the man I'd thought of as unattainable was giving me oral sex. Not only was he amazing at it, but he was in no hurry to move on either.

With my hands in my hair, I moaned and gave in to the sensation of being pampered by him, and then he inserted his middle finger and the feeling of having a part of him inside me felt intimate and bonding. "Mmmm."

"Just pretend it's my cock." His voice was low and gruff as he added another finger and moved in and out of me. Never had anyone fingered me like this and from the sound of it, I was producing all the moisture he needed to push a third finger inside me.

"Ahhh..."

"That's right, moan for me. I wanna hear what you'll sound like when I shove more than my fingers inside you."

I kept my eyes closed and my head tilted backward. My face scrunched up from the slight pain of being fingered so fiercely, but I still arched up begging for more. "Yes, oh, yes... ahhh."

"That's right. Now be a good girl and come on my hand." His voice was low and raw like he was beyond horny himself.

"Mmmm... Charles, how do you...? Ahh, jeezus... it feels so good."

"That's because your pussy knows it belongs to me." He was patient and kept finger fucking me and talking dirty until I grabbed on to his strong shoulder and cried out my orgasm.

"That's right, Saffron, come for me."

He dipped his head and sucked on my clit, sending me into a tailspin of a powerful orgasm that took my breath away. All I could do was moan out his name. "Yes Charlie, yeeess..."

I was still reeling from the climax when he moved to lie next to me. With a satisfied smile on his face, he kissed my shoulder and waited for me to look at him.

"I like that you're a screamer."

"I'm not a screamer." If my cheeks hadn't already been flushed red from my orgasm, he would have seen my embarrassment.

"You are! And my favorite part was when you screamed out my name." He kept smiling as I got under the cover again.

"I'll admit that I moaned."

Getting under the cover with me, he kissed me. "Prepare to moan a whole lot more because I'm not done with you."

"Where did you learn how to talk dirty like that? And the way you kiss and..."

He waited for me to finish my sentence.

"Who taught you to pleasure a woman like that?"

"Ah, so I take it that you're pleased with my skills?"

"Wow." I laughed. "I should take a picture of the smug smile on your face right now. You're so proud of yourself."

Raising a hand in the air, Charles grinned. "You just admitted that I'm a great lover; why wouldn't I be happy?"

It occurred to me that he had fewer tics than earlier. "Hey, what happened to your tics?"

"They come and go. I get them when I'm nervous and sometimes just for no reason at all, but it helps when I'm distracted."

"Are you saying I'm a good distraction?"

"You're the best distraction I could ask for." He hugged me tight.

When he released me again, I asked, "How long have you had them?"

"Since I was a kid. It used to be much worse. I would bite on my tongue so hard it would bleed, and most nights I couldn't sleep because of tics. And then when I finally fell asleep, I'd wake up with nightmares."

"What changed?"

"It's been a slow progress. I've tried medicine of course, but I found that things like chewing gum instead of my tongue helped, and when I couldn't sleep at night, I'd use my rocking chair and read. It calmed me down and it helped me get way ahead in school since I was always reading."

"Ah, so it's not just sex that distracts you. A book can do it too."

"Yes." Charles didn't elaborate because he had begun kissing my neck again. "Maybe we should get some condoms before we go for round two."

I couldn't suppress a yawn and it made Charles pull back.

"Okay, that sounded super enthusiastic."

"No, I'm sorry. It's not you, I just feel like I hit a wall or something." I yawned again. "I think it's the jet lag. And it's been a long day, not to mention that you gave me one hell of an orgasm, and now my body is all relaxed and tired."

"It's okay. I get it." He opened his arm for me to cuddle up against him again.

My eyes were getting heavy but I curled up to him. "I really want to make out with you some more. Maybe if I

101

close my eyes a little and then you can watch the movie. I just need a little nap to rest, you know?"

Charles kissed the top of my hair. "Sleep, beautiful. This has been the best first date I've ever had. I can't wait to spend more time with you."

"That's disappointing." My eyes closed and my breathing grew slow and heavy, making my words sound drowsy. "This has been my best date, period. For you it's only been your best *first* date. Besides, we said these two last days count for six dates, remember?"

Charles played with my hair. "I said that wrong. It's the best six dates I've ever been on, and to be honest, this has been one of the best days of my life."

It felt nice lying cuddled up against Charles, with him stroking his hands up and down my back. I wanted to smile, but sleep was pulling at me like a powerful undercurrent dragging me out to sea. Just before I drifted off, I muttered, "We'll need condoms."

CHAPTER 10
Snoring

Charles

It took me a second to orient myself when voices from the hallway outside the hotel room woke me up.

Shit, so it wasn't a dream. It really happened.

Liv was still asleep, her body lying closely against mine with one of her legs and an arm flung across me like she wanted to make sure I didn't sneak off. Playing with a lock of her soft brown hair, I replayed in my mind what had happened between us yesterday and it put a goofy smile on my lips.

Some children running and using loud voices in the hallway made Liv stir and scratch her nose.

"Good morning, sunshine."

"Good morning." She yawned and stretched. "What time is it?"

"Almost eight."

"Have you been awake long?"

"No."

"I need to pee." Untangling herself from me, Liv moved to the edge of the bed and looked for her clothes. "Where's my shorts and t-shirt?"

They were on my side of the bed so I picked them up and dangled them in my hands. "I would prefer if you didn't put clothes on. How about you just walk to the bathroom naked and let me enjoy the sight?"

"No, it's too light in here and you'll see all my imperfections."

"Maybe I'll like your imperfections."

103

She rolled her eyes but smiled. "Only if orange skin and rolls are your thing."

I scoffed. "What are you talking about? I've seen you naked and you're gorgeous."

"Until you look closer."

"Women. You're never satisfied with your bodies, are you?"

"I'm fine with my body, but not to the point where I want to get up and walk around naked. I'll need to know you better to do that."

I frowned. "But you said that you feel comfortable around me."

"I do." She snatched her clothes, got dressed, and walked to the bathroom, where she stood in the doorway and looked over her shoulder. "Would you mind turning on the TV? I don't want you to hear me pee."

"But what if that's my fetish? To hear women pee? Did you think about that?" I was smiling.

Pointing at me like a strict schoolteacher, she clicked her tongue. "Don't mess with me this early. I'm not a morning person. Just turn on the TV or I won't be able to go."

"All right." I had just turned on the weather channel when she popped her head out again. "When did you get a toothbrush?

"I got it from reception after you fell asleep. That and condoms."

"Oh... okay."

Hundreds of hours of therapy enabled me to pick up on the shy expression on her face before she closed the door. I didn't want her to think I expected her to come straight back to bed and use the condoms with me, but I didn't know how to communicate that to her.

When I heard the toilet flush and the water running, I called out, "Hey, Liv."

"Yeah?" She opened the door with a toothbrush in her mouth.

"I'm hungry. We should get some breakfast."

"Do you want to eat here or go somewhere?"

"What was that? Maybe I'll understand you better if I put my toothbrush in my mouth too?

Liv returned to the bathroom and rinsed her mouth. "I said, do you want to eat here or go somewhere?"

"Whatever you prefer."

Coming back out, she got back into bed with me. "We could order some room service and stay in bed if you're up for it. I would love some French toast. Do they make that here?"

"Let me check." I fetched the menu and handed it to her. "Here, I'm just going to use the bathroom too. Could you turn off the sound? I really want you to enjoy the sound of my urine hitting the toilet bowl."

She ignored my attempt at being funny and looked up from the menu. "They have waffles but no French toast."

"Waffles sounds good."

"How hungry are you? Do you want to share a portion?"

Damn, she was so sexy as she sat against the headboard with her nipples showing through that thin t-shirt of hers.

"Sure, but I'll need more than a waffle. Can you order some croissants and orange juice too?"

Her eyes narrowed in suspicion. "But you don't like croissants."

I winked at her. "Everybody likes croissants; you said so yourself."

"Did you pull my leg yesterday?"

"Maybe I always liked croissants or maybe you converted me. A man's got to have a bit of mystery about him." Closing the door, I smiled at my own joke.

After taking a quick shower and brushing my teeth, I walked back into the bedroom, and found Liv where I'd left her. She looked so tempting with her smooth skin and the outline of her perky breasts showing through her sleepwear.

"The food will be another twenty minutes at least."

I wanted to be respectful, but my hands were drawn to her. Getting back into the bed, I muttered, "I can't think of food when you look so pretty in the morning."

She lowered the remote control and watched me. "Then maybe you should have me as an appetizer."

My head screamed *yes!* and I was just about to answer her when my phone vibrated on the night stand. "Hang on." I reached over and answered, "Hello."

"Charles, where are ye?"

"Oh, hey, Ciara, I'm with a friend."

"Ye didn't come home last night. We've been worried about ye."

I sighed and rubbed my forehead. "I fell asleep at my friend's place and we just woke up. Sorry about that."

"When will ye be home? Conor said he needs to speak to ye."

My eyes went to Liv, who was watching me. "I'm not sure. Probably tonight?"

"Awk, ye missed our meeting last night. And now ye're saying ye won't make it today either. Who is this friend?"

"I'm not ditching you. I'm just… ehh, it's a long story."

Ciara sighed. "Try to make it back by noon. Ye know how important Sundays are to Conor."

"Yes, I know. I'll try and make it." I hung up and turned to Liv. "Sorry about that. I should have messaged my friends that I wasn't coming home last night. They worried."

She had a cute frown on her face. "Do you have to go now?"

106

"No, I can stay for a few hours." I reached for her hand, but she seemed stiff. "What's wrong?"

"Nothing."

"Liv, even I can tell something's upset you. What is it?"

She looked away. "I just thought you saw me as more than a friend."

I swallowed hard. "You mean the part about us being exclusive?"

Liv leaned her head back and closed her eyes. "Yeah, but hearing you call me a friend. It's like a bucket of cold water on my head."

"Why?"

"I think we got carried away."

"What are you talking about?"

She looked at me. "It was like a dream. Meeting the guy I had a huge crush on in college and being blinded by our amazing chemistry. But if we stop and get real for a second, being in a relationship will never work for us. I tried a long-distance relationship once and I swore I'd never do it again."

"We could make it work."

"How? I'm only visiting Dublin, while you live here. Soon, I'll be moving on to see some of Europe before I go back to the US."

My throat felt tight. "So, what you said about wanting something serious and asking if I was worth it... Why would you ask me that?"

Liv looked down. "Because I want those things and having them with you would be a dream, but not if we live in two different countries." Raising her head up, she looked deep into my eyes. "Falling in love with you would be the easiest thing in the world, Charles."

"But you don't want to." All my fear of rejection told me to pull back before she could turn me away.

107

"I do. I'm just afraid that I won't be enough and that you'll hurt me."

"No, no, no." The vulnerable expression on her face sparked my protectiveness and I cupped her face. "You're more than enough."

"You only say that because you don't know my worst sides yet."

Trying to ease the tense atmosphere, I attempted a bit of humor. "You mean your snoring, your fetish, or your indecisiveness?"

"You heard me snore?"

"A little. It was cute." I leaned in and kissed her before pulling back and locking eyes with her again. "I get that you're scared. From the moment we reconnected, everything between us has moved fast. But that's because it's so freaking natural and effortless for me to be around you. I don't think you understand how rare it is for me to say that about another person. People drain me, Liv. But not you. With you I can't get enough, and that has to mean something."

She brushed her hands down the front of my chest. "I feel the same way."

"Good." I let out a sigh of relief. "Then can we at least agree to explore this chemistry between us while we're in the same country? Let me convince you to stay a bit longer."

"And then what happens when I eventually have to go back? Will you come with me?"

I shook my head. "I don't have all the answers, but if we're meant to be together, we'll figure it out. Maybe you can stay with me and my friends for a while. I'd love for you to meet them."

"You mean the mastermind group?"

"Yes. They are the nicest people. Just the fact that they worry about me when I don't come home one night.... I

108

mean, doesn't that say a lot about their level of care for me?"

Liv didn't answer, but she moved up on her knees and hugged me tight. There was a sadness in her.

"What's wrong?"

"I just hope that you're right. That it feels so magical because we're meant to be together."

I folded my arms around her and inhaled her feminine scent deep into my lungs. "I hope so too."

Moving her head, she pressed her lips against my neck and kissed me. I was sitting on the bed and with her on her knees, she was a little higher up than me. I closed my eyes and let her place kisses down my neck, and then her tongue licked all the way up again to my earlobe. My senses went into overdrive right away and I pulled her onto my lap. Her fingernails raked over my back making my spine feel like a fuse on fire.

I growled low. "You can't do that and not expect me to want more."

"What more do you want?" Her voice was amorous and silky.

My hands slid up under her t-shirt and cupped both her breasts. "I want to see what I'm holding."

She complied and took off her shirt, and like a hungry baby, my lips were drawn to her nipples. I loved the feeling of them hardening in my mouth as I suckled, nibbled, and played with them.

"Do you like them?"

"Uh-huh." My answer was muffled because my mouth was full of one of her delicious breasts.

Pulling the rim of my shirt up, she gestured for me to undress too. I had no problem being naked with her and when she whispered in my ear to lose my briefs, I lifted her off my lap and turned to sit on the edge of the bed where I could pull them off.

109

Liv got off the bed and came to kneel in front of me. She smiled when she let her nails run from my knees and all the way up my inner thighs. I touched her hair, watching her with curiosity as she closed her hand around my cock and began stroking it up and down. My breathing turned shallow and I leaned back and rested on my hands behind me while watching her.

"Do you want to play a game?" There was mischief in her eyes.

"Yes. As long as it involves you touching my cock with your soft hands."

"It does, but the rules are that you can't touch me. Pretend that I've tied you up and I'm in control."

"Okay." I could pretend to be tied up if it made her continue what she was doing.

"You ready?"

"Mmmm."

"Good, so remember, no touching."

"Got it." I moaned as she leaned in and swallowed the crown of my cock and let her tongue roll around it. Then she leaned back again and used the moisture to stroke it up and down."

"Fuck, that feels good."

"What, this?" She did it again, leaving even more moisture.

"Yeah." I wanted her to keep giving me head, but on her knees topless in front of me, she began something that I hadn't tried before. With a tight grip at the bottom of my cock she slid her hand up, but not down. Every time, she moved her hand to the root of my cock and stroked it upward. I closed my eyes, feeling the need to rock my hips to get that usual friction of rubbing both ways, but she kept at it and it drove me wild with need.

Again and again, her hands moved from the root of my cock to the tip, but never the other way.

"Look at it."

Opening my eyes, I saw my erection was getting bigger than I'd ever seen it. It was so full of blood that it had turned almost purple. I swallowed hard and leaned my head back, forcing myself to not put my hand on top of hers and rub up and down.

Again, she lowered her head and took me in her mouth.

"Ohh…" I moaned out and squeezed the bedsheet in order to not use my hands to hold her head still and fuck her mouth.

She kept teasing me until I began arching and I couldn't take it anymore. "Please, I need to come. You're fucking killing me here."

When she finally let her hands rub up and down in a fast rhythm, I began pumping my hips, feeling desperate to ejaculate what felt like a whole ocean of semen in my balls.

I came hard and groaned on my exhalation. "Ohh, yeesss…"

My eyes were still shut tight but then I felt her soft tongue clean me up. I looked down to see her lick my cock, which was getting back to its normal color.

"I don't even wanna know who taught you that, but you should come with a warning label."

"Why, what should the warning say?"

"Charlotte Liv Christensen will drive a man to sexual insanity and make him almost lose his fucking mind. That's what it should say."

She stood up. "Is that a complaint?"

"No, I loved every part of it. It was like sweet torture, though." I reached for her. "Don't put your t-shirt back on."

"I have to, the poor man has been waiting by the door for at least a minute."

"What man?"

111

"He knocked when you were just about to come, and I didn't want to stop."

I covered myself with the sheet and turned to watch her open the door and accept the tray of food. "Let me just put down the tray and I'll sign for it." Liv placed the food on the bed and gave me a playful smile. In the door opening, a girl around nineteen stood with large eyes and red cheeks staring at me. I smiled at her but when my tics set in, I turned my back on her.

"Thank you so much." Liv closed the door behind me and came back to the bed.

"Are you ready for some waffles?"

It was mind-boggling to me how she could go from being on the floor and giving me the ultimate hand and blow job to behaving like what happened wasn't a big deal. "How can you look so calm?"

She set out the plates of waffles, fruits, and croissants, and handed me a glass of orange juice. "How should I look?"

"Like you just realized Santa is real. That's how I feel."

She drank from her juice. "I'm happy you enjoyed it."

"To say that I enjoyed it would be an understatement. Now you have my head spinning with who taught you that."

"You said that you didn't want to know."

"I don't, but tell me anyway."

"My friend Sydney told me. She learned it from a co-worker who is a bit promiscuous and very generous with tips on how to please men. I've been wanting to try it and it felt like the right time."

"Yeah, it was so good that I didn't even hear anyone knocking on the door."

"To be fair, she only knocked once and called room service. From the way you roared out your orgasm, I think she could tell we couldn't come to the door just then."

"And you still took time to clean me up."

She smiled. "I figured you needed a minute to calm your breathing before I could open the door anyway." Liv took a seat against the headboard and dove into her plate of waffles.

"I swear, everything with you just feels so right. I can't even imagine how good it will be to make love to you for real."

We smiled at each other.

"It's like that old saying about finding the right glove that fits, isn't it?" I emptied my glass of juice in one long gulp and wished we had ordered more.

"Maybe, but you might still find things about me that are deal breakers."

"I don't know, at this point, I'm having a hard time imagining it." I planted myself next to her against the headboard. "You're pretty amazing, you know that, right?"

She leaned her head on my shoulder. "Thank you."

"No, I'm serious. I can't wait to introduce you to my friends. If you're as good a match with them as you are with me, I might ask you to marry me on the spot." It was meant as a joke, but she frowned a little.

"Hey, don't worry. I'm not really going to ask you to marry me."

"It's not that. I'm just worried that if your friends don't like me, you'll let their opinion affect you."

"Sweetie, they'll love you. How could they not?"

Liv didn't look convinced but she agreed to go home with me to meet them all.

CHAPTER 11
The Mastermind Group

Liv

Charles and I took the train to Howth, which turned out to be a large fishing village in a suburban area, located forty minutes outside of Dublin. It was a tourist destination with a romantic little harbor, a number of seafood restaurants, and little tea-shops.

"The Red Manor is a bit hidden." After a ten-minute walk, Charles steered me up a long driveway with impressive, large trees on each side of the road.

"Wow, this reminds me of..." I stopped myself before revealing that I'd been at his grandfather's house back in Chicago. "I mean it's similar to a driveway back in the States. It must be so pretty in the summer, almost like entering a long cave of green all around you."

"Yes. It is."

"Oh, wow." After the narrow driveway, the grounds opened up and revealed a large estate surrounded by stone walls and hedges. "How old is it?" I was referring to the manor house that stood like something from an Irish postcard.

"I have no idea."

My eyes scanned the fancy cars parked out front and the beautiful horses watching us from their paddock. This place was like an advertisement for material success.

I didn't expect this place to be so large. The other houses we passed were tiny compared to this.

114

Charles raised his hand and pointed behind the manor itself. "Conor is having an annex with ten rooms and bathrooms built down there by the pond;, do you see it?"

"Yes."

"I love the back yard. In the summer we had bonfires and there's a tennis court that you can't see from here."

The closer we got to the house, the more nervous I got. I wasn't blinded by the loveliness of the place because unlike Charles, I knew what cruelty Conor O'Brien was accused of. The man had a long list of criminal offenses in his repertoire, from blackmailing to fraud. There were also several restraining orders against him from former members of his group. The report spoke of situations where he'd turned violent. Eileen's words from the day before yesterday ran through my mind. The cruel behavior toward Julie, who was in a psychiatric hospital right now while her daughter, River, still lived under Julie's tormentors' control. According to the report from Kit, Julie had been devoted to O'Brien, and so desperate to show her loyalty to him that she'd accepted living in a bare room without any furniture or as much as a blanket or pillow to sleep with. After a month, Julie had begged him to allow her back with the group but the monster had told her that she was unworthy and accused her of stealing from him. That's when he'd kicked her out in front of her own daughter.

Mr. Robertson, Eileen, and Kit had all warned me that O'Brien was a predatory psychopath, and now Charles was taking me to meet him.

"Don't be nervous. You'll love them." Charles held my hand and I squeezed his fingers tight as we walked up the stairs and entered the house. Inside was an entry way with a high ceiling, modern art on the walls, and a round table with flowers in the middle of the room.

115

"Come on." With another reassuring smile, Charles led me to a kitchen where three women were cooking and chatting. They looked up as we entered.

"Ah, there ye are. We thought ye'd gotten into trouble." A woman who looked to be in her late thirties and spoke with a clear Irish accent put down the knife she'd used for slicing tomatoes. "And who is yer friend?" She cleaned her hands in her apron and came to greet me with the two other women.

I shook hands with the Irish woman as Charles introduced me. "This is Liv. She and I met back in the states five years ago and now we're a couple."

"A couple are ye?" I caught a glimpse of skepticism before she stepped aside to let the other two women greet me. They looked similar with olive skin, brown hair, and noses with an arch that made them appear as they'd stepped out of a painting from ancient Greece or Rome.

One of them showed me all the flour on her hands and spoke with a lovely Mediterranean accent. "Hello, it's so nice to meet you, I would shake your hand but I'm baking pita bread for our dinner tonight. I hope you'll join us. We're having moussaka, Greek salad, and fresh pita bread."

"That's sounds amazing. It smells lovely in here."

"Oh, that's because we have a cake in the oven." Ciara's smile didn't seem genuine to me, or maybe I was just being careful not to trust anyone in this house.

"Ciara bakes something sweet for us every day," the Mediterranean woman without flour on her hands said with a loving smile to the Irish woman, who managed to look both stylish and maternal with her silk blouse, jewelry, apron, and make-up.

Charles put his arm around me. "Ciara has been with the group the longest. She runs this house and has two boys with Conor. Maya and Isabel are from Portugal. They're twins although not identical."

"Yes, we're Trinners like Charles," one of the twins said.

I looked at him because I'd no idea what a Trinner was.

"Except I teach there while you study." He gave the twins, who couldn't be more than twenty-three, a smile.

"Is a Trinner someone who studies at Trinity College?" I asked them and the taller of the twins, Maya, nodded. "How come you chose to study here in Ireland?"

"We wanted to try something different." They exchanged a glance and I picked up that there was something they weren't telling me.

"How long have you been here?"

"Almost a year. We were just supposed to stay for a semester, but then we got this unique opportunity to work with Conor, and he has helped us so much."

"That's right." Isabel chimed in. "We used to be these clueless kids who just cared about fashion and likes on social media, but now it's like we see people for what they are and we're tapping into our full potential."

"That's... eh, nice." I took mental notes that these girls fit the description of the people that O'Brien targeted. They were without their family's protection in a foreign country, and I would bet a lot of money that they came from an affluent family too.

"Conor is upstairs in the schoolroom with the children. I know he wants to talk to ye." Ciara opened her arms to Charles and pulled him in for a hug. "And don't ye scare us like that again."

Charles looked ever so happy to be fussed about, and thinking back to what I knew about him, he probably never really had that maternal figure in his life. With a grandmother who was sick, and a grandfather who was busy, he'd been left to nannies.

117

Walking up the stairs, I saw more art on the walls, spanning many styles and ages. The wooden stairs were covered by a thick oriental runner in red colors. Upstairs, we walked into a large library where books decorated each wall and two long study tables were set up in the middle. At one of them a group of five older children were sitting with their books out while a man stood leaning against the wall with his arms crossed. He was handsome, with a silver fox look, although he couldn't be more than in his early forties.

"Hey." Charles walked straight to the man, who pushed out from the wall and gave Charles a manly hug, slapping his shoulders.

"I tried to call you all night."

"I'm sorry. I got distracted." There was a large smile on Charles' face as he reached out his hand, urging me forward. "I want you to meet Liv."

The first thing that hit me was a scent of expensive cologne that matched his stylish look of dark pants and a fashionable sweater with a v-cut that revealed a button-down shirt underneath. Meeting Conor's eyes, I saw him scan me with interest as he reached out a strong hand to shake mine while still talking to Charles. "You're forgiven. I would have been distracted too." He oozed confidence, giving me a charming smile and letting an appreciative glance slide up and down my body. "Liv was it?" He held my hand between both his while keeping eye contact with me. "What an interesting name, I'm sure you know the name Liv means life and originates from the Scandinavian languages."

"Yes, I know."

His brow lifted. "I'm impressed. Americans aren't always familiar with the origin of their names."

"Well, I'm a first-generation immigrant, so my origin is still fresh."

"Liv moved to Chicago when she was eight. Her family is from Denmark."

I had told Charles yesterday during the bus trip and he looked proud to tell my story.

"And what about you?" I smiled at Conor. "How many generations have you gone back in knowing your family history?"

"Oh, that's not hard when you live in Ireland. O'Brien was a powerful clan and ruled large areas."

I knew from the report that the charismatic man in front of me was born with the last name Bricks. He might wish he was related to the mighty O'Briens, but he was a fraud. I was supposed to charm my way into the cult, but even though my side gig of escorting brilliant business men to boring events had taught me to keep a polished façade, I couldn't help myself from asking, "And whose side of the family did you get your name from? Your mom or your dad?"

"Neither." He stood with a calm smile on his face. "I picked the name O'Brien because my own family name didn't suit me."

That surprised me. Why would he tell me that?

"Come, I'm sure the children are eager to meet you too." With a hand to my elbow, he steered me to the table, where five teenagers sat watching us. "Liv, meet my children Atlas, Lumi, Nathan, River, and Maximum."

All the teens greeted me, but it was the oldest boy who caught my attention. He looked like a mini Conor except he had glasses and a much more serious expression on his face.

"Did I get your name right?" I asked him. "Atlas as in a world map?"

"Yes." The young man scratched his collarbone and it made me take in the striped polo shirt he was wearing. The small stitched-on horse and rider told me it was a

Ralph Lauren. In fact, all the teens were wearing expensive brands and looked healthy.

"And how old are you?"

"Almost seventeen."

A younger boy next to him snorted and it made Atlas elbow him. "I *am*."

"Yeah, in eight months. That's not soon, is it?"

"You can sit here if you'd like." A blond girl smiled at me and patted a seat. Remembering Eileen's words that it would be wise to make friends with the children, I took the girl's offer and sunk down on the chair next to her.

"What about you? How old are you?" I addressed the boy who had teased Atlas.

He was of mixed race and looked young. "I'm fourteen."

"You are?" I wouldn't have guessed him to be more than twelve or thirteen. Clearly age was a sensitive subject and I didn't want to offend any of them, so I quickly added, "And your name was Nathan, right?"

"Yes. My mom named me Nathaniel and later when she met Conor, she changed it to Liberty, but that's a stupid name and since she isn't here anymore, I go by Nathan."

"What do you mean when you say your mom isn't here anymore?"

"She left." He shrugged and Conor moved to stand behind him with his hands on the boy's shoulders.

"Every parent loves their child, but not every parent is fit to care for one."

Kit had told me that Nathan's mom had committed suicide, and my heart ached with sadness from the closed-off expression on the boy's face.

The blond girl looked to be the youngest of the five. She raised her hand like I was a teacher and I nodded to her.

"I'm Sun River Devine, but I only go by River. In two months, I'll be twelve years old. And that is Lumi. She's the oldest. She's seventeen but Conor says she has the maturity of someone in their thirties. Maximum is Conor's and Ciara's other son and he just turned thirteen last week.

Conor spoke up. "You're all my children, River. We talked about that. We're a family here."

"Yeah, but I meant blood-related."

"The word is biologically," Atlas corrected her. "Blood-related is a less refined word."

"Fine." River leaned back in her seat and looked down with a small pout on her face.

"Blood-related described it just fine," I said to comfort the girl.

"Actually..." Conor moved around the table at a slow pace and as he passed each teen, he touched their shoulders. "We take great care to develop the children's vocabulary. Words have power and we want them to communicate in a concise and refined manner. Using precise words, as well as the correct tone, will make people respect you, and once you have their respect, doors open up to you."

"Are there more children in your family?"

"Not at the moment." He was coming my way, and I didn't like that I was sitting while he was standing, so I got up. "I noticed that your wife has that wonderful Irish accent, but you don't seem to have one. Where are you from?"

"I don't have a wife."

"Oh, I meant the boys' mother. We met her downstairs."

"I have to correct your misconception. I'm not married to Ciara or anyone else for that matter." He gave me a smile that I would categorize as mildly flirtatious. "Ciara and I have a history and I'm bound to her in spirit, but that's the same with everyone else in my tribe. As for your question of where I come from, the answer is London, but I've lived in many places and I've acquired what some would say is a clean or neutral accent."

I tilted my head. "I don't know. It's clear to hear that you're from this side of the Atlantic. You sound like a newsreader on the BBC. Proper and well-articulated."

"Thank you, but I've lived in Ireland long enough that I tend to use some of the local lingo. Where in the US are you from?"

"Chicago."

"Oh, I see. Same as Charles. Are you old friends?"

"Yes, actually, Charles and I go back five years. We didn't meet in Chicago though. We met at Harvard and it's a funny story really, because we were both called Charlie and so I accidentally took his coffee order, thinking it was mine."

River smiled at me, but Lumi sighed. "You shouldn't use words such as actually, really, and so. An over-reliance on adverbs is a sign of weak communication. In writing it would be considered a sign of insufficient revision."

"Really?" My tone was lighthearted. "Well, I guess my degree from Harvard was a complete waste of money if I can't even communicate on the level of you smart teenagers."

River laughed and moved in her seat. "You did it again, you used really and well. You can't do that."

I liked her because of all the people in this house she was the youngest and most innocent. Placing a hand in front of my mouth, I made big eyes and then she and I laughed together. Charles pulled me against his side and laughed too.

"Charles, there is something I'd like to discuss with you. I'm sure the children can entertain Liv for a moment until we're back."

I nodded to Charles and returned to my seat when the men left. As soon as the door closed, I leaned in and whispered in a conspiratorial tone of voice. "Okay, so who wants to tell me the best pranks you've played on your teachers?"

None of them spoke, and I sensed tension around the table.

"Argh, don't tell me you never prank the adults. Then what about each other at least? I love a good prank."

Maximum, a quiet boy with blond hair and soulful brown eyes, looked over his shoulder to check that the door was closed. "One time, I pranked my parents. I told my mom that my dad needed to speak with her, but then when she went to his bedroom, he was with Sara."

I frowned. "Did they laugh about it?"

Maximum shook his head.

My heart went out to the boy. He was probably as confused about his parents' relationship as I was, and maybe it had been his way of trying to wake up his mom and make her see that his dad wasn't faithful to her. But I suspected Ciara had already known that.

"I once pranked Lumi." River snickered and moved closer to me. "She doesn't like it when I sleep with her in her bed, so I waited until she'd fallen asleep and then I snuck in and slept next to her."

"You do that all the time." Lumi gave another sigh that was worthy of a teenager. "That's not what a prank is. A prank is like the time Nathan put salt in the sugar bowl, or when he hid all the knives from the kitchen and the adults had to search the whole house to find them."

"But that wasn't funny at all," River complained. "Remember how much trouble you got in, Nathan, and you ruined the cake for all of us."

I threw my hands up. "You people aren't much in the line of pranksters, are you? Wanna hear some of the greatest pranks that I played on my parents?"

"I do." Nathan put his hand down on the table and looked at me with interest.

"No, you don't." Lumi told him and gave me a reproachful glance, before she returned to Nathan. "Why would you lower your energy to do hurtful things when you could attract bad karma because of it?"

He scrunched his nose up. "I just wanted to hear what she did. It's not like I was planning to copy her."

Pushing Nathan's book closer to him, Lumi muttered, "If you want entertainment all you have to do is read."

I stared at her with fascination. "Wow, you really are like an old person trapped in a young body, aren't you?"

"Lumi is a lot of fun when you get to know her," Atlas defended his friend, but then he scratched his collarbone again. "At least she can be."

Clearly my tactic of bonding with the kids through a bit of rebellious fun had fallen flat, so I changed tactics. "What are you all reading?"

"We're going through the hundred greatest novels ever written. I'm reading *Don Quixote*." Nathan showed me. The others showed me the titles of their books too, spanning everything from classic English literature to a book by Salman Rushdie.

When River showed me hers, I raised my brow. "Wow, you're reading *The Land of Painted Caves*? That's a big book for a ten-year old."

River squared her shoulders. "I'm a good reader."

"You must be. I was a lot older before I read that one."
I looked to the door, but with no sign of Charles, I figured
I could get some intel. "How do you like living here?"

Nathan's fingers played with the pages in his book.
"It's okay. I miss Liverpool sometimes."

"You were five when you moved here. How can you
remember anything from back then?" Atlas looked
skeptical and Lumi followed suit:

"You remember all the fairytales your mom told you,
but she romanticized it."

Ignoring them, I validated the boy. "I've never been to
Liverpool, what's it like?"

"It's amazing. There's a harbor and my dad used to
take me to this football field and we'd play together. He
was a soldier and in top shape. I've seen pictures of him
showing off his abs."

"Where's your dad now?"

Nathan's face fell and he kept playing with the book.
"He died on a mission."

"I'm so sorry to hear that." I reached over and placed
my hand on top of his.

"What about the rest of you. Do you like living here?"

"Yes, but I wish I had my own room," Atlas said.

"Me too." Nathan wrinkled his nose up. "I don't like
sharing with a girl."

From the pout on River's face, I could guess she was
the one he shared a room with.

"What's wrong with sharing a room with a girl?" I
asked him.

He shrugged, unwilling to clarify, but River was more
forthcoming.

"I used to share one with my mom, but then she went
to study yoga in India and she couldn't bring me with her."

"Your mom is studying yoga in India?" I knew it was a
lie. Eileen had told me how River's mom, Julie, had been

125

kicked out while River had been allowed to stay. "How long will she be gone for?"

"I'm not sure. She's been gone for a few months now."

More like eight or nine, I thought, but I didn't say that out loud.

"Can't you ask her when she's coming back then?"

"We can't talk on the phone because of the bad connection."

"Oh, okay. What about you, Lumi? Do you have your own room?"

"No, I sleep with my mom."

"And where is your father?"

She stiffened a little. "All I know about him is that he's white and that my mother resented him for not marrying her when he learned that she was pregnant with his child. She's from a traditional Indian family so marriage was a big thing until Father made her realize that marriage is institutionalized suppression of women. Anyway, she was lucky that Father took her in and helped her become successful on her own."

"Father, is that Conor?"

"Yes."

"We are all his children," River said, repeating what O'Brien had said not so long ago.

"Can I ask a question?"

"They nodded.

"How come none of you speaks with an Irish accent?"

"We can if we want to." Maximum changed into an accent as Irish as his mother's. "But Da says it's better if we speak a more polished English. It makes us sound more cultivated."

River spoke Irish too. "Nathan an' I sometimes speak Irish when it's just the two of us at night. I love it because it reminds me of my ma. She has a thick brogue but I always loved the way she speaks."

126

"Maybe you can teach me one day. I find it so charming."

"Aye, I can!" River guaranteed. "Try saying something in Irish."

I imitated an accent in a few sentences and it was so bad that it made the girl bend over with laughter.

"Ye're rubbish at it."

River and I were good at laughing together and even the others smiled at my willingness to embarrass myself.

I could hear voices approaching and hurried to cover my tracks in case Conor would drill them about what questions I'd had asked. "All right, but when I wanted to know if you liked it here, I didn't mean in this house, I meant in Dublin and Howth. I'm a tourist, so I'm curious to know what it's like living here."

"Howth is quiet in the winter but in the summer, we have a lot of visitors." To my surprise, Lumi was the one who began entertaining me with details as Conor and Charles came back in to the room.

"There's a castle not far from the main road, and the lighthouse is pretty. If you want to visit a café, I recommend the one just by the train station."

"Thank you, I'll check it out."

When Charles and Conor came up to us, I was disturbed by the withdrawn expression on Charles' face. Walking over to stand next to him, I muttered, "Are you okay?"

He didn't have a chance to answer before Conor turned his attention on me. "I understand you're an anthropologist. Maybe you could teach a lesson to the children about what it is you do and how anthropology works."

"Sure." I smiled, but on the inside, I was tapping my foot wanting Charles to tell me what the hell had happened to him. His energy, which had been so light, playful, and loving this morning, was sad and fearful now.

"Can I see your room?" I tugged at his hand.

"Uh-huh." He didn't take my hand but walked out the door and I followed.

His room was on the fourth floor. The air was stuffy, so he opened a window. "This used to be the attic, but two years ago it was renovated and the roof was raised to allow six additional rooms up here."

"Charles, what's wrong?" I sat down on the bed and patted the spot next to me.

"Nothing." He kept by the window and didn't look at me.

"You know how you told me that you have a hard time picking up on people's emotions. Well, I'm the opposite. I sense the smallest changes in people's mood and right now, your body language is screaming to me that something's wrong."

His hands were folding and unfolding and he closed his eyes.

"A relationship is built on trust, so trust me, Charles. Tell me what's bothering you."

Charles rubbed his forehead and sank down on a chair in the corner of his small room. "I don't know, maybe we're rushing into things, Liv."

My chest felt like I was wearing a bra two sizes too small. I'd been so sure that what we had meant something to Charles, but fifteen minutes alone with Conor and he was doubting everything. "What did Conor say to you?"

"I told you, it's nothing."

"Okay." Feeling hurt from his change of mood, I got up and walked to the door.

"Where are you going?"

It took everything in me to remain calm and not beg him to come with me. "I'm just going to give you some space to think."

"Liv." His word hung in the air like a half-hearted protest, or maybe it was an apology.

I forced a small smile. "It's probably healthy for us to get a chance to process everything that has happened since we met."

Charles got up and raked his hand through his hair, his tics making him blink and wrinkle his nose up.

"Charles." I moved close, got on my toes, and looked him deep in his eyes. "I don't know what he said to you but it made you doubt yourself and us. You went from being loving to me one second to pulling back. I was scared something like this might happen because it's happened to me before."

His Adam's apple bobbed in his throat when he swallowed hard. "It has?"

"Yes. Last time it was a dominant mother who didn't think anyone was good enough for her son, but the dynamics are the same. I don't like that Conor has this kind of influence over you. I need a man who can think for himself."

"I can think for myself."

I allowed his words to hang in the air for a moment and then I took a step back. "Then remember how you felt about us before he got into your head."

Without a kiss goodbye or any more explanations, I walked away from him. It was hard not to turn around and look over my shoulder to see if he was still standing there.

I'd only reached the stairs when Charles came after me. "Let me walk you to the train station."

"That's not where I'm going."

"No?"

"No. I'm headed to see Howth Castle. I'm a tourist, remember?"

"Do you want me to come?"

"No thanks. You just said that you worried we were rushing into things, so take some time alone."

"But when are you leaving Dublin?"

We were outside before I answered him. "That all depends."

"On what?"

I turned and walked backward, pointing from me to him and back. "On this. On us."

Charles stood with pain written on his face, like he was torn about what to do. "Liv…" The way he said my name sounded like a plea for me to stay, or maybe I was hearing what I wanted to hear.

Overwhelmed with everything that had happened between us, I raised a hand and gave a last wave before walking away. Leaving Charles in the claws of O'Brien made me want to cry with frustration. Each step away from him was forced, as if I was moving against a powerful current in a river, using my whole body to push through. I had to trust that I'd planted a seed; my intuition told me that staying would have been disastrous.

CHAPTER 12
Sunday Dinner

Charles

Everyone was praising the moussaka, the homemade bread, and the Greek salad that the twins had made for us, but nothing tasted good to me and I had no appetite.

For the first time since I moved in to the Red Manor, I hadn't wanted to come to Sunday dinner. My mind was in chaos from everything that had happened between Liv and me, and I'd rather be in my room to ruminate and make sense of it all.

Yesterday had been one of the best days of my life and I'd been on cloud nine when Liv and I defined our relationship as a committed one. With all the times Conor had told me that I could have anything I dreamed of, I'd been so darn proud to bring Liv to meet my new family and prove him right.

That's why it was surprising and confusing that Conor had questioned her motives and cautioned me to take it slow. I knew that he was only looking out for me and that my family name, Robertson, could attract gold diggers, but Liv was nothing like that. To her, I was Charles McCann, and not once had I revealed that I was related to one of the richest men in the world.

When I told Conor that Liv had called my Tourette's cute, he had scoffed and made a lot of convincing points. Each of them had felt like hard blows to my solar plexus and together they had provided a rude awakening from the dream world that I'd been in ever since I went out for lunch with Liv.

131

"We should drink a toast to Sara." Conor raised his wine glass and glanced around the long table to meet all of our eyes. Thirty-four people lived here at the Red Manor, which was also the name of the mastermind group that Conor ran from here. I sat next to Atlas, who was one of my favorites. The boy was highly intelligent like his father but introverted like me. It would have been easy for him to gloat about having Conor O'Brien as a father, but he wasn't like that. I understood the pressure of being related to someone people admired. My grandfather had built a business empire and was highly respected himself. Now Atlas and I were sitting shoulder to shoulder with our glasses raised, watching Conor praise Sara.

"Because of Sara's generous donation, three new schools will be built in Africa to support education."

We all smiled and cheered for Sara, who beamed at Conor's kind words about her.

"The Red Manor Foundation is growing every year thanks to the success and good graces of all of you. It makes me extremely proud."

"We couldn't do it without you." Sara gave him another of her adoring looks.

When I first came here, I'd been desperate for her to look at me like that, but my interest in Sara had faded once I understood that she didn't feel attracted to me, and that she was already in a sexual relationship with Conor. Now, I was comparing Sara to Liv and finding her too polished and eager to please. Liv was nothing like that. She was authentic and unapologetic.

"Your wisdom, support, and guidance means everything to us."

While Sara showered Conor with words of affirmation, I thought back to yesterday when Liv had confided in me that her lover's hand on her throat turned

132

her on. The intimacy and trust she had showed me had been so fucking sexy.

After dinner, we were gathering in the living room for our session of the day. The room was full of sofas and chairs and we all took a seat directing our attention upon Conor, who stood in front of the cozy fireplace.

"Today's topic is how to withstand critics. Many of you have felt the pressure from family and friends who don't understand what we're doing here at the mastermind group. Can you name some of the reasons people are critical?" Conor looked relaxed as he stood in front of us.

Hands flew up and he selected Lumi, who was eager to answer.

"People are jealous and wish they had access to something like this themselves."

"That's right, but is that our problem?" Conor asked her.

"No, it's your right to only work with those you see great potential in."

Conor nodded and pointed to me. "What other reasons are there for people to be critical?"

I cleared my throat. "They could be controlling."

"Can you give us an example?"

"Maybe your family had fixed plans for your future and the moment you break away, and it doesn't fit their agenda, they get critical of your choices."

"Yes." Conor gave me a sad nod. "We've seen this over and over. That's why I only extend invitations to people I believe are strong enough to withstand the outside pressure. Because let's face it, sometimes, it's not jealousy or the need to control that drives criticism. Often it's a friend or family member who is genuinely concerned and listening to horrible gossip that isn't true. They get confused and make accusations. Remember the times angry and confused people have accused us of being a cult."

People around me laughed and River repeated the joke I'd heard a number of times over the five months I'd been here. "People need to learn the difference between being cultivated and being part of a cult."

Conor spoke again, "But what about what Charles just said? Are we obligated to follow the path that our family has laid out for us?"

I loved it when he referred to something I'd said as if my words were important.

"Our destiny is our own and it's our obligation to make the most of it." Conor swung his hand to the twins. "Some are drawn to inspire others by stepping into the bright spotlight and sharing their gift." His body turned to me. "While others prefer to stay out of the spotlight and work on serving justice to victims of international crime syndicates."

I had told him that was my dream one time when he'd pushed me to define my goals in life, but the truth was that I wasn't sure what I wanted work-wise. I enjoyed teaching much more than I would have thought possible, but there were also days when I missed Solver Industries.

If only my grandfather hadn't closed his mind to what I was doing in Ireland. He had made accusations of Conor being a fraud without having even met the man. It was so typical of my grandfather to dismiss something without taking a second look. He was used to making quick decisions all day long, and decades of people sucking up to him had given him a sad God complex, where he thought everyone was interested in his opinion, and ready to follow his directives. Well, I wasn't! I could think for myself and I'd stand by my friends here in Ireland.

"How do we deal with the critics?" Conor gave us time to think.

My way of dealing with my grandfather had been to cut him off. I hadn't called or emailed him in months. At first it had made me feel empowered that I was out from under his constant pressure, but at that moment, with my being already sad and confused about Liv, a new thought entered my mind. I had accused my grandfather of not caring about me, but... thoughts were running through my mind so fast that I couldn't pinpoint what bothered me. Conor and the others kept discussing ways to set boundaries, cutting off people, and taking control of one's life, but my mind was searching to understand the gnawing feeling inside me that I was missing something. And then it came to me. I'd felt loved when Ciara called to check up on me this morning. I'd even told Liv that it was a sign of how amazing the group was. So why was it that when my grandfather left call after call, I ignored them and took it as him badgering me? The last time I'd spoken to him, he'd been angry with me for getting involved with the group. He had called it a sect and told me I was naïve. I rubbed my forehead as if I could massage clarity into my thoughts. My grandfather was my closest relative and even though we disagreed, I might regret cutting him off. Could I accuse him of not caring about me while at the same time ignoring his attempts to connect? I sighed with a heavy heart and promised myself that one of these days, I'd give him a call and see if we could somehow have a conversation without fighting.

After the initial discussion, we were asked to divide into study groups where we'd do role-playing to practice cutting off people who didn't support our lifestyle.

"You might feel that you owe your family and friends to listen." Conor's gaze landed on me. "You might even think you're in love, but trust me when I say that no physical pleasure can beat the prize of mental clarity that comes with being in charge of your own destiny."

"I'm sorry, but I'm going to have to skip this part. I don't feel good," I told Conor.

With a worried expression he placed a hand on my shoulder and pulled me to a corner. "You're upset about Liv." As always, he could read my mind. "I get it, but think about what I said. Is it possible that you projected your ideas of a girlfriend on to her? You don't know her, Charles."

I was looking down, focusing on the pattern in the oriental rug on the floor.

"It's a powerful feeling when someone laughs at your jokes and dismisses your flaws as charming. Especially, for someone like you who's never had a partner before, but I wouldn't be a friend to you if I didn't warn you that no relationship would be like that long-term. There will be fights and heartbreak. Are you ready to deal with the downsides of a relationship, hmm? You know you lack skills when it comes to communicating and picking up on social cues. I have no doubt you can get there if we work together, but I'm also sure that now isn't the right time for you to go all in. I worry you'll end up burned and bitter if you do." He pulled me in for a long hug. "I'm only trying to protect you here."

"I know."

"Tell you what. The worst part is staring at your phone hoping she'll call you. Why don't you give it to me?" He reached out his palm.

When I hesitated, he spoke in a soft voice. "You don't want to make the mistake of calling her. It's best if you give me your phone."

Looking from his palm to his face, I shook my head. "No, it's fine. I'm keeping my phone."

Conor's face left no doubt that he wasn't happy with me. "Do you not trust my judgment?"

"Yes."

"Then give me your phone." His voice got insistent and people were looking over at us.

I took a step back. "No. My phone is private and I'm keeping it."

He looked shocked and disturbed by my unwillingness to do as he told me, but I'd been pushed too far today.

Turning on his heel, Conor walked away from me and I retreated to my room with a feeling of having burned a bridge.

No, that's silly. It was just a small disagreement. Tomorrow everything will be fine.

Just like Conor had predicted, I kept looking at my phone longing to hear from Liv. She had called me her boyfriend, but with the way we'd ended things today, I wasn't sure if that was off. Obviously, Conor was right in saying that I was horrible at being in a relationship and that it was just a matter of time before Liv wouldn't find my issues cute. I hadn't even lasted two days before making a mess of things by overthinking and doubting the feelings between us. If I was a normal person, I would have known how to talk to her about the confusing thoughts in my brain, but that was part of my condition. When I couldn't make sense of something, I would shut down and hide from the world, like right now when I was in my room while my friends were together in the great room.

Stripping out of my clothes, I got into bed to write in my journal as a way to analyze what had happened today. It was a tool I'd used since childhood and when I was done, I wrote and deleted a number of text messages to Liv without actually sending any of them. I tried reading in a book, but I couldn't focus and my tics were worse than ever. Finding the meditation app on my phone, I used it to calm myself down.

CHAPTER 13
Status Report

Liv

I woke up in the middle of the night with my head hammering. Drinking some water didn't help much. Unable to fall asleep again, I checked my phone to find a number of unanswered calls on my phone—none of them from Charles.

Kit had left messages, and so had Mr. Robertson. It was three a.m. local time but only nine p.m. in Chicago.

Sitting up in my bed, I turned on some light and rubbed my eyes before I called Mr. Robertson and filled him in on everything. Even the part about Charles and me being intimate together.

"What did Conor tell him to make him pull away?"

"I don't know, Charles wouldn't say."

Mr. Robertson was quiet for a moment. "I want you to know that I never expected you to have sex with Charles."

"I know." I sighed, "but that attraction Charles wrote about in his diary. It's mutual." I felt my throat swell up. "I really care about him, and everything was going so well between us. Now, I wonder if I ruined everything by allowing the physical part of our relationship to get too far too fast."

"I doubt it. If he feels anything like I felt for Emmy when I first met her, he'll have a hard time staying away from you. It was different times back then, but from what I recall, our relationship turned physical quickly too."

"How did you meet your wife?" My question was a way for me to shift focus away from my own sad situation.

"Oh, it's been so long since I spoke about it." He coughed on his exhalation. "I was a clerk in a bank and she worked in a diner where I'd sometimes eat my lunch. Emmy was mild and shy by nature while I was full of ambition and drive. She loved me before I became a rich man and I'm grateful I got to marry the woman I loved. Our marriage wasn't perfect, but we supported each other through hard times, and in the end that's what I'm most grateful for; her loyalty and trust in me."

"Yeah, it's what we're all searching for, isn't it?" I yawned and looked at the clock. It was almost three thirty a.m. "Do you think Charles will reach out to me or should I reach out to him?"

"My advice is to be patient. There's nothing as enticing for a man as to chase a woman."

"But what if I never hear from him again?"

"Then he's a bigger fool than I can even imagine. For now, just stay calm and play your part as a tourist. I'm working with my people to build a case against O'Brien and I think we might be onto something big."

"What is it?"

"Kit has all the details and she can fill you in, but just know that I won't be satisfied until I've closed down O'Brien's entire cult. He went after the wrong man's grandchild." It sounded like a declaration of war.

"There are children there." My words came out in a soft voice.

"Yes, the report said as much."

I closed my eyes and exhaled. "It's different when you meet them in person. I knew about the children from the report, but seeing them and speaking with them makes it twice as awful. I didn't see any signs of physical violence toward the children. I mean, they had a lot of respect for O'Brien, but they weren't cowering in a corner and they looked healthy and well fed. My biggest concern was that

139

none of them seemed to interact with children their own age outside of the house. It was like they were experiencing the world through books only. None of them did team sports or had friends in the village. Isn't that strange? And they're home schooled. Did you know that?"

"No, but it doesn't surprise me. Children are impressionable. Teenagers especially tend to question parental authority and pull toward their friends. By home schooling them, O'Brien can maintain control over them."

"I want Charles out, but I want the children out too."

Mr. Robertson coughed before he spoke. "You have a good heart, Liv. I sensed it the moment I met you."

After I ended the call with Mr. Robertson, I lay with my cell phone in my hand thinking about Charles. There were so many layers to him, from the insecure man when it came to dating to the very assertive lover when it came to sex. Someone had trained him to feel confident talking dirty and taking charge. Maybe it was the female employee who had written the notes to him that he kept in his box back home in Chicago.

My mind circled everything that had happened these past days, trying to find where I'd gone wrong.

Maybe I should have tried getting inside the cult before I met up with Charles. If I'd been an insider, maybe Conor wouldn't have turned Charles against me.

The thing that bothered me the most was the way Conor had flirted with me. It had been subtle, but I'd picked it up. Why would he do that if he was adamant that he didn't want me around the cult?

If only Charles were more like an open book, so I didn't have to guess at what he was thinking and feeling.

I managed to get a few more hours of sleep before I called Kit and asked if we could meet up.

She gave me an address that took me to Liffey Street in central Dublin and when I climbed the stairs and entered the apartment, it was clear that it wasn't an office but a private home.

"You live here?" The place didn't have much furniture and seemed void of colors. A large sectional leather sofa took up most of the living room where a large TV with game equipment stood. There were nails on the walls but no paintings hung there.

"No, this is my brother's place. He lets me use it sometimes if I have business downtown."

"He's not much of a decorator, is he?"

Kit looked around. "Oh, I see what ye mean, but that's because his girlfriend more or less emptied the place when she moved out."

"How long ago was that?"

"Two, three months, I reckon. He's better off without her. Damian has awful taste in women, if ye ask me."

"Ye know that I can hear ye…" a deep male voice came from the bedroom, and I turned to see a tall man walk out while putting on a t-shirt. His red hair was copper where Kit's was close to orange and he had brown eyes where she had blue. The mere glimpse I got of his upper body was enough to see that this man spent a good amount of time in a gym.

Kit pointed to him and back to me. "This is Liv, who is a client from Chicago, and that's my little brother Damian. Our da had him with his second wife, Lucy, who he met in Thailand after he split from my ma. That's why he looks so exotic."

"Hello." He gave me a charming grin that reminded me of Joey from *Friends*. Like it was a smile he'd studied in the mirror, designed to make women swoon.

"Hey. So, you're the SWAT brother."

Damian's brow rose and then he smiled again. "I am. Did my sister already tell ye about me?"

"Yeah, she mentioned you."

"Briefly," Kit cut in, and something told me she didn't want him to know how proud she'd been when she spoke about him. "At the same time that I told her about Da and Tommy. Don't go lookin' so smug; it's not like I was trying to set the two of ye up."

He gave me an appreciative smile. "I'm single."

"Aye, ye are. Again!" Kit rolled her eyes and turned to me. "It's because he's a sex addict. Last time I saw Miriam, the poor lass couldn't walk straight. My brother thinks a normal sex life means feckin' five times a day, and no woman can keep up with that for more than a few weeks."

"At least I have a sex life," he retorted and didn't look the least bit offended that she had revealed he had a high sex drive.

"I do too. A very satisfying one where the focus is on my needs."

"That's because all ye do is masturbate."

"So? I always come, and I'll bet that's more than ye can say for yer women."

Damian threw his hands up with a smile. "I'm a great lover. It comes with practice. Tell ye what, I'm willing to prove my skills. All I need is a volunteer." He wiggled his eyebrows at me but I just grinned and held up a palm.

"Sorry, but I'm into a nerdy guy with Tourette's called Charles."

"What a shame." He turned to Kit. "I'm goin'. Don't eat all my cookies again."

"I'll make you some new ones. I promise." When she leaned in and hugged him, she gave him a kiss on his cheek.

"It was nice to meet you," I said and reached out a hand to him, but he opened his arms.

"I'm a hugger."

"Oh, okay." I felt small in his arms, but he smelled lovely and let me go quickly. Once he was by the door, he turned and looked at me.

"Oi, Liv, how long are ye staying in Dublin? I've got an extra room."

"She's not goin' to be yer roommate, ye silly man." With a light hand to my elbow, Kit moved me to a table where her laptop and papers lay spread out.

"Thanks for the offer though," I called as he smiled and left.

"Liv." Kit was already by the table and waving me over. "C'mere to me till I tell ye what I've found." Kit searched through a pile of papers. "While you were kissing with Charles, I've been doin' some serious diggin'. Look at this."

I sat down and studied the papers in front of me.

"What is this?"

"A police report from Liverpool."

There were four pages.

"Seven years ago, a woman named Patricia Maddox walked into a Liverpool police station and said she suspected her brother had been murdered by a man called Conor Bricks. No evidence was found and since Conor had an alibi and people vouching that he'd been in Dublin, no charges were made against him. Patricia and her brother were known by the police to be hustlers so she wasn't a credible person to begin with."

"Okay."

Kit's eyes shone with excitement as she continued. "Since Mr. Robertson has given us full carte blanche to use as many hours as needed on this case, I took a quick trip to visit Patricia and ye won't believe the story she told me."

My body moved to the edge of my seat. "What did you find?"

143

"According to her, Jim, her brother, owned a sleazy bar with a few guestrooms on the first floor. He had a little side hustle where he'd use hidden cameras to film unfaithful husbands getting' a quickie with their mistresses and then blackmail them for cash."

Kit looked me straight in the eye. "But one day, a black woman checked in with her wee fella. She seemed upset and desperate, so when a man showed up, Jim figured there was a story to exploit. He pushed the button in the bar that activated the cameras and went about his evening serving drinks and food in the bar. At one point, the man left with the sleepin' fella over his shoulder and that's when Jim turned off the cameras. The next day the woman stayed in her room all day, and when Jim watched the film, he knew why."

"Why?" I was eager to hear more.

"She was dead. That's why." Kit leaned back and like the great storyteller she was, she paused for effect. "Patricia has never seen the video but Jim told her how the little fella had been sleeping while the man held a knife to his throat. The mother was pleadin' for her son's life."

"Did he kill the boy too? You said Jim saw him sleeping. Did that mean he was really dead?"

"No. To save her son's life, the mother did as the man ordered. She wrote a suicide note dictated by him, and she ate fifteen pills that he gave her."

"She *killed* herself?" My eyes widened.

Kit shook her head. "Nah, she didna kill herself. She might have swallowed the pills, but it still counts as murder!"

"That's awful. And the boy. Is it Nathan?"

She nodded. "Aye. I've confirmed that his mother's body was found in the bar that Jim owned, but of course we have no way to prove that Nathan or Conor was there without the video, do we?"

144

"Wow." I leaned back too. "If this is true, Conor Bricks is a sick and very dangerous individual."

"Aye. He is." Kit shuffled some papers around. "Accordin' to Patricia, she and Jim identified the man as Conor and tried to blackmail him. Conor negotiated a smaller amount than they had first requested over the phone and agreed to meet up in person to pay the money. Only Patricia never saw Jim again."

"Conor killed him!" My words hung in the air as the most obvious reason for Jim's disappearance.

"Aye. I think he did." Kit looked grave. "Ye have to be careful, Liv. This man will stop at nothing. He's a monster."

My thoughts went to Nathan and the pain in the boy's eyes when he'd told me about his mom. "And now Nathan thinks he wasn't enough for his mom to want to live when all the time it was the man whom he calls father who forced her to kill herself." It made me sick to think about the unfairness and cruelty of it all.

"We have to find Jim's body and the video," Kit declared. "Once we have that, we can put Conor away for murder and then Charles and the others can see he was always a complete fraud."

"But how? If it's been seven years and if the police closed the case, then how will you find evidence?"

"Leave that to me. In the meantime, I need ye to help me put pressure on Conor."

"How?"

"Keep yer hook in Charles and buzz around like a feckin' bee that Conor can't kill."

"You just asked me to be careful and now you want me to provoke the sicko?"

"Aye. My da and I will be dropping by to ask him questions about Nathan's mom."

"What was her name?"

145

"Sandra." Kit found a picture and placed it in front of me. The woman in the photo was a young black woman in a white wedding dress smiling up at her white groom who stood in his formal military uniform.

"This wedding photo was from about a year before Nathan was born." Kit sounded as sad as I felt.

"It's such a tragedy."

"Aye. It is."

"Do we have a motive for Conor killing her?"

"She was tryin' to get away from him. Hiding with her son in a primitive room above a bar. Don't forget that other members who left have restrainin' orders against him. I'd say that Sandra was scared of him."

"For good reason." I sighed and closed my eyes. "How in the world did Charles get messed up in this man's net?"

Kit sighed too. "That's the thing with psychopaths, isn't it? They don't go around with warnin' labels, but they should. Conor is a good example of someone clever and cunnin' with no conscience. He has developed a fine set of skills to hold power over others. It's like when I was young and I begged my brothers to play Barbie with me. Tommy would come up with the most twisted plots and I'd be so angry with him because I wanted the dolls to fall in love and play family while he wanted them to rob, steal, and get in fights so his Action Man could come and save the day."

"Kit, I'm not really sure where you're going with that story."

"Just that Conor is destroying people's lives."

"Like Tommy destroyed your Barbies' made-up lives?"

"Uh-huh."

I could tell Kit's analogy made total sense to her, but I brought her back to what mattered, "Kit, we need to expose Conor to the world."

She nodded. "I'm on it!"

146

CHAPTER 14
Reconciliation

Charles

Monday, I went to work in a haze of misery. I stalled while teaching and banged my head against a door because I was too busy looking down at my phone instead of seeing where I was going.

Every minute that I spent away from Liv felt like time wasted. What if she'd already packed up and left Dublin?

The thought left my stomach in a painful knot. I had obsessed about her comment that she had gone through this situation with an ex whose mother didn't find Liv good enough for her son. How was that even possible? Any man would be lucky to have her as his girlfriend, and I'd meant it when I said I could think for myself.

Not that the two scenarios were close. Conor wasn't a clingy mother. He was my mentor and friend. Liv might think my issues were cute but he understood them better than she did. He wanted what was best for me, and his warnings had nothing to do with Liv's not being good enough. It was a matter of his thinking that I wasn't ready for a relationship with any woman.

Still, if he'd seen how effortless things were between Liv and me, maybe he wouldn't worry so much.

My fingers kept playing with my phone. My body screamed for me to go after my woman. That's why, when I got home that afternoon, I texted her.

Charles: Are you there?

When my phone buzzed, I was so eager to pick it up and see if the text was from Liv that I dropped the phone on the floor.

Can you be a bigger idiot? I hurried to see who the sender was. My heart felt like it was pounding right out of my rib cage when the screen said, The cute coffee thief.

"Please don't write that you're leaving," I muttered with bile in my throat from the thought that I'd never see her again.

Liv: Yes, I'm here. Howth Castle is worth a visit. Have you been?

I stared at the text. Why would she write me about Howth Castle? Did I just imagine that she was disappointed and angry when she left yesterday? I put the phone down and felt like fucking crying. Being an Aspie was like navigating the world with minimal hearing and sight. Every time I thought I understood a situation, it turned out that I'd gotten it wrong. I'd been sad and depressed since she left, obsessing about my relationship with Liv, while *she* didn't seem to be affected. Picking up the phone, I texted back.

Charles: Yeah, it's pretty.

God, my answer looked so short and cold. Like I didn't care about her.

Liv: What are you up to right now?

Pushing you away, destroying my chance of a happy life, proving to myself that I truly am the biggest loser. The long list of things that came to mind was endless.

Charles: I'm in my room. Thinking!

Liv: Me too!

Charles: Not about leaving, I hope.

There... I had to write it because I didn't want her to leave. What I hadn't been able to communicate to Conor was that I liked who I became when I was with Liv. She wasn't like other women; I'd felt relaxed when we were together. Liv didn't sulk because I said the wrong thing. She confronted me and asked for clarification. She was transparent and honest with me and that made it easy to be around her. A new text popped in.

Liv: You don't want me to leave?

Charles: NO!

Liv: Okay then. Have you had enough time to process? Are you ready to be my boyfriend and come make love to me?

A sound between a sigh of relief and a loud laugh erupted from me, like one of those happy cows that's finally allowed on grass in the spring after a long winter, I got up from my chair and did a happy dance. There was so much energy running through my body that I wanted to sprint straight from Howth to her hotel.

Charles: I'm on my way.

Grabbing my jacket, I flew out my door and ran down the stairs taking three steps at a time.

"Whoa, where are you going? Is something on fire?" Nathan, Maximum, and Atlas watched me with big eyes.

"Yes. My heart." I didn't stop to clarify but snatched a set of car keys to one of the cars parked outside. Conor had always allowed me to use them whenever I needed to, and right now, I *needed* to.

The BMW took off so fast that small stones flew up from the ground around me, but I didn't care. I could afford a new paint job for the car but I couldn't afford to waste any more time with Liv.

Maybe I wasn't ready to be in a committed relationship. In fact, there was a big chance that Conor was right and I would screw up everything and suffer from a broken heart. But I didn't have a choice. Missing Liv had made it clear that I would take every second I could get with her. If she was serious about forgiving my quirkiness and still wanted to be with me, then I'd bury my head against her warm body and stay there.

I hated that her hotel didn't have valet parking because I had to circle the building twice to find a place to park. When I knocked on her door, I was out of breath from running.

All my senses were working overtime, analyzing her footsteps as she approached the door on the other side, and the way she swung the door open wide as if she wasn't holding any part of herself back.

I was on her before she could say hi. Lifting her up and carrying her inside the room while the heavy door shut behind us, I might not be able to explain how I felt, but at least I could show her.

My kisses were deep and hungry, my breathing ragged. Liv let her tongue dance with mine and didn't complain when I placed her on the bed and began undressing her. If she asked me to slow down, I'd die. It

150

was like I was drowning and she was my life preserver that I needed to hold on to.

"I need you." It was all I could get out of the bundled-up emotions in my chest.

"And I need you." She wrapped her arms and legs around me but I still needed more.

The condoms I'd bought were on the night table and, pushing my pants down, I broke free from her hold and put one on at warp speed. Any concern about foreplay was suppressed by my urge to feel her embrace me. All of me.

I pushed inside her with more force than I normally would and she made a small sound of discomfort. Remembering what she'd told me, I placed my hand around her throat and looked into her eyes. "I can't be gentle. I need you too much for that."

"It's okay."

I pushed deeper, seeing tears form in the edges of her eyes.

"Don't stop, Charles. I want this as much as you do." Her words were underlined by the way she was wrapping her body around mine again.

"Don't leave." Another two words escaped the hard knot of bundled-up emotions inside me.

The salty taste of her tears was in our kisses. I should ask her why she was crying, but I wouldn't know how to comfort her so I kissed her tears away and made love to her instead.

I was an expert at hot dominant sex. It had been what my other lovers had wanted from me, but Liv was asking me for something none of the women in my past had ever desired. She wanted me as her partner. Not just her lover, but partner. In her text she had asked me if I was ready to be her boyfriend, and this was my way of showing her that my answer was a big fucking yes.

My kisses down her jaw line turned possessive with the way I nibbled her skin at the same time that I intertwined my fingers with hers. My initial urge to connect with her was soothing now that we were paired. I wasn't trembling any longer and I was able to look her in the eyes and watch for her reaction to the rhythm and depths of my thrusts.

No words passed my lips. This wasn't about me being horny, and I wasn't in the mood to talk dirty. Slowing down my pace, I pushed in deep and just stayed there, enjoying the feeling of being inside the core of my girlfriend.

"Do you want children?" The question came without a filter and seemed to surprise her.

"Eh, yeah, I do, but not now."

I moved again. "Good."

"Good that I want children or good that I don't want them now?"

Lowering my head to her amazing breasts, I suckled on one of them. "Both."

She tilted her head on the pillow where her long brown hair lay splayed out, and smiled at me. "Are we having children one day?"

Fuck... her talking about a future *us* made the butterflies that lived in my body take a victory lap. "We are!" I kissed her again. "But first I'm going to enjoy you. We can travel if you want, and see the world."

"What about Conor and the others?"

"They'll be there when we get back."

There was something in her eyes that I couldn't decipher. "What is it?"

"Nothing. I just want to make love to you. We don't have to plan everything right now, but will you promise me something?"

"Mmm."

"Will you come to Paris with me? It's the most romantic city in the world and I want to see it with you."

I smiled and nodded.

"Yes?" She was smiling at me as she asked me to assure her that I was serious.

"Yes!"

She moved to get on top of me, and I let her. Seeing her gorgeous tits sway as she rocked back and forth was the most beautiful sight. She had her feet placed on each side of my hips as she rode me with her eyes roaming my body and face, and intense lust shining from her. The rush it gave me to see her desire for me made my ball sack harden and my moans deepen. Liv was so fucking perfect, like that missing piece to my existence that I'd longed for but never found until now.

"I wanted to do this from the first time I saw you." Licking her lips, she pressed down on top of me, taking me to the root and moving her hips with a smile of satisfaction.

"I wish you had." I reached up and pulled her down for a deep kiss. "You're so goddamn sweet and amazing."

We kissed and moaned into each other's mouths, our fingers touching and exploring lips, hair, and warm skin.

After she had done most of the work riding me for a long while, I took a firm hold of her hips and held her up enough for me to pump in and out of her at a fast pace. Liv closed her eyes and leaned back her head, moaning deeply. "Not fair."

"Why, don't you like it?" I panted.

"Yeess, but you're making me addicted to you." Her voice was hoarse from lust and she ended her sentence with a breathy moan. "Ohh, it feels so right."

I kept going – hammering in and out of her, and enjoying the sound of sex with my balls slapping against her.

153

"Ohh… Charles, it's… oh… Yeess."

"It's okay, let it go, Saffron."

Her moans grew higher in their pitch, as mine grew deeper.

"Come on me, Liv. Fucking come on my cock."

She squeezed her hands on my chest, digging her fingers into my skin.

I was grateful that I was in great shape and could keep going until she screamed out her orgasm. "Yes, Charles, yeeesss."

The satisfying sensation of her core muscles milking my cock made me roar out my own orgasm and empty my balls in the thin sheath of rubber that protected her womb.

Her arms were holding on to me tight and she had her face pressed against my neck. Inside I felt a sense of peace fill me from being accepted, desired, and appreciated by Liv. It was so powerful that I felt tears in my eyes, but I blinked them away before she noticed how making love to her made me emotional.

As our breathing calmed, Liv placed her head on my shoulder, while my arms clasped tight around her back.

"I think this is it," she whispered.

"What is?"

"When you know you've found the one."

It was like a magic trick. She pulled a single thread and just like that, the hundreds of bundled-up threads of confusing emotions untangled in my chest, leaving a freeing sense of complete order and clarity. "Liv…"

"Hmmm?"

"I think I love you."

She lifted her head and looked into my eyes. "I think I love you too."

CHAPTER 15
Moving In

Liv

"I'm happy you came." I was circling my fingers on Charles' chest as we lay cuddled up in the hotel bed.

"Do you mean in a sexual way or that I came to see you?"

I kissed his nipple. "I'm happy you came to see me. I was looking at tickets for Rome but I just couldn't go yet."

Charles pulled me closer and kissed the top of my head. "I'm glad I came too."

"So, what happened? What did Conor tell you to make you freak out like that?"

"It's not important."

"To me it is. I don't want him to fill your head with doubt again."

"Conor wants what's best for me. He worries about my issues being too much for you and what will happen if you break my heart. You have to understand that I was in a bad state when I met Conor."

"Bad how?"

"My trust in people was low. I'm not a social person to begin with and I tend to misunderstand situations because of my Asperger's. I say the wrong things and end up offending people without wanting to. I feel like everyone is staring at me and judging when I have my tics." He paused and played with my hand. "I have few friends and every relationship I've ever had with women have been purely physical. And then there's the massive amount of pressure that came with working for Solver

155

Industries, where everyone compared me to my grandfather. I haven't told you this but McCann was my mother's maiden name. My real last name is Robertson and Charles Robertson Senior is my grandfather."

"Okaaay." Part of me wanted to reveal that I already knew that, but we had just overcome one crisis, and I didn't want to rock the boat before I was a thousand percent certain that he knew how real my feelings for him were.

He looked at me like he was waiting for a bigger reaction, but when I still said nothing, he continued, "I was working at Solver when I first came to Ireland. My grandfather is old and he has been grooming me to take over ever since I graduated."

"But you don't want to?"

"I'm not sure. I felt suffocated for so long." Charles looked up at the ceiling. "And lost. I felt so goddamn lost. Like I was locked into a position from the day I was born with no regard to what *I* wanted. I happen to love international law, but I don't recall there ever being a choice for me. My grandfather would preach about the sacrifices that we leaders must make for our employees. A lot of families depend on their salary to pay bills, feed their children, and send them to school. Being at the top might look glamorous from the outside, but it comes with a heavy burden of worries." Charles turned a little toward me. "Conor was the first to tell me that I wasn't locked down, and that I had the right to walk away. Did you know there was a king in England who chose to pass the crown to his younger brother when he felt suffocated? That empowered me to step away from the path I'd been on and take time to discover what I would want to do if it was entirely up to me."

"You know that the king you talk about abdicated to be with the woman he loved, right?"

156

"Did he?" Charles frowned.

"Yes, she was American and already married twice, which made her unsuited to be queen."

"Right, but what I got from it was that you always have a choice."

"Hmm, do you know what I got from it?"

He turned his head to look me in the eye before I continued,

"That not even a crown, scepter, and a great kingdom can make a man happy if he's not with the woman he loves."

We smiled at each other and he kissed my nose. "Good point."

"So, what you're saying is that Conor suggested that our relationship wouldn't last."

Charles scrunched his nose with a round of tics. "That, and he also pointed out that you're a distraction from the work I've been doing and that he didn't think I was ready to take such a big step."

"But you were ready yesterday morning. Remember, when I had doubts and you were the one staying strong and holding on to me?" I kept my tone serious.

"I know, but he has some valid points, Liv. I'm pretty sure I'll be a terrible boyfriend. When I get pressured, my ability to communicate my emotions shuts down. You saw it yourself."

"Yes, I saw it. That's why I left. I had to trust that you'd recognize how special this thing between us is. How many times have you experienced something like what we share?"

Charles closed his eyes. "Never."

"Me neither."

We were silent for a moment before I asked, "Are all your doubts gone or will they come back the moment he raises his concerns again?"

157

A triangle formed between Charles' eyebrows, but he didn't answer.

"Can I be honest with you for a second? I don't think Conor knows what we have. Don't you see, Charles? He's never had that with anyone. It sounds to me like he has sex but no real commitment with any of his women. You're not like that. What works for him won't necessarily work for you."

Charles lifted a hand to his forehead and his eyes went back to the ceiling. "Conor might not follow the norms of society, but that's because he sees through the conventions and limitations that are put upon us. If you knew him better, you'd know he's a genius and that getting to be one of his insiders is a huge privilege."

I wanted to scream at him: *Do you hear yourself?* but this was Charles' reality and for me to help him see the truth about the charlatan whose influence he was under, I had to tread carefully.

"What does him being a genius have to do with commitment? He has children with Ciara but made sure to point out to me that he's not married. All I'm saying is that he doesn't have to agree with our definition of a relationship. Quite frankly I'm only interested in two opinions and that would be yours and mine." I pointed to his chest.

Sucking in a breath, Charles nodded. "You're right. He always said that I shouldn't limit myself and that I should reach for the stars. That's what being with you feels like."

"Right back at ya." I kissed him and licked his upper lip. I should leave well enough alone, but with everything I'd learned about Conor Bricks this morning, I couldn't help myself. "It seems odd, though." Rolling out of bed, I walked to the bathroom. This time, I did it naked for one major reason; I wanted Charles to see that I felt bonded to him and that our relationship had moved to the next level.

He had asked me to keep my clothes off yesterday morning when I needed to use the bathroom, but I hadn't been ready at that time.

After what Kit had told me today, I would have walked naked through the street to get Charles out of Conor's claws.

"What is odd?"

"Him telling you to dream big and reach for the stars. But then when you do it, he makes you doubt it. Seems strange to me." I strategically closed the door in that moment, allowing my words to linger behind me.

When I came back out, Charles was getting dressed.

"Do you have to go?"

"I thought about it. It's stupid that you're paying for a hotel room when I live in the Dublin area. You're my girlfriend and I want you to stay with me. God knows, I pay plenty for the room I have."

"How much do you pay?"

"A lot more than you pay for this room, but it's not important."

"Why is it so expensive to live there?"

"It's not. Conor lets us pay what we want to. He encourages us to pay equal to what we're getting out of living there. Since I've been very happy with what I've gained, I've been generous in my contribution to the family."

"Ah, I see. But are you sure they will allow you to let me stay with you?"

He got my suitcase and opened it on the bed. "Tell you what. If any of them have a problem with you living with me, I'll book us into the nicest hotel there is."

"I don't want to be an inconvenience."

Charles walked over and with an appreciative glance down my naked body, he pulled me close. "Are you kidding me? You're the best thing in my life."

I melted into a puddle on the floor, or at least that's how it felt, but then he smacked my butt.

"Now pack your things, I'm double parked."

"Can I dress first?" I wiggled my eyebrows.

"Only if you promise to undress again the moment we're in my room."

Charles helped me by collecting everything from the closet and bringing it to the bed where my suitcase was. When he was about to open the drawer where my underwear was, I got nervous. That's where I kept the report and his diary.

"Hey, would you mind packing the things in the bathroom? There's a toiletry bag under the sink."

"Sure."

As soon as he obliged and went into the bathroom, I cleared out the drawer and packed the report and diary under a pile of clothes in my suitcase.

"Was that all?" he asked a few minutes later as we both looked around.

"Yes."

"All right, then let's get you checked out." He took the biggest of my suitcases and opened the door

"Actually." I bit my lip. "I've prepaid for the room for the next two days. Do you mind if I don't check out? Just in case you let Conor into your head again and I need a place to stay."

Charles stopped and gave me a serious look. "That's not going to happen. I've made up my mind that I want to be with you, and I mean it."

"I want that too, but you can't blame me for keeping a back door open, just in case you change your mind again."

Closing his eyes, he sighed. "I'm sorry for making you doubt me. I want you to feel safe with me."

"Ditto."

There was a smile between us full of unspoken promises and then he held the door for me as I exited the room with my cabin-sized bag on wheels.

All the way back to Howth, we listened to music and talked about our favorite things. We discovered that Charles preferred the fall while I preferred the spring, that his favorite color was blue while mine was green.

"But what about food? If you could only eat one category of food for the rest of your life, what would it be?"

Charles thought about it. "Maybe salad; the variations are endless."

"Salad?" I wrinkled my nose. "No way; I'd live off cake."

"You can't live off cake. There's no nutritional value in cake."

"Who said we had to think of health? I was talking about taste only."

"Salad is still the better option."

"Salad is boring."

"Then what about soup? There's a lot of different kinds to pick from."

I shook my head. "Most people I ask this question always say pizza."

"Why?"

"Because pizza is a favorite for many and you can make it into a dessert too."

"Dessert? How do you make pizza into a dessert?"

I lowered my brow. "Don't tell me you've never had a cinnamon and sugar pizza or a Nutella pizza."

Charles looked disgusted. "Is that a thing?"

"Yes! It's a big thing because it's delicious."

"Nah, I'd still pick soup or salad."

"Slugbug." I slapped his arm when a yellow Volkswagen Beetle passed us.

"Why are you hitting me and what the hell is a slugbug?"

161

I stared at him in disbelief. "You've never played slugbug?"

"No."

"My sister and I did it all the time. Whenever you see a Beetle you get to punch the other and if it's a convertible you get two punches. All kids play that game and it's one of the reasons that I drive a Beetle myself. I love that I get to carry on the tradition."

He shook his head. "I didn't have any siblings and I assure you my grandfather never shouted 'slugbug.'"

I laughed. "Then it's a good thing you have me now. You'll get used to it. Just you wait and see."

When we parked the car and walked up to the house, Charles was chatting happily. "We're going to have a challenge with closet space."

My heart was drumming fast in my chest as we entered the house with my suitcases. Eileen, who had insider knowledge from her years in the group, had told me to weave a close emotional bond with Charles and not scream about the place being a cult. This would be my chance to go undercover and gather intel that could help take down Conor O'Brien.

We hadn't made it from the entryway and up the stairs before Conor appeared with three of the children. Looking at Charles with my large suitcase, he raised a brow. "What's going on?"

Charles was a few steps above me and turned. "Liv is staying with me."

"Is she?" Conor held a calm smile on his face, but I thought I saw a micro-expression of annoyance. "I don't recall giving my approval, and no one moves into my house without my permission."

"Fair enough. Can my girlfriend stay in my room while she's in Ireland?"

Conor looked thoughtful but then he gave a firm "No."

162

"Why not?"

"I'm happy to explain if you allow me a moment of your time." He waved a hand for Charles to follow him, which made me nervous, but Charles stood his ground and didn't leave my side.

"You can talk to me in front of Liv."

Conor tensed. "What we do here at the manor isn't anyone's business. You agreed to respect the privacy and secrecy of this place when you moved in."

"But she's my girlfriend."

"I understand, but unless I have invited her, she can't stay here."

With frustration on his face, Charles threw his hands up. "Then invite her already."

"I would, but we don't have an available room, and I don't want her sleeping in your room."

"But..."

"Charles, I'm not having this discussion here. We'll continue it in the library."

We left my suitcases in the entrance and walked to the library, where we sat down in an expensive-looking sofa, holding hands.

Conor sat in a reading chair with his right ankle casually placed on top of his left knee. "The reason that Liv can't stay in your room is that if I allow you to have your girlfriend in your room, soon everyone else will expect the same privilege. I can't slack on my rules, not even for you."

I loved Charles a little more when he raised his chin and stood up. "In that case, we're staying in a hotel. Come on, Liv."

Having hoped for a chance to get insider information, I didn't leap out of my seat, but looked to Conor, who was hard to read. Something told me he was surprised by Charles' willingness to leave if need be. Conor's eyes lingered on me for a second as if trying to read my mind and see how big of a threat I'd be.

I rose from my chair and took Charles' hand.

"Not so fast." Conor gave us a smile like a parent talking to teenagers. "I understand that Liv is visiting from the US and you want her close. My concern about you and her sharing a room is that you're moving too fast. Only yesterday, I sensed doubt in you, Charles. I'm sure you've been honest with Liv and told her about your need for time alone to process the world around you. There is such a thing as drowning in your own success."

Charles shifted his balance. "Yes, I'm familiar with the expression, but it relates to business, not to love."

"Ah, but in this case, being overwhelmed with love and attention might push you back into feeling suffocated."

Once again, Charles stood his ground. "I made a promise. If Liv can't stay here, we're going to a hotel."

The door opened and River came in. When she opened her mouth to speak, Conor held up a hand, gesturing for her to wait. Pushing forward in his chair, he cleared his throat.

"I'm not an unreasonable man and if it means this much to you, I can agree to Liv's sleeping on a couch but not in your room."

There was no way I was sleeping in this house alone. What if Conor came at night and forced me to eat pills like he did with Nathan's mom?

"Liv isn't sleeping on a couch. That's ridiculous."

A soft voice sounded. "She's welcome to sleep in Nathan's and my room. We have an extra mattress for the floor."

I jumped at the chance to get some intel from the children that could aid Kit's investigation. "That's fine with me," I said a bit too fast.

"But…" Charles looked surprised. "We can go to a hotel, Liv."

"No, it's fine. I agree with Conor that a bit of alone time will be good for you, and I love kids."

Charles lifted my hand to kiss the backside of it. The appreciation in his eyes made it clear that he hadn't wanted to leave his friends here at the manor, but I was still pleased that he'd been ready to do it for me.

CHAPTER 16
Questions

Charles

River was over the moon that Liv would be sleeping in their room. It was silly to me, as I wanted Liv in my bed, but Conor had thirty-four people living in his house and I had to respect his rules even when they made no sense to me. When Liv kissed me good night and went with the children for their first sleepover, as she called it, Conor asked to talk to me in his study.

"How are you doing?" Conor sat on the corner of his desk while I was in a chair. It made me have to look up at him.

"I'm fine. No, better than fine."

"These last days I've seen a different side of you. You don't seem as interested in my teachings as usual; yesterday, you wouldn't give me your phone when I tried to help you; and you've ignored my advice several times. It worries me."

Crossing my arms, I defended myself, "I know you feel that I'm not ready to be in a relationship with Liv, but you don't know how strong our feelings are for each other."

"Oh, I never doubted that you had strong feelings. What I doubted was your skills in the area of love. And believe me, it takes skills to successfully navigate a serious relationship with a woman. It worries me that a bit of estrogen in the air will make you disregard my concern for you. As you know, I'm very picky and selective about whom I let into my circle. People would pay large sums to have me coach and mentor them, but I'm not interested in being the next self-help guru or tour the world doing get-better seminars. I believe the universe brings me the people who need my help the most. Haven't you felt better after I took you under my wing?"

I nodded. "Yes."

"If this was about money, I'd open up my house to as many as possible, but it's not and that means there are limited spots in the group. I consider everyone here a part of my tribe. My family. That's why I give you everything in a symbiosis of mutual trust and loyalty."

I looked down. "Thank you."

"You can understand how disappointing and hurtful it is to me, when a member is no longer willing to reciprocate with the same level of trust and loyalty."

I nodded.

"I'm not sensing the same interest or dedication from you. There's been a shift after Liv came into the picture."

"I'm still very loyal to the family. You mean a lot to me. You know that."

Conor tapped his chin and looked up. "Words are easy, Charles. I need to see action to be certain that you mean it."

"What kind of action?"

"Members do different things to show loyalty. Some get a tattoo with the Red Manor crest, others donate large sums to our foundation, some offer to clean or cook to be of service. It's up to you really."

"I can pay for a few schools like Sara did. Would that be enough?"

Conor shrugged. "If you want. It's important that you understand that you're not doing it for me. I'll miss our friendship if you leave, but where are you going to find a community with people who love you like we do? We want you here, but only if you're as committed as the rest of us."

"How about five schools then?"

He tilted his head. "That would be a good start, but mostly, I'd like to see you be involved again. I share everything with you. Are you willing to do the same?"

I threw my hands up. "Sure, what do you need?"

Conor gave me a long look. "I'm not talking about material things. Those are easy to share. I'm talking about what matters the most to you."

I tapped my foot on the floor, unsure what he was on about.

"What about Liv? She seems to be the most important person in your life now. Are you willing to let her be part of our group and share her with the rest of us?"

"Of course. She's already sleeping in the children's room. I was counting on all of you to accept her the way you've accepted me."

"Good." Conor leaned forward and patted my shoulder. "Good."

A knock on the door was followed by Ciara walking in with a red-haired woman and a tall gray-haired man who looked winded after walking up the stairs.

Ciara introduced them to us, "This is Kit and David O'Rourke from O'Rourke Investigation. They're detectives and have come to ask you some questions about Sandra."

"Sandra who?" Conor asked.

Both of the detectives were tall people and I guessed them to be father and daughter. She had a pad and pen in her hand and walked over to shake Conor's hand. "Sandra, your wife."

Ciara shook her head. "You got that wrong. Conor isn't married."

"No, he's a widower, we know." The female detective took a seat without being asked to. "But you were married to Sandra Hamilton for seven months before she committed suicide, isn't that correct?"

Conor stood with a stoic calmness. "It's nine thirty at night; why don't you come back at a better time?"

The old man cleared his throat and spoke with a thick brogue. "Oh, we're on a busy schedule and try to come by when people are home."

"Well, I'm happy to set up an appointment and sit down to answer your questions about Sandra at a different time."

"That won't be necessary, this won't take long." Kit tapped her pen on the pad. "A witness saw you in the bar in Liverpool where Sandra's body was found; can you confirm that?"

"He's already been asked those questions years ago and I vouched for him being here and not in Liverpool. Ciara fiddled with her hands. "Nothing has changed, except you got the detail wrong about Sandra being Conor's wife."

"No, I'm pretty sure that part is accurate. The insurance company paid out quite a nice sum in her life insurance to her husband, Conor O'Brien," Kit said in a matter-of-fact tone.

Ciara opened her mouth and closed it again, looking at Conor to deny it.

"Sandra and I had a practical marriage. She wanted a father for her son, Nathan, and I took them both in."

Kit tapped her pad again. "When you say practical, do you mean there was no sexual relationship between you?"

"Oh, there was sex, but it wasn't a traditional marriage."

"You were *married* to her?" The pain on Ciara's face was clear, but Conor looked unaffected as he addressed Kit.

"I wasn't there when Sandra died, but she left a note and begged me to raise Nathan as if he was my own. I've kept true to her wish."

169

"So how come ye were seen carryin' out the boy from the bar that night?"

"That's impossible. As I said, I was here. Ciara already confirmed it."

Ciara's hands were shaking and her lips disappeared, leaving only a thin line in a face full of tension.

Kit turned her head and spoke to Ciara. "It looks like there might be video evidence of Conor bein' with Sandra that night. It's crucial that ye tell the truth or ye could get implicated in Sandra's murder."

The accusation was ludicrous and to my relief, Ciara was quick to defend our mentor and friend. "There was no murder. Sandra was mentally unstable and killed herself. Why would I lie about Conor's whereabouts? I'm telling the truth." Her words came out in a small hiss as she raised an eyebrow at Conor. She didn't say the words, but her eyes shouted, *Unlike you.*

It surprised me that she didn't show more trust in him. Conor was the most trustworthy person I knew. If he'd married Sandra and not told anyone, there had to be a logical explanation for it.

Clearing his throat, Conor leaned back in his seat with a bored expression. It comforted me that he didn't seem the least bit worried when he asked the detectives, "Who hired you to investigate Sandra's death and what video evidence would you be talking about?"

"We can't tell ye who hired us, but it's someone who cared for Sandra."

"She killed herself and left me a suicide note. I still have it."

"Would ye mind showing it to us?" Kit asked.

Conor got up to fetch the letter from a folder and handed it to Kit. After reading it, she placed it on the desk and took a picture with her phone.

Conor kept a standing position next to his chair. "You didn't answer my question about what video evidence you're talking about."

"Oh." Kit looked up. "We've contacted all the stores in the street of the bar to see if they have video surveillance cameras, and some of them did."

"From seven years ago?" Conor scoffed. "That sounds unlikely."

"Ye're right. It's unusual since most stores delete it after a month or so, but it turns out that one of the owners in that street is a bit of a voyeur, and so anal about his surveillance that he saves snippets from all the way back to when he first got his shop. When we reached out to ask about that night, he happened to have a tape and he said it contains a man carryin' a child over his shoulder out of the bar. He saved it because it was the same night a woman died in the bar and he always figured there was a connection. Accordin' to him, he tried to tell the police back then, but they weren't interested." Kit leaned forward. "The bloke wouldn't stop talkin' when he understood that we're quare interested."

Conor leaned on his desk. "Let's see the tape and you'll see that I wasn't that man."

The tall detective hadn't said much, but he brushed his left eyebrow, and turned his head. "We'd love to show it to ye, but my son and business associate got delayed in the airport. Ye see, he went to pick it up himself."

"Then why didn't you wait for him? Why come here late at night and bring up traumatic memories for us? If you had only waited for the tape, you would see that I wasn't there."

Kit looked at her father. "He has a fair point, Da. I told ye we should have waited."

The older man shrugged. "Why wait to do tomorrow what ye can do today? I thought the witness sounded

171

credible and it does no harm to ask questions. I've done this for a while, ye see, and in cases like this, it's usually the husband who is behind the murder."

Conor squared his shoulders and spoke with a deep authoritarian voice. "You two are out of your mind. Sandra was a depressed and paranoid woman who committed suicide. There was no murder. Please leave my house immediately."

"As you wish." The old man moved to the door but the red-haired woman gave me a curious glance as if I might have details from the night Sandra died. Just before the two of them exited the room, she gave me another glance and I thought I saw a small and very satisfied smile on her face. But that couldn't be, because their investigation was a waste of time and all their accusations that Conor was connected to Sandra's death had been shot down by him.

"Wow." I exhaled noisily. "I can't believe they just came in and insinuated that you killed a woman."

He moved behind his desk and sat down. "I guarantee that it's some disgruntled former member who is trying to get back at me for asking them to leave. People get emotional and vindictive when their dreams come crashing down."

"But to accuse you of murder. That's just crazy. I can't believe how calm you are about it."

"That's because I know I'm innocent. Now do you see why loyalty means everything to me? Critics, haters, and jealous people will do anything to get you down if you're successful. With great power come enemies; it's the way of life."

"Maybe you should think about hiring security. I've never lived in a place that didn't have armed security before. My grandfather always feared someone would try and rob us, or kidnap one of us to get a ransom."

"Hmm... I'll think about it."

"Okay." Getting up from my chair, I walked around his table to hug Conor. "Don't let them get you down. Once they see the video you'll be cleared."

"Yes." He hugged me tight. "Sleep well, my friend."

"Same to you." My eyes locked onto his and I gave him a reassuring smile.

CHAPTER 17
Stirring the Pot

Liv

I woke up early and untangled my body from River, who had crawled down from her own bed to sleep with me last night.

Tiptoeing through the house, I entered Charles' room and whispered his name.

"Charles, wake up. It's me."

He was on his side facing the wall, his naked back uncovered and the rim of his briefs visible.

Getting into his queen-sized bed, I snuggled up against him and it made him jerk awake.

"It's me." I let my hand slide up his thigh and smiled when he turned around to hug me tight.

"Mmmm, come here, my lovely Saffron." His voice was hoarse from sleep. "Did you have nice dreams?"

"River, Nathan, and I talked until midnight and then I slept cuddled up with River. That girl is the sweetest."

"I know. She's cuteness overload. Too bad about her mom."

I soaked up the scent of his cologne mixed with his natural smell that worked like a direct link to my libido. My hands drifted up his chest while his hands pulled at my shorts.

"Did I tell you, I'm a big fan of morning sex?"

"No, you didn't." I smiled at him. "But it just means we have another thing in common. The only thing I'm not a fan of is kissing with morning breath."

"All right, then I won't kiss you on your mouth." He turned me to face away from him, planting kisses down my neck and shoulder while pulling my butt against his crotch. I almost purred at the feeling of his massive morning wood pressing up against me.

I could hear the sound of foil being ripped as he found a condom and put it on.

Sliding his fingers inside me, he muttered into my ear. "Mmm, I love how warm and wet you are for me."

"That's because I crave to feel you inside me."

"You do?"

"Uh-huh." It came out as a moan. I wanted to bond so tightly with him that if I ever had to make an ultimatum and make him choose me over the cult, he wouldn't hesitate. Charles might be introverted and shy, but he was a fiery lover and with a hand around my throat, he kept me right where he wanted me while taking his time to go slow, fast, circle his hips, and whisper dirty things in my ear.

"Ahhh..." I was pushing back against him and molding my body to his.

"You have no idea what you're doing to me." He bit my shoulder. "I can't lose you, Liv. Promise that you're really mine."

"I'm really yours." My eyes were closed and my head leaned back against him. With all of my heart, I wanted to be with Charles. "This is amazing."

"Yeah? You like being fucked by me?"

"I love it."

"Good, because we're doing this every morning from now on." We could hear people waking up in the house and someone on light feet running upstairs, probably River.

Our bodies had found a perfect rhythm and worked in harmony like we'd been lovers for years.

175

"God, Liv. Yes! Take every inch of me. Do you feel it?"

"Yeess." We were panting and chasing that place of euphoria we'd been in yesterday when we made love and when it finally came, Charles had to cover my mouth to dampen my screams while growling against my neck.

"Fuck, yes... I'm coming, Liv."

With my insides cramping around him, I grabbed his hand, closed my eyes, and felt the purest sensation of connectedness that I'd ever experienced with a man. I wasn't screaming anymore and he removed his hand.

He moaned in my hair. "I'm never letting you go."

We kept spooning for a few minutes, until he pulled out of me and tied a knot on the condom.

"Have you ever had sex without a condom?" I propped my head up to look at him.

"No. Have you?"

"Yes. In long-term relationships."

He lay back down and let his fingers run up and down my arm. "Part of me hates that someone else had you for a long time, but at the same time I wonder if they helped make you the amazing woman you are."

I played with his earlobe. "You've had other women too."

"Yeah, but nothing serious."

"Who were they?"

"Older women, mostly."

"How old?"

Charles looked at me. "Are you sure you want to know?"

"You're twenty-nine, it's not like I expected you to be a virgin. You can tell me."

"All right." He sighed. "When I was sixteen, one of our housekeepers and I began an affair. She was a hot-blooded Latina whose husband had been in a work accident that left him paralyzed from the waist down. She never pretended to love me, but she taught me about carnal pleasure and allowed me to experiment with her. Carmen was twenty-eight at the time."

"How long did it last?"

"It was daily while I lived at home and after I started college it slowed down to whenever I was home on vacation. But then she and her husband moved away when I was twenty.

"And after her?"

"There was a personal trainer at my gym. She was in her thirties and going through a divorce. I was a fun distraction, I suppose. I've never been good at connecting with women my own age, but older women, they..."

"They what?"

"They are more aggressive and know what they want. With them there was never any pressure of going on dates or trying to impress them with my dance moves. They didn't want my kids, money, or my love. All they wanted was to have fun without a commitment. It would be a bottle of wine, some casual talk, and sex. That was it!"

"But you said that you loved morning sex. That would imply you've spent the night with some of your lovers."

"There were a few weekend trips with the divorcee."

"Oh, I see."

"Are you sure that you're okay hearing about this?"

"Of course. I want to get to know you better. I can only do that if you tell me about your life."

Charles kissed my left breast and sucked on my nipple. "Well, in my case, I don't mind that you have a past, just as long as you agree that I'm your future."

Warm smiles and unspoken promises passed between us and then he rolled over to sit on the edge of the bed, reaching for his clothes.

"I couldn't sleep last night."

"Why not?" I watched him put on his shirt.

177

"Something crazy happened after you went to bed. I was with Conor when a couple of detectives came to question him about Nathan's mom, Sandra. She used to be a member of the mastermind group."

My whole body stiffened and I was happy he had his back to me and couldn't see it.

"It was a father and daughter, as Irish as you can imagine. Red hair and strong brogue."

"What did they want to know?"

Charles turned to me. "They more or less insinuated that Conor had been involved in Sandra's suicide. It turned out that Conor and Sandra were married and from the way Ciara reacted, I'd say that she had no idea."

"Conor was married to Sandra?"

"Yes."

"That must have been a blow to Ciara. I mean, Conor and she have two boys together, but he hasn't married her."

"I know. It's weird." Getting up, Charles closed his pants. "But either way, the detectives had it wrong and they left when they couldn't prove anything."

"No wonder you couldn't sleep. What if there's something to their accusations?"

"There's not!" Charles' tone was firm. "I shouldn't have told you. Now you'll have a bad impression of Conor but he's the kindest, most thoughtful guy you'll ever know. He'd never do anything to hurt a person. Especially not a member of his group. We're family to him."

"If he didn't do it, he'll have nothing to worry about." I picked up my shorts and t-shirt and changed the subject. "I was hoping for a shower."

"It's down the hallway. Come on, let me show you."

When I was in the bathroom with the door locked, I let the water run and called up Kit.

"Hello."

178

"You were here. Charles just told me."

"Aye, my da and I stirred the pot last night. We told Conor that there's a videotape to prove he was in Liverpool the night Sandra died."

"But I thought you didn't have that tape."

"We don't. It disappeared with Jim when he tried to blackmail Conor, but we came up with a story about a shop owner who has a security tape."

"You *lied*?"

"Aye, but it's more like gettin' creative and puttin' a bit of pressure on the target. Ye'd be surprised how many times it helps the investigation along. Criminals get stupid when they're paranoid."

"But if you think he's a killer why would you provoke him? What if he comes after you?"

"Me?" Kit got quiet.

"Yes, Kit. If he made Sandra kill herself, what makes you think he couldn't do the same to you? I swear, I'm not staying one second longer in this house than I have to. Not when I know what he's capable of."

"Ye're in the house?"

"Yes. Charles moved me in here last night. I'm sleeping with the children. I was going to text you, but I haven't had a moment to myself."

"This is excellent. Keep yer ears and eyes open and report back to me."

"That's the plan. But I have to take a shower now. Just be careful, Kit."

"Aye, and the same to ye."

I showered in record time to compensate for the minutes I'd been whispering on my phone with Kit.

At the breakfast table, only the children, Conor, Charles, me, and five of the residents were present.

Conor was quiet and ate without conversing.

179

"Is something troubling you," one of the Portuguese twins asked him.

I expected him to say it was nothing, but he put down his cup of coffee and pushed his plate of toast away. "Yes, something *is* troubling me."

Right away, everyone around the table fell silent.

"It seems that the timing of my session on how to deal with haters and critics was the universe sending me a reminder that I need to be strong and that trouble is coming. As you all know, I firmly believe that our souls have lived many lifetimes and that we've each experienced events that were designed to teach us about forgiveness, grace, patience, love, and other virtues. I've never been afraid of dying as I know it's not the end, but merely the beginning of a different life."

I listened intently, drawn in by his calm voice, which was low and yet filled the room.

"Rumors are circulating that I was somehow involved in Sandra's suicide."

Nathan dropped his knife and stared at Conor.

"The only armor I have against these nasty lies is this letter that Sandra wrote to me before she decided to move on to her next life." He held up a piece of paper that had been next to his plate and passed it to Nathan, who sat across from him. "I want you all to read it so that you'll see that Sandra was sick from depression and had given up on life."

Nathan's eyes ran over the letter before his hands fell down.

"Can I see it?" Atlas held a hand to Nathan's back and took the letter when Nathan put it down on the table. One by one everyone at the table read and passed the letter along. When it reached me, I read it in silence like the others.

Dear Conor,

I'm so sorry to write you this letter. I know you'll be disappointed that despite all the hours of friendship and support that you've given me over the years, it still wasn't enough.

Somehow, I thought that coming back to Liverpool with Nathan would be better, but it's been worse. If anything, it has proved to me what a useless mother I am.
Nathan deserves more than what I can ever give him.

We've talked about this.

My mind is sick and darkened by demons that make me see things that aren't real. I even imagined that you and Nathan would hurt me when I know that the two of you are the only ones who love me despite all my flaws.

Please forgive me for asking you this one last favor. Love Nathan as your own son. He will be without parents but with you to care for him, I know he'll have the best father he could wish for.

Remind him often that I loved him and that I'll see him in our next lifetime.

Sandra.

Tears were streaming down my face as I imagined Sandra scared in her room, watching Conor hold a knife to Nathan's throat and forcing her to write this vile letter to save her son's life.

Conor gave me a sad look. "Yes, it's tragic to read her talk about demons in her sick mind, but at least, I've kept my promise to her and raised Nathan as my own."

Nathan sat with his shoulders slumping low and his chin shivering like he was fighting his tears.

"Ciara has already confirmed to the gardas that I was here the night Sandra died, but it worries me that cruel people would rip open this sad and dark chapter again when we worked so hard to close it behind us. That's why I was quiet this morning."

With his having Sandra's letter next to his plate it seemed to me like he had just been waiting for someone to ask what was wrong. He had planned this speech.

"How can we help you?" Sara, a pretty woman in an expensive-looking pantsuit, asked. I had met her last night and knew that she was the lawyer who had invited Charles to meet Conor. I also knew from the children that Sara and Conor often slept together.

Conor watched her and then he glanced around the room at all of us. "Children, please take your plates out, go upstairs, and begin reading. It's almost eight and I'll be up in a little while."

We waited for the children to disappear and then Conor continued. "If any of you think that I could harm one of our family members, then it's best if we part ways. You're all successful people and you'll do fine out in the world."

"No, no..." All around the table protests sounded.

"I know I seem invincible, but it's a blow to have someone accuse me of harming a woman I loved."

"We're here for you." Ciara reached out and placed her hand on top of Conors.

Conor was quiet as other members assured him that they couldn't imagine him doing anything to Sandra.

"Yes. Whatever you need." Sara, who sat next to him, leaned her cheek against his shoulder. "We're here for you in this lifetime and the next."

"How do I know?" His voice was low and when he raised his gaze to look at Sara, warning signals flared up in me. For just a flash, I saw the crazy behind the façade. I looked to Charles hoping he'd seen it too, but he sat with deep frown lines and an expression of sympathy for his friend who was claiming to be wrongly accused.

Sara blinked her eyes. "You know we'd all die for you, just as you'd die for us. That's not a question."

Whoa, whoa! My eyes widened as Conor let Sara's words hang in the air while meeting the eyes of the people sitting at the table.

Ciara nodded to support Sara's statement and so did the twins and the others. This was so uncomfortable and intense that a sound escaped my throat like a protest to their talk about death.

For a long second Conor's eyes lingered on Charles before moving on to me. His penetrating glance felt like he was assessing me and I was searching for something to say to change the heavy subject.

Turning his attention back to Sara, Conor spoke in a soft voice that still filled the silent room like he had screamed the two words. "Prove it!"

Sara flared her nostrils at his challenge but gave a short nod.

While I looked on in disbelief, Conor pushed his chair back and walked to a painting in light colors portraying a woman in white walking through a field of corn with her hands reached out to each side, touching the crop with the sun shining down on her. Pushing the painting aside, Conor opened a safe and retrieved a gun.

My eyes were wide as I squeezed Charles' hand and gave him a *what the fuck?* look. He looked as stunned as me and so did everyone else at the table.

Putting down the gun in front of Sara, Conor looked at her. "It's ready to fire, so prove it."

She licked her lips and swallowed hard. Her eyes fixed on the gun in front of her. When no one said a word, she picked it up with her hands shaking.

I elbowed Charles, who finally seemed to wake from his shock.

"Sara, don't be stupid. Put the gun down."

"No." Conor kept staring at Sara but pointed at Charles. "Sara knows what she's doing. Words mean nothing. Only action does. Don't say you're willing to die for someone unless you're ready to back it up."

Sara was breathing heavily but she kept her eyes on Conor and lifted the gun to her head with her shaking hands.

"Don't do it." I moved to the front of my seat preparing to intervene.

The moment felt like slow motion as I looked around the room hoping someone would stop this madness, but they all sat transfixed by the silent conversation taking place between Conor and Sara.

When I turned back to Sara, her eyes were large and moist while the barrel of the gun was pointing at her right temple and her finger was on the trigger.

"Would you die for me?" Conor's question was a low mutter meant only for Sara, but we all heard it.

The gun was shaking in her hand and perspiration showed on her forehead. "Yes."

Conor leaned closer to her. "Show me."

Sara's closed her eyes and took a deep breath before there was a click of the gun.

Loud gasps sounded from all of us. And then Conor bent forward, cupped Sara's face and kissed her on the mouth. When he pulled back, she had tears running down her cheeks.

"That's what loyalty looks like." He was holding a finger under her chin, and beamed at her with pride. Taking the gun from her, he put it on the table and pushed it to the center of the table. "Anyone else willing to show me?"

Ciara reached for the gun.

"Careful." Conor had a sly smile on his lips. "Maybe it's loaded with a single bullet and Sara just got lucky."

Ciara pulled the gun toward herself, but with a hand on top of hers, Conor stopped her. "I know you'd die for me just like I'd die for you." His eyes turned to Charles. "Can you say the same?"

Next to me, Charles, paled and swallowed hard. My heart was speeding and I recognized the acute stinging pain to my scalp from the time I barely missed a car accident and adrenaline rushed through my veins, alerting me to the danger. If this was Conor's idea of Russian roulette then there was a chance that the gun was loaded.

"Charles?" Conor kept staring at him and pushed the gun closer to our side of the table.

My fingers dug into Charles' thigh under the table not caring that it might be painful for him. I couldn't speak my mind freely, but I could show him that he wasn't alone.

"Where did you get a gun?"

"That's irrelevant," Conor said without breaking eye contact with Charles.

The atmosphere was thick and tense as the two men sat looking at each other.

Don't do it. Don't do it, I repeated over and over in my head as if Charles would be able to pick up my message.

Charles' tics were making him bob his shoulders and blink his eyes. "I don't think I should touch that gun. With my tics I might aim at me, but end up shooting one of you instead."

Conor's laughter was like letting out air from a balloon that had been blown up too hard. Looking around the room, he grinned. "Come on, don't look so shocked. You didn't think I'd hurt any of you, did you?"

Laughter of relief filled the room as everyone assured him, and each other, that they always knew it was only a playful test.

Charles smiled too while I just sat there like an observer getting a brutal insight into the power Conor held over them.

"Wow, I think I sweated through my shirt. That was intense." I forced a laugh when all I wanted was to run the hell away from this asylum.

"It was a joke, Liv." Charles and some of the others laughed as if collectively trying to normalize what had just happened.

Feeling Conor's eyes on me, I played my part and elbowed Charles. "You should have warned me that the humor in this house is pretty dark."

"Well, now you know." Charles used a sing-song voice and took his plate to the kitchen while talking over his shoulder. "I have to be at Trinity in an hour and I'm taking Liv with me. She wants to see the buildings from the inside."

"Will you be home for dinner tonight?" Ciara asked as if this were any regular morning.

"I'm not sure. We might go out for dinner downtown. I'll call you when we know our plans."

When Charles and I were outside and walking to the train station, I waited until we were out of earshot from the house before I stopped him and burst out, "You have to admit that was crazy."

Charles let out a deep breath and looked back the way we'd come. "Yeah, that stunt surprised me. I don't know what that was about. I've never seen anything like it."

"Ciera and Sara were literally ready to die for him. What the fuck?"

Charles shook his head. "I know. But that's the kind of people they are. It's authentic and real. They live life to the fullest – they walk the walk and talk the talk."

I stared at him. "Who in their right mind would ask someone to shoot themselves to prove their loyalty?"

"Conor knew the gun wasn't loaded. It was a test. He wasn't going to let us kill ourselves."

The way he was defending Conor worried me. I had been so sure that after this stunt, Charles would see that Conor wasn't a nice guy.

We began walking again. "What if I hadn't been there? Would you have pulled the trigger to prove your loyalty to him?"

"Nah-uh. I'm a loyal person, but I don't' mess around with guns. Besides, that whole thing about dying for each other is illogical to me. What would my loyalty be worth if I was dead?"

I kept walking with his hand in mine. "Do you think he got mad when we asked Sara to put the gun down?"

"Maybe, but we had to. We couldn't know that the gun wasn't loaded."

"At least the children weren't there to see it. I was really scared."

"Conor is super protective of the children. Of course, he wouldn't do it in front of them. They wouldn't understand that it was just a joke."

I didn't argue with him or point out that jokes were supposed to make people laugh and not almost pee themselves in fright. They could call it a prank all day long, but it had been a test of Conor's control over not just Sara but the rest of them too. Not one of them had intervened or protested, except for Charles, but he'd only done it when I pushed him to. I was well aware of how cult leaders pushed people to accept irrational behavior as normal, and this morning, the Red Manor group had just been pushed further.

Sitting in the train, we were both quiet, until I asked, "When you say Conor is a genius, what do you mean? What makes him so special? What kind of work does he do?"

"He used to work for the government as a code breaker. Most of his work was classified so he can't talk about it, but he was recruited because of his insanely high IQ."

"Then why did he stop? Seems a bit young to be retired."

"He's not retired. He just didn't like being used as a tool by the government. Conor managed to take the salary he made and invest it in a way that makes him a multi-millionaire today. He's extremely gifted that way and keeps making a lot of money on investments. That's why he now runs the Red Manor Foundation, which works on philanthropic projects to benefit children around the world. At the same time, he's taken a lot of time to travel and study with gurus in East India where he learned to connect his energy to a higher vibrancy. Now, he's careful of who he lets into his circle but those of us lucky enough to learn from him benefit tremendously. I'm telling you: if you can sit down and have a deep conversation with him, you'll understand how rare he is. It's like he can read your mind and look into your soul."

I managed to change the subject and talk about something else, because if I had to listen to one more minute of Charles' adoration for the psychopath who'd just challenged his followers to kill themselves, I would throw up in a public train.

CHAPTER 18
Brainwashing

Charles

For three days everything seemed to work fine.

Liv spent a lot of the time with the children and there were times when I'd almost get jealous because they took too much of her attention. Every morning Liv would make me feel like the happiest man in the world when she came to my room. We'd make passionate love and start our mornings discussing our future.

She no longer talked about her next destination, and I didn't bring it up. I'd promised her that we would visit Paris together, and an idea was starting to take root in my mind. I could invite her to Paris over Christmas and if everything was still amazing between us, I would propose to her.

She had called Paris the most romantic city in the world and for that reason alone, it seemed like the perfect place for us to exchange engagement rings. My grandfather had only known my grandmother for a few months when he proposed to her, and my parents had been quick to get engaged too. It ran in my family; now that I'd found the perfect woman, I had no need to wait around for a few years to test the waters.

I was happy to see that Conor had taken a liking to Liv too. Last night, he'd talked to her for at least an hour about her past and her plans for the future. She told him about her dream to work as a forensic anthropologist to help police departments identify mysterious or unknown remains. It didn't surprise me that with Conor's vast network he knew someone who could help her achieve that dream.

The episode with the gun on Tuesday morning had freaked Liv out, so I was grateful that she got to see the real side of Conor that we all loved so much.

On Friday afternoon, however, Liv and I came home to a house that was buzzing with half of the residents gathered in the kitchen.

"What's wrong? Why are you all in here?" I asked Sara, who stood closest.

"Because the garda is here again."

Liv and I exchanged a glance. "What do you mean again? I wasn't aware they had been here before. Those two who came by on Sunday night were private detectives."

"I know, but Tuesday the garda stopped by to ask questions."

"About what?"

"We don't know, but we're assuming it's those awful rumors about Sandra." Sara's long brown hair was braided in a circle around her head, her make-up was perfect, and she was in another of her smart pantsuits with high heels that made her at least five-ten. Like Ciara, Sara was born and raised in Ireland, but after living with Conor for four years, she had adopted his clean accent and spoke without an Irish brogue.

Liv's eyes were wide open as she leaned in and whispered to me, "Maybe the police got the videotape from the surveillance camera that the detectives talked about."

"Yes, maybe. But in that case, it's good news because the video will show that Conor is innocent." I turned to Sara. "Is he alone with the police?"

Sara nodded. "Yes. I asked if he wanted me there, but he declined."

191

"We're lawyers, Sara. We need to be by his side."

She rubbed her wrist. "I know, but he said no."

I wasn't about to let someone pin a murder on my mentor. After asking Liv to wait with the others, I went upstairs to Conor's study and knocked on the door.

"Come in."

Opening the door, I saw one guard standing close to the door and another sitting in front of Conor's desk with a notepad in his hands. Conor looked calm when he asked, "What is it, Charles?"

"You shouldn't talk to them without a lawyer present."

"Yes, Sara already told me that, but since I'm innocent, I'm not concerned. I'd prefer to do this alone."

Walking into the room, I shook my head. "That would be crazy. I'm staying."

His jaws clenched but he didn't insist on my leaving.

The two officers shook my hand and introduced themselves as O'Hara and Williams before they went back to questioning Conor.

"I would like to get back to the time before ye changed your name to O'Brien. Can ye tell us more about the three restraining orders against ye?"

Conor, for once, looked visibly annoyed. "It was in the early days of my mastermind group and I wasn't as finely tuned to whom I worked with as I am now. You could say my desire to help and fix people brought me in contact with some troubled individuals. There was a woman named Janet that I took in after she had experienced severe violence from her ex-partner. I hid her from her ex for her protection, but he found her and it's my biggest regret that I wasn't there to stop him when he dragged her back home with him. Of course, I went after her, and in my eagerness to save her from him, it got to an altercation between us. In the end, she chose to stay and filed a

192

restraining order against me, but I always knew it was done under his influence."

"And what about Clara Nielson – accordin' to her file, she accused ye of rapin' her."

"That was dismissed."

"Aye, it says she withdrew the charge but there was still a restrainin' order."

Conor shrugged. "I always take a risk when I allow wounded souls into my life. Clara was disturbed and the trouble started after I found out that she was using drugs. I had to kick her out and that's when her accusations began. It was a simple act of revenge on her part."

"And Nina Evans?"

Conor sighed. "Oh dear, I'd forgotten about her. It was so long ago. Well, in her case I take the blame. She was my first love and I took it hard when she broke up with me. I was eighteen or nineteen and a romantic at the time. I'm embarrassed to admit it, but I would serenade her below her window, send her flowers and love poems. Unfortunately, Nina was overwhelmed and felt that I was stalking her."

I was starting to see why Conor cared so much about loyalty and trust between him and his members. With a history of wrongful accusations made against him, he would have learned his lesson.

"Why did ye change your name to O'Brien?"

"I had moved to Ireland and was fascinated with the history of the O'Briens. It's a strong name that holds power, and it fit me well."

"Ye weren't trying to hide yer troubled past?" The officer looked down at his pad. "Besides the restrainin' orders, ye have a history of fraud and blackmail."

That piece of information made my tics act up and it didn't escape me how the officer by the door stared at me.

"Look, I've never asked for anything from my members. They only contribute what they want to. The rule is that they give to the Red Manor Foundation according to the value they feel they're getting from working with me. The charges you are referring to were made by a father to one of my members who couldn't understand that his daughter would have been generous enough to donate a large sum. He was sure she was a victim of fraud and blackmail."

The officer frowned. "These weren't just charges, Mr. O'Brien. Ye were found guilty of fraud and blackmail."

Conor rolled his eyes and sighed out loud. "Yes. I'm still disappointed when I think about how the girl didn't take responsibility for gifting my foundation the sum. I suppose it's a bit like when a woman is confronted with having had sex and she doesn't want to admit that it was voluntary so she screams rape to look like the victim."

"Ye seem to have a long history of people blamin' ye for things ye claim you didn't do." There was an undertone of skepticism in the officer's voice.

"As I said, I've gotten better at vetting the people I let into my life now."

"We've been receivin' alarmin' calls from family and friends of members in yer group. There are concerns that ye're brainwashin' and exploitin' people. What do ye have to say to that?"

Conor gave a bored smile. "Those aren't new accusations. Many of the people living here come from families with high expectations and when they rebel against the chosen path for them, I'm accused of brainwashing them, but I'm really just helping them see that they have a choice." He looked to me. "Charles here is a brilliant lawyer and dreams of serving justice to victims of international crime syndicates. But he's also the sole heir to one of biggest business empires in the US, so you

194

can imagine the pushback he received from his family when he said he didn't want to take over the family business."

Both officers studied me.

"What is yer last name?" the one with the pad asked.

"Robertson."

His eyes lit up with recognition before he turned back to Conor. I figured it was because he knew of Solver Industries.

"If O'Hara and I walked around and asked everyone who lived here if they were here by their own free choice, what do ye reckon that they'd say?"

Conor swung his hand to me. "Charles, why don't you answer that question?"

I squared my shoulders and tried to calm my tics. "They'd say that they are all honored to be here. It's a privilege."

Conor smiled at me with satisfaction while officer Williams scratched his gray beard. "Is it?"

"Yes." I gave a firm nod. "There's no one better than Conor to help you find your true potential and unleash it. He pushes us to be the best version that we can possibly be. What he offers is a complete package of coaching, friendship, and family in one, and he's right when he says that he never asks for anything in return except the same amount of loyalty that he's showing us."

"All right." Williams crossed his legs by his ankles and tapped his paper pad with the pencil. "Does that mean ye haven't paid anything to be in this so-called program?"

"No. I've made contributions to the foundation, but that was all voluntarily."

"Huh. Could ye give us an estimate of how much ye've paid?"

I hesitated. "About four hundred thousand."

His eyebrow shot up. "Euros?"

"Yes."

"How long have ye been living here?"

"I moved in about three months ago."

O'Hara whistled and crossed his arms. "It would take me a decade to raise that kind of money."

I looked away, aware that for a normal worker, four hundred thousand euros sounded like a lot of money, but for me it was a write-off as charity on my tax return.

"Would ye mind if we take a moment to question everyone living here to see if they are as enthusiastic about being here as Charles?"

Conor threw his hands up. "Go ahead. I have nothing to hide."

Williams stood up. "Thank ye for your time."

Conor moved around his desk and shook the men's hands. "Charles can take you downstairs to meet the others, I'm afraid I have a class to teach. The children will be wondering what is taking me so long."

I showed the policemen down to the kitchen, where the white noise from voices went silent the moment we entered.

"Everyone, this is Officer O'Hara and Officer Williams. They have some concerns about whether or not we're here of our own free will and if we're being brainwashed by Conor. Because of that they would like to speak to each of you alone to confirm that you're fine."

"Oh, for God's sake," Sara exclaimed and gave the officers an angry stare. "What a waste of time."

"Liv, why don't you start by going with the officers into the living room?" I gave her hand a squeeze and looked at Williams, who seemed to be the senior of the two officers. "I assume you want to speak to each member in private?"

"Yes, please."

Talking loud enough for anyone to hear me, I offered, "If you don't feel comfortable speaking with the garda alone, Sara or I will be happy to stay in the room. You have the right to have an attorney present."

Liv walked off with the policemen without requesting my help. It seemed logical because her conversation would be short as her part in all of this was new. Still, my protective side made me follow and listen at the door. My biggest worry was that she would tell the officers about Conor's weird prank on Tuesday where he pulled out the gun and challenged Sara to show him loyalty by shooting herself. I couldn't blame Liv for telling that story because I knew she'd been shaken by the incident, but I hoped she didn't because it would make things worse for Conor.

"Yer full name, please."

"Charlotte Liv Christensen."

"Age?"

"Twenty-six."

"American?"

"Yes."

"Are ye a resident here?"

"No, I'm a guest. My boyfriend lives here and I'm staying with him while visiting Ireland."

"Who is yer boyfriend."

"Charles McCann – I mean Robertson."

"How long are ye planning to stay?"

"I'm not sure. I'm hoping he'll travel around Europe with me but right now we're just taking time to get to know each other better. The relationship is still new."

"How new?"

"We go back five years, but we reconnected when I bumped into him about a week ago."

"Ah, okay."

"Can ye confirm that ye're here of yer own free will?"

"Yes."

"Do ye feel that ye're being brainwashed in any way?"

197

"No. I'm spending my time with Charles and the children who live here. I'm not really a part of the mastermind group."

"What's yer impression of Conor O'Brien?"

"He's... ehhm, pretty intense."

"In what way?"

I folded my hands into fists, afraid that she would tell them about the incident with the gun, but just as I was about to enter the room and hopefully distract her from saying it, she answered, "He makes the children study classes meant for college. He encourages them to speak with eloquence and refinement. They can't use casual speech and they're so damn smart that it's frightening. He's a great teacher, but I find him intense, that's all."

"Ah, okay. Thank ye."

"Can I go now?"

"Yes, and will ye please send in the next person?"

I moved away from the door and touched Liv's shoulder when she exited. "Was it bad?"

"No. It was fine. You wanna go for a walk?"

"Later. Right now, I have to check in on Conor and see if he's okay. They asked him some tough questions."

"Like what?"

"I can't tell you." I kissed her nose. "As a lawyer I can't discuss that sort of thing."

"Okay, but Charles..." She pulled at my collar and pulled me in face to face, speaking in a hushed tone. "I don't like all these accusations. My father always said: where there's smoke, there's fire."

I jerked my head back. "Trust me. It's all a misunderstanding. I was in the room when they questioned Conor and I heard his explanation for all of it. If you'd been there, you would know it wasn't Conor's fault. He didn't do anything wrong."

Liv let go of my collar and there was disappointment on her face. "No one is perfect, Charles. Not me, not you, and not Conor. People aren't always who they say they are."

"What is that supposed to mean?"

"You didn't tell me you were a Robertson until a few days ago. I'm sure you didn't mean to lie to me and that you had your reasons. Maybe it's the same with Conor. He's only telling you what will serve his relationship with you. That's normal human behavior. If he did any of the things that he's accused of doing, he wouldn't tell us about it, would he?"

My eyes darted around, not liking her intense stare. "No, probably not."

"My point is that you can't trust that you know everything about him."

"Fine, but I know he's a good guy who does amazing things for others."

She sighed. "I'm going to get some fresh air while you go and check up on him. I'll be down by the harbor."

I hugged her tight. "Liv, I'm so sorry about all of this. It wasn't like this before you came. Things were happy and amazing. It wasn't supposed to be this way."

She hugged me back. "As long as I'm with you, things are still amazing, if you ask me."

CHAPTER 19
The Body

Liv

"Why is it that when it's just me here, you can't be bothered to spend two minutes with me, but the moment Liv arrives, yer like an annoyin' fly buzzin' around us all the feckin' time." Kit scowled at her brother Damian, who was stuffing his mouth with the cookies that I'd brought. "Stop eating all of them. Shouldn't ye be smooching on a protein shake like ye always do?"

"Aye, but these are so good."

"Honestly, Damian, ye're like a child with no self-control. It's embarrassin'." She gave me an apologetic eye roll.

"I don't mind him eating the cookies. I want to lose a few pounds anyway."

Damian stopped with another cookie to his lips. "Why? Ye're gorgeous."

"Thank you." I smiled at him and loved the boyish grin he shot back at me.

"There has to be somethin' to grab and squeeze on a lass. That's the best part." He was demonstrating with his hands and it made Kit hit his shoulder.

"Don't be vulgar. We know ye like to grab and squeeze. Why don't ye stop annoying us, and go for a walk or somethin'?"

Damian nodded to the window where rain was pummeling down outside his apartment. "It's pissin'."

"Then go hang out with that neighbor ye talked about."

"What neighbor?"

"The one who invited ye in for some coffee." Kit's eyebrows wiggled suggestively.

"Are ye daft? Not even the tide would take her out. She's fifty and missing two teeth."

Kit sighed. "What do I care? I'm tryin' to work here, and do not forget that Liv is a payin' client. Or Mr. Robertson is anyway. We have a case to crack and ye're not helpin'."

"All right, detective. What do we have?" Damian clapped his hands together and looked at the papers on the table.

"Oi, now ye want to help?" Kit shook her head. "Seriously, go find some shite to blow up or some criminals to shoot at. You're an action guy, not a detective."

He pouted. "I've got brains too."

I interrupted the sibling rivalry. "As I was saying, I keep planting little questions in Charles' mind. The pressure from the police has made Conor moody and the atmosphere in the house is tense. Yesterday, he gave the children a day off from school, and it was the first one ever."

Kit lit up. "Told you that stirrin' the pot was a good idea. We just need to keep the pressure up until he cracks with guilt for all the shite he's done."

"That's not going to happen." I drummed my fingers on the table. "If Conor is truly a psychopath, he won't feel the least bit of guilt or remorse. That's why psychopaths are so good at what they do."

Damian picked up a picture of Conor from the pile of papers. "From the things Kit has told me about this bloke, he sounds more like a bloody sociopath." Damian crossed his arms.

"There's no difference," Kit said, as if her brother had no clue what he was talking about.

"Aye, there is. A sociopath is a step up from a psychopath."

I held up a hand and stopped them. "You're both wrong."

"Nah, I'm pretty sure I'm right." Damian lowered his brow with authority. "We learned about this during my trainin'. Psychopaths, sociopaths, and narcissists."

"Well, you got it mixed up then. They all share the same traits, but out of the three, the psychopath is the worst because the person is born with a personality disorder leaving them unable to feel empathy of any kind.

A sociopath on the other hand, is a product of their environment. They actually do have a sense of right or wrong but it's too weak to hold them back from their antisocial behavior."

"What kind of environment are we talking about?" Damian asked.

"The kind no kid should grow up in! Each case is different, of course, but it could be a criminal environment where the parents are volatile and unpredictable. Stealing and hustling might be a way of life for the family and they teach their child to disrespect authorities and disregard rules. Typically, there's mental and physical violence around the child and they are taught never to trust anyone and to always expect the worst from people. In that kind of environment, there's no room for empathy or softness. To survive, a person would have to grow callous and cold-hearted, but if that same person had been born into a loving and supportive environment, things would have been different."

Damian scratched his stubble. "So, what ye're sayin' is that a sociopath is programmed to not care?"

"That's right. And where a psychopath is always a narcissist, a narcissist isn't always a psychopath."

"Say what?" Damian scratched his stubble.

"My professor taught us to categorize the narcissist as *dismissive* because everything is about them, and it's impossible to ever have a healthy relationship with a narcissist since they have a high need for control and a low level of empathy. They're right, you're wrong. It's all about their needs, and they are critical of everything you do. With the sociopath the word is *schemer*. They are highly manipulative and feel that rules don't apply to them. They will cheat and lie without remorse because they have no set of morals. But the psychopaths are in the worst category, which my professor would have us headline *predator*. They can range anywhere from your worst nightmare boss to a cold-blooded killer. Therapy is useless, as psychopaths have no desire to change. They have zero compassion and use people for their benefit. They also tend to have a criminal mind. In fact, if we look at statistics for North America, we know that although only one in a hundred adult males are psychopaths, they make up between fifteen to twenty-five percent of the males incarcerated."

Damian whistled and looked to Kit. "Did ye know that?"

"Sort of."

"The medical term is antisocial personality disorder, not psychopath or sociopath, although that in itself is an ongoing debate in the field of psychology."

"How do ye know all of this?" Damian took another cookie.

"I have a degree in psychology."

"Gorgeous *and* smart." He winked at me, and gave me one of his charming and very flirtatious smiles, which made his sister kick him under the table. "Stop flirtin' with my client."

"Och, stop it. It's a wonder I'm not a sociopath with a violent sister who kicks me." Damian gave Kit a blameful look and turned to me. "How do ye diagnose a psychopath? Could be Kit is one."

She rolled her eyes, while I answered his question. "The doctors use a checklist. If a person scores high it's because he shows a variation of antisocial behavior such as a sense of entitlement and a lack of empathy. They are unremorseful, lie, manipulate, are apathetic to others, conscienceless, blameful, cunning, cold, and irresponsible." I drew in a deep breath. "Some say that sociopaths are more hot-headed and will explode if you don't give them what they want, while the psychopath is cold and cunning and will plan your demise if you're in his or her way."

Damian narrowed his eyes at Kit. "Are ye remorseful for kickin' me?"

"It was ye're own fault."

"Oi, I bloody knew it." Pointing to Kit he looked at me. "She has no empathy and is blameful too. I'd say that's antisocial behavior right there."

She pushed at him. "Shut yer cakehole. I'm no psychopath."

Damian was clearly riling her up, but couldn't keep a straight face and cracked into a smile.

Kit exhaled. "Bricks is the true psychopath here. When I asked him about Sandra, he sat in his chair and lied straight to my face. There wasn't the least bit of remorse in his eyes."

I bit my lower lip. "If he did the things that he's accused of then he's a cold-blooded killer who would fit the classification of a psychopath."

"Why can't his followers see it?"

I sighed. "Because in order to get away with his cunning behavior he has developed a smooth and inviting personality that sucks people in. I've spent time with him these past two weeks, and it's impressive how well he has perfected how to read people and tell them what they want to hear. Even though he can't relate to their pain, he's highly capable of mimicking what empathy looks like. They think he's their friend, while he's spinning a net around them with his charm and lies. River and Nathan have opened up a bit and told about some things that are truly alarming."

"Like what?"

I thought about how to describe it. "He makes them question their own sanity. River confided in me that she's sick like her mother but that Conor is protecting her from ending up in an asylum. She says she hallucinates and has false memories, but I think he's the one messing with her head. Narcissists are **notorious for** gaslighting people. They lie with such confidence that it makes the people around them question what's up and down. It would be like Damian blaming you for eating all the cookies. You tell him you were right here when he stuffed at least ten in his mouth, but he shakes his head and looks at you like you're crazy and tells you straight to your face that you only imagined it, and that you're wrong, confused, and seeing things that aren't there. No matter how much you scream at him that he ate the cookies, not you, he refuses to admit it and over time you start wondering if you really are crazy."

Damian held up both hands. "Nah, I have no problem admitting that I ate the cookies."

"Good, but to a psychopath it's second nature to lie and confuse people. Poor River doesn't trust her own mind. She thinks Conor is helping her escape ending up in a psychiatric hospital like her mother."

"But didn't River think that her mother is in India?" Kit asked.

I shook my head. "She admitted to me that her mother is sick. She told me the story about India because she's embarrassed about it."

Kit raised her voice. "Are ye sayin' the poor lass thinks Conor is protectin' her from the same sad destiny as her ma, when the truth is that he's probably the one who pushed her ma to need psychiatric help in the first place?"

I nodded.

"Och, that's just wrong. And what about Charles? Is he still blinded by Conor and his disciples?" Kit snatched the bag of cookies from Damian when he reached for another one.

"As I said, I keep planting little questions in his mind, but Charles is particularly susceptible to Conor's deceit because he has Asperger's and doesn't read people as well as others do. I don't blame him for not seeing Conor's true colors. I mean, I came in knowing Conor is a con man, but if I hadn't been warned, I might have been sucked in by him too."

"Nah, ye're too smart for that," Damian said.

"It's not a matter of intelligence. You haven't met Conor, but he can take on the persona of someone witty, charming, intelligent, and knowledgeable, and when he talks, it's with such confidence that it's easy to buy into it. When I told him that I regretted never learning how to play an instrument, he insisted that I let him teach me to play a melody on the piano right then and there. He makes you feel like you're the only one that matters and that he would make the moon and stars align in order to help you to be the best version of yourself. It's a powerful feeling to have someone show that level of interest in you."

Kit wrinkled her nose up. "God, ye sound like ye admire the bastard."

"No. I'm just trying to explain to you that Charles and Conor's other followers aren't fools. It's easy for me to see why they're so blinded by Conor. That's all."

"But haven't ye been able to open Charles' eyes to the other side of Conor at all?"

"I thought he was starting to see, but it's like the new pressure on Conor has enhanced how protective and loyal Charles is. Maybe because he's been acting as his legal adviser. It's weird because Charles was in the room when the police listed a whole number of legal problems from Conor's past, and he still believes every excuse Conor gave for why he was really the victim in those cases." Feeling restless and frustrated, I drew a doodle on the paper in front of me. "You would think that hearing of Conor's criminal past would make Charles question things, but no."

Kit snorted. "That's bollocks."

I brushed my hair back. "Yeah, it sucks, but even if Charles wanted to leave, I couldn't abandon the children. They are innocent in all of this and after Conor's stunt with the gun last week, I want to make sure he doesn't do something awful to the children."

"But are you and Charles still good?"

My face softened. "The more I get to know him, the more amazing I think he is. He's so…" I smiled.

Damian and Kit exchanged a grin, and he whistled low again. "Geez, she's a goner, that one."

"I can't help it. Charles has this way of looking at me across the room as if he doesn't quite believe his luck. It melts me every time."

Kit cleared her throat. "Excellent. It helps to have an undercover observer, and if everythin' goes right, it won't be for much longer. Mr. Robertson is throwin' some serious cash into this investigation. We have put together a team of five private detectives in Liverpool to find Jim

Maddox and the tape he was using to blackmail Conor. Several of the detectives have strong connections and their pressure on the Liverpool police is workin'."

"Working how?" I asked.

"The Liverpool police have been in contact with our gardas, not to mention that Mr. Robertson has used his powerful connections from the US. Five days ago, the American ambassador made an inquiry to the Garda Commissioner, who is the highest ranking in the Garda Síochána. He discussed Mr. Robertson's concerns and the old accusations made against Conor O'Brien. That's why the garda came to question him. Conor is under their microscope right now," Kit explained.

"That's great news but tell them to work fast." I looked at the clock. "Charles is done teaching in an hour. I told him I'd be working from a café and meet with him after he was done at four."

"It's fine." Kit pushed her chair back and stood up at the same time as me. "Ye're doing amazing, Liv. Just keep soaking up everything you see and report back to me. If Conor makes a mistake, I want you to be there to catch it. Ye have my number. Text or call me anytime, night or day."

"Okay."

I hugged Kit and Damian before making my way through the streets of Dublin in the pouring rain. When I got to Trinity College, I waited for Charles under the cover of one of the old historical buildings, which looked like a bell tower in the middle of the square. There was something amazing about the rain bouncing off the cobblestones and the tourists moving in packs with their umbrellas.

My head was full of thoughts about the investigation and what would happen when Charles realized that Conor was a fraud. Would he be relieved that I'd come to rescue him? Or would the shock of how wrong he'd been about

Conor overwhelm him to the point where he'd get suspicious of my motives as well?

The thought of Charles pulling away from me left a chill up my spine. If only I had a way to tell him that our meeting hadn't been a coincidence but that my feelings for him were one hundred percent real.

"Liv."

Hearing my name, I turned around to see Charles jogging toward me with his bag above his head to shield him from the rain. The sight of him made me reach out my arms and as soon as he was close, I hugged him like I hadn't seen him for a year.

"Mmm, I missed you," I whispered in his ear.

Charles pulled back, giving me a wide smile that created soft crinkles at the edges of his eyes. "I missed you too, Saffron."

Our deep kiss made someone whistle and when we looked over, Charles spotted some of his students.

"Do you think you'll get in trouble for kissing me in front of them?"

He laughed. "I'm just a guest teacher. I don't think they care and I doubt any of the students will make complaints. They're just jealous that I get to kiss the prettiest woman in the world."

We were nose to nose, with locked eyes. "You want to kiss me again? Just to make sure they know I'm yours."

"Mmm…" With a hand behind my neck, he pulled me in again, giving me a long demanding kiss that left my panties as wet as my rain jacket.

"You want to get out of here?" Charles had such a playful gleam in his eyes that I knew he wanted to be alone with me and make love.

"I do!"

His eyes widened and he took my hand. "Standing under a bell tower and hearing you say the words *I do* just gave me the craziest chills up and down my spine." He lifted our intertwined hands to his mouth and pressed his lips against the back of my hand. "I hope that I get to hear you say it again in the future."

I caught his reference to a future wedding between us and beamed at him before we ran together through the rain. We were like a couple in a romantic scene from a cheesy rom-com until we got into the streets and a car drove by, splashing a load of water on us.

"Oh, for fuck's sake." Charles and I stood frozen with our clothes soaked. We tried waving down a taxi but all of them were full.

"Hold this." Charles gave me his bag and ran to an intersection where cars were waiting at a red light. Knocking on a car window, he spoke to a man in his fifties and turned to wave me over. "Get in."

I was soaked and ready to get a hot shower, so I didn't question why we were getting into the backseat of a stranger's car.

The driver turned to look at us. "Are ye really givin' me five hundred euros to take ye to Howth?"

"I am." Charles pointed to the light, which had turned green. "Could you turn up the heat? My girlfriend is wet and freezing."

At that moment, I didn't feel my wet clothes. All I could feel was the heat pumping through my body with an acute arousal for Charles. It was such a turn-on to see him be assertive and take charge. From our first lunch we'd put the cards on the table. He knew that I wanted the whole package with marriage and kids, and his comment about hearing me say "I do" told me that he was as serious as me.

Leaning in, I whispered in his ear. "When we get back to the house, can we take a shower… together?"

A smile spread on his lips as his shoulder bobbed up with a tic and he wrinkled his nose.

210

God, he was so cute when he did that.

CHAPTER 20
A Cry for Attention

Charles

Liv and I had just made it into the bathroom when we began kissing and undressing each other. Our wet clothes fell to the tile floor one piece at a time. I couldn't get her naked fast enough, because being inside Liv had become an addiction to me.

"I thought about you while I taught today. At one point, I stood with a goofy grin on my lips."

"Yeah?" She licked my neck. "Did you imagine yourself pressing me against the shower wall?"

I pulled my sweater over my head and turned on the water in the shower. "Actually, I was replaying our lovemaking from this morning." With an expectant smile, I walked to the rack where beige towels were neatly stacked. Like my room, the bathroom was on the top floor in what had once been the attic. A large skylight window gave a beautiful view of the large grounds that belonged with the Red Manor. Despite the rain falling on the window, I caught something out of the corner of my eye and stopped to stare. "What in the world?"

"Charles, what's wrong?" Liv came to stand next to me, looking out too.

"There, in the pond." I nodded, unsure if my eyes were playing tricks on me.

"Is that... what is he doing?

I had no idea why Nathan was sitting in the pond. "The water must be freezing."

212

Liv was already putting her clothes back on, but when her wet pants gave her trouble, she settled for her panties, sweater, and socks and ran out the door with two large towels in her hands.

"Hey, wait up." I was cursing as I hopped on one leg, forcing my foot through my pants leg.

Unlike Liv, I took time to put on shoes while she was already down the stairs, shouting Nathan's name. Trying to catch up, I slid down the railing like I'd done as a child in my own house.

Liv had swung open the French doors in the living room, leading to the back yard, and she was already by the pond as I stormed after her.

Running across the lawn, I watched Liv pulling Nathan out of the water shouting questions at him. I couldn't hear his answers but she looked back up at the house, and wrapped him in the towels she'd brought.

When I got there, I began with my own questions, "Nathan, what were you doing? You'll get pneumonia It's far too cold to swim this time of year."

The boy was naked except for his boxer shorts and the two towels that Liv was rubbing his body with. His lips were blue and quivering. Being of mixed race, Nathan's normal skin tone was golden brown, but now it had a sickly pale color with dark circles under his eyes.

"I... wa... wasn't swim... swimming."

Liv was rubbing his back but with the rain coming down, the towel she'd wrapped around him was getting as wet as him.

"Come here." While Liv bent to collect his clothes, which had been placed in a pile on the grass, I picked up the boy and jogged back to the house with him over my shoulder.

When we got to the living room others were gathering to see what the commotion was about.

"What happened?" Conor stepped forward and frowned at Nathan.

Nathan was shaking and trying to answer, but he was too cold and his lips wouldn't work.

"He said that he was meditating." Liv reached for a soft blanket from one of the couches and removed the wet towels. "Come here, honey." Wrapping the large throw-over around him, she nodded to me. "Help him remove his wet boxers. They're only cooling him down."

With the blanket covering the boy, his privacy was intact as I pulled down the soaked fabric and placed the water-dripping boxers in a ceramic bowl that stood on the coffee table.

Liv wrapped two more blankets around him, making him look like the Michelin guy. "Let's get you warmed up." Sitting down in a large reading chair, she pulled Nathan down on her lap. Wrapping him tight in the blanket, she placed his head against her chest. "River, please get that other blanket from over there and wrap it around his feet. A foot rub will help him."

River was eager to help her friend and did as Liv had instructed.

"Why would he meditate in the pond?" I looked from Nathan to Conor.

Conor shook his head with deep disappointment. "Nathan, how many times have I told you to think about your actions?"

"Bu... but... you said..." Nathan struggled to get the words out.

"What did I say? If you're trying to make everyone here think that I'd ask you to go kill yourself by meditating in a pond in October, then you're worse off than I thought."

Nathan closed his eyes and Liv rocked him back and forth like a little boy despite the fact that he was fourteen.

"Maybe he's confused," I suggested. "He's cold and it's hard to think when…"

Conor cut me off. "Don't make excuses for him. Nathan has a long history of going about seeking attention in destructive ways. It's something he and I are working on."

"What do you mean?" Liv asked with her hand on Nathan's forehead, holding him close to her.

"With his mother's history it's understandable that he's longing for constant validation that I won't leave him too. He creates dramatic and dangerous situations that put him in a position of needing rescue. For years it's been nightmares about snakes in his bed, and then there was the time he got stuck in a tree and couldn't get down."

"You told me to… to climb… that… that tree." Nathan stuttered with his jaws shivering.

"Nathan, stop it!" Conor squatted down in front of Liv and the boy. "It's one thing to come up with imaginary snakes, but to put yourself in danger like this is reckless. I won't have it. We've talked about it. I would never ask you to do this. It's all in your mind." Conor's face softened as he rubbed the boy's shoulder. "We all love you and we don't want to see anything bad happen to you."

River sat on the floor next to the couch and was rubbing Nathan's right foot under the blanket. She had her eyes down and seemed as sad about the situation as the rest of us. Looking around, I saw that the room was full of the children and residents. Everyone was looking on with crestfallen faces too.

"How do you feel, Nathan?" I asked.

The boy hid his head against Liv's chest as if he was too embarrassed to talk.

Conor rose back up. "How about we all go back to what we were doing? Nathan, you and I will come back to this incident and find an appropriate consequence for your error in judgment. Right now, I want you to go to your room and think about how wrong it is to lie."

Liv's voice was shaking a bit when she spoke up. "Maybe it would be wise for him to see a doctor. Just to be sure he doesn't have frostbite and that his vital signs are fine."

Conor turned to the others in the room. "Ciara, please make the boy some tea and toast. He'll take it in his room."

"You're not going to let him see a doctor?" Liv asked again.

"No. All he needs is to warm up in his bed for half an hour and then he'll be fine." Conor tilted his head and gave Liv and me an appreciative smile. "It was a good thing you found him and brought him inside. I thought he was meditating in his room."

"Can you walk?" Liv whispered to Nathan but I could tell he was too weak.

"Let me take him." Nathan was quiet as I carried him to his and River's room on the second floor. It was the last room in a long hallway, the next after Conor's room. Liv followed me and when the boy was in his bed, she went to get clean underwear from his closet. With the attitude of a nurse, she helped Nathan, who was under his duvet, get his feet into the boxer shorts and pulled them up to his knees.

"Can you pull them up yourself?" she asked and without words he did.

"Good." Liv kneeled down next to him. "Nathan, listen to me. River is going to lie next to you and offer you her body heat. This time, you won't tell her to go away. Do you understand?"

He nodded and River, who was right behind us, didn't need any further instruction than that. She climbed onto the bed and spooned Nathan.

Turning to me, Liv gestured for me to follow her and once we were outside, she spoke in a soft voice the way you do around people who are sick or sleeping. "I'm going to stay with them until Nathan feels better."

Her concern for Nathan touched me. I couldn't remember anyone loving me so unconditionally as a child, and Liv hadn't even known him for that long. "Okay, do you want me to stay as well?"

Closing the door to the room, she wrapped her arms around her waist. "Charles, I'm worried for the kids. What if Nathan told the truth and Conor really did tell him to go meditate in the pond?"

"That's crazy. Why would he do that?"

Her eyes were alight with fire. "For the same reason that he'd ask Sara to put a gun to her head and pull the trigger."

"But Conor didn't even know Nathan was out there."

"Yes, he did. I saw him looking out the window from the schoolroom. He knew!"

I rubbed my forehead feeling myself getting defensive. My mentor had already suffered with people spreading untrue rumors about him. The last thing he needed was us insiders to turn on him. "Conor probably just heard you shouting and running through the house. That's why he went to the window to see what was happening."

"But why would he go to the window to the back yard? Why not come downstairs to see what was wrong?"

"Saffron sweetie, you're overthinking this. You heard what Conor said. Nathan has a history of creating drama. We shouldn't fall for it."

"Fall for it?" Her tone was incredulous. "That boy in there almost died trying to prove his loyalty to O'Brien."

The accusation was so far out that I scoffed. "No, he didn't. Conor had nothing to do with it."

217

She crossed her arms and raised an eyebrow, but didn't speak.

"You really choose to believe Nathan?" I asked.

"Yes!"

I was stunned and took a step back. "Well, I'm taking the word of the adult. Conor wouldn't lie."

We stood staring at each other with a wall of frustration suddenly feeling like a physical barrier between us.

Footsteps made us turn to see Ciara with a tray in her hands. "I've got the tea and some toast for him."

Liv took it and I opened the door for her to enter the room. Ciara and I didn't question that Liv was the one to care for him. After all, she had slept in Nathan's and River's room since she got here, and she'd been the one to pull Nathan out of the pond. I was, however, upset that Nathan's desperate call for attention had come between Liv and me.

"I'm taking a shower. I'll talk to you later?"

She nodded before closing the door, but there was no smile from her and I got the feeling that she wasn't happy with me.

CHAPTER 21
When Adults Lie

Liv

When the Red Manor had been built for the first family who lived here in the late eighteen hundreds, River's and Nathan's room had housed five children. Their governess had slept in the room next door, which was now O'Brien's room. Nathan had told me as much on my first night sleeping in here when I'd asked about the connecting door.

After Nathan fell asleep that first night, River had told me that both she and Nathan suffered from nightmares and that's why Conor insisted on keeping them close so they could run to him if they needed comforting.

I'd only experienced Nathan's having a few nightmares in the time I'd shared their room, and both times he'd woken up screaming about a yellow snake in his bed. I looked to calm him down, but of course there was nothing there.

River didn't scream in her dreams. She made small whimpers, and I found that the easiest way to calm her down was to hum a melody and hold her hand.

As the younger sister in my own family, I hadn't had small siblings to care for like this, but I found that it came natural to me. In fact, my bond with the children was growing fast.

"Is Nathan going to be all right?" River asked in a brittle voice.

"Yes." I gave her a small smile of reassurance. "You and I are going to warm him up again. I just need to change out

219

of these wet clothes." I changed in the hallway powder room and hurried back into the children's room. It was large. Even with my mattress on the floor, and the two beds that were placed against opposite walls, there was room for River's toys, a large closet, and Nathan's collection of Star Wars ships that spread out over his side of the room.

I got into Nathan's bed and positioned myself sitting against the wall while helping him sit up against me to sip from the tea cup. He was shaking less than he had downstairs and his breathing was better too.

"River, were you there when Conor asked Nathan to go meditate in the pond?"

River had moved to sit at the foot end of the bed and was rubbing Nathan's feet again.

"River?"

She looked down.

"It's okay. You can tell me. I know Nathan would never do something like that on his own accord."

River stayed quiet while I helped Nathan take a tiny sip more.

"Are you afraid that Conor will get mad at you for telling me the truth?" I asked her.

She bit her lip. "It's just that sometimes we children get confused."

Looking straight into her eyes, I kept my voice calm. "Did you hear Conor tell Nathan to go meditate in the pond? I won't tell a soul outside this room. All I want is for you to tell me what you heard."

Still biting her lip, she nodded her head. "I did."

"Do you think he was making a joke?"

A line formed between her eyebrows. "Conor was angry. He said Nathan wasn't trying hard enough and that he didn't appreciate everything Conor is doing for him."

I stroked the boy's hair and helped him drink another sip while asking him in a soft voice. "And did you feel like you needed to prove that you do?"

He nodded, pulled the duvet higher, and spoke in a weak voice that was still shaky. "I'm not ungrateful. I know that… that I owe Conor everything. I'm an orphan and he took me in. If not for him…. I wou… would have been in an orphanage."

I kept stroking his hair, relieved to see the color in his lips returning.

"Nathan, I want you to listen to me." I paused to be sure he was focused. "I believe you!"

He closed his eyes.

"I believe you." I let the words hang in the air.

"I'm sorry Conor made you look like a liar. It's not right, but I want you to know that I believe you over him."

He still had his eyes closed but tears were running down now.

Hugging him from behind, I rocked his body. "And I also want you to know that there are a ton of people out there who would love to have a son like you. You're kind, smart, funny, and driven. Conor is lucky to have you in his life. Do you understand?"

Nathan's chest bobbed as he was sobbing now.

River's face was drooping with sympathy. "Liv is right. I feel lucky that you're my brother. I know you think it's annoying that you have to share a room with me, but you still let me play with your Star Wars and you wake me up from my nightmares and hold my hand. Remember that time when you sang for me? I don't think many big brothers would do that." She and I were tearing up too.

"Nathan." I said his name in a soothing voice and kept rocking his body as I held him against my chest. Reaching for a tissue on his night table, I dried his nose, which was running, and like a small child, he turned his body and clung to me while sobbing his heart out.

"It's okay. I'm right here."

At fourteen, Nathan was small for his age but in that moment, it felt like the seven-year-old boy whose mom had committed suicide was letting out all his grief in my arms.

"It's okay. I've got you, and I believe you. You're not crazy and you didn't lie." I kept repeating words to soothe him while letting him cry out his sorrow and frustration.

River and I stayed with Nathan and when he ran out of tears, we gave him tissues to blow his nose and dry his eyes.

"Ciara made you some toast. Do you want to eat it?" I reached for the plate to offer him the food.

Nathan shook his head. "No. I'm not hungry."

"How do you feel?"

"I'm still cold but it's better now."

"It's because of River's foot rubs, isn't it?"

My heart leaped when Nathan's lips lifted in a tiny smile and he looked to the blond girl. "Yes, I think it is."

It only made River massage his feet with more gusto.

I hadn't planned on bringing it up again, but then Nathan turned his head and asked me, "Why does Conor lie so much?"

Telling them the truth was a big risk. I couldn't take the chance that words like psychopath or narcissist might find their way back to Conor. Not until we had enough evidence to arrest him.

"Conor lies because he's a proud man who doesn't want to admit he was wrong." It was the most diplomatic answer I could give them.

"I hate when he does it," Nathan mumbled low.

"Adults shouldn't be allowed to lie," River chimed in.

"No, they shouldn't." I was thoughtful for a moment before I asked. "Did you ever hear the story of the two brothers?"

"What brothers?" Nathan was still leaning against me.

"There once were two brothers. One had become a drunk and a criminal who ended up in prison. When he was asked what the reason for his failure was, he answered, 'My father.' Now, the other brother was extremely successful in life with a beautiful family and a great job. When he was asked what caused his success, he answered, 'My father.'"

Both children looked at me and then each other.

"I don't get it." River played with her hair. "Is it because the father was only nice to one of them?"

Shaking my head, I stroked Nathan's hair. "No, the point is that one brother let his father's behavior break him, while the other grew up with a clear image of what he didn't want to become himself. The story is to remind you that you two get to decide what kind of adults you want to be. You're smart enough to see that not all adults behave in the best manner. But here's the good news; you get to observe and think to yourself., *I'm never going to do that when I grow up*, or if you see something you like, you can put that on the list of things to strive for."

"I'm never going to lie!" Nathan declared with a solemn expression on his face.

I squeezed him a little harder. "If you grow up to be one of the few adults who can live up to that promise, then being cold in a pond for a few hours will be worth it. Maybe the universe put you through this pain so that you could become a better adult than the rest of us."

"You think?"

I placed my chin on top of his hair, still with my arms wrapped around him from behind. "No matter how old you get, I think you'll always remember the trauma of

223

what happened today. Ten or twenty years from now you can look back and be filled with rage that Conor's pride cost you so much pain and suffering. Or you can look back and think of this day as a defining moment in your life that made you a better person."

"I guess." He turned his head to look at me. "But why does he hate me so much?"

The pain in his beautiful brown eyes made my throat swell up with emotion. I wanted to tell him that he didn't want the love of the man who killed his mother anyway, and that he was way too good for Conor, but I had to be careful with my words. "We're all flawed people, Nathan. Not everyone has the capacity to love unconditionally. Conor's pride makes him say and do things he shouldn't, but his shortcomings have nothing to do with you." I stroked his hair again. "You're a precious and beautiful young man. I've only known you for a few weeks and I already love you. That's how easy you are to love."

Nathan lifted his hand to hold my wrist and then he squeezed a little. "Thank you, Liv."

"What about me? Do you love me too?" River's eyebrows were knitted closely together.

"You know I do!"

The worried expression on her face lifted as she lit up in a smile. "I love you too, Liv. I wish you were my mother."

"Aww, that's so sweet. I can be a fun aunt if you want."

"Aunt Liv." Nathan smiled. "Yeah, I'd like that."

I held out my hand. "All right, then let's make a pact. From now on I'll be your crazy but fun aunt, whom you can always call if you need to be pulled out of a pond or something."

Nathan placed his hand on top of mine, and River sandwiched our hands with her right palm under my hand and her left palm on top of Nathan's.

"Family for life on three. One, two, three..."

"Family for life." We all said it loud and clear.

Nathan fell asleep less than half an hour later, his body and mind exhausted from the stress he had been through.

River and I were talking in low voices when a light knock on the door was followed by Charles popping his head in.

"How is he doing?"

"Better. He's sleeping."

I got the feeling that Charles hadn't moved on from the tension that had been between us earlier, because he had a hard time looking me in the eye.

"Dinner is ready in twenty minutes."

"Okay. Thank you." I turned to River. "I'm just going to take a shower before dinner but I'll meet you down there, okay?"

"All right."

I was right about Charles being on edge. When I walked out the door, he was serious and would have come across as cold and uninterested if it weren't because I knew this was his Asperger's showing its ugly head. Charles had warned me over and over that he was bad at communicating his emotions and this was what it looked like. I had zero doubt that he loved me and wanted us to be close, but tension between us made him hide his head like a tortoise.

I had just poured out all of my love to Nathan and River and I needed to recharge before I focused on getting Charles and me back on track. "How about I meet you downstairs?"

I caught the sideways glance and the press of his lips. "I thought you might want to talk."

"I do, but I also need a minute to get my head straight. Hopefully a shower can help with that."

He nodded and we walked side by side in silence until I took the stairs up and he went downstairs. I thought about saying something encouraging, but I was upset with him for believing Conor's lies.

I was walking down the corridor and had just opened the door to the bathroom when I heard someone call my name.

"Liv, wait up."

I turned to see Conor jogging toward me and froze halfway into the bathroom.

"I just need to talk to you in private." Looking over his shoulder, he placed a hand on the door and pushed me gently inside before he closed the door behind us.

"What is it?" My body was stiff and alert from being in an enclosed room with Conor.

"I hope you understand that I'd never hurt Nathan. I see him as my own son. "

It seemed the wisest to agree rather than challenge a crazy person, so I nodded. "Uh-huh."

His face softened. "Charlie said that Nathan is sleeping now."

"Yes."

"That's fine. We can set aside some dinner for him."

"Great. Now, if you don't mind, I would like a shower before we eat."

"Yes, of course." He turned and put his hand on the door handle, but changed his mind and turned back to me. "Oh, before I forget. I talked to Mike Hanson like we discussed and I was right. He does have connections to other forensic anthropologists around the world. He didn't know anyone in Chicago, but he mentioned Denver, Boston, and LA. He'd be happy to meet up and talk to you. Mike could open a lot of doors for you if you play your cards right." Conor's smile seemed so genuine and warm that it was unfathomable that this was the same man who had hurt so many people.

226

"I have his contact information if you want it and I'm happy to be there at your first meeting and make the introductions."

"No, that won't be necessary. I'm sure I can handle that part myself." I gave him a polite smile, relieved that something good might come out of this whole ordeal if I could get in contact with the right people who could help me achieve my dream job.

"Yes, I'm certain Mike will be as taken with you as the rest of us." Raising his hand up, Conor stepped into my personal space, letting his finger stroke down my bare shoulder and arm.

I rolled my shoulder to signal that I didn't like it, but he ignored my rejection.

"You're a beautiful woman, Charlotte."

For him to use my first name annoyed me when he knew perfectly well that I preferred to be called Liv. It was almost like he was demonstrating that he did as he pleased.

A few fingers stroking me became hands rubbing up and down my arms while pulling me closer to him.

"Please stop. I'm not interested. Charles and I are a couple."

He chuckled. "Charles doesn't mind sharing you with me. I asked for his permission already."

That stunned me and I shook my head, refusing to believe him. "Charles would never share me."

"Maybe you don't know him as well as you think you do. Charles likes you but he values my friendship and didn't hesitate when I asked him if he'd share you with me."

I was so stunned from what he was telling me that tears formed in my eyes. When had Conor asked Charles for permission to come on to me? Was this why Charles had been so withdrawn before?

Before I had a chance to push Conor away, he was kissing my neck and grabbing my butt.

Anger rose inside me and I pushed at him.

"Ah, yes, Charles told me you like a man to take charge." Without warning, Conor placed his hand on my throat and strangled me. My eyes grew to double size and I tried to say no, but it hurt to push out muffled sounds, and I was busy trying to keep him from pushing down my shorts with his other hand.

His hand on my throat felt like it was burning my skin and made it impossible for me to scream.

"Don't worry, I had a vasectomy a while back. I won't get you pregnant." His voice was raw and horny as he pressed me against a cabinet. My head was pushed back by his hand tight around my throat and my shorts were already down to my knees as he unzipped his own pants. "I've always enjoyed a rough fuck myself, and you Americans are so freaky in bed."

My hands were pushing at his chest trying to create distance between us while I struggled to push the word "No." past his painful hold on my throat. He tightened his grip. "There's no need for you to pretend you don't want this. I've seen you look at me and I'm finally going to fulfill your fantasy." With the cabinet behind me, I had nowhere to go as I struggled against him.

"Liv." The sound of Charles' voice outside the door made Conor cover my mouth and whisper in my ear. "Tell him to go away."

I was scared for my life, and in desperation, I banged my head back against the cabinet, making as much noise as I possibly could.

"Liv, are you okay?" The door handle moved but the door was locked. "Open the door, Liv."

When did he lock the door? It had to be when he pretended that he was about to leave.

228

Conor's grip on my throat tightened even more making it hard to breath, so I couldn't bang my head again, but I used my hands to make as much noise as possible.

CHAPTER 22
Deal Breaker

Charles

The banging sounds coming from inside the bathroom, and the fact that Liv didn't answer me, made my protective instinct flare up.

I was pushing at the door handle, but it was locked. "Liv, open the fucking door."

When she still didn't answer, I knocked at it with my shoulder.

Taking a few steps back, I prepared to do it again, but then I heard footsteps and the door unlocked and swung open.

I stared at Conor, who stood with his pants unzipped, and then my eyes moved past him to Liv, who was red in the face and pulling her shorts back up.

"You... you..." I didn't know who to get mad at first.

"Charles, we were in the middle of something. Maybe you can come back later."

So that's what the banging sounds had been; the two people I trusted most in this world, having sex behind my back.

Conor's words made me see red. "You bastard. How dare you touch her?" I pointed a finger at her. "And you... I trusted you."

Liv stared at me, her fingers to her throat where marks from his fingers were red against her creamy skin. Her fetish to be held around her throat was a detail she only told her lovers.

My tics went into beast mode and it felt like I was having a seizure with the way my body jerked. Why the fuck couldn't I be like normal people. "How long has this been going on?"

Liv was heaving for air, unable to speak.

"Charles, there's no need to get upset. Remember when I asked you if you'd share Liv with the rest of us? You gave your consent right away. Did you think I wouldn't make a move on a beautiful woman like her?" Conor spoke to me in that tone he used when he was explaining something rather obvious to someone who was a bit slow. "Let me be clear. This doesn't mean Liv likes you less. Love shouldn't be limited in its expression, and it's not like there's less for you just because I dip in and take my share. I'm sure Liv can handle both of us."

I took a step back. "No! Liv and I were *exclusive*. We made a promise to each other."

Liv was coughing and then she tried to say a few words. "You told him..."

We both looked at her, waiting for her to finish her sentence.

"You told him about the throat thing."

"No. Of course I didn't tell him." My eyes darted from her to him. If she hadn't told him... then... "How did you know?"

Conor zipped his pants and looking into the mirror, he made himself look presentable again. "Call it intuition."

"No. You said Charles told you." Her voice sounded rusty and forced.

"He did."

"Why would I tell you something that private?"

"Because you trust me. You're just confused right now, but you sat in my office and told me that Liv got turned on from being strangled."

"I didn't!" Lifting my hands to my head I felt myself going over every conversation I'd had with him. Why couldn't I remember that I told him?

"Well, then I must be a mind reader." Conor tried to move past me, but I intersected him.

And then the obvious explanation came to me like a lightning bolt. "You fucking read my diary, didn't you?" It was the only explanation, and suddenly his ability to read my thoughts made sense.

"Charles, you're being very dramatic right now."

"I don't care. What you just did is a deal breaker. Not only did you violate my privacy by reading my diary, but you're spinning my words against me because we both know I *never* agreed to you having sex with my girlfriend."

A small voice by the door, made me turn to look over my shoulder and see River standing behind me.

"Ciara sent me up to see what's taking you all so long. Dinner is ready."

"Tell Ciara that Liv and I won't be eating dinner. We're leaving."

River paled. "You're leaving? When are you coming back?"

"We're not!" I gave Conor a cold stare. It was clear to me that whatever had happened between him and Liv didn't mean she loved him. Liv hadn't said much but she'd scowled at him a few times.

River ran to Liv and clasped her arms around her. "But we made a pact. You can't leave me. Family for life, remember?"

It seemed dramatic, but I reminded myself that River was already suffering from the absence of her own mother.

"Liv?" I said her name like a question.

She was holding River in her arms and looked like someone had asked her if she wanted her right or left arm amputated.

"I'm not staying a single moment longer with this asshat." I nodded my head to Conor. "I don't know if we can save our relationship after your betrayal, but…" I trailed off, hoping that she would at least apologize.

Liv's face was still red and she had tears in her eyes as she stood with her arms around River, who was clinging to her. "I'm staying."

"You're staying?" Her rejection felt like she'd impaled my heart with a fork only to take a knife and slice it into a million small pieces that could never be sewed back together.

I couldn't stay to ask her why, or sit down to have a civilized and rational conversation about it. The two people I loved most in the world had betrayed me and by leaving, I'd leave behind the only real family I'd known.

Maybe I should stay and fight for her.

As fast as the thought came, I pushed it away. Staying would mean accepting sharing my girlfriend with someone I had trusted and thought of as the big brother that I never had. The trust in others that he'd helped me restore over these past few months had come crumbling down and I could already feel the bitter and vile taste of disappointment fill my mouth.

"There's no need for you to leave, Charles. You have an entitlement issue that we need to work on, but once you accept that Liv is free to have other lovers, you'll see that it's for your best as well. I told you that you weren't ready for a relationship and I was right. You are angry right now, but take some time to reflect about how you're overdramatizing the situation and blowing it out of proportion. If you let this serve you as a learning experience, you can take a step upward and become a more grounded, less controlling and possessive partner to Liv.

"No." Backing away, I took in the scene with Conor tilting his head to one side while Liv cried in the background with River in her arms. The woman I loved was choosing Conor over me, just like Sara had done when I first arrived. How could I have been so naïve to think that I'd ever be enough for her?

Slamming the door to my room, I called a taxi and tore all my clothes from my closet, filling my two suitcases in under five minutes. What I couldn't fit, I left behind. Carrying them down to the entrance, I was met by Atlas, Lumi, and Maximum in the foyer.

Atlas tried to step in front of me. "Please don't leave."

"I have to."

They were trailing after me as I walked outside to wait for the taxi.

"You don't have to leave, Dad said so himself," Maximum insisted.

"Was that before or after he fucked my girlfriend?" I regretted my harsh words immediately. It wasn't their fault and I was directing my anger at the wrong people.

Lumi looked down while Atlas kicked some gravel. "Why did you bring her here when you know what he's like? You know he sleeps with every woman who comes here."

"He hasn't slept with Estelle or the twins," I said in my defense.

Pushing his glasses up, Atlas rolled his eyes. "Yes he has. The twins gave in months ago and had a threesome with him."

"How would you know?"

Atlas and Maximum exchanged a glance, and then the younger brother answered, "Because Dad's room is right next to ours."

"And Liv? Have you ever heard her in his room?"

They both shook their heads. "No. We would have heard it. The walls are thin."

"And you're sure, Liv was never with Conor in his room."

"Yes!" Atlas confirmed.

Lumi touched my elbow. "Are you sure they were really together? I always got the feeling that Liv didn't like Conor much."

I lowered my brow. "Why would you say that?"

It was cold and the teenagers didn't have any jackets on. Lumi folded her arms, making herself smaller. "It's like she's always fishing for dirt on him every time she's alone with us, and her smile becomes fake around him."

"No, Liv is just critical of people in general. She clearly likes Conor."

"Then maybe I just misread the situation." Lumi's eyes were drawn to the taxi coming toward us.

"I hope you all know that my leaving so suddenly has nothing to do with you three." I gave them each a hug.

Lumi teared up and Maximum was biting his lip with a pained expression.

I was already in the car and about to close the door when I looked back at the house one last time. Liv stood right outside the entrance, her eyes large and her body stiff. I waited a few seconds to see if she would run to me, but she only took a small step forward before she was stopped by Conor, who stepped up behind her and put a hand on her shoulder.

I squeezed the inside door handle of the car and suppressed the strong urge to run up to them and punch his face for touching her. There were tears on her face and even from this distance I could tell her lower lip was quivering, but she stood by her choice to stay and didn't move off the spot.

235

With my heart left in pieces somewhere on the top floor of the Red Manor, and my pride stinging like this whole fucking cab was made of nettles, I told the driver, "Go!" My jaws were so tensed up that it was hard to speak.

Without a plan, I ended up checking into the hotel I'd first stayed at when I arrived in Dublin for a conference.

I tipped the bellboy when he brought my luggage up and handed me the key card.

Now what?

Letting myself fall on the bed, I looked up at the ceiling trying to piece everything together. No matter how much I tried, I couldn't find a plausible reason for Liv and Conor to be half undressed unless something sexual had taken place between them. That meant she had betrayed me.

Unless…

The thought that he could have forced her entered my mind, but if that were the case, she wouldn't have chosen to stay with him.

Arghhh… it was all so confusing and my head was exploding with questions like: could this be it? We had talked about a future with children and made love like we couldn't get enough of each other. I wasn't ready to let go or say goodbye to Liv, but I couldn't share her either.

The need to understand made me pick up my phone and text her.

Charles: Was it all a lie?

Staring at my phone I hoped for an answer but she didn't answer me.

Walking over to the window, I looked out over the lights of Dublin. It was early November and below me on the street, strangers were moving about like the world still made sense to them. Placing my hand on the floor to ceiling window of the suite, I wondered how long it would take someone to fall from here and if it would be an instant death.

A memory of Liv and me visiting the cliffs of Moher and discussing how many times you could say shit on your way down from the cliffs, came back to me. That day had been so perfect. For the first time in my life, I'd walked around holding hands with a woman I fancied.

My mood was as dark as this November night.

When my phone rang, I wanted it to be Liv so badly that I didn't even check caller ID before I pressed it to my ear. "Liv, is that you?"

"Hello, Charles." My grandfather's voice made me stiffen. I hadn't talked to him in almost three months and it had been on my mind to call him. Of all the times in the world, now was the worst time for him to call. I didn't want to hear his 'I told you so' and I had no energy to argue.

"Where are you, Charles?"

My tone was flat. "In a hotel. The same as when I first arrived."

"Oh, good." He sounded relieved. "You had me worried there for a second. Liv told me you left after a dramatic incident and she was worried about you."

I frowned. "Wait a minute. How the f..." I stopped myself before cursing. My grandfather had always looked down on vulgar speech. "How do you know Liv?"

"I'll explain everything if you come home to see me."

"No. Tell me right now." I couldn't stand still, so I paced the floor.

"All right." He sighed. "But you have to promise me that you won't hang up until I'm done explaining. Things aren't as black or white as you think."

"I'm listening."

"I did my research and Conor O'Brien isn't who he made you believe he is. His real name is Conor Bricks and he has a long list of criminal behavior from his past."

"I know all of that, but it's all lies." I rubbed my forehead, annoyed with myself for defending the man who had seduced my girlfriend just to prove he could have her.

"Charles, you believe the best about people and he's good at lying. He has perfected it over his entire life, but the man leaves a trail of misery in his path. We believe he killed the boy's mother to gain her life insurance."

"What boy? Are you talking about Nathan?"

"Yes. His mom was scared of Conor. That's why she hid in England, but he found her and forced her to commit suicide."

I closed my eyes and rubbed the spot between my eyebrows. "That's absurd."

"Yes, it is. But we're dealing with a man without scruples."

"Does this mean you were the one who hired those private detectives?"

"Yes."

I snorted. "They were amateurs and came to make accusations with no proof to back it up."

"They weren't there to prove anything. They were there to put pressure on Conor. I would like for you to meet up with Kit tonight. She can answer a lot of your questions. I'm also happy to send over the report we've gathered about Conor Brick's dark past and current deception of his cult members."

"It's *not* a cult. Don't start with me again. I've already told you."

"How much did you pay him?"

I rolled my eyes and sighed out loud. "Not much."

"Are you saying that you didn't pay at all?"

"No."

"How much, Charles?"

I hesitated before giving him my answer. "Four hundred thousand."

"Is that it?"

"Yeah, the truth is that I was going to transfer another one hundred and fifty thousand dollars, but that was a donation for his foundation. It would build three schools in Africa."

"His foundation is a scam. Kit can tell you all about it. No more than ten percent is used for philanthropy. The rest is channeled into his own pocket."

"But he doesn't need the money. Conor is a millionaire himself."

My grandfather scoffed again. "Only because he's scammed rich people like you, Charles. It's what he does."

"No, he used to be a code breaker for the government. He's a genius."

"Charles, use your common sense. The man is a convicted criminal. I know you heard that straight from the Irish police, so stop defending him and ask yourself, how someone with his criminal record would get a security clearance. Bricks might have wished he was a code breaker, but I assure you it's just another lie."

My chest felt heavy and I found it hard to breathe. How could I have been so blind?

"About Liv..."

"Yes?"

"She came to get you out."

"What do you mean?"

He coughed. "I found your diary from that time at Harvard where you met her. It's an old proven method that cults will lure people in by using attractive members to do the invitation. I believe that's what happened to you too."

I was going to protest, but Sara had flirted with me at the conference and made me think I had a chance with her before she invited me to join her mastermind group.

"I'm not sure. Maybe."

"Well, I figured we could reverse the method and send someone to lure you out."

"Are you saying that you paid Liv to be with me?" It felt like an iron band was squeezing my lungs making it hard for me to breathe. "Was she just acting?"

He sighed again. "Here's where it gets tricky. You see, when I told her about you being wrapped up in a cult, Liv was eager to go and help. I offered her money but she didn't want it. I think she was genuinely happy to connect with you again."

"Then why is she there and not here? She made me believe she was in love with me." My head was about to explode with confusion and my eyes were getting moist.

"She *is*, Charles!"

I made a sound of skepticism and sat back down on the bed.

"Whenever she called me to report about the progress that she was making, she would talk about falling in love with you. I believe that part was very real."

"You're just saying that."

"Don't insult me. You know me better than that. I'm sorry Liv chose to stay at the manor. It wasn't part of the plan."

I was quiet, trying to calm my emotions and think rationally. "So, what was the plan?"

"To open your eyes and see Conor for the Machiavellian character he is."

"Only you would use a word like that. Can't you just say villain?"

"I'm old and I'm using old words, but you know what I mean."

My chest rose and fell. "Why did she sleep with him then? Was it her way of showing me that I couldn't trust him? Was that her plan to get me out?"

"Liv slept with Conor? No. That makes no sense. She would never do that."

"That's what I thought, but tonight, I found Conor and Liv in a bathroom with their clothing disheveled. She was pulling her shorts up and he was unzipped."

"Oh."

"Yeah. Big oh."

"That's surprising."

"Uh-huh. I got mad and asked her to leave with me, but she wouldn't."

"That's strange. I only received a text from her saying that you left and that she worried about you. I wonder…" My grandfather coughed again. "I wonder if it's because of the children. She has been talking a lot about wanting to save the children from Conor."

The image of River clinging to Liv and asking her to stay came back full force. "Actually…"

"Yes?"

"Today, Liv and I found Nathan in the pond. The boy said it was Conor who had told him to go and meditate in the pond, but he denied it. Liv believed the boy while I believed…"

"Conor," my grandfather finished the sentence for me. "It's because she knows Conor is nothing but a liar and a cheat."

"Do you think that's why she stayed? To protect the children?"

"It sounds like Liv. She is surprisingly willing to put herself at risk to save others."

I shook my head. "It's not like anyone in that house is a danger to her. They're good people."

241

"Charles." My grandfather sighed. "Open your eyes. Conor drove River's mother crazy and she's now in a mental institution. We are building a case to prove that he killed Nathan's mother, and Jim Maddox too."

"Who's that?"

"A man who blackmailed Conor. He had a recording of Conor forcing Sandra to write her suicide letter and swallow the pills that killed her. Conor is a murderer and from what I understand he has a gun in the house."

"Yeah, but…" It was like my brain was trying to catch up to everything my grandfather was saying. "You really believe he's a killer?"

"Yes, and it's only a matter of time before we can prove it. I'm telling you that Conor will be in jail soon. If we can't prove murder then we can go after him for using the Red Manor Foundation to commit major fraud."

I was quiet and thinking everything over.

"Are you there, Charles?"

"Yes, I'm still here."

"It's a lot to take in, I understand."

"My head feels like a hoarder's house with too many questions and thoughts."

"You need to talk to Kit. She can help you with answers."

"Is she the tall ginger who came to the manor with her father?"

"Yes. She's the private detective who has been working with Liv to get information on Conor and get you out."

"Yes, I want to talk to her, and I want that report you mentioned."

"Kit has it. I can text you her number." He coughed again.

"Are you okay? You sound sick."

"Yes. That's why I want you to come home and see me. I might not have long left and I worry that I won't get a chance to make peace with you before I die. That's all."

"Make peace with me; what do you mean?"

"The last time we talked, you told me I had never loved you and that you had found the family you always longed for, but never had."

My left hand lifted to rub my face. "I only said that because you kept pushing me to come back to work at Solver. It should be my choice, and nothing in my life ever felt like I had a choice!" My voice rose a bit.

"I'm sorry that you felt that way. But for all it's worth, Charles..." He sighed. "I always wanted for you to be your own man and I see great strength in you. If you don't want to listen to me, that's fine. I'm just grateful that you're no longer under Conor's power. I've hardly done anything but worry about how to get you free of his mind control."

The sincerity in my grandfather's voice moved me, but we had never been used to sharing our emotions with each other. "Yeah, well, we can talk about it next time I'm back. I have to figure out what's up and down with Liv, Conor, and the Red Manor group."

"You do that, and I'd appreciate an update when you can."

"Okay. Don't forget to send me the number of the private detective."

"I'm old but I'm not senile. You'll have the number as soon as we hang up."

My grandfather was in his seventies and the type who couldn't both talk on the phone and navigate his contact list, so I ended the call and waited a few minutes until a text came in with a local number for a Kathy O'Rourke.

CHAPTER 23
Unhinged

Liv

My heart felt like it had been stabbed, stomped on, and beaten up by a madman all at once. To see the confusion and disappointment on Charles' face, when I chose to stay instead of leaving with him, had just about killed me.

I'd flown all the way from the US to get him out of this cult and when he'd finally been ready to leave, I had failed him.

If only I could have told him my reason for staying.

Bile rose in my throat from the mere thought that Charles believed I'd chosen to stay because I was attracted to Conor. Nothing could be further from the truth. My reason for staying was the safety of the children.

With the way Charles had stormed out and my still feeling shocked from the way Conor had pushed himself at me in the bathroom, I hadn't managed to talk to Charles before he was gone.

A quick text message from the bathroom, to Mr. Robertson and Kit, was all I'd been able to do for Charles. My hope was that they would find him and explain what I hadn't been able to tell him.

After Charles left, Conor had been determined to love-bomb me with compliments and encouragement. "You made the right decision. I'm so proud of you for setting your boundary and not allowing Charles' jealousy to limit you. From the moment I saw you, I sensed there was something special about you, Liv. You're meant for great things and I'm going to help you achieve it."

Conor had misinterpreted my resentment toward him as sadness.

"You're upset that Charlie left. I understand. It's an awful feeling to see your relationship come crashing down like that. I promise you, though; the rest of us will take good care of you." Conor had opened his arms to hug me but I had made an excuse and run upstairs to finish the bath I had attempted to take twice already.

I'd skipped dinner and gone straight to check up on Nathan. By nine o'clock, the five children were all in River's and Nathan's room. Lumi had crawled up on the foot end of Nathan's bed and was pulling the sleeves of her purple sweater over her hands. "It's a shame that Charles left you, but I think you broke his heart when you slept with Conor."

I was on my stomach using my hands as a pillow, my elbows to the side. Sighing, I looked at Lumi. "I didn't sleep with Conor and I never will. Charles misunderstood the situation."

Lumi rubbed the bridge of her nose. "Maybe you can talk to him. If I ever find love, I'll fight for it. My mom loved my dad and I'm sad that she let him go. She said he was the most brilliant man she ever knew."

"More brilliant than Dad?" Atlas, who was sitting on the floor next to Nathan's bed, looked up at Lumi.

"Yes. That's what she said, but I doubt it." Pain crossed her face. "I think of him as stupid for not fighting for my mom... and me."

"Where's your dad now?" I asked.

She shrugged. "I don't know. My mom doesn't like to talk about it. Their relationship was forbidden."

"How long have you and your mom lived with Conor?"

"Since I was eleven. Before that we lived in London, where my mom worked as a CPA. Conor was one of her clients but they became friends and he helped her get a better job here. Today she's a partner in Munster and Son."

"Yes, she told me."

"Despite having me, my mom still graduated with the highest score from her university."

"Wow. The apple doesn't fall far from the tree. You're gifted too, Lumi."

The girl looked down. "We all are. Atlas in particular."

Atlas frowned. "We had the best teachers, that's why." Looking at me, he continued, "Charles has been more than willing to help me. He's very knowledgeable, did you know that?"

I nodded and lowered my gaze with sadness.

"We all liked Charles." Atlas spoke on an exhalation and I could tell he was sad too. "Over time you'll get used to people leaving."

"Why do you think people leave?" My question made Lumi and Atlas exchange a look.

"For different reasons," Atlas said in a diplomatic way, but from the corner of the room, a more honest answer came from his younger brother.

"It's because of Dad." Maximum used a matter-of-fact tone, while touching one of Nathan's Star Wars space ships.

Like a hunter on a trail, I turned my head to him. "What do you mean?"

All the children were quiet. Nathan, who had been woken up by the commotion in his room, was sitting up in his bed under his duvet with his knees pulled up in front of him. "You can tell her. Liv isn't like the others. She believed me over Dad."

Five sets of eyes were on me and it suddenly felt like a defining moment. If this had been poker, I'd been called out and it was time to show my cards. "I still believe

Nathan didn't come up with the idea to meditate in the pond by himself."

"You think Conor lied?" Lumi narrowed her eyes. There was a test in those words.

"I do! But you tell me. You've known him a lot longer than me."

She raised an eyebrow. "Conor wouldn't like it if he knew you called him a liar."

I stood my ground. "Probably not, but are you gonna tell him?"

There was a quiet tension in the room as Lumi and I kept looking at each other. Finally, she exhaled sharply and cranked her head from one side to the other before rolling her neck. "No. I won't tell him."

"We can trust Liv," Nathan insisted before turning his attention on Maximum. "Stop touching my Millennium Falcon. It's an original."

Maximum, abandoned all the Star Wars toys and came to sit around the bed with the rest of us. River was with me on my mattress and had crawled up to lie on top of my back while Atlas sat with his legs stretched against the wall.

"You don't like Conor as much as the others, do you?" Lumi asked me.

I shook my head.

"How come?"

It was a balancing act of saying the right thing without saying too much. "I don't know. There's just something about him that makes alarm bells ring in my head. It's like there's a different side to him that he's hiding."

"There *is*!" Nathan crossed his arms as if to challenge anyone who dared stop him from saying so.

I turned to Maximum. "What did you mean when you said that people leave because of your dad?"

He shrugged. "Either people are asked to leave or they run when they find out what Dad is really like."

Atlas didn't say anything, but he gave Maximum a warning glance not to say too much.

Like a bloodhound, I pushed a little further, "Tell me more."

Maximum had seen his brother's warning and looked away so I turned to Atlas. At sixteen, he was a bit younger than Lumi, but he seemed to be the leader of the children.

"Dad is good at getting his way," Atlas said.

"You mean he manipulates people?"

Atlas shrugged.

"Does he manipulate you too?"

He frowned. "No. I don't know. Maybe sometimes."

"If Conor told Nathan to go meditate in the pond but then refused to acknowledge that he ever said it, only to point fingers at Nathan for making bad choices, then that's manipulation. Wouldn't you say?" My question was directed at all of them.

"Yes!" Nathan dipped his head to rest his chin on top of one of the knees he'd pulled up to his chest. "It's not just the lying. I also feel like he's hiding something. Sometimes I wish I could go snoop in his room and look into some of his closets that are locked."

"What do you think is in there?" I asked.

"I don't know, but one time I came in when he had the closet open and he slammed it shut so fast that I'm sure it's something important," Nathan explained.

"Probably porn."

Everyone looked at Lumi, who had said it.

"What?" She raised her hands up. "Adults look at porn. My mom says it's normal."

Atlas squirmed in his seat and I got the sense that he was feeling guilty.

248

"Do you know what your father is keeping in those locked closets?"

"No." Atlas shook his head while Maximum rolled over on one end of my mattress to lie on his belly, propped himself up on his elbows, and admitted:

"Neither do I, but I have a good idea where he's hiding the key."

"Where?" River whispered in a conspiratorial voice.

"Under his mattress. I can show you," Maximum told River. "But I doubt you'd be brave enough to use it."

She moved down from my back. "I'll do it if the rest of you go with me."

Lumi shook her head. "We can't! If Conor finds out, he'll be furious and he'll..." She didn't finish her sentence. "Besides, it's not right to invade people's privacy."

Nathan's voice was icy when he spoke. "It's not right of him to lie either. You were there, Lumi. You heard him tell me to show that I'm serious by doing my meditation in the pond."

"He didn't think you'd do it."

"I don't care. It's not like he tried to stop me either." Nathan was staring at Lumi. "I was so scared of him throwing me out, but you know what Liv told me?"

They all looked to me again as Nathan continued. "Liv said that Conor is lucky to have a son like me and that there are people out there who would adopt me. Maybe it's not true that I'd be in an orphanage. Who says Conor hasn't lied about that too? For as long as I can remember, I've been scared of him giving up on me like my mother did. But sitting out there in the icy water made me think that an orphanage might be better."

"Don't say that." River's face fell. "I don't want to lose any of you. You're my siblings. We're family."

Nathan pushed his duvet off and swung his legs over the side of his bed. "Come on, let's go see what Conor has in his closet."

"He's going to throw a fit if he finds us in his room," Lumi warned again.

"No, because we'll be quick and he won't know that we looked in his closet." Nathan pushed up from the bed and moved to the connecting door. "Let me just make sure he's not there." Knocking lightly on the door, he waited with the rest of us, but there was no answer.

The rest of us got up, except for Lumi, who kept to the corner of Nathan's bed, and Atlas, who was still on the floor.

We all looked at them, and then Atlas got up and drew a deep sigh. "Lumi is right. We shouldn't be doing this, but there's a lot of things Dad shouldn't be doing either." He gave me a pointed look. "He shouldn't have come on to you without Charles' permission. When I have a girlfriend, I'm never introducing her to my dad."

A knot in my throat made it hard to speak, but I understood his position and listened without interrupting.

"Charles was my friend and I'm angry at my dad for hurting him, just like I'm angry at him for hurting you, Nathan." Atlas looked to Lumi. "Are you coming?"

"No, what you're doing is wrong!"

Atlas nodded. "I know, but I'll make sure they don't touch anything. Can you a least keep an eye out while we go in?"

With an annoyed huff, Lumi crawled out of the bed and walked out in the hallway.

"It's just going to be a quick peek!" Nathan declared, while I hoped we would discover something the police could use to finally arrest Conor O'Brien.

Nathan stood in front of the connecting door to Conor's room. With one hand on the door handle, he turned around to look at each of us while putting a finger to his lips gesturing for us to be quiet.

We all gathered close to him and then he turned the doorknob. The door creaked as Nathan opened it and took a careful step, as if Conor might jump out at him.

"Turn on some light," River whispered. "I can't see."

My heart was galloping in my chest. For the kids it was a matter of curiosity and a bit of a teenage rebellion, but for me there was so much more on the line. We were breaking into a cold-blooded murderer's room while he was in the same house.

A small "click" sounded and then lights came on.

"Where is it?" River whispered to Maximum, who walked to his father's bed like he was in a museum and attempting not to set off an alarm.

Placing his hands on the bed, Maximum let himself squat down and then he lifted the mattress a little. It took him a solid five seconds that felt like minutes until he held up a key with triumph shining from his eyes.

Holding out his hand, Nathan took the key from Maximum and tiptoed to a large closet that was placed against the opposite wall next to a beautiful antique mirror.

There were three closet doors and first he unlocked the one to the right. I held my breath as it opened and revealed five shelves full of clothes and a few boxes.

I pointed to a black box hoping one of the kids would be curious enough to look inside it. River moved forward and took it out for me to open the lid. As soon as I did, I put it back on. It was full of sex toys.

River looked confused and I hoped she hadn't gotten a good look.

"What was it?" she whispered.

251

I put the box back and gave a dismissive swing of my hand. "Adult stuff."

Disappointed with the content of the first closet, Nathan moved on to the second and I spotted five binders on the top shelf that I'd like to look at. What if they contained incriminating information that he was hiding? Of course, such boring stuff didn't interest the children and they moved on to the last closet door.

The jolt of Nathan's body- and his soul-crushing scream made us all react very fast. Atlas moved forward to cover Nathan's mouth and hissed for him to be quiet while Maximum bent down to pick up the key that Nathan had dropped.

Everything happened so fast. With one hand still covering Nathan's mouth, Atlas picked him up and carried him back to his room. River retreated too.

I held up my phone and snatched a picture just before Maximum closed the closet door and locked it with shaking hands. He was moving to the connecting door when I hissed at him. "Put the key back."

He ran to the bed and stuck his hand under the mattress and then sheer panic spread on his face when we heard Conor's dark voice in the hallways outside the room.

"Lumi, what are you doing out here?"

I stabbed my finger through the air pointing to the connecting door but Maximum moved to turn off the light. Afraid that the change in light would be visible to Conor from under the door, I grabbed Maximum's arm and nudged him away,

"I'm waiting out here for Atlas' smelly fart to be gone. He did it on purpose. It was disgusting."

"Hmmm… is that why someone screamed?"

"Yeah, that was me."

Maximum and I made it into the children's room, and I could have kissed Lumi when she shouted:

"Atlas, you better not have farted again. Dad and I are coming in."

Her loud voice covered the small creaking sound of the connecting door closing after us.

Maximum let himself fall onto my mattress where he'd been before. I fell to my knees and reached for a strand of River's hair, pretending to be playing with it. Nathan was back in his bed with his face to the wall. His shoulders were bobbing like he was crying without sound.

"Are you done farting?" Lumi asked when she walked in with Conor behind her.

Atlas sat on the floor against Nathan's bed, blocking the view from the door to Nathan. His performance was worthy of an Emmy Award when he pointed to the window and spoke in an annoyed tone. "Why don't you just let in some fresh air if it's that bad?"

Conor gave me a smile. "Hey, Liv, if you get tired of teen drama come join us downstairs."

I smiled back in pure relief that he hadn't caught us red-handed in his room. "It's fine. I promised River that I'd braid her hair and I think I'm going to try and sleep soon."

"How is Nathan doing?" Conor craned his head to look behind Atlas.

"Much better. He's just tired." I lowered my voice a little. "He had a nightmare but fell asleep again."

"All right. I was going to discuss the consequences of his foolish behavior with him, but I can do that tomorrow." He waited for a moment as if I might have a comment, but I didn't and just focused on braiding River's blonde hair.

"Sweet dreams then. Don't let them stay up too late."

"I won't."

The moment Conor closed the door and left, we held our breath and listened for his footsteps. They stopped outside his room.

Please don't go in and see that the lights are turned on.

As if a guardian angel was keeping a hand over us, my silent prayer worked, and Conor walked on.

A collective sigh escaped all of us, except Nathan, who was still on his bed facing the wall.

"Nathan." I got up from the floor and moved fast to pull at his back. "Look at me!"

His body was shaking and his eyes were red-rimmed from tears. He was quiet but the way he stared into the wall with wide eyes made me sure that he was experiencing a panic attack. If Conor had walked into the room and taken a better look at Nathan, he would have seen pure terror on his face.

"Help me get him up to sit," I instructed Atlas as all the children came to help. "You're not crazy, Nathan. We all saw it."

"Saw what?" Lumi asked and reached out to touch Nathan, who was fighting us when we tried to turn him to face us.

The excellent performance the children had mastered before with Conor in the room was gone now, and River had tears in her eyes too. "I don't understand."

"What happened?" Worry coated Lumi's tone.

"We found this in Conor's closet." I held up my phone and showed her the picture.

Lumi covered her mouth and stared at the picture of a large bright yellow snake facing the camera with its large fangs and a forked tongue sticking out. "No." She shook her head.

"Yes." I couldn't disguise the indignation and anger in my tone. "Nathan, listen to us. You were never crazy.

Conor just made you think you were. The snake is real. We all saw it."

"You saw it too?" Lumi asked Atlas, who nodded.

River who was standing behind me, spoke up, "It was scary."

"The snake is real," Atlas confirmed and placed his head in his hands like he was thinking hard and hating every thought in this head.

"Did Dad place the snake in Nathan's bed on purpose or did it escape by accident?" Maximum was pacing behind me.

My tone was harsh. "I think it's safe to assume he did it on purpose."

"But why? Why would he do something that cruel?" Lumi asked.

"Someone who likes control." I turned to River. "Didn't you say you once saw the snake too?"

"Yes, but I thought I was just dreaming. Dad explained how all Nathan's nonsense about the snake had infiltrated my dreams as well. I can't believe it's real."

"Oh, it's very real and very large," I said in a dry tone.

Nathan whimpered so I caressed his hair and spoke in a soothing voice, "That snake won't ever come near your bed again. Here's what we're going to do. The six of us are going to come up with a plan and go to the police tomorrow. What Conor did to you is child abuse and that's illegal."

"No," Lumi objected. "We can't go to the guards. If we talk about this to anyone outside the room, social services might come and try to separate us. We can't let that happen."

"Then what do you suggest we do? Conor has deliberately been trying to drive Nathan mad and I'll bet he has done awful things to the rest of you that you haven't told me about yet. We have to speak up and stop this

255

unacceptable behavior, Lumi. Tell me that you understand."

Lumi ran her hands through her hair. "We'll make sure that Nathan never sleeps alone. From now on, we'll take turns to watch over him. Just promise that you won't call the guards."

"But, Lumi…"

Her large dark eyes were pleading. "Liv, please!! We've lost so many people. We can't lose each other too. Promise that you won't call them."

Closing my eyes, I sunk down on Nathan's bed. "Okay. I won't say anything to the police tomorrow, but I can't keep this secret for long. We all need to get out of here. A man deranged enough to do something that evil isn't safe to be around.

They were all quiet.

I touched Atlas's arm. "Tell me you understand what is happening here isn't right."

"Of course it's not right, but you don't understand."

"What don't I understand?"

When he lifted his head from his hands, there were deep frown lines on his forehead. "We're talking about our dad. Not some kind of monster."

I jerked back. All my psychology knowledge told me that this was going too fast for the children, who had no idea how long the list of Conor's despicable behavior was. I should have gone slow, but I was shocked myself and couldn't hold back my honest response. "Your father is intentionally fabricating Nathan's nightmares in order to control him. No one likes to think of their parent as a monster, but if you ask me, the description fits."

Atlas got up and moved to the door. "Come on, Maximum. It's time to go."

Lumi leaned down and gave Nathan a kiss on his head. "I'll see you tomorrow. Liv is here and from now on we'll make sure that you never sleep alone again."

Nathan was holding my hand and when it was just him, me, and River again, he moved down to my mattress and let me spoon him.

"I thought I was crazy."

"You're not! Conor is."

CHAPTER 24
Heat

Charles

Kit came to my hotel room and presented me with the report my grandfather had talked about.

"It's a messy affair ye got yerself into. That Conor is right up there with the devil himself."

I took the report and began reading it while the red-haired woman sat down on a chair in the corner with her legs crossed and a foot dangling.

The few times that I looked over she was on her phone.

"Are ye done?" she asked when I put down the report.

"Yes." I sighed. "It's difficult to believe half of the things that are in this report."

"Ye'd better believe it, 'cause it's the truth." She got up. "Are ye hungry?"

I shrugged and looked at the clock on the night table. It was a little past eleven at night and I hadn't eaten yet.

"Come on. I know a good kebab place close by that's open all night."

Taking my jacket, I walked with her. Kit didn't say much and seemed to understand that I was trying to process everything that was in the report.

As we approached the kebab shop, I found my voice. "It can't be true. I mean, Conor introduced me to some powerful people. There's no way they would have been fooled by him."

"Why not? Ye were fooled."

"Yes, but I'm not..." I trailed off as Kit held the door open for me and we entered a small place with four tables and a greasy menu. There were no other guests but us.

"Ye're not what?" She raised an eyebrow. "Were ye going to say that ye're not as powerful and influential as the people he introduced ye to?"

"Yes. I met some of my biggest idols through him. Conor is friends with a lot of interesting business people that donate to his foundation to help children. He associates with celebrities and politicians."

"Did ye forget that ye're the sole heir to one of the biggest business empires in the US?"

I creased my brow.

"Others are going to be impressed with him for knowing someone like ye."

"But no one knew. I was using my mother's maiden name."

"Argh, don't be naïve. I'll bet he told people who ye were. One of his former members characterized Conor as a collector of people. I'll bet ye that he sees ye as a diamond in his collection. He probably expects that ye'll be back and if not, he'll find ye and use that lyin' tongue of his to gaslight ye into thinkin' that what happened tonight was yer fault and not his."

"It wasn't like that. I wasn't some trophy of his.'"

"Aye, it was exactly like that. Ye just don't want to believe it."

"But to think that Conor would force a woman to kill herself. It makes no sense."

Kit patted my shoulder. "Hold that thought." Turning around, she gave her food order and pulled out her credit card. "What are ye havin'?"

"I think I lost my appetite."

She rolled her eyes and turned back to the man behind the counter. "Let's get him a shawarma sandwich and some chips."

"No, it's fine," I objected, but Kit waved a hand.

"Look, my brother does this all the time. He says he's not hungry when I order my food, but once I get it, he eats half of it. I hate when people do that."

"At least let me pay for it."

"No need. Yer grandfather has been very generous. I can afford to buy ye a sandwich and a Coke."

Kit finished paying and took a seat by the window where I joined her. "I understand that it's hard for ye to wrap yer pretty head around the fact that someone ye trusted and thought was a friend turned out to be a liar."

"Are you talking about Conor or Liv?"

"Conor of course. Liv couldn't tell you that she knew about his tricks. Ye wouldn't have believed her anyway."

"She still lied to me."

"Aye. But ye would have done the same if ye were the one tryin' to save her."

I looked down at the food in front of me. "I didn't need saving."

She crossed her arms. "For feck's sake, man. I can't believe how gob-smacked Liv is with ye and then ye're this thick-headed."

"I'm not thick-headed. I just don't like being lied to."

"Then ye shouldn't have joined a bloody cult." Kit plunked her crossed arms down on the table. "Liv risked a lot to save ye. Conor has killed before and her being undercover is dangerous."

I rubbed my face. "Okay, so I'll admit that I saw a side of him today that I hadn't seen before, but the things about him being a killer and dangerous? That's just crazy."

"Of course it's crazy, but that's because we're dealing with a sick person."

260

Her phone buzzed and she fished it out of her pocket. "Hang on, it's my da." Picking up the phone, she spoke with an even stronger accent. "What's the craic?" I listened and watched her body language tense up as she leaned back. "Ye're serious? Wow, that's good news. Aye, I'm with Charles now. Hang on, Da." She looked up and met my eyes. "Our sources say that the Liverpool police just dug up a body believed to be Jim Maddox."

"Who?"

"The man who tried to blackmail Conor."

"Oh, right. When will they know?"

"Da, how long before they can confirm that it's really him?"

I heard his short answer: "Soon."

"Keep me updated, will ya?" She finished the call just as our food was ready.

"This is excitin'. I love a good breakthrough in a case." Kit took a big bite of her sandwich.

My stomach was in a knot. "You really believe that Conor killed a man for trying to blackmail him?"

She nodded and dried her mouth with a napkin. "I believe he killed Sandra too."

"But..." I picked up a French fry only to put it down again. "The thing you said about Liv being in danger." It was like I couldn't articulate my question because I didn't want to think the thought through.

Kit answered anyway. "He's unpredictable. I told her so, but Liv stayed because of the children; she's a good person."

I sat in a light trance watching Kit eat her sandwich while my head was searching through all the excuses Conor had given for his criminal past. "He made it sound like he was the victim."

"Aye, that's classic for blackguards, isn't it? They're experts at cheatin' and lyin', and they always make it

261

sound like they're being unfairly treated. I'll bet he sounded credible too."

I looked down. "He did. I was there when the police came to question him."

My phone lit up with my grandfather's name on the screen.

"Yes, this is Charles."

"Charles, I just spoke to the ambassador. It seems the police in Liverpool found the man they were looking for. Did you read the report yet?"

"Yes. I'm with Kit."

"Good, good. Now that we have a body, they can connect it to Conor and make an arrest."

"*If* he killed him." Part of me still didn't want to believe it.

"Oh, he killed him!"

"You don't know for sure."

"According to the ambassador, they found evidence in Jim's grave that he'd been trying to blackmail Conor. The Irish police are cooperating with the people in Liverpool and they already obtained DNA from Conor from an earlier arrest. Right now, technicians are working on securing DNA from the body to see if there's a match."

I was quiet.

"Charles, did you hear me? Tell me that I can trust you. This is confidential information and if you..."

"What kind of evidence?"

"What?"

"You said that the police found evidence that Jim was trying to blackmail Conor."

"Oh. I'm not certain. I can ask, but does it matter? Conor is a cold-blooded killer and if you don't believe that yet, then at least acknowledge that his foundation is a scam. You saw it in black and white in the report."

I groaned. "Yes, I saw."

262

"Conor O'Brien is going to prison. If not for murder then for financial fraud."

Kit, who had been eating the last bite of her sandwich and checking her phone at the same time, gave a muffled outburst that caught my attention.

"What is it?"

She chewed fast and handed me her phone. The name Liv Christensen made my heart beat faster. Letting my eyes run over the text, I felt all the blood disappear from my face.

Liv: Remember I told you Nathan has recurrent nightmares of a yellow snake in his bed? Tonight, the kids and I went snooping in Conor's room and unlocked a large closet. Look what we found.

I stared at a picture of a terrarium holding a large yellow snake with its head lifted before I read on.

Liv: Nathan and River are sleeping now, but I'm still so angry that I'm shaking. We need to take this monster down, Kit. I mean it! He deliberately makes the children think they're crazy.

"Do ye believe us now?" Kit asked and took back her phone while nodding to my other hand, where I was holding my own phone.

"Charles, hello, are you there?"

I lifted the phone to my ear again. "Yes, I'm here. It seems I've misjudged Conor O'Brien."

My grandfather sighed. "You and many others, my boy. I'm just grateful you're finally seeing him for the charlatan that he is."

"I need to get Liv out of there. If anything happens to her it'll be my fault. I'm the only reason she's there to begin with."

"Yes." My grandfather sighed. "I'm not comfortable with her being in his house either."

Kit was texting away on her phone across from me while I ended the call with my grandfather. "I have to go, but call me if you hear anything."

"Yes, same to you."

My grandfather and I ended the call and Kit gave me a quick glance. "I'm telling Liv that the police found Jim Maddox's body."

With a look of determination, I got up from my chair. "I'm going to Howth to get Liv."

"Whoa, stall for a second." Kit got up too. "Ye cannot just barge in at midnight like a jealous lover and demand that she leave with ye. Liv is there because of the children and the best we can do is help her get them out too."

"But if the police have all that incriminating information on him, why haven't they made an arrest yet? If his foundation is nothing but a front to pile up the money for himself, then it's illegal and he should be brought to justice."

"Aye, and he will be, but these things take time." She pointed to my untouched shawarma sandwich. "Are ye not gonna eat that?"

"No. All I can think about is how to get Liv out of there."

Kit brought my sandwich and fries to the man behind the counter and had him bag it to go.

When we left, she took a detour back to my hotel and stopped by a homeless woman sitting in a sleeping bag and looking miserable. Kit squatted down in front of the woman. "Here ye go, my love. You'll sleep better on a full stomach."

264

The homeless woman had greasy hair sticking out under her knitted hat and she was missing a front tooth, but her smile lit up her face and made her look younger than at first sight. "Oh, bless ye."

Kit patted her shoulder and stood back up. "Stay warm, Millie. The cold is fierce tonight."

"I know."

"Do ye have the jumper I gave ye?"

"I do. It's wonderful and warm. Ye're an angel."

Kit laughed. "Ask my mother and she can tell ye differently. See ye around, love."

When we walked away, I looked back to see the woman opening the wrapped sandwich with a smile.

"So, what's the plan?" I asked.

"The plan is to wait for the DNA match. Once the English police have it, the gardas will arrest Conor and Liv can go home with you."

"But what if that takes days?"

"Then we wait days."

I stopped her with a hand to her shoulder. "I can't just do nothing."

"Do ye think it was easy for us to be patient and not get ye out of there by force? Three weeks Liv has waited for ye to wake up." Like the rest of the Irish, Kit didn't pronounce the letter h in words like think and three. "Now, I'm asking ye to be patient as well."

"But maybe I could pretend that I've changed my mind and go back to be with Liv. I could help protect the children." I shook my head and gave a rumbling sigh from my chest.

"What is it?"

"I just remembered something that happened after Liv and I came home from work today. We found Nathan sitting in the pond in the back yard, blue lips and all. Liv tried to tell me that Conor was behind it, but I refused to

265

believe it. In order for him to do something like that he'd have to be a…"

"A psychopath?" she suggested.

"Yeah."

"He *is* a psychopath. A sneaky, cunning predator who spins a net of lies so tight around people that they can't see what's real or not. He has zero empathy and God only knows what else he has done to mess up those innocent children. He certainly had no qualms about placing a snake in a child's bed to give him nightmares."

"Jesus Christ." I looked up to the dark sky above us. "I can't believe I trusted that man. I saw him as my friend and mentor."

"Aye, but at least now you see behind his polished façade."

"I should go back and help Liv. It's not right that she's there as a one-man army."

Kit kept walking. "Conor would read ye like an open book and ye'd make everything worse. Ye're not the lying type, are ye? The moment he starts to press ye, I reckon ye'd tell him what a grand gobshite he is."

"Probably." I ran to keep up with her.

"I don't blame ye. I would too. It's impressive that Liv has been able to keep her mouth shut this long."

We had reached my hotel and stood outside with our hands in our pockets to keep warm.

"Do you live far away?"

"About forty-five minutes, but I'm staying at my brother's place tonight. He's got an apartment in the city and since he's working tonight, he won't be disturbed by my late arrival."

I rocked back and forth on my feet. "I know it's late, but if I go to bed now, I won't be able to sleep. I still have so many questions. How about a drink in the hotel bar?"

"Sure!" Kit smiled at me. "That sounded American, didn't it? I've practiced, ye see."

"Very impressive." I opened the door to the hotel and we walked through the lobby to the hotel bar.

"Tell ye what, ye get us a round, while I head to the jacks. I'll just have a mineral."

I had lived long enough in Ireland to know that the jacks was a restroom and a mineral a soft drink.

"Coke okay?"

"Aye."

Finding a place at the bar, I ordered a beer and a Coke, and took off my jacket. With Kit gone, I took out my phone and texted Liv.

Charles: I'm sorry for bringing you into this. I had no idea who Conor really was. Tell me what I can do to help.

There was no answer. It had been half an hour since Liv had texted Kit and it was now close to midnight. Either she had fallen asleep or she was mad at me and ignoring me on purpose. I closed my eyes and blamed myself for being such a naïve fool and for not listening the many times Liv had tried to warn me that Conor might not be who I thought he was. Looking back, I couldn't believe how patient she'd been, just waiting for me to wake up and see the truth. She had been so subtle with her hints, until today when she took Nathan's side. Why hadn't I listened to her?

Confusion and fear crept down my neck. Why had she been in that bathroom with Conor when she knew what he was like? And what would happen now that her mission of getting me out was over? I couldn't bear the thought of never seeing her again, but at the same time I could understand if Liv was disappointed with me for leaving her without at least talking to her to get her side of the story.

Lowering my head, I ran a hand through my hair. I'd been such an idiot for believing Conor's lies. A headache was brewing from the overload of drama in my life and the realization that I'd blown it with Liv.

Emptying my glass of beer, I nodded to the bartender. "I'll need another one, please." I would need a lot of alcohol to numb the crushing pain of self-blame in my heart.

CHAPTER 25
The Next Level

Liv

"Liv, wake up. You have to wake up."

Opening my eyes, I saw Lumi shaking my shoulders.

"What's wrong?"

"It's Conor. He wants everyone to gather downstairs. He doesn't look like himself. Did you tell him that we know about the snake?"

"No. What time is it?"

Lumi bit her lip. "It's one in the morning and he's waking up everybody. I think he found out that we were in his room. He's very upset."

Like me, Lumi was in her sleepwear. Hers consisted of a blue chemise in a flower pattern with a kimono over, and big bulky Mickey Mouse slippers that looked like she'd stuffed her feet into two Mickey Mouse teddy bears.

"Okay. You stay here with Nathan and River, while I go down to see what's going on."

"He wants *everyone* to come down."

"Until I know what he wants, I want you to keep Nathan and River here."

"But my mom is downstairs."

"Lumi. Please stay with River and Nathan. Your mom or I will come and get you if we want you there."

Music sounded from downstairs and I heard doors opening and closing. The whole house was waking up. With a bad feeling in the pit of my stomach, I put on some casual clothing and walked downstairs. What I saw made the blood in my veins pump faster.

Music was playing in the great room and bottles of champagne stood on the table next to trays of flute glasses. Conor was motioning for everyone to come in and take a seat on the floor or in one of the chairs or sofas.

He waved me closer, but the expression in his eyes scared me and my instincts told me to run the other way. What if he'd heard the news about the police finding a body in Liverpool? If Conor had killed Jim Maddox, then he would know that his time was running out.

I knew from my time here that Conor had powerful people in his circle of friends. Maybe someone had called to warn him.

"I just need to use the bathroom real quick." I diverted to the small powder room, where I called up Kit.

"Hello?"

"Are you awake?" I whispered into the phone.

"I am."

"Conor has gathered us all for some kind of meeting. He looks a bit unhinged. I'm going to record the meeting so I can play it for you later."

"No, just keep me on the line."

"Okay."

With my phone in my pocket I walked back into the living room, where Maximum and Atlas stood in the back of the crowd with morning hair. I stayed next to them and gave a silent nod before I took out my phone and held it in my hand along my leg.

Maximum yawned but nodded back while Atlas looked away. He was probably conflicted that I had called their dad a monster and threatened to go to the police to rat him out for what he did to Nathan. I didn't blame Atlas. The boy had shown rebelliousness by going into Conor's room to see what his father had hidden in the locked closet. For us to discover the snake in there had to have

270

been even more shocking to Atlas than me since he loved his father, and I didn't.

"Are we all here?" Conor asked and after a quick count it was established that River, Nathan, and Lumi were missing.

To buy time, I lied, "They're on their way down. Lumi is waking up the two sleepyheads."

"Good, because we have something to celebrate." Conor's words made the people in the room exchange smiles of anticipation.

"Let's all share a toast." He pointed to the two trays where champagne had been poured in beautiful glasses.

When a few said no thank you, Conor pointed them out. "I'll take it as a personal insult if you don't share this toast with me."

In the end, we all stood with glasses in our hands as Conor made his toast in a tone of importance. "Let's cheer the fact that it's time for us to take our group to the next level. Cheers!"

Everyone drank but I was paranoid and only pretended to drink before I discreetly emptied the glass in the plant behind me.

"We have become too powerful for the government to control and they hate it!" Conor's words sounded strong and confident. "Throughout human history, free thinkers and progressive groups like ours have been at war with the establishment. They don't understand that we're not content with following their directions. We're the true influencers of the world and our strength scares them. Our message confuses them. And just like Jesus was silenced with violence, I fear that retribution is coming our way as well. There are people who want to harm me."

"No. We won't let them." Carlos, a famous cross dresser with a huge social media following, called out. He wasn't wearing any make-up, which told me that like the rest of us, he'd been sleeping when he was called down to this meeting.

Conor continued his speech. "A friend alerted me that if we don't act now, outside forces are going to force us apart?"

"What do you mean?" Sara asked and concerned glances were exchanged around the room.

"You know how much I love you all, but the haters have found a new way to destroy the beautiful bond between us. The same bond that they can never be part of."

"They can try, but we won't let them," Sara declared and raised her chin.

Conor walked over to her and placed a slow kiss on her cheek before addressing the rest of us, "Sara is right. We can't let them split us up, but trust me; at this point nothing they do truly scares me because I have a way to make us untouchable." Raising his glass again, Conor scanned the room for those who still had champagne in their glasses. "Cheers. Bottoms up. This is the good stuff, let's not let it go to waste."

Conor waited until everyone had emptied their glass before he continued, "Going against the stream has always come with a high price. Jesus was persecuted and hung on the cross when his only crime was helping people and spreading a message of love and kindness. As we speak, I'm being framed for crimes that I didn't commit and soon they're coming for you as well."

People began booing and Conor let them express their frustration before he held up a hand and silenced them. "All of you in this room are old souls who cannot be fooled by their threats of control over us." He pointed to the entrance door and boomed, "They cannot control us!"

As if he had just cast a powerful spell, everyone around me raised their hands and shouted out their support.

"They cannot control us."

"They cannot control us."

"They cannot control us."

Again, Conor silenced them and spoke. "Like magnets we've been drawn together as a family because our souls vibrate when we're close. The family in this room aren't like the young souls out there who are happy to be numbed by their government's lies. We see the deceit with a clear mind. We know their false accusations are a matter of control. But what they fail to understand about us is that we hold tremendous power that we can take with us to the next level."

I tried to refrain from frowning at his constant mention of the next level.

What is he talking about?

"We don't have to stay and suffer through endless persecution from an establishment who fear us and attempt to imprison us and control our minds."

"How dare they?" Carlos, who was wearing a pink kimono, snapped his fingers in the air with an attitude worthy of his popular drag queen performances, but he swayed and sounded slurred in his speech, which made me look around at the others.

"Are you okay?" I asked Maximum who was squinting his eyes as if seeing was difficult for him.

"Mmm, I'm fine." Maximum giggled low and elbowed his brother, whispering. "Does Dad's head look gigantic to you?"

Atlas was swaying too and his eyes were rolling up in his head.

Looking down at the empty champagne glasses in their hands, I felt guilt. Why hadn't I stopped them from

273

drinking it? What if Conor had poisoned all of them like that Jonestown cult leader did back in the seventies?

I was panicking as Conor kept rambling about the threat of outside powers trying to split us apart. His words made no sense to me. The others, however, behaved like they were high and once again they chanted:

"They cannot control us."

"They cannot control us."

When they began jumping up and down in what had to be mass psychosis, I backed to the entry door and unlocked it because I wanted an escape route if things got weirder.

"Liv, come here." Atlas seemed to have forgotten all his troubles and reached out for me. "Why are you outside the group? Come and hug with us."

I had no choice but to walk back and be swallowed up in hugs by Atlas, Maximum, and Lumi's mom, Aisha, who kissed me on both cheeks.

"Where's Lumi? My daughter loves a good party." Aisha's voice was slurred and she leaned against me with her arm around my waist.

Conor fed on their adoration and support. "Raise your hand if you're ready to go with me to the next level."

People jumped and cheered.

"They cannot control us."

"They cannot control us."

"I'm a hundred percent loyal to all of you, but are you loyal to me?" Conor screamed to the group, hyping them up.

The hairs on my arms stood up from memories of what happened the last time he used those words.

"My family. I have a way for us to stand up to the tyranny of the establishment. Who's with me?" Conor's eyes shone with fire and determination as he jumped with Carlos, Sara, Estelle, Ciara, and all the others.

In order not to stand out, I swayed and smiled too when Conor screamed one more time:

"Who's with me?"

Loud whistling gave the impression that Conor was a rock star who had just asked if his audience wanted another song.

The hair on the back of my neck stood up when Conor bent down and pulled out a bag from under a chair.

"We're going to leave this level and go the next where we can be free to be together and live our lives as we want to."

My eyes doubled in size as he took out the first gun, and then the second, third, fourth, and fifth. Some of the members moved closer to him asking questions while others had confusion written on their faces.

"I need a group of pioneers." While talking Conor handed out a gun to Sara, Estelle, the twins, and Carlos, who batted his eyes and smiled at Conor.

"Darling, you're honoring me. You know I was born to be a pioneer."

"I'm selecting you five to go first on this journey. The rest of us will follow right after."

Under the pretense of a sneeze, I turned and spoke into the phone. "Get help, *now*!" My words were muttered and I was unsure if Kit would understand what was going on here.

Conor put down the empty bag, and gestured with his hands for everyone to stand up. "I want you all to give space for our five pioneers. Yes, that's right. Sara, you sit down on the floor. I want you to lead the first group. The rest of you will sit behind Sara." The twins were having a hard time getting down on the floor with the guns in their hands. They were giggling like it was a party game while I was freaking out on the inside. What if these guns weren't empty like the last time he'd told Sara to shoot herself?

My mind was racing to find a way to interfere. *Where's the fire alarm?* My eyes darted around, but this wasn't a public building and there was no glass to break nor did I see any smoke detectors or sprinkler systems. I could run, but then what about the children?

The selected five sat linked together with Carlos in the back and Sara in front.

"I don't know, Conor, I would have preferred to have a man between my legs," Carlos joked and it made people laugh.

Don't they understand what's going on here?

I stared around me, hoping to find an ally among the drugged cult members, but they were caught in the mass psychosis and were oblivious to what was really going on.

"Give them space." Conor got us all to move out of the way so that we were standing in front of them.

"Your job is to prepare for the big welcome party that we'll have on the other side," Conor instructed them. "The rest of us will be right along."

"Oh, leave it to me to arrange a fun party." Carlos slurred and gave an exaggerated laugh while his movements were slow from the drugs.

"We're all going to count down from five and then you'll press the triggers." Conor turned up the music, which blasted with a heavy bass, and then he raised his hands in the air and did a few dance moves.

I couldn't believe how easily he controlled the minds of the poor people around me who danced along with him with uncoordinated movements revealing just how intoxicated they were. It was mindboggling how quick they'd been to accept this impromptu meeting as a party when it was anything but.

"Let's do it!" Conor shouted over the loud music and Sara and the other four raised the guns to their heads with big grins. The last time Sara had been in a similar situation her hands had been shaking, but this time, she didn't seem the least bit concerned. Maybe she was convinced the gun would be empty again, but most likely it was the combination of whatever drug had been in the champagne and the hyped-up atmosphere around her.

What if he killed them? I should say something to stop them, but I'd gone into survival mode and was terrified of drawing attention to myself. Keeping in the background, I dug in behind Maximum and spoke into the phone again. "He's having people shoot themselves. *Send help, Kit*!"

"One!" Conor led the countdown but everyone counted along with him.

"Two!"

"Three!"

"Four, get ready to be freeee!!!" Conor was smiling from ear to ear and blew his five followers a kiss.

Sara pursed her lips and sent an air kiss back while I tugged at Maximum's and Atlas' t-shirts and gestured for them to pull back with me. They turned to me just as the group shouted, "Five!"

The gunshots were loud enough to be heard over the music. Sara, Carlos, Estelle, Maya, and Isabel, who had just been grinning and joking a few seconds ago, were now quiet and lifeless as they half sat, half lay in that bizarre way as a human train.

Conor gave a jump with excitement and turned to the group. "Our pioneers have gone before us. Let's follow and keep the party going on the other side. Who wants to go next?"

Maximum swayed on his feet and raised his hand with a few others, but I jerked him back.

As if he was trying to understand what had just happened, Atlas stood quiet with his eyebrows drawn inward.

"Wait, are they dead?" Aisha asked with a hand to her face. She leaned forward squinting her eyes as if she wasn't sure what she was looking at.

"No, they're not dead my love. They just took the elevator to the next level. And now, we're all going to join them." Conor took the guns from the corpses on the floor and dried the blood off with a beige-colored cloth before handing them to the next people in line who were getting down on the floor to continue the human chain.

"What about you, Liv? Why don't you go next?"

I felt Conor's eyes on me and people turned to look. Swaying on my feet, I felt sweat drip between my breasts and from my forehead as I pretended to be as drugged as them. "Sure, just hang on. I don't want the children to miss out. I wanna go with them. Come, on boys, let's go and fetch the others."

Without waiting for Conor's response, I pulled the boys along and staggered to the stairs.

"Hurry back down here. We'll do a special round for you and the children after this one."

I felt like screaming with terror when the boys weren't as fast or as willing to move as I wanted them to. It was like seeing a shark in the water and not being able to move away fast enough.

"I wanted to go next," Maximum complained when we were half way up the stairs.

The music had been cranked up again, but I spoke into his ear. "Snap the fuck out of it. He's killing people"

Maximum giggled. "That's a bad word. You can't say the F word."

Another collective countdown sounded and looking over my shoulder, I saw another round of five people pull the trigger and kill themselves. Pushing the boys to move faster, I screamed into the phone to overpower the music. "Kit, I need help right now."

278

If she answered, I couldn't hear it over the music and it took all my focus to get the boys moving down the long hallway. When I finally opened the door to River and Nathan's room, Lumi came at me.

"What's going on? We hear loud music and fireworks."

"That's not fireworks. Conor has lost his mind. He's having everyone kill themselves and he wants us to come down and kill ourselves too." I slammed the door shut behind me and locked it just as another round of shots were heard from downstairs.

Lumi's golden skin paled in front of my eyes and her hands covered her mouth.

"But they're not doing it, are they? They wouldn't kill themselves." River moved closer too.

"I wanted to go next, we're going to an awesome party on the other side," Maximum repeated but this time I shook his shoulders.

"Wake up, boy. There is *no* party."

Maximum and Atlas sat down on Nathan's bed and only now that the music was playing low in the distance, and no one was giggling, did they seem to wake up a little.

Loud bangs were heard and I closed my eyes, understanding that another five people had just killed themselves. That would make it twenty in total.

"Wait..." Atlas pushed his glasses up. "Sara and the others. It's not real, is it?"

"Yes, it's real. They're not waking up, Atlas. That champagne you all drank. It was spiked with something."

"But..." Atlas shook his head. "But it was just for fun."

"No!" I moved over to stare into his eyes. "People are really dying down there."

"My mom?" Lumi shrieked and if I hadn't stopped her, she would have run out the door.

"No, Lumi, you can't go down there. None of us can. We have to find a way to escape."

279

"But my mom…"

"Your mother wouldn't want you to die too. Tell me you understand." As I stared into her large brown eyes where worry and tears showed me how scared she was, my heart beat in my chest like a war drum alerting about the severe danger.

"I understand."

"Good!" I left her to open the window and look down. "Nathan, River, we'll have to tie the sheets from your beds together and crawl down."

Bang! Again shots were heard and this time I wasn't there to hold Lumi back. Before any of us could stop her, she sprinted over to unlock the door and ran down the hallway.

"Nooooo!" I ran after her, the phone dropping from my hands. "Lumi, stop. Stoooppp!"

CHAPTER 26
Flying Bullets

Charles

"Liv... Liv... what's happening? Answer me." Kit drove like a crazy person and still I wanted her to go faster. I was holding her phone and every sound that we'd heard so far had scared the crap out of us. The countdowns, the shots, Liv's panicked voice. I would never forgive myself if something happened to her.

"I'm calling her back." My foot was tapping on the floor of the car as the ringing went unanswered.

Kit and I had been in the hotel bar when Liv first called and told us Conor was waking people up for a meeting. I had insisted that we leave immediately, and the drive to Howth that normally took at least thirty minutes had taken less than twenty. It was night and the streets were for the most part empty.

Before we could drive up the driveway to the house, we were stopped by four uniformed police officers that motioned for us to stay back. Two police cars marked with the word Garda were parked to block the road.

Rolling down the window, I called out to the one closest. "We're the ones who called you. My girlfriend is in there."

"I'm sorry, but ye cannot go any closer and ye'll need to move the vehicle."

"Why the hell are you out here when there's a crazy man killing people inside?" I threw my hands around with agitation.

281

"I'm moving the car right away." Kit put the car in reverse and as she turned in her seat and looked out the back window, she explained, "Regular guards are not armed here in Ireland. Protocol doesn't allow them to enter a house when there's been a report of an armed incident in progress. All they can do is secure the area and protect the public from goin' in while they wait for an armed support unit or the emergency response unit."

"So why aren't they here yet?"

"The ERU are coming from Dublin like us. They'll be here any second."

"I'm not fucking waiting when Liv is inside." As soon as Kit had stopped the car, I got out and ran in the direction that I knew would take me to the trail leading to the back garden of the house.

Kit followed me. "Where are you goin'? Backup is on their way."

I was too busy running to answer her and soon I arrived at the back yard over a small trail. With the night air singing with the sound of sirens, I stopped to look up at the house and heard Kit's running footsteps catch up to me. "That window on the corner, where the lights are on, is River's and Nathan's room. I can crawl up the drain pipe and get them to let me in."

"What if ye fall?"

I ignored her and moved forward.

"At least be careful," she called after me.

It was dark and when I reached the building, I heard gun shots from inside. Adrenaline gave me tunnel vision and all I could see was the pipe that would take me up to Nathan and River's window. The bass from the loud music they were playing inside was like the soundtrack to a movie I didn't want to be in. I crawled up as fast as I could, ignoring the many scratches I got on the way because the pipe was so close to the wall that it didn't leave much room for my hands.

Looking through the window, I saw Maximum sitting on the floor while Nathan and River stood to the side of the door with white sheets in their hands.

When I knocked on the glass, River dropped her sheet and ran to the window. "It's Charles."

I didn't get a chance to ask her questions before she started talking. "We don't know where the others are. Lumi ran down to save her mother, and Liv ran after her. We tried to stop Atlas from going because he was acting strange, but he wouldn't listen to us."

Climbing through the window, I scanned the room again, and noticed that furniture had been pushed in front of the two doors. "What's with the sheets?" I asked Nathan, who stood holding the edges of the fabric.

"I couldn't find any weapons to defend us, but if someone storms in here, I'm going to make a surprise attack and throw a sheet over their heads so they can't see. And then we'll run."

"Is he all right?" I nodded to Maximum, who looked to be in his own bubble as he sat surrounded by Star Wars toys.

"No, he's being weird. River and I didn't want him to go downstairs, so I told him he could touch everything tonight." Nathan was panting from talking fast and breathing with fear. "Liv said Conor is making people kill themselves downstairs and we hear sirens. You have to stop them, Charles."

"Did you hear the shots being fired?"

"Yes, at first we thought it was fireworks."

"How many rounds of shots have you heard?"

"A lot."

"Two? Three?"

River and Nathan looked at each other. "More like five."

"Shit." I knew from listening to Liv's phone that five people were killing themselves at a time. With Liv, there were thirty-four people living here, and five rounds of shooting could mean that twenty-five group members were already dead.

"Stay here. I'm going down."

River nodded and the kids helped me push the table to the side that they had used to block the door.

"Lock the door after me," I ordered before I ran down the hallway. The music got louder the closer I came, and when I was by the staircase I walked down far enough that I could spy on the group and get a sense of what was going on. If I was to save Liv and the others, I needed a plan.

Think Charles, think!

But my mind was paralyzed from the sight of my friends sitting in a long line between each other's legs. Each was tilted backward or to the side with a bullet hole in their head.

My hand grabbed for the bannister of the staircase as my head spun and I felt like vomiting. The loud music was still playing as I stared at all the dead bodies in a line so long that it went out of the living room and into the foyer towards the main entrance. It was unfathomable.

"No, Mom, don't do it." Lumi was pulling at her mom, who was moving to the front of the line.

Conor had a gun in his hand but held up his free hand and spoke over the music in a placating tone, "It's okay, Lumi, you can join your mom and the two of you can go together."

It was as if I saw him for the first time. How had I not seen what a sadistic puppet master he was? His eyes were crazed as he handed a gun to Ciara and picked up another one to give to Atlas. "See, Atlas and Ciara will go together with you, your mom, and Liv. I'll bring Maximum, River, and Nathan and then we'll all be together again."

When he pushed a gun at Liv, she stepped back. "No, I don't want to kill myself and nor should any of the others."

Lumi kept pulling at her mom, who got back up from the floor with a careless giggle. "It's okay, darling. We'll be fine. It's a new beginning. We can trust Conor."

Lumi's eyes were wet from tears as she pleaded with her mom. "No, we'll die. There's nothing waiting for us. Don't do it."

"You don't want to go?" Aisha raised a hand and dried away one of Lumi's tears in a clumsy way. She was so drugged that she spoke in a slurred way and had a hard time balancing on her feet. "Don't cry, sweetheart. There's nothing to be scared of but if you don't want to go, I'll stay here with you."

Lumi wrapped her arms around her mother and wept. "Thank you, Mom, thank you."

"No! I love you all too much to leave you behind." Conor lifted the gun in his hand, his voice sharp and demanding. "We're doing this *together* as a family."

Lumi shook her head and clung to her mother. Aisha seemed confused but her love for Lumi made her step in front of her daughter and confront Conor with her palm up. "Stop, Conor, you're scaring her."

"Dad, this isn't right." Atlas stood leaning against the doorframe as if he found it hard to balance. His speech was slow and slurred and his eyes on the gun in his hands.

I needed to find a weapon, but nothing in my proximity would match the gun in Conor's hands.

Conor pointing to the long line of our dead friends. "Trust me, son, we're so close and we don't want to let the others wait. Come on, get down."

Atlas pushed out from the door frame and took a step toward the twenty-five dead people. By now, the only

285

ones left in the house were Ciara, the five children, Liv, Aisha, and Conor himself.

"No, Atlas don't do it," Liv pleaded and held on to him while shouting at Conor over the music. "You've killed enough people."

"Oh, but dear Liv, I'm not killing anyone. They all made a choice."

Her voice shook with anger. "And now we're making one too. If you want to join them, go ahead, but the rest of us choose to stay here."

Conor leaned his head to one side and narrowed his eyes. "It's not nice to reject an invitation. I'm afraid that I have to insist that we all go *together*."

The moment Conor pointed his gun at Liv, my brain shut down. Nothing could have held me back, and I stormed down the stairs without a plan; I just knew I couldn't let him kill Liv or the others.

"Charles." The surprise on Conor's face, as he looked up the stairs to understand where I'd come from, was quickly exchanged for a smile. "I'm so glad to see you. You're just in time for the biggest event in the group's history. I always knew you'd be back. We're the only family you ever had."

I pushed Liv behind me and spread out my arms to make myself large enough to shield both her and Atlas. "Conor, stop this. The guards are outside. There's no need to kill more people. Just let us go."

He waved his gun through the air and scrunched up his face. "Why are the guards here? I've done nothing wrong. All the accusations against me are malicious and untrue. You know that Charles, I already explained it to you."

My voice rose as my hand pointed to the train of bodies. "You *killed* them."

286

Stepping closer to Liv and me, Conor lowered his voice to a threatening sneer. "They poisoned your mind against me. I'm not letting anyone stop our family from moving on to the next level together. Either you all get down on the floor or I'll shoot you right here."

"Conor, what are you doing?" Aisha blinked her eyes while comforting Lumi, who was crying and clinging to her. "This isn't like you."

Ignoring Aisha, Conor turned to Ciara. "My love." He nodded his head in the direction of Atlas.

"You heard your father." Ciara walked over to take Atlas's hand but Liv wouldn't let go and I stepped between Ciara and her son.

"Ciara, you're drugged. You don't know what you're doing. This is crazy!"

Her eyes were foggy when she blinked a few times and looked around. "Where's Maximum? We need to go now."

Atlas took his mother's outstretched hand and broke Liv's hold on him.

"No, Atlas, don't do it." This time it was Lumi who reached out for him with her face red from crying.

"Don't!" Conor turned his gun on her chest and it made Aisha once again step in front of her daughter.

The bang sounded like someone had dropped a pan on a kitchen floor, and then Aisha's white silk pajamas grew red in front.

Time stood still as I stared at Aisha.

"Nooo!" Lumi's large brown eyes were double the size as she failed to keep her mom from falling. "Mom. Mom." Lumi fell to the floor with her mom, cupping her face and calling for her.

With disbelief in her eyes, Aisha looked at Conor, and then she gasped for air one last time before she closed her eyes.

287

"Noooo…" The wail from Lumi was heart wrenching and sent chills down my spine.

"She's not gone Lumi, you'll meet her again in a minute." With Conor aiming his gun at Lumi's head. I reacted on instinct and threw myself forward in a tackle.

Conor flew down on his back with me landing on top of him fighting to get a hold of his gun.

In that moment, the entrance doors slammed open and men dressed in black came storming in, shouting for us to get down. They looked like a SWAT team with their helmets, bulletproof vests, and assault rifles. The officers kept shouting for everyone to get down. I was already on the floor and rolled away from Conor, afraid that they would mistake us and shoot me. I had managed to get the gun from him and placed it to my side. Lumi, was on the floor too, holding on to her mom while screaming as the men came toward us. Liv got down on her stomach and held her hands on top of her head, while Atlas looked confused.

The music with the heavy bass kept playing and my eyes went to Conor, who picked up another gun he'd dropped when I knocked him over.

"Drop your gun! Get down on the floor," the guards shouted at Atlas, who kneeled down and placed the gun he'd been given earlier on the rug in front of him. A garda kicked it away and pushed him down all the way to the floor, where he handcuffed Atlas.

Ciara put down her gun too, but Conor was determined to carry out his plan and went for another of the five guns used tonight. I didn't have a chance to react before he fired at me. His shot went over my head and took down a vase, but in response to his opening fire, a police officer shot Conor in his shoulder. Still on the floor, he screamed in pain and threw himself around.

"No, don't kill him." Ciara got up and held out her arms to shield Conor from the officers pointing their gun at him.

Deep male voices screamed at her to get down.

With the music blasting, the guards shouting, Lumi sobbing, and Conor screaming in pain, my head was exploding from the noise and inferno of human angst in the room.

"You can't control us," Ciara shouted just as a large guard in ballistic vest and helmet went for Conor, who twisted his body and managed to fire his gun one more time before he lay dead with a bullet to his brain.

"Nooo…" Ciara's loud scream penetrated the noise of the music as she threw herself down next to Conor.

"Garda down."

Through my sensory overload, I saw a guard on the floor in the direction Conor had shot. The man was on top of Lumi, covering her with his body.

Another loud shot made me turn my head back to Ciara. "Shit!" She lay in front of me with a gun in her mouth and dead eyes. The garda behind her had blood all over his pants and was swearing out loud.

"Is the girl all right?" Someone called out. "Is she shot?"

"No, Rook took the bullet."

It seemed like there were police barking orders at us from every angle.

Twenty-eight people with great careers and bright futures lay dead around us. I was stunned and my body was shaking with adrenaline and fear when a garda pulled me to my feet and handcuffed me. As we walked outside, I stared at the long line of dead people that I'd called family a few days ago and knew their faces would forever be burned into my memory.

"There are three children upstairs in the room at the end of the hall to the right," I told the guard who led me outside.

289

"We'll find them." He motioned for me to sit down on the cold ground. Soon, Liv and Atlas were walked out too and sat down next to me.

"Do any of you need medical attention?" the garda leading them asked us.

I shook my head and looked up when a large man came out carrying Lumi in his arms.

"Is she okay?" Liv asked and got up.

"Sit down," a brute of a policeman ordered, but Liv had reached a boiling point and pushed her jaw out.

"I'm not the enemy here. That girl over there just watched her mother get killed and I need to go to her and comfort her. Right now!"

I was quick to support Liv. "We're the ones who called you to come in the first place."

"The house is cleared." Three officers came out with River, Maximum, and Nathan. "We're going to secure the scene and let the technicians take over."

"Liv." River shouted and ran to us. When the girl wrapped her arms around Liv, the handcuffs made it impossible for Liv to hug her back. Instead she tried to compensate by lowering her head to River's hair.

"Hang on." The guard left for a second and then he came back. "I just spoke with the sergeant and we're takin' off yer handcuffs, but don't go anywhere. We'll need yer statements for the report."

"Thank you."

Liv, and I walked with the children to Lumi, who sat in an ambulance where a paramedic was looking at her ankle.

"What happened to you?" Liv asked and crawled up to sit next to her.

"I'm afraid it was my fault." One of the ERU guards stood on the ground in front of the ambulance. He had removed his vest and taken off his helmet. "I landed on her ankle when I fell on top of her. That's why I carried her out here."

"Damian?" Liv's voice was full of disbelief. "I didn't recognize you with all your equipment on."

"Nah, ye would nae but I recognized ye." He turned his attention to the paramedic who was wrapping Lumi's ankle. "How is she?"

"Minor injury. She'll be fine."

"Good." Looking back at Liv, he sighed. "Ye and Kit were serious about that guy being a lunatic, eh?"

"Where's Kit?" I looked around for her and pulled out my phone to call her. "Last time I saw her, she was behind the house."

Kit came running a few minutes later. "Jesus, Mary, and Joseph. I was so scared that ye'd all been killed."

"It was close." Damian picked up his vest and studied where the bullet had hit him.

"Ye took a bullet?" Kit leaned in to see.

"I just saw him swingin' a gun in the direction of the girl so I threw myself on top of her." Damian, whose hair was wet from sweat, nodded to Lumi, who sat in the ambulance with Liv next to her.

Lumi turned to look at Damian and there was such sorrow and pain in her large brown eyes that it tore at my heart.

"Thank you for saving Lumi's life." I reached out my hand to shake his. "You're a true hero."

"Nah, it's what I'm trained to do. Do not worry about it. It's my pleasure."

"Let me see where the bullet hit ye." Kit pulled at Damian's uniform shirt and he took it off and turned his back on her. The man was ripped.

"Bloody hell, I see a mark." Kit's hand touched his back. "Yer goin' to be well purple, I reckon."

"It's not too bad." He shrugged and gave Lumi a small smile. "For ye, my love, I'd take a bullet any day."

His kind words only made Lumi tear up, but River tugged at his sleeve.

"What about me? Would you take a bullet for me?" River asked with large eyes.

Damian looked down at the blond girl and tousled her hair. "Of course. Any of us men here would. It's why we go to work. To stop the bad guys from hurting innocent people like yerself."

"But what happened?" River looked back at the house. "That man over there covered my eyes and carried me outside. He said that we didn't need to see it."

We all turned to look at the guard in question and when he saw us watching him, he came to join us and placed a hand on Damian's shoulder. He was in his early forties and looked weathered, with wrinkles and dark circles under his eyes.

I reached out my hand to shake his, just as I'd done with Damian, and I lowered my voice, "Thank you for not letting the kids see the bodies. It's enough that the rest of us will have that image haunt us forever."

"I've been with the Gardai for almost twenty years and I've never seen anything like it. Being a father myself, I reckoned that I wouldn't want my kids to see something that gruesome." Turning to Damian, the older guard patted his shoulder hard. "Ye did good rookie, but I wonder if maybe ye should have become a bodyguard instead. Throwin' yerself in front of flyin' bullets and all." He shook his head.

"I acted on instinct."

"Aye, I could tell."

A stern-looking man came over. "We would like to interview the witnesses. Are you done here?"

Damian picked up his vest and helmet and leaned in to give Kit a kiss on her cheek. "I'll talk to ye later, sis." When he walked away, he looked back over his shoulder, and then turned to walk backward. "Hey, Lumi."

The girl gave a nod to show she had heard him.

"I'll check up on ye later, okay?"

She answered with a tiny nod.

We gave witness statements and answered the same questions over and over. A social worker came to take care of the children, but River and Nathan wouldn't be separated from Liv, who argued with the social worker that they had already been traumatized enough.

In the end, the older woman agreed that Liv and I should accompany the children to a temporary facility until she could figure out what their family relations were.

Liv looked exhausted and it made me protective of her and the children. In the end, I refused to answer any more questions until we'd had some sleep. At the facility the five kids, Liv, and I were given a family room with extra mattresses on the floor and as we were trying to fall asleep, the children's questions started.

"Is my mother with Conor and the others now? On the other side, like he said?"

It was Liv who answered Lumi's question. "No, sweetheart, I don't think that's how it works. I think your mom is with her ancestors."

"Good. I don't think she would have liked to meet Conor again in the next life. Not after he shot her." I was surprised that Lumi wasn't crying while speaking about it, but then she had already cried on and off for the last five hours.

The light in the room was dimmed, with only a bit of light coming from the bathroom. Liv and I were on two mattresses on the floor with River sleeping on Liv's other

293

side. The other four children were in two bunk beds along the walls.

"At least your mom put herself between you and my dad. Aisha took a bullet to save your life while Ciara helped my dad try and kill us all," Atlas muttered.

Lumi was in the lower bunk with Nathan above her. She was on her side with her hands under her cheek. "I just wish my mom had survived."

I moved closer to Liv, who was holding River's hand. "I wish they all had survived."

"Conor too?" Nathan asked.

"Yes. I wish he hadn't gotten away so easily. It would have been better if he'd been forced to spend the rest of his days behind bars, reflecting on what he did to the people who loved him."

"But why did he want everyone to die?" River asked. "I don't understand it. He told us he was excited that Carlos was going to teach us all about quantum physics next week. Carlos used to be a science professor before he started doing drag shows, did you know that?"

I answered her with the only explanation I could find. "No, I didn't know that, but to answer your question, I think what happened tonight was that Conor lost his mind. He knew the guards were coming for him and he didn't want to go down alone."

"Did you say that twenty-eight people died tonight?" The question came from Nathan.

"Yes," Liv answered.

I swallowed hard, and Liv and I intertwined her free hand with mine. For a while we were all quiet before River asked in a small voice. "What's going to happen to us now?"

Nathan sniffled and only now did I notice that the boy was crying. "They're going to split us up and send us to orphanages."

"No, I don't want that," River cried and pressed her face against Liv's shoulder.

I propped myself up on an elbow and spoke with all the confidence I could muster in a situation like this. "No one is going to an orphanage. Liv and I will take care of you until we find your other family. Right?" I looked at Liv, who nodded.

"That's right."

As the children finally fell asleep, Liv and I lay close and whispered.

"What happened in the bathroom between you and Conor?"

"He tried to force himself on me."

"Then why didn't you leave with me?"

"Because I had promised the children that I'd be there for them. I always knew he was dangerous, and after what he did to Nathan, I couldn't just leave them defenseless."

"I wish you would have told me. I would have killed him then, and then everyone else would still be alive."

Liv sighed. "First of all, you didn't give me a chance to explain, and you're not a killer."

She was right of course. I squeezed her hand. "The thought of him forcing himself on you makes me so angry. I should have been there to protect you. If I'd known what he was really like…"

We fell quiet for a moment, until I looked into her eyes. "I know about the report and my grandfather asking you to come here."

She held her breath. "Are you disappointed that it wasn't a random meeting between us?"

"I'm confused about what was real and what was not."

She pointed from me to her. "This is real."

My Adam's apple bobbed in my throat. "You sure? I mean it feels real, but it turns out that I'm not the best judge of character."

"I love you, Charles." She moved closer and kissed me. "You can trust that."

"Why would you be with someone stupid enough to fall for a scammer like Conor?"

"You didn't do anything wrong. None of you did. He was a master at deception and if I hadn't been warned before going in, there's a real chance that I would have fallen for his charm as well. And for what it's worth, I'm happy you brought me here?"

I pulled back a little. "How can you say that?"

She frowned. "Look around you. Five children are alive because you brought me in there. Who would have stopped him? Who would have called the cops? Who would have insisted three of the children stay away from the meeting? Without you becoming a member, things might have turned out very differently for these kids."

"Huh." I thought about it. "I see what you mean, but if I hadn't been there, my grandfather wouldn't have started an investigation, and then there wouldn't have been the same pressure on Conor. People might still be alive if he hadn't been pushed to a breaking point.

"It would have happened sooner or later. I'm only sorry that the police didn't arrest him before he lost his shit."

I yawned. "And I'm sorry that I believed all his lies."

Liv let her finger run from the tip of my nose to my lips. "It was his lies that brought me to you. Are you sorry about that?"

I pulled her in and kissed her. "No. For that I'm grateful. The day I met you again was one of the best days in my life, and I will happily spend the rest of my life making up for all the awful things that I've put you through."

"The rest of your life, huh?" She smiled at me as we lay nose to nose.

"And every life after that." I moved forward, placing a long soft kiss on her lips.

"Wow, that's commitment."

"Yeah. It is." I let my hand slide up her arm. "Does it scare you?"

"No. If anything it excites me."

For a moment she was quiet. "Charles."

"Mmm."

"I worry about the children. What are the chances of them staying together?"

I groaned. "Slim. If Nathan has family, they're most likely in England where his parents were from, and I'm pretty sure Ciara had sisters up in the northern part of Ireland. I remember her talking about them."

"What about Lumi? Aisha was from India, right?"

"Yeah, but she grew up in London. Her family shunned her after she got pregnant outside of wedlock."

"But if her family cut her off then why was she of interest to Conor? Did they still give her money?"

"Yes, she used to joke that they were paying her to stay hidden to avoid bringing public shame to them. I don't know what story the family has been telling their social circle, but they never wanted anything to do with Lumi before, so I doubt they'll want her now."

Liv bit her lip and whispered, "And River? Her mom is in a psychiatric hospital. What if she'll never be capable of taking care of her daughter?"

"I don't know. Maybe there's some other family."

Liv closed her eyes and opened them with a sigh. "I can't bear the thought of them being split up and maybe never seeing each other again. They need each other."

"Maybe a fresh start for them isn't so bad."

"They've suffered a severe trauma and I guarantee you that it will stay with them for the rest of their lives. Can you imagine growing up in a suicide cult and having no one who understands what it was like? They have a shared history, and only the five can relate to the issues that they're bound to have in the future. I would adopt them all if I could but I doubt the Irish would let a foreigner adopt here."

Stroking her hair, I kissed her again. "Try not to worry about it. The social services will find a solution. I'm sure of it."

She didn't look convinced, but she cuddled up in my arms and closed her eyes. "Good night."

"Good night." I was on my back staring up at the ceiling. My thoughts were all over the place, analyzing and processing. Her breathing had slowed down when I said, "I'm a dual citizen."

"What?" Her speech was drowsy.

"My mother was Irish and before she died, she made sure I had both Irish and American citizenship. That's why I can live in Ireland."

"Oh okay." She closed her eyes again, probably half asleep.

"Maybe we could adopt the children as a couple, with me being Irish."

Her eyelids were heavy but she opened them enough to look at me. "You would do that?"

"To keep the children together, I would. But I don't know if I'd be any good as a parent. I didn't have much of a role model."

That made her eyes open wide. "Darn it. Did you call Mr. Robertson – I mean your grandfather? What if he reads in the paper that twenty-eight people were killed?

He's going to die from a heart attack before he finishes the headline."

"I don't have the energy to call him right now." I reached for my phone on the floor. "I'll text him instead."

Charles: Liv and I got the children out. We're safe and I'll call you when we've had a chance to sleep.

Liv read the text on my screen and the minute I pressed send, she closed her eyes again. "Thank you."

I put the phone on silence before placing it back on the floor, and then I wrapped one arm around Liv. "It's me who should be thanking you. I don't know what's going to happen, but as long as it includes falling asleep with you in my arms, I'll deal with it."

"Yeah, me too." She yawned and two seconds later her breathing told me that Liv was fast asleep just like the five children around us.

When I first came to Ireland, I'd felt lost. My role as the heir to Solver Industries brought me only an empty feeling of misery, because the outlook of living as a copy of my grandfather felt meaningless.

Then I'd found a family in the Red Manor Group and my life had blossomed with meaningful conversations, laughter, personal growth, and a deep sense of connection that I hadn't known before.

The Red Manor Group was gone now, but as I lay with my arm around Liv, my heart was bursting from a new sense of purpose. The bravest and most selfless woman in the world needed me, and so did five truly amazing children. I had wealth, connections, and I knew about international law. If anyone could find a way to make sure these children stayed together, it was me. In that quiet moment, I made a vow to dedicate my life to making sure that the six people sleeping around me would wake up to a better tomorrow. I would work night and day to make sure they had each other and everything else they needed to heal from this tragedy.

CHAPTER 27
Goodbye

Charles

The hardwood floor in the old house creaked as I walked to my grandfather's room. The light was low and the sound of a machine beeping made me take in the changes since I'd last been in here.

"He just woke up." A nurse stood by his bed and with a trained eye, she did a last check on the machines around the hospital bed that had replaced the four-poster bed that used to be here. "I'll give you privacy."

Looking down on the man in the bed, I hardly recognized my grandfather. His cheeks were sunken and everything about him looked gray, from his lips to his skin color, eyebrows, and the few strands of hair that he had left.

"Charles." His hand shook as he tried to lift it. A needle was inserted in a vein on the back of his hand with a piece of tape covering it.

"I'm here." I tried to swallow the hard knot in my chest and took his hand as I sat down on the bed.

"Did Liv come with you?"

"No, she had to stay with the children."

He sighed. "Ah, yes. I had hoped to thank her in person. Liv is your guardian angel. I hope you know that."

My nose twitched from talking about it, as I was trying to hold back tears at seeing my grandfather dying.

"How was the flight?"

"Fine. I would have come sooner but we're trying to find a way for Liv and me to adopt the children and it's taking most of my time."

There was a small lift of his lips. "Hurry. I would like to know that I have five great-grandchildren before I leave."

I leaned in. "Then I think you'll be happy to know that Liv and I married last week. I was planning to propose to her in Paris, but things have been crazy with getting the social services to cooperate. One of the lawyers said that our chances of adoption improve if we're married, so we made a quick decision."

"Was it a nice ceremony?"

"It was at the city hall. The kids were there and we invited Kit, the detective you hired, and her brother Damian. Remember I told you he was the policeman who saved Lumi's life?

"Yes, I remember."

"We went out for a lunch afterward to celebrate, but we'll have a proper wedding later. Liv promised her mom."

"Ah, so she's talking with her parents again, is she? That's good."

"Yes, she called them and they talked for hours." I smiled. "There was a lot of catching up to do and apologies to be made, but her whole family is flying over in a few weeks."

"How are the children?"

"Traumatized but better than expected."

"I wish I'd had time to meet them all."

Pulling out my phone, I showed him a picture of all the children that I'd taken before I left. "You'd love them. They are all academically ahead and very smart. Atlas and Lumi are the perfect candidates to take on leadership roles at Solver. They are sharp and analytic by nature."

"Charles."

"Mmm?"

"Don't make the same mistake I did. Never put pressure on them to get involved in Solver. They have to want it. Not you."

A twitch pulled at my upper lip and I scratched my neck. "Good point, old man."

He smiled back with his sunken cheeks and for a second, I recognized the powerful man trapped inside the fragile and old body.

"Anyway, I'm talking to one of my college professors about Atlas."

"Why? Does he want to study law?"

"He's still figuring out what he wants to focus on, but he's so academically advanced that he'll need to be challenged."

"And the girl?"

"Lumi?" I drew a deep breath. "She's grieving more than the others. Atlas and Maximum saw some of what happened that night, but they were drugged and only have blurred memories. Lumi, however, remembers everything vividly. I don't think she'll ever recover from seeing her mother killed in front of her."

"No, I suppose not."

"She's seeing therapists and getting help, but she's having a hard time finding joy in anything."

"Don't give up on her." My grandfather coughed and I helped him drink through a straw.

"We won't. I'm grateful that you never gave up on me. If you hadn't hired Kit, and convinced Liv to go to Ireland, I might have been dead like the others."

My grandfather looked tiny and frail in the bed and when he spoke it was so low that I had to sharpen my ears to hear him.

"When are you coming home?"

303

"I don't know. We might split our time between the US and Ireland. It's only been a few weeks since the incident, but the social services pushed for the kids to begin new routines and they're starting to make friends. Nathan joined a soccer club, River is on a dance team, and Maximum wants to play rugby. Liv says it's important for them to establish a new life with as much familiarity as possible so for now we're staying in Ireland. I found a large house with a pool thirty minutes outside of Dublin.

"What about work?"

"I'll get there, but for now, I'm using most of my time with the lawyers trying to secure the signatures from the children's relatives to let us adopt. It helps if the child and their closest relatives all agree. Maximum and Atlas have two aunts up in Northern Ireland that were more than happy to sign the papers since they have a lot of children themselves and broke off contact with Ciara more than sixteen years ago. We also secured signatures from Nathan's grandparents, who are in bad health and unable to care for a teenage boy."

"When I die..." My grandfather coughed again and the beeps on the machine became faster. "There's a folder in my office. I've made all the preparations for the funeral. Please be there."

"Of course." I squeezed his hand.

"And I should tell you that I'm not leaving everything to you. Some of it will go to a young lady."

"What young lady?" I frowned and looked to the door. My grandfather wouldn't be the first rich old man to be scammed by some young gold digger. "Is it the nurse?"

"It's Liv." He was too weak to smile, but the tiny lift at the edge of his lips told me that if I'd had this conversation with my grandfather when he was healthy, he'd would have had a satisfied smile on his face. "I said I'd pay her a million dollars to get you out and even though she has

304

refused to take the money, I'm earmarking it for her in my will. A million with a tip."

"You're tipping her?" I smiled at the irony because my grandfather had never been a generous tipper.

"Yes. One million for getting you out and nine million for loving you as much as I do."

This was the first time I'd ever heard those words from my grandfather and it made my eyes moist.

"I love you too, and I'm sorry for everything that happened and the things I said. Liv is going to be very surprised when she hears that she's in your will."

He sunk deeper into his pillow. "I've lived a long life and it gives me joy that I can leave something behind that might make a difference in someone else's life."

"You understand that Liv is going to use the money on others, right? It's how she is."

"I know. But you're going to make sure that she lacks for nothing."

"Of course. I can promise you that."

He locked eyes with me. "I don't need to tell you that material wealth will never be enough. Liv and the children will need more than expensive gifts from you. Be generous with your time and affection or there will come a time where they won't want any of it.

"I will."

He closed his eyes and it was clear that our conversation was exhausting to him.

"Maybe you should rest a little. I have a meeting with the board in a few hours but I'll check in on you after. Okay?"

He gave a minuscule nod. "Charles."

"Yes."

"When you go into that board meeting, straighten your back, and don't be intimidated. You might be young, but you're my blood and none of them would have their job if not for our family. You're a Robertson and we stand our ground."

I nodded. "Count on it."

"They have read articles about what happened. The whole world knows about it. Don't let any of them judge you for what took place. When I was thirty-three, I almost lost the entire company because I was swindled. Rockefeller was scammed by convincing con men, and so were many other successful men before you. You have learned the hard way to be skeptical of people and it will serve you in business. People will underestimate you because of your tics. Let them. They will come to regret it later."

I smiled. "Rest now. I'm not the same man who left for Ireland. Don't worry. I've got this."

"I know you do." With a last squeeze of my hand, he let go and closed his eyes to sleep. I stayed in the room for a while, watching the peace on his face.

Before I made it back from the board meeting that night, my grandfather had taken his last breath.

EPILOGUE
Pool Party
10 months later

Liv

The melody of the doorbell chimed and made me hurry from the garden through the house to open up.

"Why didn't you just come straight out back?" I opened my arms to hug Kit and Damian, who stood wearing shorts and t-shirts while holding towels under their arms.

"Sorry to give ye such short notice, but we're meltin' in this heat and ye're the only friends we have with a pool."

Waving my hand, I laughed. "Come in, come in."

Damian walked in and looked up at the large chandelier. "See, sis, this is how the other half lives."

"Oh, stop it. You say that every time you come here." I closed the door and gently bumped his shoulder.

"That's because none of my other friends live in small castles and have people to scrub their toilets."

"That's different. Charles and I are Americans. We're used to big houses."

Damian grinned. "I could get used a grand house like this myself."

"Charles and River will be here soon. He took her to a dance class, but the others are out back."

"Here." Kit gave Damian her towel as he headed for the pool while she followed me into the kitchen.

"Why do you always bring towels? I told you that we have plenty."

307

"That's what Damian said, but I don't want ye to have more washin' because of us."

"Silly woman." Shaking my head, I got a tray ready with cold drinks and some snacks.

"So, did you get the signature?" Kit asked.

I turned to look at her and had to keep myself from squealing with joy. "We did!"

Kit lit up and opened her arms. "Oh, come here. That's wonderful." Hugging me tight she added, "Does River know yet?"

"Yes, we told her last night and she cried with joy. It was a beautiful moment and we celebrated with a low-key movie night, all of us together. Charles and I offered that we could go out to a restaurant, but River just wanted some family time and she even let the boys pick the movie."

"Kudos to Charles for working his magic. Now the kids can have peace knowing that they're legally siblings and can always stay together in some way." We let go of each other but kept holding hands for a moment. Kit and I had only known each other for less than a year, but in that time, she'd been the best friend anyone could ask for. She loved the children as much as we did and made sure to come by often. During our hardest days, her dark humor had brought us smiles, and she and Damian had become an extended part of our family.

"But while ye're on a roll, can ye adopt me too?" Kit tilted her head and made deer eyes.

I laughed. "Very funny. As if five adoptions weren't enough."

"Aye, ye should be proud of yerself. Not only did ye save the prince, ye adopted the peasant children too. It's such a beautiful story."

A snort escaped me. "Peasant children. Where do you get it from?" I gave a nod to the large French doors leading outside. "Come on."

Kit carried a bowl of sliced melon while I took the tray with drinks. As soon as we stepped out, the sun was beating down on us from above while the ground burned my feet. "Hot, hot, hot," I exclaimed as I hurried to my sunbed while balancing the tray in my hands. "I should have put on my flip-flops."

"Just come into the pool with me. It'll cool you down." Damian splashed water in my direction.

"Stop it." Lumi, who was on a sunbed by the pool reading, shielded her book from Damian's splashing, but it only made him splash a little more.

"Kit, do you wanna come play with us?" Nathan and Maximum waved at Kit from the lawn, where they were playing around with a soccer ball.

Kit put down the melon on a side table in the shade and looked over at the boys. "Thanks for the invite, but I came for the pool. I always forget this place comes with pesky kids too."

The boys grinned and Maximum shouted back, "Just admit it. You love us."

Kit sent them an air kiss and turned to Lumi, who had gotten up from her sunbed and opened her arms.

"Do you want a hug from a pesky kid?"

Kit's orange-colored hair mixed with Lumi's black hair and there was a big contrast between Kit's milky-colored freckled skin against Lumi's golden brown tan.

"Ah, don't be daft. You'll be eighteen in less than a month now and officially no longer a child. When I was yer age, I was making good money as a spy."

Damian shook water out of his hair. "Don't listen to her, Lumi. She always makes it sound like she was 007

309

when the truth is that all Kit did was tedious surveillance jobs with our da."

Kit smacked her tongue and planted herself on a sunbed, arranging her towel as a pillow. "I'll have ye know that I also spied on people having extramarital affairs. Sometimes I even took pictures of them in intimate situations. Not something I'd describe as kid's work, so my point is that at almost eighteen, Lumi is no longer a child while the boys have a way to go." She nodded to Nathan, who was fifteen, and Maximum, who was turning fourteen in less than two months.

Damian did a handstand in the water and popped his head up again. "Ahh, I know I've said it a million times, but I'm so happy ye bought this house. This pool is world class."

"I'm glad you think so. You know you're always welcome to use it," I offered.

Kit was applying a thick layer of sunscreen on her freckled skin and had her large sun hat on. "Don't tell him that. Soon, he'll be havin' all his lads over for pool parties. Damian might be twenty-seven, but mentally he's their age." Kit's thumb pointed to Nathan and Maximum.

Damian did another handstand and came back up splashing more water around him.

"Also, I'm not convinced that my brother didn't just trip over his own feet with the perfect timin' to catch a bullet. It's not like him to do somethin' noble for others. I can't even get him to walk into the kitchen and bring me cookies from the press when I'm visiting."

"That's because you practically live in my apartment. Ye can get yer own bloody cookies." Damian tilted his head from side to side as if trying to get water out of his ears.

"You forget that I saw it with my own eyes," I said. "I know what someone tripping looks like, but he threw

310

himself to save her. It was the most heroic thing, and we're all forever grateful."

Damian didn't say anything but he was smiling from my praise.

"Ach, no wonder he loves comin' over here. Ye all treat him like he's feckin' Rambo." Kit handed me her sunscreen and turned around. Since she'd already applied it on her legs, arms, and face, I figured she wanted me to smear sunscreen on her shoulders and back.

"Hey, Damian." Nathan came over with the ball under his arm. "You said you'd come play with us when you'd cooled down. Wanna play now?"

"Aye, I can beat ye in football if ye want."

Nathan grinned. "You can try."

"Challenge accepted!" Damian's muscles flexed as he pulled himself out of the water, dripping as he jogged with the boys to the lawn, where a small soccer goal was positioned away from the house.

"It's crazy how much Nathan has grown," Kit said as we watched them sprint around and play soccer.

Damian growled when Nathan tried to trip him up. "Ah, ye little plonker." Using his shoulder, Damian pushed at Nathan, who pushed back.

"You're too slow, old man." Nathan was agile and athletic and got the ball from Damian, who cursed out loud.

"Yes, he's taller than me now. Nathan finally hit puberty and to be honest it feels like he's using sports to deal with his grief. He's either running, working on ball control, or doing strength and conditioning at the gym. He doesn't like to talk about what happened, but I think keeping physically active helps him numb his grief."

"Whatever works." Kit shrugged, but I wasn't sure that she understood the level of obsession that Nathan had with sports or how suppressing grief wasn't healthy.

"What about Maximum?" Kit took a sip from her glass.

I lowered my voice. "It's hard for him. He misses Atlas, and some kids at his new school have been bullying him."

The second I said it, Kit lowered the glass and narrowed her eyes. "Tell me who bullied him and Damian and I will go talk to the little wankers. I'll have Damian show up in his uniform and scare the shite out of them."

"Thank you for the offer, but the principal is on it." I sighed. "It's inevitable that being Conor O'Brien's son will affect him for the rest of his life. It's too big to hide with the story being international news for weeks, everyone at his school knows what happened."

Kit looked thoughtful. "Kids can be brutal if you have the wrong shoes or a big nose. I can't even imagine what it would be like to have a dad who was a mass murderer. I can imagine the other parents telling their children to keep a distance just in case it's inherited."

I watched the handsome boy run around and voiced my concern to Kit. "Yeah, it's tough being him, and it's like Max is taking on the guilt and shame of his father's actions, even though we keep telling him it wasn't his fault."

Lumi lowered the book she was reading. "It's Maximum, not Max. I told you that Ciara was always adamant about us not shortening her boys' names."

"I'm sorry, Maximum told me the same thing this morning; it's just so natural for us Americans to shorten names."

"What about Atlas, is he helping his little brother cope with all of this? They seemed so close," Kit asked.

Lumi answered, "Yes, they talk often. Atlas called last night."

"And how is our local genius doing at Harvard?"

Lumi gave Kit a shrug of her shoulders. "He said that his professors aren't too happy with him. Apparently, he got into trouble again."

312

"Why?" I frowned. "What did he do this time?"

Lumi got defensive and crossed her arms. "Nothing! It's not his fault."

Kit gave me a *what's going on* look, so I sighed and explained. "Atlas has gotten in trouble for correcting his professors while they're in the middle of teaching a class. I can't figure out if it's because he's unfamiliar with a normal classroom setting, or if it's because he's rebelling against authority due to what happened. His disrespect for his current professors could very well be a projection of his anger toward his father, who used to be his teacher."

"But was he right?" Kit asked.

"About what?"

"Ye said that Atlas corrected his professor. Was Atlas right or was the professor right?"

Lumi gave a proud smile. "Atlas was right of course. He's not one to speak just to be heard. He felt it was too grave a mistake to stand uncorrected."

"What did the professor say?"

"That Thomas Edison invented the electric light."

Kit looked to me, "But he did, didn't he?"

I shrugged. "Apparently not."

Like a small lexicon, Lumi began. "It's a common myth that he invented the electric light, but in reality, he improved on an invention already made by Sir Humphry Davy forty years earlier. The problem was that although many scientists tried, none of them could find a way to make the carbon filament glow for more than twelve hours. Davy's invention brought electric light, but it was the inventors in Edison's lab who found the right filament that would burn for days on end."

Kit tilted her head. "Huh. I had no idea."

"That's okay, but a history professor should know better."

"That might be, Lumi, but Atlas humiliated his professor and that's not smart." I leaned forward. "So, tell me. What did you mean when you said he got into trouble again?"

"It's just that they don't understand his way of studying."

Kit and I exchanged another glance and then she snickered, "What are ye on about? Does he do it at midnight, under a full moon with a cape on? How can there be a wrong way to study?"

"They say it's not enough that he takes all the classes. They want him to write reports and do exams too."

I pushed my sunglasses up. "Duh! Exams are part of going to college. How does he think people get their degrees?"

"But that's just the thing. Atlas isn't studying to get some degree or title. He doesn't care about that sort of thing. All he wants to do is search for answers. The rest is just noise to him."

I gaped and then I scrunched up my face. "That makes no sense, Lumi."

"It makes complete sense. A degree is a useless external validation while the knowledge you've obtained to get it is what truly matters."

"I don't understand. What's wrong with a degree?" Kit asked.

"It's redundant," Lumi declared.

I snorted. "No, it's not! It's proof to everyone else that you've mastered the knowledge you've been studying."

"But Atlas has no interest in others knowing what he studied. Learning should be about getting answers and finding a deeper understanding. Not getting a certificate to show off your degrees. Right now, he's working his way through class after class to understand."

"To understand what?" Kit shook her head. "What is he searchin' for?"

Lumi looked at her as if Kit were slow of thought. "Answers to why it happened, of course."

Kit looked confused. "Is Atlas trying to find answers to why his father behaved and acted the way he did?"

"Yes."

"But I thought that he studied history."

"Yes. More precisely, he studies dictators throughout history. He wants to understand what makes people follow psychopathic narcissists like Conor."

I crossed my arms. "As I've told him, I can see his fascination with that subject, but if he wants to understand the dynamics of persuasion and mind control, he should study psychology."

Lumi brushed her hand over the towel on her sunbed. "He'll get to that. He's working his way through every class that can offer insight into what happened. Unless of course, he's kicked out of school first."

Kit looked to me. "Can't ye have Charles talk to Atlas?"

I nodded and it made her turn back to Lumi.

"Did Atlas say anythin' about how he's liking Harvard? Does he have a girlfriend yet? Someone told me that American women love a man with a British accent; is that true?"

I chuckled. "Don't look at me like that, Kit. I don't know what all American women like. We're as different as Irish women."

Lumi answered in a matter-of-fact tone. "Atlas gets his fair share of attention from females. He just finds them all insufferable, but he did tell me that he made a new friend."

"Did he?" I lit up. "Who?"

"Some professor in astrophysics."

"Nooo…" I bit my lip. "We really need to get him to socialize with the other students.

"Are you sure you want that?" Lumi bent one of her long golden legs and adjusted a blue ankle chain. "Atlas just turned seventeen and according to him many of his classmates are binge drinking on the weekends and smoking pot." I knew Lumi said it to get a reaction from me, but I wasn't taking the bait.

"He doesn't have to drink or smoke to go to a party. He can just socialize and get to know people. It's a part of the American college experience, which you would know if you went to one."

"No, thank you. Trinity College is plenty crazy for me."

"Is it?" I tilted my head "Then how come you haven't been to a single party yet?"

"I don't know, let me see." Lumi tapped her lips. "Could it be that the word *party* has bad connotations for me? I remember a party from last year where champagne was served and people had this party game where they shot themselves and left for another world."

I drew a deep sigh. "That's not what I meant and you know it. I'm talking about a fun party with people your own age."

"All right. I'll make you a deal. When Atlas and I have our own company and we're making a million a year, I'll throw a party. How about that?"

"Can I be an investor?" Kit asked.

Lumi wrinkled her nose. "You want to invest in a company we haven't founded yet?"

"Aye, a hundred percent. Ye two are legit geniuses and I want in on the fortune ye're goin' to make."

Lumi was smiling now. "I'm flattered. How much do you have to invest?"

"Let me see." Kit picked up her bag and took out her purse. "I have a tenner."

"Eh, all right then." Lumi raised her book again.

316

"Oh, I see." Kit waved the crumbled money note in her hand. "Are you too laudy daw for my money?"

"No, of course not, but I can't take it until we have an actual company, can I? And please don't call me laudy daudy; I'm not a snob."

"Then how come ye're too good to party with the Irish?"

"I never said that I was." Lumi looked hurt. "I wouldn't party with anyone, no matter their nationality."

"Damian, come here for a second." Kit waved her hand for him to see her.

He came jogging over and I couldn't tell if he was still wet from the pool or his bare chest was sweaty from playing soccer.

"Now, ye listen to me, Lumi. Since my brother saved yer life, I think it's fair he has a little say in what ye do with it." Kit turned to Damian, who looked confused. "Can't ye tell Lumi that she needs to go out more? She's a book-readin' hermit and it's not healthy. Ye have a party gene bigger than anyone that I've ever met. Can't ye give her a motivational speech or somethin'?"

Damian sat down on his sister's sunbed and his wet shorts made the thick blue cushion darken in color around him. He reached for the glass of lemonade that stood on her side table. She didn't protest when he emptied it before he addressed Lumi. "Why won't ye go out? Parties are fun."

Even with her wearing sunglasses, I could tell Lumi rolled her eyes. "Parties are not fun. They're boring."

"Then ye've been to the wrong kind of parties." He leaned over and pushed at her knee. "Go dance and kiss a few lads. I'll bet ye have a long line of suitors."

Lumi stiffened and then she lifted her hand to lower her sunglasses and look at him. "Why do you assume that I have suitors?"

317

"Ehmm… Because ye're wicked smart and ye're as pretty as Princess Jasmine from Aladdin."

Lumi wrinkled her nose up again. "She's a cartoon character."

"So?" Damian leaned back and it made Kit push at him because he was taking up too much space on her sunbed. "Cartoons are great. I used to fantasize about Jessica Rabbit when I was younger."

Kit laughed. "I'll bet ye still do."

"Ha." Damian's smile grew. "Not for a long time, but maybe I should watch her movie again."

"And Jasmine, did you fantasize about her too?" Lumi put aside her thick book and sunglasses.

Damian opened his mouth to answer, but closed it again.

"Ye'd better say no." Kit told him, but he never got a chance to answer because Lumi spoke to me.

"I'll go to *one* party if you stop bugging me."

"Three parties." I held up three fingers. "You're almost eighteen. Live a little."

She got up from the sunbed and looked gorgeous in her bright yellow bikini, which complimented her golden tan. Standing in front of us she raised her arms and made a ponytail of her long black hair. "I'll go to two parties this summer, that's all I can agree to."

"I'll take it." With a triumphant smile, I mimed "thank you" to Kit and Damian.

Passing me on her way to the pool, Lumi had a satisfied smile on her face and when she stopped by the edge of the water, she looked back over her shoulder. "You forgot to specify how long I needed to stay at the parties. Don't be surprised if I'm home early."

I opened my mouth, but before I could object, she made an elegant dive into the water.

Damian sat with his eyes on Lumi and chuckled. "That lass is too clever for her own good."

As if she had heard him, she swam a few strokes, turned on her back, and called out to him. "Wanna play, Damian?"

I saw the small frown on his face and then he looked to me and Kit. I didn't confirm that I'd heard the flirting undertone in Lumi's voice or that it wasn't the first time I sensed Lumi goading Damian either. I could understand a teenage girl's fascination with him. Damian was tall, strong, fit, and playful, but he was also almost ten years her senior. To my relief, he knew better than to feed into her teen infatuation.

"Maybe later. I still need to show Nathan who's the better football player." He chucked down another glass of lemonade and headed back to the boys.

Kit must have caught on to the situation as well because she began talking about Damian's newest girlfriend using a voice loud enough to guarantee that Lumi couldn't avoid hearing it. "Megan is so pretty with big doe eyes and she can cook too. The other day she made us mushroom soup and homemade bread. It was delicious! I told Damian he should hurry up and marry her before she finds out what a tool he really is."

"I heard that," he shouted at her.

"I meant it in a lovin' way." Kit grinned and then she lit up when River came running around the house with Charles walking behind her.

"I saw Damian's car out front." River was smiling from ear to ear when she ran to give Kit a hug.

"Didn't I tell ye to stop growin'?" Kit hugged River and moved her around to stand back to back. "Liv, tell me that I'm still the tallest."

I got up to measure. "It's a tie."

319

Kit rose up on her toes and River followed until Kit turned around and pressed her palm down on top of River's head.

The blonde girl laughed. "Next time you see me, I'll be taller than you for sure."

Kit gave up, waved a hand, and took her place on the sunbed again. "We'll never know, 'cause it's the last time I'm letting anyone measure the two of us."

"Charles says that Nathan and I are growing like weeds."

I kissed River's cheek when she came to hug me. "River sweetie, go get your swimwear and jump in the pool with Lumi. It's so nice today."

She was quick to comply and disappeared into the house.

"Oh, that lass is such a charmer. If ye get tired of her, I'll take her." Kit turned her sun hat a little.

"Can you take all of them for a week?" Charles sat down next to me and pushed my long brown hair away to kiss my shoulder. "I could use a little alone time with my wife."

I melted like I always did when he kissed me.

"No problem. Damian and I are happy to help."

"I'd like that." I wiggled my finger at Kit. "But I'm warning you. Our kids may look idyllic, but they come with a lot of issues."

"Are ye talking about the nightmares?"

"Uh-huh. River and Nathan have them the most, but those are just some of the things that we're working on."

Charles moved to sit behind me and I leaned back against his chest as the three of us sat in silence watching the others in the garden for a moment.

"I wish I could peek ten or fifteen years into the future and see where the children are in life," he said and massaged my shoulders.

320

"Me too," I sighed.

"Me three." With Kit's accent making her not pronounce the h, it always made me smile.

"I guess we'll just have to wait and see."

"Aye, and if Atlas finds the answer to what makes people follow lyin' psychopaths, I for one would like to know. It's scary!" Taking her sun hat off and waving it in front of her, Kit got up from the sunbed and called out to Lumi. "Wanna watch me make a bomb?"

Lumi swam to the side just in time to get out of the way before Kit ran to the pool, jumped up with a loud howl, and pressed her body into a cannonball making the water splash in all directions.

Maximum had seen it and came running to make his own bomb and soon Damian and Nathan followed with impressive splashes of water.

Charles and I watched them with goofy smiles on our faces. "They're crazy." I laughed.

"Yes, but the good kind of crazy."

"Aww, look at how happy the kids seem."

"I know. It must be because they have the world's coolest adoptive parents in the world."

"If we say so ourselves." I squeezed his hand just as he bit my earlobe and whispered into my ear, "I need to show you something."

"Okay. Now?"

"Mmmm…" Charles stood up and offered me a hand. Kit and Damian were having fun with the kids in the pool and even Lumi was allowing Nathan to put her on his shoulders and throw her into the water.

"Liv and I will be right back. We just need to look over some papers that have to be signed." Charles led me through the house and up the stairs. I recognized the look he gave me. It was pure desire and lust, and as always, it gave me butterflies in my stomach.

321

"We're not signing papers, are we?"

"Nope."

The laughter from outside reminded me that everyone in that pool was capable of looking out for themselves. I could steal a moment with Charles, couldn't I?

Like two naughty school kids, we intertwined our hands and ran up the stairs and into the bedroom, where we locked the door and laughed together, like we had pulled off some great escape plan.

"Come here." Charles kissed me while nudging me to the bed. "I've missed you all day, and coming home to see you in that bikini made it hard for me to think. Wanna know why I placed myself behind you?"

I smiled when he took my hand and placed it on his hard erection.

"Wow, is that all for me?" My laugh was swallowed by our kissing.

"Every inch is yours." Charles growled low and removed my bikini top. "God, you're so tempting."

"So are you."

He looked into my eyes with a serious expression. "I can't tell you what this last year has meant to me, but I know that you feel it when we make love."

My face softened. "I do!" Kissing him slow and enjoying his soft lips on mine, I admitted, "The truth is that sometimes you still make me shy and nervous, like I can't believe I scored the guy out of my league."

"I was never out of your league. If anything, you were out of mine."

We looked deep into each other's eyes and then he kissed his way from my mouth to my earlobe and then down across my neck and collarbone. With a small moan, I leaned my head back in surrender. Charles was a master at seducing me and sure enough, his thumb ran down over my throat just as a reminder that he was in control.

322

"This bikini looks amazing on you, but I still prefer you naked." He pushed the fabric of my bikini bottoms down and they landed next to my top that he'd already removed. Heat spread at my core and I fisted my hands into his dark hair, when he bent down to lick and suckle on my nipple.

Right then his tics came out and in response, I tightened my grip on him. "I love you so freaking much. Do you know that?"

Charles responded by picking me up and placing me on the bed where he pushed me down on my back and got nose to nose with me. "I know it, but I'm still not sure I understand it. You're like a dream come true with the way I can be myself around you. I never have to hide my issues or my tics."

"And I can be open about my weird fetish."

He rolled down next to me on the bed before lifting his hand to my throat with his dominant smile that made my body vibrate with lust. Pushing myself against him, I lifted my thigh to his hip.

"Mmm." He growled low against my ear. "There's something amazing about two quirky people finding each other and making it work."

"Are you calling me a weirdo?"

"A sexy weirdo." He licked my lip. "*My* sexy weirdo."

I gave a seductive smile. "How about I show you how sexy a weirdo I can be?"

"I was hoping you would." Biting my shoulder with just the right amount of pressure, he moved to position himself between my legs. "But first let me taste you."

The warmth of his breath on my pelvis bone made my most sensitive parts tingle with anticipation.

"Liv… are you in there?" The doorknob wiggled.

We both stopped moving and I called out, "Yes. What's wrong, River?"

"I can't find my blue bikini. I've looked in Lumi's room and my own. I've even looked through the laundry. Can you help me?"

Charles closed his eyes and moved onto his back, letting go of me.

"Just a minute, sweetie," I called back to her before turning to him. "We signed up for this. Five children, remember?"

"I know, but I'm so fucking horny for you."

Taking deep breaths, I tried getting my breathing under control. "How about we let Damian and Kit move in here while we go away for a few days? They've offered several times and we need it."

"Yes! When?"

"Maybe tomorrow? I'll talk to them."

I was rolling off the bed, when Charles reached for my arm and made me look at him. "I can't wait for some wild undisturbed sex."

The door handle wiggled again. "Liv?"

"I'll be right there love." I put my bikini back on, and just before walking out of our bedroom, I looked back at him. "Are you coming?"

"I'll need a moment alone first."

My eyes fell to his mid-section with longing, but there was a child on the other side of the door. "I love you."

"I love you too, Saffron, and I still think you're the most precious spice in my life."

"I'll see you downstairs at the pool." I was just about to open the door when I paused and whispered to him, "It's so hard to leave when I'm dying to finish what we started."

Charles had a look of pure devotion on his face when he whispered back, "You and I will never finish; I'll always want more of you. Always."

I felt like a schoolgirl with a huge crush when I smiled back and walked out the door.

River was waiting on the stairs and looked up when she heard me. "How come you look so happy?"

I walked over and gave her a sideways hug and led her down the stairs. "Why wouldn't I be? I'm surrounded by people I love. I feel very lucky that I get to be here with you, Charles, and the others."

"You mean that?"

I gave her a genuine smile. "One hundred percent. Now let's find that bikini, shall we?"

This concludes Charlie – Cultivated #1

Thank you so much for reading Charles and Liv's story. If you liked it, I hope you'll take a moment to leave a review on Amazon and spread the word to your friends.

The truth is that your review is a big part of other reader's buying decision and therefore makes a massive impact for a self- published author like me.

Want more?
When I first had the inspiration to write the Cultivated series, I wanted to take on the issue of smooth talkers who slowly gain control of you without you even realizing that you're under attack. The psychopaths who are skilled at making you trust them until you're in their net and they hold power over you.

No one deserves to have mentally or physically abusive relationships. If you're in one, I would feel honored if this book helps you reflect on your relationship while giving you some valuable insights to recognize the traits in people who look oh so inviting but are toxic for you.

Charlie, the book you just read, was supposed to be a short prequel to the five stories about the children surviving the cult. For some reason, I don't know how to write short stories. It's the second time I try, and they always end up the same length as my other books, but it's all good.

In the next book, we'll jump ahead eleven years and see what's it like for Atlas to carry the fear of becoming like his father. As a bonus to you, I've included the first chapter from Atlas – Cultivated #2 on the following pages.

Atlas – Cultivated #2

Jolene is a clinical psychologist down on her luck. With bills to pay, she accepts a job at a test center but quickly realizes that her boss, Atlas, might be handsome and mysterious, but he's also eccentric and obsessed with finding answers to why people follow narcissistic liars so blindly.

Afraid that Atlas might use this information to mind-control innocent people, Jo digs into his past. What she discovers shocks her. Atlas' father was the leader of a cult who left Atlas and his siblings traumatized. The psychologist in her wants to help him heal his mental wounds, but to do so, she must find a way to make him open up to her. Is that even possible for someone as guarded as Atlas?

Atlas is the second installment in *Elin Peer's* romantic suspense series, *Cultivated*. For the best reading experience and to avoid spoilers, it's recommended that you start with the first book in the series, called *Charlie*.

Elin Peer is the author of the popular series, *Men of the North, Clashing Colors*, and the *Slave Series*. Her books are fast-paced, thought-provoking, and always offer humor and a solid romance story at the core.

If you like stories with authentic characters that will stay with you for a long time after you've finished reading, get this book today!

Atlas – Cultivated #2 will be available around December 7th.

BONUS
Read the first chapter from Atlas – Cultivated #2

CHAPTER 1
Red Manor House
Atlas

Complete silence filled the car the moment we drove into Howth. Nathan was driving and from the way his knuckles turned white around the steering wheel, I could tell he felt as tense as me. I was in the passenger seat and took a quick look at the back seat where Maximum sat between Lumi and River. All three of them had solemn expressions on their faces as they looked out the window.

The gravel driveway leading up to the house had once been a beautiful sight with the pruned trees creating a canopy above, but now the trees were overgrown and some of the branches scraped the top of Nathan's Jeep as we drove through.

"Look at all the weeds," Maximum said from the back.

My eyes fell to the ground lit up by the headlights of the car as he continued in a low mutter:

"I used to love using the flamethrower to burn weeds from the gravel."

"You were probably the last one to do it." River's tone was dry as she leaned forward to see the manor come into sight in front of us.

When Nathan stopped the car, all five of us got out. No one spoke as the sound of car doors closing filled the night.

We gathered in front of the stairs leading up to the main entrance.

For a moment we stood shoulder to shoulder and then I felt a hand in mine. River was the youngest of us and even though she was twenty-three now and no child, I squeezed her hand.

"Why did we have to do it at night?" she whispered. "The house looks scary, and we haven't even gone inside yet."

I answered her in a calm voice hiding that my heart was beating fast too. "Because we don't want anyone to see us. We don't need a stupid article about how the five surviving children from the suicide cult in Howth returned to confront the demons of their past."

River sighed. "No, you're right."

"Come on!" It was Lumi who took the first step and we all followed up the stairs, watching her unlock the double doors.

Stepping inside, Nathan turned on the light so we could see, and it made me gasp. The entrance that led into the living room had always been bright and welcoming with fresh flowers and a constant scent of home-cooked food. Now the place looked like a squatter's house. Only a few pieces of furniture stood around, and walls and floors had been painted with graffiti.

We were quiet as we moved further into the house and it was only then that I realized that it wasn't graffiti. "It's markings from where the bodies were." I counted the outline markings of the twenty-eight friends and family members whom we lost that night.

"Why are most of them in a line?" Nathan had frown lines on his face as he took in the twenty-five markings in one long line and the three that were spread out in the living room.

"You don't know?" I asked him.

330

"Why would he?" Maximum walked closer to Nathan. "Some of us had no interest in seeing pictures or reading articles. Nathan and River were led out of the house without getting a look at what happened here, or did you forget that detail?"

My brother, Maximum, hadn't wanted to come tonight and his tone told me he was pissed that I'd pressured them until they agreed for us to go together.

Lumi stood with a stern expression looking at the drawings on the floor. "Conor had them sit in a long line, like a human train on their way to the next destination. My mom fell down over here, and those two markings are of Conor and Ciara."

I took a step closer to her, placing my hand on her shoulder. Of the five of us, only Lumi and I had been in the room that night eleven years ago, when the emergency response unit had stormed the house and saved us from my father's madness.

"If any of you want to see photos, I have copies."

River looked up at me. "You have copies?"

Nathan shook his head at me. "You can keep them. I'm happy the guards made sure we didn't see the bodies then, and I have no need to see it all now."

I shrugged. "No one is forcing you to."

Maximum walked around the living room and stopped by the dusty French doors to look into the darkness of the garden. "I wonder how it looks out back. The garden is probably overgrown."

"Yeah, probably," I agreed.

His hand rested on the doorframe and his eyes glazed over. "The garden was my favorite part about this house. The bonfires in the evenings, the tennis court, and the hours of playing Petanque with Carlos." Maximum turned to us. "He always cheated, but I still played with him."

"I want to see our old room, but I don't want to go alone." River stepped over to Nathan. The two of them had shared a room when we lived here. He gave a short nod before moving to the staircase. We all followed.

"My heart is beating so fast right now," River whispered when we got to the second floor and began walking down the long corridor.

Mine was too, but I'd always been the leader of our group and even though Lumi was technically older than me, I took on the same role as I had back then. "It's going to be fine. It's just an empty old house."

"With lots of memories," Nathan added. "My heart is trying to climb out my throat. I fucking hate this."

"It wasn't my idea to come back here," Lumi muttered.

Letting out a deep sigh, I spoke: "I never said it would be fun, but we need to face our fears of this place. When we leave, it will no longer matter to us. We've been here, seen it, and we can move on."

"Speaking of moving on; am I the only one who feels like we're not alone? It's like someone is watching us."

"No, I feel it too." River reached for Lumi's hand and looked scared.

"Now you're just riling each other up. There's no one here but us," I scolded them.

We had reached the end of the hallway when my brother challenged me, "How would you know? Twenty-eight people were killed because of a crazy man. If ever there was a haunted house, wouldn't this be it?"

"No!" I shot him a *you're not helping* look, but he persisted:

"I'm with Lumi and River. I feel it too. There's something in this house. What if it's Dad and he's still crazy? What if he tries to trip us up so we fall down the stairs and break our necks? He was a cold-blooded killer

332

when he lived, and if he's the one haunting this place, I don't think we should be here."

"Enough!" I opened the door and walked into what had once been River's and Nathan's room.

"What happened to the furniture?" River asked.

"It was sold in the estate sale," I told her.

River walked further into the almost empty room and touched a dresser that had been left behind. "How come you and Maximum never sold the house?"

I snorted. "And have it turned into a tourist attraction as a haunted bed and breakfast? I don't think so."

"But leaving it to rot like this…" Lumi didn't finish her sentence. The way her hands peeled at the water-damaged wallpaper spoke for her.

The sound of a creaking door made me look over to see Maximum opening the adjacent door leading to what had once been our father's room.

With hesitation Lumi and River followed and entered while Nathan stayed in the doorway.

"It's not in there," I told him.

"I know." Perspiration formed on his forehead and his upper lip.

"Snakes don't live that long, and someone would have removed it back then."

"It's not like I'm scared of a snake anymore." Nathan's words were contradicted by his wide eyes and shallow breathing.

"You want to see this," Lumi called from the other room.

Giving my adoptive brother a reassuring look, I nudged Nathan into the room.

"The closet is still here." Lumi was standing in front of the closet we had opened eleven years ago when we all decided to snoop in Conor O'Brien's room.

We'd been shocked to find a terrarium inside with a large yellow snake. For years, Nathan had suffered from nightmares of a yellow snake in his bed, and it turned out my sick father had been behind it.

"Is that the dead snake?" Lumi pointed but didn't walk closer.

Maximum lifted a long gray snakeskin. "No, this is just skin that it shed. I wonder what happened to the snake and what kind it was."

"It was a yellow corn snake."

They all turned to me and stared.

"Charles told us. You just don't remember."

"When did he tell us what kind of snake it was?" Nathan asked.

"A few days after. The question came up and he looked into it. Don't stare at me like that. It's not my fault you're all trying to block out what happened."

"Why would you remember a detail like that?" River walked over to look closer at the snakeskin. "I remember it as a large python in size."

"No, it was a corn snake. I found it interesting because it's one thing to place a snake in a boy's bed, but it's another as to whether or not Nathan was in actual danger from the snake. A corn snake isn't venomous. In fact, it's a common pet snake because of its docile nature and reluctance to bite. It does look similar to venomous snakes like the copperhead but it's described as harmless."

"There's nothing harmless about what Conor did to Nathan." Lumi straightened up. "He placed that snake in his bed to control him through fear, and then he had the nerve to pretend he couldn't see it when Nathan screamed for help. He made Nathan think he was crazy."

I sighed. "True. I was merely pointing out that it wasn't Conor's goal to kill Nathan and that he used a harmless snake rather than a deadly one."

"Don't defend the man." Maximum moved to the exit.

"I'm not defending him. You were the one who asked what kind of snake it was, and I happened to know."

The others left the room and I made sure to turn off the light before I followed. We walked through bedrooms, bathrooms, and the kitchen before we ended up in Conor's office.

"I'm done with this house. Can we leave now?" Nathan was leaning against the doorframe with his arms crossed.

"The office no longer had a desk, but the reading chair was still in the corner and there were books scattered on the built-in bookshelves on two of the walls.

Lumi and I both walked over to scan the titles and pulled out a book each.

"What's wrong?"

I turned my head to Maximum, who had asked.

"Nothing. Why?"

"I was talking to River."

Instant worry filled me when I saw how pale and frightened she looked. "River, what's wrong?"

"I don't know what it is, but that book makes me want to run away."

"What, this one?" I reached for the red book to pull it down from the shelf. It was stuck so I pulled harder.

Click. A narrow opening appeared at the end of the shelves.

Lumi, Maximum, and even Nathan moved closer, while River took a step back.

"Don't open it."

I frowned. "Why not? Aren't you curious?"

"I have a bad feeling. What if he had someone chained up in there and the person was never found?"

With a snort, I pushed the door open and watched dust fall. My hands searched for a light and found it to my right.

"Holy Christ!" We all stared into a room that was about the same size as the office we were in.

"I don't want to go in there." River's voice was brittle.

"How did you know about the book? Have you been in there before?" I asked her with some confusion.

She shook her head. "I don't think so. I can't remember."

Maximum pushed past me and walked in, with me and Nathan right behind him. A day bed and two leather chairs were on the floor, but it was the walls that made my blood freeze to ice.

"What the fuck is this?" Nathan scanned the walls with his face scrunched up. "Do you recognize any of them?"

I studied the photos, pinned to the wall. Everything in Conor's life had been well organized but these photos were placed in random order, some on top of each other. "Maybe Conor didn't know this room existed. Maybe these are from a previous owner."

"No, I recognize this girl." Maximum reached for a photo and took it down. "Remember Heather? She was my age and lived here with her mom for about a year." He handed me the picture of a girl who sat naked against a wall, looking away. She couldn't be more than eleven or twelve.

"Hmmm." I gave him the picture back and walked around looking at the girls and young women in the pictures. Several I recognized but in most of the pictures the girls had their back to the camera so it would be hard to identify them.

On a low shelf, a combined TV and video stood and underneath it at least fifty videotapes were lined up.

My hands tore through my hair. "Conor was a psychopathic killer who lied and deceived people, but he wasn't a sexual child molester. We would know if he was. We were children living in his house."

336

Maximum looked around. "I don't know. It's all females. Just because he never touched you and me doesn't mean he didn't touch others."

I spun around to face Lumi. "Did Conor ever touch you?"

She shook her head. "Not that I remember."

"River, did Conor ever touch you inappropriately?"

River had never entered the room and still stood in the office looking in. "Do you see any photos of me?"

"I can't tell." Using my phone, I documented what we'd found while Maximum began taking down the photos.

"Stop, what are you doing?"

He kept going. "We need to find the children. This isn't right and they need to know about it."

"Maximum, stop!" I raised my voice.

He already had five of the pictures in his hands when he stopped and listened to me.

"None of these girls are children anymore. It's been eleven years, which means every girl in those pictures is an adult now. Why would you tell them? What if they blocked it from their memory and are now living healthy lives? We don't know what really happened but even if there are worse things on those videos, we can't just show up with proof that they were molested. It might start a chain reaction and they could end up worse than before they were told."

"What can be worse than not knowing?" Maximum argued.

I shifted my balance. "Taking an overdose or drinking yourself to death in order to forget is worse. Look, it's not like we can put our dad in jail. The man is already dead."

"But what if they have all sorts of issues but don't remember why? This is a piece of a puzzle. They deserve to know."

My hands were shaking. "Do any of you want to go through another round of publicity? You know the press would be all over this, and then what?" I gave Maximum a direct stare. "You and I are the sons of a mass murderer and now you want to tell the world that he was a pedophile too?"

Pain crossed Maximum's face before he looked away.

"With dad gone, who do you think the press is going to come for?"

My brother didn't answer. While I'd been shipped to the US after it happened and few at college had known about my back ground, Maximum had been younger and stayed here in Ireland. For him school had been a nightmare with all the bullying and exclusion from people who judged him as the son of Conor O'Brien.

Lumi's voice sounded from behind us. "I say we burn it all. This room is a shrine to misery and evil, and nothing in here deserves to be spread or seen by anyone."

"Yes. Let's take all the photos down and burn them. The tapes too," Nathan agreed.

"No, I need to document this and see what's on the tapes," I objected and stuffed four flash drives from the pile of videotapes into my pockets.

Maximum, Lumi, and River were now all taking down the hundreds of pictures in the room while I snapped pictures with my phone. What they didn't understand was that I'd been searching for answers for eleven years and those pictures could hold information that I needed.

Once they were done taking down pictures, they took the videotapes, and if it hadn't been that River's pile was too high and she dropped two of them on the floor, I would have never gotten to see what was on them. While the others left the room to burn everything in the garden, I took the videotapes and closed the door.

338

I tried to distance myself from what I might see, and turned on the TV as I pushed in the tape.

Please let it be a Hollywood movie.

The sound of my father's voice made the hair on my arms stand up. I only had to see a few minutes of my father's gift of persuasion to be sweating like I'd run a marathon. Not even the young girl's giggles and assurances that she wanted him to touch her made the bile in my throat lessen.

I had come here to prove to myself that Conor O'Brien held no power over any of us any longer, but as I stopped the tape, I stood with a feeling that he was right behind me, hissing low into my ear. "You can never outrun me, son. You're my blood and I live on inside you."

As if I'd felt a physical touch to my neck, I shivered and rubbed my skin, and then I hurried to the others in the garden.

"There was still split wood in the shed and lighter fluid," Maximum told me when he stepped back from the fire he had made.

"Cover your noses. Burning plastic isn't healthy," Lumi warned and threw the first tape on the fire.

I didn't like the smoke. "What if the neighbors notice the smell?"

"This is Howth. Nothing happens after midnight."

"Nathan is right," Lumi said. "It's December. They're all sleeping inside with their doors and windows closed.

We stood for a while throwing tapes onto the fire and watching them melt. I had been one of the first to throw my two tapes and there was a sense of relief when the fires engulfed them.

"I'm sure we're breaking all sorts of environmental rules right now." River was just about to throw another tape on to the fire when she hesitated and her eyebrows drew close together.

"What is it?" I was terrified she had read her own name or Lumi's on a tape, but she looked to Nathan.

"Wasn't your last name Hamilton before we all got adopted?"

"Yeah?"

"And wasn't your mom's name Sandra?"

I swallowed hard as all our eyes were on Nathan. His hands folded into fists. "Is it from the night he killed my mom?"

River held it out to him. "It could be."

Nathan took the tape and looked completely lost.

"Do you want me to look at it first?" I offered although I had zero desire to see what was on that tape.

"No, I'll do it when I'm ready."

Maximum, Lumi, River, and I all moved over to stand around Nathan, our hands on him to offer our support.

"Don't watch it alone," Lumi whispered. "At least let us be there for you."

Nathan was looking down with tears making his eyes wet but he nodded as a silent promise that he wouldn't watch it alone.

Without words, we gathered closer around Nathan and gave him a group hug. When we moved back, he squatted down in front of the fire and used a stick to stir up the flames.

"We should burn down this whole house. No one will ever want to live here anyway."

When none of us answered him, he turned his head, "No, actually, we should blow it up. Once and for all. One giant explosion to get it out of our lives." He lifted the burning stick in his hand and it made me take a step forward.

"Don't. Arson is a crime and you don't want to go to jail."

River frowned. "How can it be arson if you and Maximum own the house? It's not as if you'd press charges against him, would you?"

"No, but what if the fire spreads? Burning down the house isn't going to solve anything."

Nathan had been small for his age back when we were children, but he'd grown into a large man with a muscled body from his obsession with sports. It saddened me to see the proud man he'd become, dry his nose and scrunch his face. "Don't pretend you wouldn't feel a sense of satisfaction from seeing this place burn to the ground. We all hate this house and *him*."

I raised both palms. "You're right, but we aren't mindless teenagers, and setting the manor on fire would be reckless. If you need to see it burn down, then I'm fine with it, but we're doing it the right way."

"And what way is that?"

"I don't know. Maybe the local fire department can do it for practice."

"No! *I* want to set the torch."

"I'm sure that can be arranged, Nathan. But not tonight."

He threw the stick back onto the fire and took a step back.

Lumi was right there to give him another hug. "Atlas is right. We don't know if there's something that could explode inside, and the neighbors are sleeping in their houses. It's not safe."

Nathan stabbed his index finger at me. "I want to see our childhood and this fucking haunted house in ashes." He stormed off in the direction of the car and River ran after him.

"Are you happy now?" Maximum tucked his hands in his pockets next to me and rocked back and forth on his feet. "That speech you gave us about proving to ourselves

341

that Dad doesn't hold any power over us..." He scoffed. "The man planted so many phobias and traumas in us that he'll continue to hold power for as long as we live. We're cursed people."

"No!" I refused to believe that. "We can get past it. "

"How? We're all fucked up in one way or the other, and you know it."

My tone was defensive. "That's why I'm searching for answers. We just need to understand what he did to you and then we'll know how to fix it."

Maximum stared at me and gave an incredulous chuckle. "What he did to *us*? Don't you know that you're as fucked up as the rest of us? You're the one obsessing about needing to understand what happened, but you never will. Dad was crazy, Atlas. Crazy and evil!" He nodded to the melted videotapes on the fire. "I wish we hadn't come here tonight, and I wish you wouldn't insist on digging for answers. All you find is more dirt and depravity."

"Maximum, I..."

He cut me off. "That research project you're running; who is it for?"

"It's for us and anyone else who is broken by someone like Dad."

Maximum shook his head. "I know you're trying to fix the situation, but you can't. No one can."

"Give me time." I took a step forward but that only made him back away.

Shaking his head again, my younger brother walked away while I stood back with a heavy heart, promising myself that I would dedicate the rest of my life to finding a way to heal what my father had broken.

"Typical." Lumi came to stand next to me.

I gave her a sideways glance. "What's typical?"

"Others start the fire and leave it to us to put it out. It's the curse of being the older siblings that we always get left

342

with the clean-up." Her brown eyes, which always shone with her sharp intelligence, told me we weren't talking about the fire in front of us.

Feeling grateful for the support of my strong adoptive sister, I gave her a sideways hug. "Then we'd better get to it."

Atlas – Cultivated #2 is available on Amazon.

OVERVIEW OF ELIN PEER'S BOOKS

Men of the North:

1 prequel and 15 romantic stories that take place 400 years in the future where women rule the world.
These stories are unlike anything you've ever read and have made several bestselling lists on Amazon.
It's a tug of war between the crude alpha men on one side of the border and the altruristic women on the other side.
Can they find a way to integrate?

Clashing Colors:

These 5 contemporary romance stories dive into the theme of opposites attract.
From romantic comedy to dramatic scenes offering food for thought; these books will make you both laugh and cry.

The Slave Series:

5 intense "enemy to lovers" books portraying strong women who won't be defined as victims.
Expect some dark scenes and steamy sex.

Cultivated

Set in the USA and the gorgeous Ireland, these six contemporary romance books take on the question of mind control.
They're suspenseful, fast-paced, and full of humor.
As always, they carry Elin's unique style of writing, which readers refer to as 'self-help that reads like fiction.

ABOUT THE AUTHOR

With a back ground in life coaching, Elin is easy to talk to and her fans rave about her unique writing style that has subtle elements of coaching mixed into fictional love stories with happy endings.

Elin is curious by nature. She likes to explore and can tell you about riding elephants through the Asian jungle, watching the sunset in the Sahara Desert from the back of a camel, sailing down the Nile in Egypt, kayaking in Alaska, river rafting in Indonesia, and flying over Greenland in a helicopter.

After traveling the world and living in different countries, Elin is currently residing outside Seattle in the US with her husband, daughters, and her black Labrador, Lucky, who follows her everywhere.

Want to connect with Elin? Great – she loves to hear from her readers.

Find her on Facebook: facebook.com/AuthorElinPeer
Or look her up on Goodreads, Amazon, Bookbub or simply go to elinpeer.com

CPSIA information can be obtained
at www.ICGtesting.com
Printed in the USA
BVHW041934260121
598790BV00020B/419